QUAESTOR

Also by David M Allan

The Empty Throne

QUAESTOR

DAVID M ALLAN

Elsewhen Press

Quaestor
First published in Great Britain by Elsewhen Press, 2019
An imprint of Alnpete Limited

Elsewhen Press, PO Box 757, Dartford, Kent DA2 7TQ
www.elsewhen.press

British Library Cataloguing in Publication Data.
A catalogue record for this book is available from the British Library.

ISBN 978-1-911409-47-2 Print edition
ISBN 978-1-911409-57-1 eBook edition

Designed and formatted by Elsewhen Press

CONTENTS

LIFTER

"Ready?" asked Lirrov.

Anarya nodded. She liked the way he checked before starting a coordinated Lift. He was good looking too. Under other circumstances she might fancy getting to know him better. Pity he was a thief.

She felt the block of marble stir slightly as Lirrov exerted his talent. In the Oversight she saw red bands extending from his hands to wrap around the stone. More bands appeared as she used the talent she had borrowed from him and added her strength to his. The slab rose into the air, just high enough to clear the tailgate of the wagon waiting for it.

"Careful," Anarya shouted, "It's too far left."

"I know," replied Lirrov. "I'm sorry about this. I like you, but I'm afraid you've been too nosey. You're a snitch and you're about to have an unfortunate accident. Goodbye."

Instead of guiding the block to settle gently on to the wagon Lirrov destabilised the Lift with a push, then withdrew his grip.

Anarya saw Lirrov's contribution to the Lift disappear. She wasn't strong enough to support the marble herself. It was coming straight towards her. She didn't have time to think, just react.

She dived under the wagon and rolled towards the other side. A surge of Lift applied to one of the nearside wheels knocked it off its axle. The wagon tilted. She kept rolling, hoping the incline would be enough to divert the falling stone.

There was a crash as the stone hit the slanting load bed of the wagon. *Is that the last thing I'll hear*, she wondered as darkness washed over her.

"Hacira! Hacira! Can you hear me? Are you all right?"

The voice belonged to another member of the work gang. It took Anarya a moment to understand that he was addressing her; Hacira was the name she was using for this job. It wasn't one she used frequently and she didn't recognise it at first.

She used several names, depending on the talent she was borrowing. She had to remember to keep them separate, and who she was supposed to be. It would be too dangerous if anyone realised she was a Sponger and could use different talents.

Her head throbbed. She could feel something sticky trickling down her face. *It's blood. Holy Quarenna aid me.*

She tried to move and realised she was trapped between the stone, the wagon and the loading dock. She couldn't Lift anything. *I must have lost it when I was knocked out.* Her mouth was full of stone dust and she had to cough to clear it before she could say, "I'm alive, but I'm stuck."

"Stay calm, Hacira. We'll get you out."

O

There wasn't another Lifter in the work gang. Without one it took most of a chime to extract her from the debris.

"What's happened to Lirrov?" she asked.

"Never mind about him," said her client, Jemis Gotheer the owner of the warehouse. He glowered at her from behind his desk. "That was an expensive accident," he said. "That marble is ruined. If you were really one of my staff I'd be dismissing you for incompetence. As it is I'll be complaining to the man who organised your contract – Rhyanek, isn't that his name – and wanting compensation. What have you got to say for yourself?"

"I've found your thief. It's Lirrov. He realised I was investigating him and tried to kill me. He's probably put the blame for the accident on me saying I was too weak or too inexperienced for that job."

Gotheer snorted. "You'd better be able to back that up. Lirrov's a good worker. He's well paid. He doesn't need to steal."

"He might not need to, but he does. I can tell you where he hides what he steals. There's an old sea chest by the side door in warehouse three. It's got a false bottom and I've seen him move things from the cargoes into it when he thought nobody was looking. Just like you told Rhyanek, it's small, valuable items that he takes, things he can move easily with his talent without anyone noticing. You'll find a flask of carad oil there. It came off *Maiden's Dream* this morning."

"Carad oil! Some of that goes missing every time we have a shipment," said Gotheer. He looked up and said to the warehouse manager who was standing behind Anarya. "We need to look into this. Is Lirrov still here?"

"Yes. He wanted to go home. Said he was upset by the accident and Hacira's death. I was sure you'd want to question him so I didn't let him go. He's in the office in warehouse one."

"He thinks Hacira's dead?" said Jemis Gotheer.

"He does."

"He's in for a surprise then. Let's go see him."

Lirrov's reaction was to try to run. Anarya was ready for him. The Oversight showed her how he was trying to use his talent to push people out of the way. She borrowed his talent again and diverted his Lifts long enough for the warehouse manager to bring him down with a couple of punches.

"Thank you, Hacira," said Gotheer when he found the flask where she said it would be. "The perfume makers pay well for that. It's worth considerably more than the marble and I think we'll forget about the damage to that. You've fulfilled your contract. It was for two dukals a day and it's well worth the fee." He passed her a small pouch, saying, "I'm impressed that it only took you two days to find the thief. There's another dukal in there too, as a bonus."

"That's very generous of you. Can I ask what are you going to do with Lirrov? I don't fancy him wanting revenge on me."

"Don't worry about him. We'll 'entertain' him for a couple of chimes, then he can put his talent to good use in the mines. He won't be coming after you."

Anarya was feeling shaky. She asked the warehouse manager, "Can you get me something to eat and drink. I need to rest a bit before I go home."

"Can do," he said. "There's a couch in the back office of warehouse two. I sometimes sleep there when we're working late. Use that."

A mug of weak beer, a slab of cheese and a not-too-stale piece of bread made Anarya feel better. She dozed off and was wakened by voices from the outer office.

"… not right, I tell you. My cousin works in Wsurauf's

mansion and she says…"

"Don't be a fool. Keep quiet, and tell your cousin to keep quiet too. She'll be in big trouble if the Three hear what she told you. And so will you be for listening to her."

"You know everybody would like to see the king take over from the Three."

"I'm saying nothing."

"Come on, you know it's true. It's said the Three won't let him piss without permission."

"I don't care. Crossing them is too dangerous. Look what they did to that man who spoke against them last year. Do you want that to happen to you?"

"Huler's beard, no! But somebody's going to have to do something."

"Well, it's not me, and, if you've got any sense at all, it's not you neither. Come on, we're finished here. Time to go home."

Anarya heard the two men leaving. She didn't know who they were and she didn't want to. One of them was a Crowner, and walking into trouble if he carried on thinking like that. *Duke Wurauf has too many spies. So what if he bullies the king, somebody's got to rule.*

O

Feeling better and in control of her limbs again, Anarya headed home through the dying light of the early evening, walking quickly through the labyrinth of the Western Docks of Carregis, negotiating the tangle of warehouses, workshops, inlets, bridges and dry docks with the ease of familiarity. She hummed softly to herself, feeling pleased with the result of the contract, despite the almost disaster.

Her decision to become a quaestor had been a good one. She had been certain that being able to absorb and use any other magic user's talents for a short time would give her an advantage in the business. She knew she was taking a risk because Spongers like her were regarded with suspicion. A lot of people felt it unfair that someone could access all the magical talents when so few had any talent at all. Many Spongers had been killed when their ability was discovered, but she thought it was worth the risk to be able to use her talent. Doing nothing with Quarenna's gift would feel wrong.

It was the evening before the equinox and, like most people, she was looking forward to the start of festivities. Everyone seemed to be making a quick start to the next day's celebrations by going home early; the docks were almost deserted. She knew there were guards inside the warehouses where particularly valuable cargoes, like goldenwood, silks and perfumes were stored. However, they weren't making their presence known and she hadn't seen anyone for quite some time. She heard the slap of water against the wharves and the creaking of cordage but nothing else. The smells of pitch, sawdust and seaweed were there but were muted, as if the evening was waiting for something to happen.

There was no reason for her to expect trouble. She patted her pouch and smiled at the quiet jingle that action produced. *Five dukals, five! That's enough to pay for my lodgings and food for at least three months, with enough left over to let me go to the Arenafest.*

Anarya crossed a bridge over a canal, and then her pleased humming stopped abruptly as she took in the scene in front of her. She was at one corner of a cobbled, roughly rectangular space bounded by one of the larger warehouses, a building that housed a ropewalk, the canal she had just crossed and a slipway where barges could be hauled out and repaired. The space wasn't empty.

Three big men, like her wearing the canvas trousers and aprons of dockworkers, were confronting a woman who was backed up against the wall of the warehouse. She was small, a good half a head shorter than Anarya, and was swathed in a dark-blue travelling cloak with the hood pulled up concealing her features.

"It's 'nox eve, little lady," one of the men said, "Time for a bit o' fun. Treat us right and y'll walk away. If you don't want to play with us – well, that'd be too bad."

Anarya paused briefly. She used the Oversight, wanting to check if any of the men were magic users before intervening. None were, but in the Oversight the woman stood out like a flame. She had a brilliant orange aura. The colour told Anarya that the woman was a Voyanter and the brightness and extent of the aura said she was very powerful. Unfortunately, being able to see and hear at a distance, through walls and round corners, wasn't going to do her much good in this situation.

Three to one odds were unacceptable in Anarya's opinion. Three to two was still poor but Anarya could do something about that. She still held some of the Lifter's talent; not much, but she could use it to change the odds. She reached out, seeing the red bands extending from her hands to grab one of the barge chocks lying by the slipway. *Got it!* she thought, *Holy Quarenna, it's heavier than I realised.*

Grunting with the effort, she used almost the last vestiges of the Lifter's talent to throw the chock. It soared through the air to hit one of the men on his right shoulder and neck, the impact sending him stumbling forward. He crashed to the ground and lay there groaning. One of the other men started turning towards his fallen companion as Anarya ran forward. She kicked him behind his knee. His leg collapsed.

She hadn't exhausted her borrowed talent but she had come very close to it and felt rather dizzy. When the man she kicked fell into her path she stumbled and tripped over him. She saw a flurry of movement where the third man was as she converted her momentum into a forward roll. Back on her feet, she spun round. Putting her back against the warehouse wall, she looked around to see what the men would do. Her jaw dropped. The third man was on the ground, unmoving. The woman was turning away from the man Anarya had tripped over and he wasn't moving either. She bent over the man Anarya had hit with the chock and his groans stopped abruptly.

The woman reached up and pulled her hood back. She inclined her head towards Anarya. "Thanks for your assistance give I and am grateful I," she said. Then she frowned slightly and shook her head. "Forgive please. Misspoke think I. I have no Katelish spoke for long time. I think I should said, I am grateful for your aid and offer my thanks. While able to subdue all of them myself might have been I, your help made it easier."

Anarya gaped at the woman. Close cropped hair so pale it was almost white and skin as dark as likos root was a stunning combination. Grey eyes looked out from an oval face with a smooth complexion marred by smudges of dirt on her forehead and left cheek. Then she recognised the formality and the odd cadence of her speech and blurted out, "You're a Sitrelker."

"*Su Sitrelku-fa,*" the woman agreed, "I am from Sitrelk. How did you know?"

"When I was growing up my closest friends were the children of Sitrelker refugees. You sounded just like their parents do when they're trying to speak Katelish. *Sitru kesstu-fa nela.* I am reasonably fluent in Sitru if you're more comfortable with that."

A slight crease appeared between the woman's eyebrows. She said, "I fear your accent leaves something to be desired, although worse have heard I. Please, may we continue in Katelish. It more appropriate would be in any case now that here am in Carregis I."

"Fine by me," said Anarya. She waved at the men on the ground and added, "I think we should leave here before they wake up."

"They will not wake," the woman said. She had a short cane in one hand and used it to point at one of the men. "That one rushed me somewhat and I was forced to use a killing stroke. Afterwards, to kill the others also I prudent judged."

Anarya stared at the woman, startled by the cold-blooded way she had dismissed killing the men. Then she remembered what the parents of her childhood friends had said – life was cheap in Sitrelk, that's why so many people left. *She kills easily. Am I in danger?* She looked again at the Sitrelker and felt a shiver of something. It wasn't fear, she didn't know what it was. It was almost like recognising someone she had never seen before.

"All the more reason to leave," she said. "The Duke's men will take us in for questioning if they find us here with bodies lying around. But they're not going to waste time investigating an apparent dockside brawl if there's nobody obvious to blame. Let's go."

"I do not know where to go," the Sitrelker said. "To Carregis am new I."

"There aren't all that many Sitrelkers here," said Anarya, "but I know where to find them and I can take you there."

"No, I do not wish this."

"Most of the refugees who arrive here want to move further away. A lot of them end up in Hemeark. That's where I grew up. It's about three day's travel upstream by coach. You could go there."

"No! I will not."

Anarya looked at her, surprised by the vehemence of her reaction. "Up to you," she said, then she shrugged and started to walk away, heading towards the alley between the warehouse and the ropewalk.

As Anarya expected the woman followed her and they walked on in silence for a while. Then the woman said, in what Anarya recognised as a direct translation of very formal Sitru, "Benefactor, I regret my outburst. My reaction was inappropriate and excessive. I should not have behaved in that way. Sorry am I."

Anarya had to think back to her childhood and an incident when she had inadvertently insulted the mother of one of her friends before she could recall an appropriate response. "No insult is perceived and clean air lies between us," she said, then repeated it in Sitru, *"Heru-ven ti lusegri-gal,"* to make it clear that she knew what she was saying.

"You are gracious," said the Sitrelker, inclining her head towards Anarya. "Please understand that I have left Sitrelk behind me and I do not wish to associate with others who will remind me of it."

"Why did you leave?"

"I do not want…"

"… to talk about it. I get the idea."

There was another short silence while they made their way through gaps between the buildings and along the wider access roads out into the area occupied during the day by the chaos of the carters and hauliers loading and unloading their wagons.

Then the Sitrelker said, "I do not wish to be reminded of my past or what I have left behind, and talk about it will not I. Returning to Sitrelk would be dangerous for me as I have broken the law by leaving. Can you understand that? No matter what I have lost by coming here I am *not* going back."

Anrhyna looked at the woman walking by her side. She was obviously quite skilled with using that cane as a weapon and her casual attitude to killing might be typical for a high-status Sitrelker, but it was a bit alarming. She said, "I'm not going to force you to do anything you don't want to do. It was partly to escape that sort of pressure from my parents that I left Hemeark."

Holy Quarenna guide me, she thought. *She's beautiful. I can't let her wander off when she doesn't know anything about the city and she stands out like a beacon. She'd attract all the wrong sorts of attention. She can handle herself but I'd hate to think of anything happening to her because I let her go off on her own.* For some reason, she felt as though she needed to get to know this strange woman. "It's getting late. Why don't you come home with me, at least for tonight, while you sort out what you're going to do?"

"Why are you helping me when you are under no obligation to me?"

"It's part of what I do. I'm a quaestor."

"I do not know what that is."

"It's a sort of combination of investigator, advisor, helper, recoverer of lost property, and lots of other things. The kind of person people come to when they need help and don't know what to do."

"We have no equivalent in Sitrelk. Forgive me for saying so, you look very young for such a task."

Anarya's shoulders slumped. "A lot of people seem to think that. Surely twenty-three is old enough."

"Twenty-three? You look younger than that. Tell me, how long have you been performing this function?"

"I took my first contract just before the last equinox, but it takes time to get established and I haven't had many yet."

"A quaestor works to a contract?"

"Yes. When someone wants me to do something we negotiate a fee. It depends on how much my client wants whatever it is and how long it's going to take me to do it. I've just finished a very good contract." She sneaked a look at the woman walking beside her and saw an eyebrow rise slightly. *There's something about her that makes me want to impress her, but I'm not succeeding.*

"I really have," said Anarya. "It was a good one. The best I've ever had in fact, but I've got to admit I've had some bad ones too."

"How do you find your clients?"

"Verbal advertising, mostly. I stick my nose into an inn or tavern and declare I'm available. I think I must know every tavern in Carregis now. Also I listen to rumours and follow up any clues to people who need help."

"I see. Will a contract to help me settle in Carregis take you?"

"I don't need a contract for that. I'll be happy to help."

The Sitrelker bowed, touching her right hand to her heart, and said, "You have the gratitude of Yi… Yisyena."

If she wants to change her name to make a complete break from her past that's her business. I'm not going to worry about it.

"Will you also help me to improve my Katelish?"

Anarya smiled. "I will do my best if you will help me with Sitru."

Yisyena frowned.

Oh! She said she wants a clean break, and here I am asking her to remember her past. I'm stupid sometimes.

"Very well," said Yisyena, sounding reluctant. "I will try."

O

It was dark by the time Anarya led Yisyena into the street where she rented a room above a carpet shop. She nodded, waved and called out greetings to several people as they went along the street. Then she turned into an alley, said, "Be careful of the second step, it's a bit rickety," and climbed two flights of stairs.

The room was small but she kept it clean and tidy. The walls were whitewashed. A narrow bed occupied one wall under a shuttered window. In the middle of the opposite wall was a fireplace with a small stove, pots and a kettle. One plain chair stood at a wooden table, which was scrubbed clean and supported an earthenware basin and ewer. A cupboard and a wardrobe stood partly open and held food and clothes. There was a fairly good quality russet rug on the floor. The only other decoration was a statuette of Quarenna in her aspect as the Friend and Comforter standing in a niche in one of the walls. Anarya inclined her head towards the statuette and touched her right thumb to her forehead. She lit the oil lamp standing on the table and said, "*Veru-nel hesh-fan.* Welcome to my home." When she opened the shutters some voices from the street came in, as did enticing cooking smells and a couple of flies.

She watched uneasily as Yisyena looked around. A Sitrelker speaking Katelish always managed to sound very formal and rather stilted. Even taking that into account, Anarya was fairly sure from her manner and way of speaking that Yisyena was used to better surroundings than this simple room, comfortable though it was.

Yisyena shrugged off the travelling cloak and draped it on the back of the chair. Underneath it she was wearing a loose linen shirt and trousers. They were a pale blue and were clearly good quality, but in places they were stained with what looked like oil, tar and fish scales. A braided cord acted as a belt and supported an empty-looking purse. She sank to her knees, wrapped her arms around her shoulders and hugged herself. "I have been afraid for days," she said, "and so tired of it I am. Safe here I feel, it is wonderful. I cannot thank you enough."

Anarya was embarrassed. She went over and helped Yisyena to her feet. "I'll heat some water," she said. "You'll feel better after you've had a wash. There are towels in the cupboard and you can borrow some of my clothes, if there's any that will fit."

Yisyena started to take her clothes off and Anarya hurriedly said, "I'll go out for half a chime to give you some privacy."

"No. Please do not go. Privacy is not important to me. I would prefer to have your company."

Anarya knew from her childhood friends that body modesty was an unknown concept in Sitrelk, but she was still astonished when Yisyena stripped naked in front of her to wash. *She's beautiful! Quarenna aid me. Sharing the bed with her is going to stretch my self-control to the limit.*

"Try that," said Anarya, taking a cotton sleeping robe from her cupboard. "It might fit well enough."

"It is a little tight," said Yisyena, wriggling her way into it. "I am somewhat larger in the bust than you are, but it will suffice."

"I don't have much food to offer but I can go out and get something. There's a shop just around the corner that does skewered lamb and peppers – or maybe you'd rather have grilled fish. What would you like?"

"Not fish, please. I came here on a fishing boat and the smell was pervasive, unavoidable and overpowering. I do not wish to eat fish any time soon."

Anarya couldn't help laughing, then she apologised.

"I am forced to agree," said Yisyena, "There is a humorous element. I am not offended."

When Anarya returned with the food she found Yisyena sitting on the bed looking half asleep. She had her cane in her hand. Anarya didn't want to risk being the target for that weapon so she deliberately made a noise.

Yisyena jumped to her feet, looking around with her cane raised and ready for action.

"Don't worry," said Anarya. "It's just me."

Siting back down, Yisyena said, "I was almost asleep. May I go to bed after we have eaten?"

"Of course, but we will have to share the bed."

"That is acceptable."

Yisyena climbed into the bed first and scrunched up as close to the wall as possible.

Anarya extinguished the lamp and got in too, trying to avoid touching Yisyena any more than she had to. She said, "Quarenna bless you, Yisa. Good night."

Yisyena sniffled quietly then started sobbing.

Anarya rolled over and put her arms around Yisyena. "What's wrong?"

"You called me Yisa. That's what my sister used to call me. I miss her."

"I'm sorry. I didn't mean to be too familiar."

"It is foolish of me to be upset. It was a surprise. I think I would like you to call me Yisa, and I shall call you Anra." She turned in Anarya's arms and kissed her.

Anarya froze. *Was that an invitation? I hope so, or I'm going to frighten her away and feel very foolish.*

She returned the kiss, trying to stay calm.

"I have little experience of being with women," said Yisyena, "I do not wish to give offence, but I would like to be with you tonight, if that is acceptable to you."

"Yes," said Anarya, surprised. "Very much so. I've been attracted to you from the moment we met, and I don't think it's just that I've not had a lover for a long time. But I didn't want to be pushy, particularly after your meeting with those men."

"Is it common in Carregis? Sex between women, I mean. And acknowledged?"

"Yes. Nobody really cares as long as both partners agree. Is it different in Sitrelk?"

"Very. Same sex partnerships are frowned upon. They happen in secret and are considered shameful."

"It's up to you," said Anarya. "I'm not going to force you to do anything you don't want to."

"I am nervous," said Yisyena. "In Sitrelk I could not admit to my previous experiences with women. They happened when I was overwrought and in need of comfort…"

"Don't worry about it. It's up to you to decide." Anarya kissed Yisyena gently.

Moments later the return kiss was fierce and demanding, a clear invitation to take things further.

O

Much later, with both of them hot, sweaty and naked, Yisyena pillowed her head on Anarya's shoulder. "Anra, are you familiar with the concept of *galgalis*?"

"No, I don't know the word."

"It means a recognition of mutual destiny. It happened to me tonight shortly after we met. It's one reason I want to be near you. Also there is something about you that makes me feel safe and secure. Please do not think it is just gratitude for your kindness that makes me want to stay with you. Is it possible?

"You can stay as long as you want to."

"You said you don't have another lover?"

"Not since I came to Carregis. I guess I've been too busy."

"How fortunate for me that this is so. *Gal-mussen-hu ven galis*."

"What does that mean?"

Yisyena hesitated then said, "The closest I can come in translation is 'Your soul sits within mine.'"

SPONGER

"Wake up, Yisa. It's equinox today. I've been looking forward to the Arenafest for months. Do you want to come with me or stay here? It's going to be great. Caseir will be fighting."

Yisyena stretched and lay back on the bed, looking up at Anarya, "Why is the equinox significant?"

"It's a festival, a day for relaxation and fun. You must have those in Sitrelk."

"We do, but not at the equinoxes. We celebrate at midsummer, midwinter and Revelation Day, when The God was first recognised in Sitrelk."

"Is that all?"

"Is that not enough?"

"We party at midsummer and midwinter as well as the equinoxes and several other times as well, like the King's Birthday and the First Fruit Festival. And you only have three a year! Now I know why people leave Sitrelk."

Yisyena sat up and glared at Anarya, "You have *no* idea why!"

Anarya shivered at the look she was getting. *I didn't mean to offend you. Don't want to lose you when I've only just found you.* "I'm sorry, Yisa. I didn't intend to upset you. I was making a joke."

"It was *not* funny."

"I don't know why you left – No, don't get angry. I'm not going to ask, I know you don't want to talk about it. Please forgive me."

Yisyena glowered for a moment, then she took a deep breath, stood, wrapped her arms around Anarya and whispered *"Heru-ven ti lusegri-gal."*

Anarya found she could breathe again. Telling herself to be more careful in future, she kissed Yisyena, pulled her back down on to the bed and said, "Breakfast can wait."

○

Anarya stirred rice, onions and peppers into scrambled eggs for breakfast and made two mugsful of lemon and mint tea. She dragged the table across the room so that she could perch on the bed and reach the tabletop while Yisyena used the chair.

"You mentioned an Arenafest," said Yisena. "Are such events always part of your celebrations?"

"There are always some fights on a festival day but Arenafests only happen at the equinoxes. They're more than just fights. There are all sorts of demonstrations and competitions as well as the races and the fights."

"I believe I would like to go with you. I would not wish to upset your plans for the day and, in any case, I want to be with you."

"You'll enjoy it. Like I said, Caseir is fighting today. He's the greatest."

"Tell me about him."

Anarya wrapped her hands around a fresh mug of tea, sat back a bit and said, "He's won fifty-seven solo bouts. That's more than twice as many as anybody else in history. He doesn't fight often these days. It's over a year since his last appearance. There have been rumours that this might be his last fight, but they said that last time too. It's said he's been getting a cut of the gate money as well as the winner's purse for the last few years. He can afford to retire."

"You seem very sure he will win today."

"Of course he will. I'd never wager against him. You'll see. He's magnificent."

Yisyena indicated the crumpled sleeping robe she was wearing. "I cannot go dressed like this and I have no body paint."

"Quarenna's mercy! You couldn't go painted anyway. The Sitrelkers I know back in Hemeark said you don't wear clothes if you're painted."

"What would be the point of clothes? Nobody could see the body art."

"Trust me, Yisa. Body paint isn't an option, it would cause a riot. Let's see what I've got that might fit you. We've got to find you something. You've got to dress well for the festival."

"You have many different styles of clothes," said Yisyena

as they pulled garments from the wardrobe.

"That's because I don't know where my business will take me. A quaestor has to be prepared for anything and I've got to be able to go almost anywhere and be inconspicuous. I even have to dress as a man at times."

"I could not do that convincingly but, in appropriate clothes, I believe you could."

"Never mind that for now. I like dressing up when I get the chance," said Anarya. "This is what I was planning on wearing today." She displayed a heavily embroidered cream silk waistcoat, a yellow cotton shirt and a voluminous floor-length skirt striped in various shades of red.

"I could never wear that," said Yisyena. "You are so much taller than me that I would be constantly tripping over the skirt, and I would bulge out of the waistcoat in a most unbecoming way."

Eventually they settled on a loose green chemise over a purple velvet skirt with an assortment of necklaces and bangles.

"It will have to do, I suppose," said Anarya, looking critically at the outfit, "but it's not really festive enough. Let's go. The arena will start filling up about a chime before noon. We've got time for me to show you a bit of Carregis while I try to attract some business."

"Wait a moment, Anra," said Yisyena. She picked up her purse and upended it on to the table. A pair of pearl and amethyst earrings fell out. "I could not bring much with me but if you tell me where I can sell these I can repay some of your kindness."

"But…"

"Do not worry. They are mine. They were given to me by my sister to mark my Awakening."

"Awakening? What do you mean?"

"It is what we call it when someone is revealed as talented – my talent is being able to see things far away and out of normal sight. I think the Katelish word is Voyanter."

Anarya sat down with a thump as if she was startled. *I know what you are,* she thought, *but I'm glad you brought it up because I can't explain how I know without revealing what I am.* "Voyanter is the right word," she said.

"Please do not be alarmed. I know you have Voyanters and

those with other talents here or Katelish would not have words for the abilities."

"I'm not frightened, just surprised," said Anarya. "Talents, as you call them, aren't that unusual in Carrhen. Something like one person in a hundred has one of some sort. I'm startled because I got the impression from my Sitrelker neighbours that talents are much less common in Sitrelk. And here you are with one of the rarer skills."

"Rarer?"

"The gods don't make many Voyanters. They…"

"The gods? What have they to do with the talents?"

Anarya was glad she was sitting down or she might have fallen from the sheer shock of that question. As it was she almost spilled her tea. "What do the gods have to do with the talents? Everything. They are gifts from Quarenna." She turned to the statuette and touched her right thumb to her forehead. "At least they are for women. It's Huler who gifts them to men."

"Your gods, Quarenna and Huler. Their names are known but they are not revered in Sitrelk," said Yisyena. "There is only The God, and he receives gifts of talents, he does not give them. In Sitrelk the talents run in families. About half of my relatives are Voyanters like me and the others are mostly Lifters or Scratchers – I think those are the correct names in Katelish. It is true that occasionally a person born outside the families is discovered to be talented and is adopted into one of them, but it is very rare. I have seen twenty-five Revelation Days and it has only happened once in my lifetime."

Anarya was speechless for a moment, then said, "The gods are definitely involved with the talents here. A woman has to spend the night of her first blood at a shrine of Quarenna, meditating at the altar of the Maiden. At dawn she discovers if she has received one of the gifts. I'm sure men must have an equivalent ritual but I don't know any details. I've never heard men discussing it. Talking to men about the rituals of Quarenna isn't forbidden, but it's just not done. Maybe it's the same for men, they don't talk about Huler to women. Men never enter a shrine of Quarenna or women a temple of Huler."

"That is very different," said Yisyena, shaking her head.

"In Sitrelk it is also at first blood when a woman's talent appears but there is no ritual such as you describe. As far as I know there is not a specific event which triggers a man's Awakening. It happens overnight when they are around eighteen years old, sometimes as early as seventeen or as late as twenty. They have a dream and waken up with their talent. An Awakening is a cause for celebration within the family."

Anarya blinked. *That can't be right! If the gifts don't come from the gods, where do they come from? I'm going to have to talk with one of the priestesses about this,* she thought. *Why would it be different here and in Sitrelk? Saying the gods aren't involved sounds so wrong. Is it blasphemy?*

Yisyena said, "Can you help me convert these earrings into money?"

"Oh... Yes... I suppose so." Anarya had trouble concentrating on the mundane. "If you're sure that's what you want to do. But wouldn't you rather keep them?"

"I would. However, I have no money on which to live and I cannot presume on your kindness."

"Are you going to stay in Carregis?"

"I believe I will," said Yisyena.

"Well, if you want to stay with me..."

"I do."

"... you could work with me. A Voyanter could be very useful in my business."

"Work with you? As a partner in your business?"

"I wasn't thinking partnership, after all you don't know Carregis or anything about being a quaestor."

"This is true. However, you wish to utilise my talent. What do you offer in exchange?"

I want her to stay. It feels right for us to be together. Could this be that galgalis, *that destiny she talked about?*

"I'll give you an opportunity to learn if you like being a quaestor. Then, if you do, a partnership as well as a home here with me."

Yisyena was silent for a while, then said, "That seems to be a sensible and satisfactory solution. I accept."

"Keep those," said Anarya, pushing the earrings back across the table. She took some coins from her own pouch and gave them to Yisyena. "You can't go to festival with no money in your purse. Take these."

"But I have not earned them."

"Consider them a loan which you will repay by working with me."

Yisyena studied the coins. "I do not know what these are."

"This is a bit," said Anarya, pointing to one coin. "The smaller one is a half-bit and the smallest is a quarter-bit. The bigger ones are worth five and ten bits. Fifty bits make a dukal." She pulled one from a box in the cupboard and let Yisyena see it before putting it away again. "There's also a gold coin, called a regal. It's worth four dukals, but it's not likely you'll ever see one. Now let's go and enjoy ourselves."

O

As they made their way through the streets towards the arena Anarya went into every tavern they passed and announced "Quaestor for hire. Reasonable rates. Leave your messages for Anarya with the warden at the shrine of Quarenna by the Arch. Quaestor for hire."

Most of the time she was shouting over the hubbub of conversation and was ignored but sometimes heads turned towards her.

"Does no one ever come to you directly?" asked Yisyena. "It seems to me that it would be easier than using a message drop. This does not seem to be an efficient way of finding clients."

"Sometimes you'll get a direct approach, but not very often. This is the traditional way of doing it. Wait in any tavern long enough and you'll hear lots of people advertising their services, not just quaestors."

Sure enough, almost as soon as Anarya finished her announcement in *The Piebald Mare* another voice called out. "Laundry, get your laundry done. Fast and cheap. I'm Hilech and my shop's in Pargol Street. Get your laundry done within a day."

"See what I mean, Yisa?"

Another man walked in and called, "Whisperer! Links in Voro and Verenthe. Your messages passed in complete confidence. Whisperer for hire! Contact me through Nairin at his bakery in Bread Street."

"Common people have access to Whisperers here?" asked Yisyena.

"Of course, why shouldn't they?"

"In Sitrelk all the Whisperers work for The God. They pass messages, petitions and decrees between the governors and other authorities. Ordinary people can't use them."

"Really? Here anyone can hire a Whisperer to send a message anywhere in the country. I'd be a bit worried about using him, though," said Anarya, nodding towards the man who was just leaving. "I don't like the way he emphasised 'complete confidence'. No Whisperer should need to do that because nobody would ever trust them if they gossiped about the messages they handled. Also most Whisperers have a fixed place of business where they can be found. It's usually a tavern. It makes me suspicious that he doesn't."

All seven of the taverns in the Great Square were crammed full and the patrons were spilling out into the square itself. Anarya said, "They're always like that at a festival. I'm going to give them a miss today because it would be pointless trying to make myself heard in there."

The usual market stalls in the square had been cleared away for the festival and in their place there were booths, tents and tables offering food, drink, trinkets, games of chance and games of skill. Acrobats, singers, jugglers and musicians wandered through the crowd. Three carts drawn up side by side against the wall of the temple of Huler provided a stage for players acting out a comedy based on the misfortunes of a legendary wise fool.

"Do you like beer?" asked Anarya.

"I do not know. It is not a Sitrelker drink. I would rather have wine."

"You won't get a decent wine here today. The vintners take advantage of the demand at festivals to sell off their poorest wines. Why don't you give the beer a try?"

"Very well, I will."

They wedged themselves into a corner of one of the beer tents. Anarya dropped a half-bit on to the tray carried by one of the circulating servers and took two mugs of beer from it. "Here, try that."

Yisyena took a cautious sip and made a face. "I do not think I can drink that. It is unpleasantly sour."

Anarya tasted her beer. "Oh, I'm sorry! It's usually quite good. This tastes as if it was brewed just this morning.

They left the beer tent and wandered out into the crowd. "There's usually a candy maker around here," said Anarya as they pushed their way towards the centre of the square. "She makes the most delicious mint toffee. Do you like candy?"

"I am afraid so. As a child I would make myself sick eating too much of it."

They set out to find the candy maker's stall but were diverted when Yisyena said, "What is that wonderful smell?"

Anarya sniffed. She smelled burning charcoal, hot fat, sizzling onions and pungent spices. "That? Oh, it's just somebody selling sausage-in-a-bun."

"It smells delicious. I have never had one of those. I would like to try it."

Anarya shrugged. "If you want one, I don't see why not. But you probably shouldn't ask what sort of meat it is."

Yisyena took a bite from her bun, used her tongue to catch a fragment of onion that had dropped to her chin and said, "This is good." She was about to take another bite when someone bumped into her, throwing her against Anarya. She dropped her sausage-in-a-bun to grab the arm of a young man and twist it. "Slitpurse," she said. "He has your money."

The man swung round, the concealed blade in his left hand lashing out at Yisyena. She ducked and brought her elbow up to slam into his face. He fell and screamed as she twisted his arm against his falling weight and dislocated his shoulder. The money from Anarya's pouch scattered on the cobbles.

Aided by some of the bystanders, Anarya recovered twenty-seven and a half bits. She was sure that she had had more than that. Some must have disappeared into the pouches of her helpers, but she was grateful to get back as much as she did.

"What do we do with him?" asked Yisyena, twisting the man's arm and provoking another scream of pain.

"Don't worry about him," said the stall keeper. He pointed at a red and black banner hoisted above the roof of the stall. "I've called for help, I have. Duke's men'll be here soon. You did good work catching him, you did. Here, let me give you another sausage-in-a-bun to make up for the one you had to drop."

Anarya saw two men wearing the red and black tabards of the Duke of Carrh pushing their way through the crowd towards the stall. "You'd better let me do the talking. Your accent will attract their attention and they might want to take you away for questioning."

Yisyena relinquished her grip on the would-be thief's arm and moved away, deeper into the crowd on the other side of the stall.

The Duke's men listened to what Anarya and the stall keeper had to say, then marched the slitpurse away.

"What will happen to him?" asked Yisyena when she rejoined Anarya.

"He'll be flogged. And he might lose a finger if he's been caught stealing before," said Anarya with a shrug. "Time's getting on. We'd better head for the arena or we won't get a decent place."

PYROMANCER

Admission to the arena cost them two bits each. "We'll have to stand," she told Yisyena, "I can't afford even the cheapest seats, they cost half a dukal each."

"Standing does not worry me," said Yisyena looking around "This place is large. How many people can it hold?"

"I think it's somewhere between eight and nine thousand, but it's nowhere near big enough."

The arena was a horseshoe of terraces closed off at the end by a cliff face. They climbed three levels above the sandy floor and joined the crowd packed into the angle between the terracing and the cliff. "This is about as good as we'll get. That slitpurse delayed us too much."

Over on the other side of the arena they could see canopied and cushioned seats in enclosures of various sizes at floor level. Most of them were still unoccupied. Anarya inclined her head to indicate them and said, "It's considered lowering to arrive before someone of lesser rank. They'll all fill up later, more or less in reverse order of status. It's quite fun watching who arrives when. Sometimes there are squabbles when a family gets the timing wrong."

"How much do seats like that cost?"

"I've no idea. You can't just buy one, the rights to them are jealously guarded and passed on from generation to generation. Even then you have to be considered 'suitable' to be able to occupy one. See the green and purple seahorse badge?"

"Yes."

"That's the badge of the Gilruan company. There was a great fuss a couple of years ago when Mueaba, the old woman who owned it, died. She left her four seats to a favourite nephew, along with her holdings in a shipbuilding firm. Everything else went to her granddaughter. The legacy was just in time to save the nephew from bankruptcy. He had a bad reputation and wasn't thought to be socially acceptable. He was turned away when he tried to use those seats at the next Arenafest. They've stayed empty ever since. There's a three-way legal battle going on between the nephew, the granddaughter and Graumedel. Every so often there's a new argument in court and the gossip about it is always interesting."

"Who is Graumedel?"

"He's the Count of Carregis. He owns the arena. That's his badge, the golden beehive."

"Why is he involved in the legal battle?"

"He maintains that the seats are not sold but leased and that he can refuse entry if he wants to. Anyway, I don't think any court is going to find against him."

"I do not understand. If this Count Graumedel owns the arena why does he not have the best seats. Those under the red bear are better positioned."

"The red bear is the badge of Wurauf, the Duke of Carrh. He outranks the Count." *That's not all,* thought Anarya, *but this isn't the best place to be talking politics. That'll have to keep until we get home.*

O

The noise level rose as the dozen men raking the sand left the arena and the Arenamaster, in his long white cloak, entered. He strode to the centre of the arena, bowed to the canopied seats then turned on the spot quickly enough for his cloak to flare out revealing the blood red lining.

"Citizens of Carregis," he declaimed. His voice was clearly audible everywhere in the arena, thanks to a Chemer's potion. "I give you greetings on this auspicious day."

The audience answered with a chorus of blessings and invocations of Huler or Quarenna. As usual the response contained some jeers, boos and admonitions to get on with it. Almost certainly, although Anarya couldn't actually hear any, there were also uncomplimentary remarks directed at Duke Wurauf and Count Graumedel.

The Arenamaster swirled his cloak again. "It gives me great pleasure to announce that, for your entertainment, the Honourable Guild of Blacksmiths and Farriers presents a display by two of its most accomplished members. They are among the strongest Pyromancers in the city. I am confident you will agree that their mastery of fire is astonishing. I entreat you to give welcome to Terraum and Faetilla."

Anarya used the Oversight to watch the two Pyromancers make their way to the centre of the arena. It was like looking through a mask of fine silk. She could still see, but everything, except for the auras of magic users and whatever they were manipulating, was slightly blurred. The bright purple auras of the Pyromancers stood out. She could see a scattering of other colours throughout the crowd showing where other gifted people were but she wasn't paying attention to those. The opportunity to watch expert Pyromancers at work was one she couldn't ignore. Control of fire was an ability she had used before, but not one she was particularly comfortable with. She knew from experience that she could hold it unused for less than half a chime and could use it for only about a tenth.

The closer she was to a talented person the easier it was to absorb their gift. The Pyromancers were probably just within her reach. She visualised a thread stretching out from her own rainbow aura to touch the brighter of the purple ones. It was getting very thin when it made contact and turned purple.

For a moment, before she pulled the thread back, it felt as if she was in two places at once, watching from the terracing and standing on the hot sand of the arena with the sound of the crowd beating down on her. Then she was back in her own body and had duplicated the Pyromancer's gift within her own mind.

Terraum and Faetilla stood facing each other about ten paces apart. An anticipatory hush fell. A spark of brightness appeared at head height in the air between them and grew until it was as big around as a sweet melon. Then it rose high overhead and burst into dozens of multi-coloured fist-sized balls spinning through a complicated interlocking spiral pattern and provoking gasps of awe from the audience. Anarya was entranced by the delicacy of control they had, far beyond her own capabilities. It was as if they were juggling with fire, passing control back and forth.

Then, while one of them kept the display spinning, she saw a network of purple threads travel to the end of the arena and turned to watch it go. A cascade of fire poured down the cliff face at the near end of the arena. At the bottom it formed itself into a river and rushed the length of the sandy floor, splitting around the two Pyromancers, who were left standing on an island in the river of fire. Finally, it splashed upwards like water from a fountain and disappeared in mid-air.

The fire's cold, Anarya realised. *How do they do that?* The Oversight showed her faint purple threads reaching out from the Pyromancers to the mass of flame as they controlled and directed it. Some of the threads were braiding in an odd way, forming a hollow tube with the fire contained within it. Before she could study the braid in detail the last of the flames surged up the fountain, turning blue as they did so, and vanished. *Now I know it's possible to have cold fire, and I got a glimpse of how to do it. I'll have to practice that, it could be useful.*

Cheers rang out as Terraum and Faetilla bowed and waved before leaving the arena floor.

The Arenamaster's assistants hurried out, pushing handcarts containing stone columns which they placed in a line down the middle of the arena. Once the carts were in place the Arenamaster appeared and announced, "For your entertainment and delight, the best contestants from this year's Carregis races will compete for a purse of twenty dukals, sponsored by the Beghroth company. The race will last a minimum of ten turns around the arena and a maximum of twenty. If two or more reach the end of the course then the prize will be divided between them. Prepare yourselves to greet the fastest and most skilful racers in Carregis."

Twelve men entered and lined up, jostling for position, on a line drawn in the sand at one end of the arena. The Arenamaster kept them waiting while he strutted slowly to the other end. Then he signalled to a trumpeter and the blast he sounded started the race.

Three of the men fell before they took more than a few paces, tripped up by their opponents. The rest of them formed a tight bunch as they ran the length of the arena for the first time. Elbows thumped into chests. Some staggered as they were pushed but managed to stay upright. Feet got tangled and two more fell.

"Are they allowed to obstruct each other like that?" asked Yisyena.

"Of course. It's a no-holds-barred race. Anything goes. If

they're down they're out."

"It would not be permitted in Sitrelk. There races are non-contact and the winner is the fastest, not the most aggressive."

"Where's the fun in that?" asked Anarya, looking quizzically at Yisyena. "It must be boring to watch."

Yisyena shrugged. "It's exciting when they are evenly matched."

The first turn around the stones took its toll with another two fallers. The five who had managed to stay on their feet separated and became strung out into a loose bunch. Shouts from the crowd urged them on.

Turns of the arena passed with no changes in position. By the eighth turn the leader was visibly tiring. The second runner swung wide to pass him, but not wide enough. He got an elbow in his ribs for his trouble, staggered and fell back to third place.

Halfway through the eleventh turn the man in third place increased his speed. He clipped the ankle of the man in front of him and sent him tumbling to the ground. Hurdling over the faller he stayed on his feet but the man behind him didn't.

The three remaining runners were completing the twelfth turn when the leader stumbled, grabbing at his leg and falling. The others ran past him. The new leader looked around, slowed and turned round to grapple with his last opponent. Shouts of encouragement greeted this manoeuvre and the race became a wrestling match. The shouts changed to groans when one of the leader's legs collapsed and he fell, taking the other man with him.

"There is no winner," announced the Arenamaster to a chorus of jeers from the spectators. "However, thanks to the generosity of Keiret Beghroth the last two men will share half the original purse."

"That's not unusual," said Anarya. "The last two racers often end up wrestling, but they're not generally very good at it and both fall. You'll see some better wrestling later on, after the strength contests."

After the carts with the stone columns were cleared away the Arenamaster strutted out again, twirled his cloak a few times and declared, "Citizens of Carregis, now it is time for you to demonstrate your generosity and clemency."

The statement was greeted by jeers and catcalls.

"We are pleased to present, for your enjoyment, an unarmed mêlée between convicted criminals who have agreed to participate today in the hope of mitigating their punishments. They will fight for a quarter chime." He paused while his assistants shepherded about thirty men into the arena. "If there is only one still standing at the gong he will gain his freedom, otherwise those remaining will be presented to you one by one. You may choose to free as many of them as have fought well enough to please you."

"I presume these are all men sentenced to death," said Yisyena.

"That, or many years down a mine or chained to an oar. Some of them genuinely think they can win but most of them are desperate to avoid punishment and just hope Huler is with them."

Anarya suddenly thought that Lirrov might be among the contestants and might gain his freedom to come after her. *No, he can't be, can he? Jemis Gotheer said he was bound for the mines, but he might have volunteered for this instead.* She breathed more easily when the Oversight showed her that all the contestants were untalented and she realised that Lirrov wouldn't have recovered from the beating he was going to get in time for this event.

The men were chivvied into a rough circle. A hush of anticipation swept through the audience. Then a gong sounded, the men jumped at each other and the sound level jumped too. Some of the bigger men found themselves under attack from several sides at once. One of them, in a green tunic, managed to get hold of and lift a slighter opponent. He spun around using him as a flail to scatter the others. Cheers greeted this manoeuvre.

Heads clashed and blood flowed. Despite his attempts to free himself, on the opposite side of the mêlée another big man was swarmed by half a dozen others and disappeared under a pile of bodies. When it cleared he and two others were lying motionless on the sand.

The human flail was discarded by Green Tunic, sent flying into a group of three men pummelling each other. All three stumbled and fell. A chorus of approval roared out as the big man's fist made sure they wouldn't rise again.

Two men fighting a private battle on the edges of the mêlée stopped battering each other and formed an alliance against Green Tunic, jumping him from behind. He reached over his shoulder, grabbed one of them and threw him to the ground. He fell himself but rolled as he fell, landing on top of his other assailant. Green Tunic staggered to his feet. He kicked the man he had landed on and looked around for more victims.

A stroke of the gong brought the mêlée officially to an end, although two men carried on fighting until separated by the Arenamaster's assistants. Four men were still on their feet. One of the survivors was swaying so much he looked as if he could fall at any time.

"That small man with the ginger pigtail was very good," said Yisyena.

"Didn't notice him, I was watching the one in the green tunic. He was brilliant."

"He was powerful but had no finesse," said Yisyena. "I saw Ginger take out two men by himself with excellent grappling and throwing and he assisted with two others. From the way he acted I am sure he must have had military training."

The assistants consulted with each other, then one of them reported to the Arenamaster. The combatants who could be got to their feet were ushered out of the arena. Eight of them had to be carried out. Anarya wasn't sure if they were unconscious or dead.

The noise level subsided as the Arenamaster walked to the centre. "People of Carregis, each of the remaining contestants awaits your decision."

He pointed at a man in a leather jerkin. His face was a little battered, his nose was swollen and bloody, and one eye was partly closed. Anarya hadn't particularly noticed him during the mêlée and turned to Yisyena for help. However, she hadn't seen him do anything either.

"This man was convicted of assault and robbery and sentenced to serve three years in the mines. In the mêlée he defeated one man singlehanded and two with assistance. What is your pleasure?"

People nearby started hissing. The sound grew and grew as more of the crowd joined in. The man's shoulders slumped.

"As you decree, people of Carregis. There is no relief for

this man. He will serve his sentence."

The man with the ginger pigtail was called forward. "This man was convicted of murder, although he claimed it was self-defence. Four men fell to his skill in the mêlée. What is your pleasure?"

A chant of "Freedom, freedom…" started and grew louder until most of the audience were shouting for him. The man stood up straighter, grinned and waved his arms overhead.

"The people of Carregis have given their decision. You are free to go," said the Arenamaster.

The man who was swaying on his feet was indicated next. He took two unsteady steps, pitched forward, vomited and went into convulsions. The seizure didn't last long and when it stopped he was obviously dead. There was a gasp from the crowd which quieted until the body was removed.

"That's a shame," said Anarya. "He wasn't all that good but he might have made it."

"I do not think so," replied Yisyena. "He was not as good as the one who failed to impress."

Green Tunic was greeted with the 'Freedom' chant even before his crime was announced. Anarya joined in enthusiastically and applauded as he left the sands.

VOYANTER

The Arenafest continued with throwing contests and wrestling matches. These were followed by trials of strength in which men competed to carry the largest possible rocks from one end of the arena to the other in the shortest time.

The arena was hot. People wandered up and down the terraces selling water, beer, handmeals, wine and fruit. When she had the chance Anarya spent another half-bit for two cups of water. Some of the handmeals smelled good but Anarya said "We'll eat when we get home. It's not worth paying extra for food here."

"Is that Count Graumedel?" asked Yisyena when a man in black and gold took his seat under the beehive banner.

"Yes, that's him. That means it's nearly time for the swords. That's all he ever comes to watch."

"Where is the Duke?"

"He probably won't come. Rumour has it he's not well."

The first three bouts of swords were fought to first blood between men hoping to make names for themselves as arena fighters. One of the newcomers fought particularly well, unexpectedly beating a better known fighter in only a few strokes. He was rewarded with a purse thrown by Count Graumedel. Then there were several bouts between men who were already established names and who put on a better display than the novices. Their fights incited the crowd to fresh levels of enthusiasm.

Anarya jumped up and down with excitement, applauding the skills of the contestants and groaning in dismay when something went wrong. She relished the heat of the sand, the bright crimson splashes of blood soaking into it and the smells of sweat and hot blood.

When the Arenamaster walked to the centre wearing his cloak inside out she turned to Yisyena, grabbed her and shouted in her ear, "Death bout. It's got to be Caseir. Now you'll see something worth watching."

Even with his voice amplified by magic the Arenamaster

was barely audible when he announced, "People of Carregis, I am proud to bring you, for a purse of one hundred and fifty dukals, a death bout sponsored by His Excellency Count Graumedel."

He paused and the noise level dropped slightly. "From Getruva – with sixteen wins in the last three years, the last four of them in death bouts – it gives me great pleasure to present to you the exciting arena sensation – Ristaion."

The man who entered the arena was tall and muscular. He raised his arms, waved to the audience, inviting them to cheer. The crowd responded. Then he cartwheeled, somersaulted and tumbled his way across the sand to the centre. This exhibition produced even louder screams and applause, but it was nothing compared to the eruption of noise when the Arenamaster said, "And now, needing no introduction, fighting for the fifty-eighth time, the greatest fighter in the history of Carrhen: Caseir – The – Unconquered."

Anarya had seen him fight several times; the first had been years ago in the arena at Hemeark before he became really famous. Each time she was surprised by how short he was, because in her thoughts he was a giant. Without thinking about it she borrowed Yisyena's Voyanter skills to study him closely. As always she felt, for a moment, that she was in two bodies at once. The sensations she got from Yisyena surprised her. There was a conflict of emotions with a mixture of uncertainty, apprehension and, strangely enough, hope. She wanted to know why Yisa felt like that but couldn't say anything without giving away how she knew. All she could do was hope for an opportunity to discuss her feelings later on.

She turned her attention to Caseir and tried to count the scars on his arms and torso. There were so many she lost track of which ones she had counted. He walked a straight line to the centre of the arena with no flamboyant gestures. He looked unstoppable.

The Arenamaster's assistants stuck a sword into the sand ten paces from each end of the arena. Ristaion and Caseir stood back to back at the centre. The Arenamaster waited until an anticipatory hush settled over the arena, then he shouted, "Fight!"

Ristaion was fast. He reached his sword while Caseir was still half a dozen paces from claiming his. He was so fast that Anarya used her Oversight to see if he had magical assistance. She didn't see an aura around him, but she saw a dark blue one around Caseir. That didn't surprise her, she had seen it before. It meant he was a Daimoner. The first time she had seen it she had been shocked to discover that her hero could get help from the insubstantial denizens of the Darkworld. She had watched to see if he actually invoked a daimon during a fight and was relieved when he didn't. It was the same in each fight she had seen. He didn't use daimonic assistance. He was actually as strong, fast and skilful as he seemed to be and didn't need help.

Caseir plucked his sword from the sand moments after Ristaion had claimed his. He turned, stood in place and waited while Ristaion ran towards him. The crowd gasped as Ristaion stopped just in time to avoid running on to Caseir's sword. The first clash of swords raised the intensity of the crowd's screams again. There was a flurry of action which Anarya found difficult to follow even with the advantage of the Voyanter's talent. Then the parries and thrusts slowed slightly and she could begin to appreciate the skill of the two fighters.

"They are more closely matched than I thought they would be from what you told me," said Yisyena, and Anarya was forced to agree.

There was a difference in styles with Ristaion dancing around, trying to attack from different angles, while Caseir merely turned on the spot keeping his opponent in front of him. First blood went to Caseir. A backhanded cut opened a gash in Ristaion's shoulder as he recovered from a lunge. The sight of blood intensified the crowd's reactions and Anarya roared with them. The sight of her hero fighting for his life made her twitch with every movement he made. The feeling of tension increased and she gasped with everyone else when Ristaion managed to draw blood from Caseir's right forearm.

The fighters separated briefly, then Caseir went on the attack. He drove Ristaion back, wounding him twice more at the cost of a slash across his ribs.

Anarya's hand went to her mouth when blood poured from the chest wound, and her fist pumped the air whenever Caseir drew blood.

Ristaion swept Caseir's sword to the side. Before he could get his own into position for a telling stroke, Caseir stepped forward to grapple with him. They stood body to body for a few moments, then Caseir head-butted Ristaion who staggered back. He managed to leave his sword embedded in Caseir's left thigh. The pommel of Caseir's sword hammered into Ristaion's temple. He dropped to his knees in front of Caseir and blood fountained as Caseir's blade slammed into the back of his neck.

There was a hush when the crowd realised it was over. Then shouts and screams erupted and thousands of voices bellowed Caseir's name.

The Voyanter's ability let Anarya hear Caseir mutter between gasps for breath, "Too close, too cursed close. You were good, but not quite good enough." Then he lifted his sword in salute to his opponent.

"Caseir is still the Unconquered," shouted the Arenamaster over the tumult of noise. Caseir dropped to one knee, then pulled the sword from his thigh and waited while a tight bandage was wrapped around it. He hobbled across towards the beehive banner and caught a purse thrown by Count Graumedel.

"I told you, didn't I. He's the greatest," said Anarya, jumping up and down and bubbling with enthusiasm. "Ristaion was good, but not quite good enough."

"That was – interesting," said Yisyena. "There is much to talk about. Is that the end? Shall we go back to your room now?"

FIGHTER

"Haven't you had enough yet?" asked Siklisha.

Caseir looked up from the bench he was lying on in the basement of the arena. The tall auburn-haired woman bending over him was closing the gash in his thigh made by Ristaion's sword. He felt a hot, prickling, dragging sensation as the wound was drawn closed by her magic. It was an unpleasant, familiar feeling which he relished because it confirmed he was still alive.

"What do you mean?" he asked.

"You don't need to keep on putting your life at risk. You're rich enough. When are you going to give up?"

"Fighting is all I know. What else would I do?"

"No, it's not. Your sister gave me one of your carvings a few years ago. It was after that fight when you nearly lost a couple of fingers."

"That would be Jemser."

"I don't remember their names, just the wounds they made that I've had to repair. Anyway, that carving is beautiful. Why don't you do that for a living instead of fighting?"

"Didn't know Caerina had given you one. Which is it?"

"A woman on her knees praying, with tears running down her cheeks. She said you called it 'Hope and Fear'."

"Oh. That one. Well, I've got to admit it's one of my better pieces. I wonder why she picked that one for you."

"She didn't. I chose it. It's just so right for the way I feel when you're fighting."

Caseir started to sit up. Siklisha pushed him back down and said, "Keep still. I'm almost done."

"Why is it right?"

Siklisha dipped her head letting her hair fall across her face and made a noise he couldn't interpret. She made one more gesture, moving her hands in the way that gave her skill its usual name. She was a Scratcher, who controlled her magic with the gesticulations that people said were like scratching symbols into the air. The last bit of the wound jerked closed and Caseir winced.

"There, it's done. You can sit up now."

Caseir grunted, swung his legs over the side of the bench and pushed himself into a sitting position. "Why is it right, Siklisha?"

"Quarenna's grace! Maybe you are stupid after all. It's right because it says what I feel every time you fight. I haven't watched you in the arena since you started fighting in death bouts. I'm too afraid. I don't want to see you die. You were lucky this time. That sword missed the main artery by less than a finger breadth. One of these days one of these near misses won't be a miss and that'll be the end of the Unconquered." She started sobbing. "That's why I'm quitting. You're going to need to find another healer because I can't stand it anymore. Six years and nineteen bouts is too much. I don't care how much you pay me, I can't face patching you up any more."

He stood up and wrapped his arms around her. "You seem to be saying you care about me."

"Of course I do, you fool."

"But…"

"Shut up and kiss me goodbye."

He drew her head down to his level and did as she asked. "But it's not goodbye," he said. "That was my last fight. That is it was my last if you will marry me."

Siklisha lifted her head. "You mean it?" She gazed into his eyes. "Yes! Yes, you do. Of course I'll marry you. I've been in love with you for years."

"I didn't know that. And I didn't know until now that I'm in love with you too," he said. "I'm so used to having you around that I'm not sure I could stand it if you weren't there."

He stepped back, felt for the bench behind him, sank down onto it and pulled her down on top of him.

She gasped.

"No?" he asked.

"Oh, yes, yes. But not here, anybody might walk in."

"Then come with me."

O

Caseir took Siklisha to see his sister and her husband and tell them the news.

"You'll come and live here, of course," said Caerina, hugging Siklisha.

"We can't do that," said Caseir. He looked around the conservatory, smelled the rich aroma of the plants and heard the quiet trickle of water from the fountain. "This is your home. We can't intrude."

"It wouldn't be an intrusion. After all it was your winnings that paid for this house. It's at least as much yours as mine and it's big enough for all of us," said Caerina. "You can't take Siklisha into that tiny place you live in."

Siklisha started to object but was shushed by Caerina. "It might be good enough for Caseir on his own but you deserve better, Siklisha. Particularly since you've persuaded him to retire."

"I agree," said the rich baritone voice of Veluth, Caerina's husband. "You're welcome here until you find somewhere else, so don't argue."

Veluth guided Caerina to a chair and sat down beside her.

"It's amazing what you don't see when you're not looking for it," said Caseir, taking Siklisha's hand. "I never realised there was a gap in my life until Siklisha filled it."

"That doesn't sound very romantic," said Caerina.

"Oh yes it is," said Veluth. "I know exactly what he means. You did the same for me when you saw past the rough surface and into my heart."

Caerina smiled. "Now Veluth, you know perfectly well that I didn't 'see' anything. I used to curse that attack of brain fever that left me blind but now I almost bless it. I learned to appreciate the world of sound in a way I never had before. In that world it was very easy for me to fall in love with you."

Caseir looked fondly at his sister. Looking after her had been his main interest since their parents died. More than half of his winnings had gone to support her and make sure she was well cared for.

She had been attracted by the power and clarity of Veluth's singing and fell in love with his voice before she met the man. Bringing them together was one of the most satisfying things he had ever done, and one of the easiest. His fame had ensured his own introduction to Veluth and he took advantage of that to introduce her to him. He hadn't expected Veluth to fall in love with her but was delighted when he did.

It gave Caerina the security he had tried to provide by supporting her with his winnings.

"What are you going to do now that you've retired?" asked Veluth.

"I don't really know. Siklisha suggested I do more carving and that's certainly a possibility."

"I've had an idea," said Veluth. "I remember you telling me about learning Sitru from another arena fighter."

"That was years ago. It was just a way to pass the time between fights."

"But you've kept it up and you speak Sitru better than anyone else I know."

"Not that well. I've been told my accent is terrible."

"I wasn't thinking about speaking it but translating it. The Sitrelkers have a tradition of sung dramas and the Carregis Chorus has been talking about putting on some of them. The problem is not enough people in Carregis speak Sitru well enough to follow the plot. You could do the translation."

"Worry about that later," said Caerina. "Let's get you settled in here first. Now don't argue, Siklisha. It's settled. You're living here, at least for a while."

SPONGER

"Wasn't he great?" said Anarya as they walked back to the lodgings. "I told you, didn't I – got to admit I was worried when he got that gash across his forearm, but it didn't slow him down at all – and that riposte that almost took Ristaion's ear off – it was brilliant."

She kept talking, principally about the final bout but ranging across almost all the events of the day.

Yisyena answered her in monosyllables, if at all.

"I've got some fairly decent wine," said Anarya, walking towards the cupboard as soon as they got home. "I think the Arenafest was worth a glass or two. Want some?"

"Turn around."

The brittle tone of Yisyena's words penetrated Anarya's excitement. She turned, saying, "What's ..." and froze.

Yisyena had picked up her cane from the table. Her left hand was supporting it at shoulder height and the right was driving it forward, end first, towards Anarya's throat. It stopped fingerbreadths away.

"What are you?" said Yisyena.

Anarya started to take a step back but stopped when Yisyena said, "Do not move. Answer me. What – are – you?"

"I don't understand."

"You led me to believe you are untalented, but that is a lie. You have a talent of some kind which I do not recognise. I want to know what it is."

Anarya swallowed and said, "I'm not a danger to you."

"You have not answered my question."

Anarya hesitated before saying, "You're right. I am talented but I don't let it be known. It's too risky."

"For whom?"

"For me," said Anarya, with a sigh, "only for me. I swear by Holy Quarenna that I'm not a threat to you."

Yisyena stood ready to strike for a few more moments, then she lowered her cane and said, "Sit. I saw you praying to this god of yours this morning and you have invoked her name at other times. I believe you to be devout and I do not think you would swear falsely by her."

"Thank you," whispered Anarya. She sat on the bed shaking. *She could have killed me!* "What did I do wrong? How did I give myself away?"

"There were several things. At first I thought you were a Lifter because you threw a block of wood at one of my assailants."

"I thought you didn't see that because you weren't looking in that direction."

"You forget I am a Voyanter, I can see everything around me. I saw you appear on the scene and I did not know if you were going to join the others against me. Naturally I paid attention to you."

"Oh."

"However, you did not admit to being talented when we spoke of such things yesterday and I wondered why. At the arena I observed you turn, apparently anticipating what the Pyromancers were going to do, but I thought you might have seen a similar display before. Then you repeated the exact words Caseir used about his opponent when you should not have been able to hear them. I have seen too many things for them all to be coincidences."

"Quarenna aid me! I've been really careless. It must have been the excitement."

"I do not know of any talent which would enable you to do all of these things. You have still not answered my question. What are you?"

Anarya's head drooped, she sighed and said, in a quiet voice, "I suppose I have to tell you but, please, I beg you, don't tell anyone else. I'm a Sponger."

"What is that? I have never heard of this talent."

Anarya looked up. "But there are so many stories... Oh, they'll be stories that aren't told in Sitrelk. You won't have heard them."

"I have not."

"I don't know what a Sponger is called in Sitru. It's someone who can absorb another magic user's talent, like a sponge absorbing water... No! Stop."

Yisyena was halfway across the room towards Anarya with her cane swinging in a backhand stroke towards her head.

Anarya threw her hands up to try to deflect the cane. She just managed to duck under the blow which glanced off her right wrist. "Stop. What's wrong? I can't hurt you. I swear it."

Yisyena's face paled as much as her skin colour would allow. "Impossible. That is the power of The God. He takes gifts of talents from the *cranil* and they die."

"But you're not dead. I borrowed your talent at the arena – that's how I knew what Caseir said – and you're not dead. And anyway it can't be the same. Only women are Spongers, never men."

Tears came to Yisyena's eyes and her face crumpled. She sat down on the bed beside Anarya. "I want to believe you, but I do not understand how this can be."

"Spongers have the rarest of Quarenna's gifts," said Anarya, cradling her wrist and wincing. "The priestess who accepted my first blood offering told me that less than one in a thousand of the gifted are Spongers. She also told me to keep it a secret."

"I do not understand. Why would she tell you to keep it a secret?"

"Because people who are revealed to be Spongers generally regret letting others know of their abilities. Some of the ungifted are jealous of any magic user. I'm sure that's the same in Sitrelk. They're particularly envious of Spongers who, they think, can do anything. Even many of the talented resent the capabilities of Spongers. When the blessèd priestess was warning me she said, 'jealousy breeds hatred and hatred leads to violence'.

"There are a lot of stories about Spongers and in most of them they came to bad ends. For example, Tilua told me about one called Geala. About thirty-five years ago she decided she would use her skill to help anyone who asked. There were some things she couldn't do because a Sponger can't use all talents equally well and some of the things she was asked were impossible. Many people didn't understand her limitations and thought she was arbitrarily refusing to help some people. The resentment this caused overflowed one day. She was only nineteen years old when she was attacked in the Great Square by someone she was unable to help. She died in the riot that followed, along with five or six other people who tried to protect her."

"How awful."

"That's why I beg you not to tell anybody what I am. I don't want to have to leave Carregis and go into hiding."

Yisyena blotted tears from her eyes. "I am sorry I frightened you and have injured you when you have been so good to me. I was afraid of you, and your talent which seems so like The God's. Can you forgive me?"

"I scared you just as much. And I think I've worked out why. You said the talents run in families in Sitrelk and The God takes talents from the *cranil*. I've heard of them, but I've been slow and I didn't realise until now that you must be a Godspeaker."

Anarya could hear the reluctance in Yisyena's voice when she said, "You are correct, I was. I had hoped to keep that a secret."

She slipped from the bed, knelt in front of Yisyena and said, *"Vores tenyekku, hi-cranil."*

"No! You must not kneel to me or ask me for a blessing."

"But you're a Godspeaker and I'm just the daughter of a woman who runs a dairy."

"I have left that behind me. I ran away from The God. He does not permit *cranil* to leave Sitrelk. I will be killed if I return. Now I am simply Yisyena and my rank is the same as yours." She pulled Anarya to her feet and kissed her. "It seems we both have secrets. Let us agree to protect each other's."

Anarya drew in a deep shuddering breath, "Yes. Let's do that."

"Have I broken your wrist?"

"No. It hurts, but I don't think it's broken."

"Where is that wine you mentioned?"

"Bottom shelf of the cupboard, at the back. Glasses on the second shelf."

Yisyena poured for both of them. *"Gu-merin-li tisseta,"* she said, lifting her glass.

Anarya frowned. "We shall shine like the wings of the meri. What does that mean?"

"It is a toast used in Sitrelk to celebrate the formation of a new partnership. The meri are beetles with iridescent wings found in the south."

"I like it," said Anarya, lifting her glass in reply to the toast.

"Now", said Yisyena. "If we are to work together, I must know more about this talent of yours. You said a Sponger cannot use all talents equally well."

Anarya took a sip of wine and said, "You know, it's strange but I'm almost relieved that someone knows about my talent now. I've kept quiet about it for six years and it's been difficult. I've sometimes felt rather lonely keeping it to myself. Not even my mother knows, she thinks I'm untalented. The only other one who knows is the priestess I told you about."

"I take it that this priestess is also a Sponger. Do not worry. I will keep that knowledge to myself."

Anarya didn't acknowledge Yisyena's guess. "It's complicated and I'm not sure where to start." She paused briefly. "Well, I guess the first thing is that there's a way of looking at people and things, it's called the Oversight. It lets me see magic. With it I can identify other magic users and know what their ability is and how strong it is. I've been told that Daimoners can recognise each other in the same way but I don't know of any other talent group who can."

"Voyanters cannot, and I did not know that about Daimoners. They are extremely rare in Sitrelk."

Anarya stood and started pacing around the room. "It's difficult to talk about this when I've kept it secret for such a long time. It feels – wrong."

"Come here, Anra," said Yisyena, reaching out to give her a hug. "Take your time."

Anarya sighed contentedly as she snuggled up to Yisyena. "I suppose the next thing is, I can borrow someone else's skill and have it available for a while. If I don't use it, it gradually fades. If I do use it, it goes faster. Some skills are – more comfortable, I suppose – than others and I can hold them and use them for longer. But it's not as simple as that. The stronger the talent of the person I borrow from, the longer I can hold it for."

"Which talents can you use most easily?"

"Whisperer and Scratcher and Voyanter are the ones I can hold longest. Those skills will last at least three chimes, maybe as much as four. Sometimes I can add a second skill and hold both at the same time, but sometimes trying to take a second means losing the first. It's easier to have two if one of them is from somebody really strong, like you."

"Which are the poorest?"

"I can't be a Seeker for long and it's a waste of time me trying to be an Aeromancer or a Aquamancer, they just last a breath or two."

"It is unfortunate that being a Seeker is not easy for you. If I understand your business correctly then it would be a useful skill for a quaestor."

Anarya snorted. "It would be very useful. But my range is short and I can only hold it for about twenty, maybe thirty, breaths. No more than that."

"What of the other skills?"

"I've never been a Daimoner. I might try it in a pinch but the idea scares me too much. There are too many stories of what can happen if a Daimoner fails to control a daimon he's summoned. I've never met a Stealther, so I've no idea what that's like. All the others fit somewhere between Scratcher and Seeker."

"You said you have used my talent."

"Yes. I took it to watch Caseir's fight from close range."

"I did not feel anything."

"Nobody ever does. That's because I don't steal a skill, I copy it and the owner still has it. Borrowing a talent from somebody doesn't weaken them or affect them at all. Just as well, it means I don't have to ask their permission."

"I think I understand."

"I have to be careful. If I overuse a borrowed talent or try to keep using it as it fades then I suffer for it."

"Suffer? How?"

"Headaches, shivering, weakness, nausea, loss of vision."

"That sounds unpleasant."

"It can be worse than that. I've been told that Spongers can burn out their talent for a day or two, maybe even permanently, or kill themselves by trying to do too much with a borrowed skill."

"You must take great care. Now that I have found you I do not wish to lose you. I will be most displeased if you take risks."

"There is a cure for talent exhaustion. It's quite simple – food and rest."

"You must not put yourself in the position of needing a cure."

"There's one more thing. I can also absorb – the feel – the ambience – the atmosphere of a place and fit into it so well I'm unnoticeable. I'm not invisible, people are aware I'm there and will avoid walking into me, but I'm just not worthy of attention and I get ignored. It's easiest if I dress and behave appropriately, but if I wanted to I could walk into a dockside tavern wearing silks, satins and lace and nobody would think me out of place. It's a very useful ability for a quaestor."

"Does the ambience affect you in return? I am wondering because you seemed to be more aggressive, more blood-thirsty when we were at the arena. Were you responding to the atmosphere?"

"I don't know," said Anarya. "It's possible, I suppose. I've never thought about it, but then I might not notice if it does."

STEALTHER

"Boy! Boy! Where are you, you useless, good-for-nothing little git?"

Baram heard the shout clearly over the clop of hooves and the rumble of wheels on the cobbles of the yard. His heart sank. *He's back early. Wasn't supposed to be back until tomorrow!* Baram wished he could ignore him or hide from him, but that would just make Uncle worse.

He patted the horse he was grooming, carefully closed the stall behind him and ran out into the yard. He looked up to see his uncle, a big swarthy man with unkempt, greasy looking hair, glaring down at him from the box seat of the wagon.

"Well, don't just stand there. You should know what to do by now. Huler's beard! You'd think he'd have learned something in the fourteen years he's been here, but he just stands there doing nothing." Uncle's voice trailed off into a muttered litany of complaints. He jumped down from the box and slapped Baram's head in passing as he shambled towards the house on the other side of the yard from the stables. "Get moving."

Baram shook his head to clear it. He'd had worse, much worse, from his uncle in the past. Beatings featured regularly in his life. *He'll get drunk tonight and beat me again.* Baram hated his uncle, who had never seemed to want him around. *I do a better job of looking after the horses than he does but it'll never satisfy him. I wish he was dead.* He unharnessed the horses and led them to the stables. The animals towered above him but it was years since he had been worried by that. He had been at first, but everything had been strange after his mother died and her sister had taken him in. Since then he had learned that horses were gentle creatures who wouldn't hurt him; unlike his uncle.

He made sure there was fodder and water available for the horses, thumped them affectionately and said, "I'll be back to look after you later, but I've got to go now."

He dropped the tailgate and looked into the wagon. There were only half a dozen sacks instead of the twenty or thirty that would be a good load. He opened one of them to find it contained turnips and shook his head. *This poor load is going to make him worse than ever.* Grunting with the effort, he dragged the sacks out of the wagon and into the store. Each sack weighed about the same as he did, really more than he could comfortably handle. His uncle was much bigger and stronger than him and could have managed them easily, but he knew he would have to do it himself. Uncle had stopped helping him to unload five or six years ago. *He'll blame me for being slow when he could do it himself in half the time.*

By the time he had finished unloading, looking after the horses and closing the yard gates it was starting to get dark. He went into the house to find his uncle, as he expected, slumped in a chair with a mug in one hand. The remains of a rabbit pie were on the table in front of him.

"You've took too long. No dinner for you tonight," his uncle said.

Baram gritted his teeth, trying to ignore the rage he felt and the empty feeling in his stomach. He wasn't really surprised by his uncle's decision. Starvation was a favourite punishment for his supposed misdemeanours. His aunt would have fed him earlier in the day if they had known his uncle was going to be home so soon. Resentment made him scowl and clench his fists. He forced himself to open them again in case his uncle saw and he kept his head turned away as he squeezed past the table. When he came within reach of his uncle's empty hand he tried, but didn't quite manage, to dodge the expected slap. He scampered up the ladder to the loft where he slept and curled himself into the corner. He imagined himself standing up to his uncle and shivered in fear. *No, I can't do that. He's too big and strong. He'd kill me.* He started sniffling and struggled to keep quiet to avoid provoking his uncle anymore.

"Let me give him something," he heard his aunt say. "You're always complaining he's too small. He won't get any bigger if he's not fed."

"No. He's got to earn his keep."

"But …"

"No buts. No excuses. He gets nothing, not until he learns

to do things faster. Understand me? Nothing. I'm going out."

Baram heard his uncle leave and relaxed a bit. *At least he's gone. I don't have to worry until he comes back.* About an eighth of a chime later his aunt called his name.

"He's gone to get drunk. It's safe to come down. He won't be back until the tavern closes," she said. "I've got a bit of bread and cheese for you. It's not much but I can't risk him noticing anything missing from the larder."

Baram was sitting at the table eating when the door burst open.

His uncle stormed into the room. "Cash!" he roared, "That misbegotten, Huler-be-damned tavern keeper wants cash. Cash from me that he's known for years; no more credit he says…" His voice faded as he saw what was happening.

His fist slammed into Baram's jaw, knocking him to the floor. Then he turned to his wife. "I said no food, didn't I? Didn't I? So why are you feeding him?" He grabbed her shoulders and shook her. "Why?" he bellowed with each shake, "Why?"

"Look at him," she managed to say. "He's too thin. He needs building up."

"Won't do no good. He's weak. Just like the rest of your family. He's a weakling. Your sister died birthing another one even weaker than him. And you're no better. None of the sons you've given me have lived more than a couple of days. It's all your family's fault." He shook her again then threw her aside.

She stumbled backwards, fell over a chair and crashed to the ground. Her head hit the corner of the oven with a dull thud that sounded like an egg breaking. Blood spread in a pool around her. She twitched briefly then stopped moving.

Baram crawled towards her but his uncle's boot caught him in the ribs. He curled up in a ball. He tried not to scream because that always made his uncle angrier and the beating worse. However, he couldn't help sobbing as he suffered more kicks until one hit his head and everything went dark.

When he opened his eyes again it was to the warm golden light of a summer morning. He felt sick, his head throbbed, he was seeing double, breathing was painful and coughing agony. Movement sent a stab of pain through his left arm. He looked at it. The unnatural angle it was lying at made him feel even sicker and he had to swallow several times to avoid vomiting.

There was no sign of his uncle. His aunt lay where she had fallen. He crawled over to her, whimpering every time he bumped his arm.

She was cold and her eyes stared blindly at the ceiling.

Tears filled his eyes. He started crying but it hurt too much. *She's dead. What am I going to do now? I'll kill him*, he promised himself. *Somehow, I'll kill him. I'll find a way. Huler help me, I'll find a way.*

Baram managed to pull himself to his feet. Cradling his arm, he pushed open the door to the lane and stumbled through it. Darkness pulsed in time with the throbbing in his head. He staggered along the street, not knowing where he was going, or why. He had flashes of lucidity interspersed with blanks. He found himself on the ground more than once and struggled back to his feet. Then the world went away again.

"Drink this," a voice said.

The liquid was bitter and he tried to turn his head away.

"No," said the voice. "Drink. It will do you good."

He obeyed the insistent voice and soon fell into darkness once more.

O

"Are you awake?" said a voice he vaguely remembered.

Baram opened his eyes. A ruddy-faced man with blue eyes and grey in his neatly trimmed beard, wearing a tunic with a red border and embroidered with a sun symbol, was smiling down at him.

"You're a priest," said Baram.

The man nodded. "Yes, you're right, I am a priest of Huler. My given name is Raifen. Are you feeling better?"

Baram sat up with difficulty. He was clumsy with his arm strapped to his chest but there was no pain. He looked around. The room was small and held little more than the soft pallet he was lying on and a chair for the priest. Light streamed in through a small window high on one wall. "Where am I? What happened?"

"The where is easy. You're in the temple of Huler on the

Oxway. The what is a little more difficult. A man brought you here two days ago and left without giving his name. He said he had found you in the street. He didn't know who you were. Tell me your name and what you remember."

Baram told the priest what had happened, describing his uncle's rage and his aunt's death.

"I see," said Raifen, with a relieved expression on his face. "That explains something that was a talking point for a day or so. Your aunt's body was discovered in the afternoon when a neighbour called to visit. The neighbour told the Duke's men there was a boy missing. They suspected that he was responsible for her death."

"No! I didn't kill her."

"I know. The state you were in I doubt if you could have killed a flea. But I'm sure you can understand why we wondered about you – we have a missing boy and, not too far away, an unidentified boy. Are they the same?"

"Oh."

"It was obvious that you'd been beaten quite badly but we didn't know by whom or why. Your injuries had us worried for a while. Apart from your arm and at least four broken ribs, you had concussion. This is the second time you've woken up. The first time didn't last very long and your ramblings didn't make any sense. You sound more rational this time. I hope that means you're going to stay with us."

"What about my uncle?"

"There were only two wagons and three horses in the yard. The neighbours said that meant he was out on the road somewhere with another wagon."

"There aren't any others. Just the two. Uncle's business has been getting worse for the last couple of years. He sold off the other two wagons he had, and the horses and tack to go with them as he got fewer and fewer jobs. The wagons were in poor shape because he hadn't been looking after them. He didn't get much for them and he drank it all. People stopped trusting him and he couldn't get valuable cargoes any more. That last one was just turnips."

"Don't despise turnips," said Raifen. "Have you any idea where your uncle might have gone? The Duke's men will want to speak to him."

"He must have taken one of the horses, there should be four

in the stables. I expect he'll have gone to Nuruye. His brother's a farmer there."

"Nuruye. That's in the duchy of Alrem, isn't it? He'll be safe there. The Duke's men won't follow him across the border into another duchy."

"Blessèd one, I don't know what I'm going to do. I've nowhere to go and nowhere to stay."

"You can't do much at the moment, but you can stay here until your arm has healed. There are always little tasks that need doing."

"Thank you."

Raifen frowned slightly. "You will need to tell your story to the Duke's men."

"But, blessèd one, you said they thought I killed my aunt."

"Don't worry about that," said Raifen. "You called me 'blessèd one' and you're right. I have been blessed with one of Huler's gifts. I'm a Feeler. As well as knowing people's emotions I can tell when they are lying. You haven't been, and I will say as much to the Duke's men."

He knows what I'm feeling! He'll know I hate uncle and I want to kill him!

"How old are you? And how long did you live with your aunt and uncle?" asked Raifen.

"I'll be twenty a week after Yearsend, my birthday's the same day as the king's. Auntie took me in when I was five, after my mother died."

"You look younger."

"I know," said Baram, with a grimace. "That was one of the things uncle complained about. He always said I was too small and too weak and feeble."

"You're old enough to inherit your uncle's business. His actions, killing your aunt and running away, make it forfeit. You can claim it."

"No. I don't want it. And I can't claim it anyway, I'm still a boy."

"What?" Raifen's eyebrows shot up. "You're almost twenty and you haven't sacrificed your beard to Huler!"

"Uncle said it would be a waste of time because I'd never make a real man."

"That is not your uncle's decision to make. If you wish to offer your beard to Huler as a first sacrifice I will be pleased to accept it in his name. Then you can inherit the business, or sell it if you don't want to keep it."

"Yes! Oh, yes please," said Baram. "I wish I could see uncle's face when he hears my beard's been cut."

"Good," said Raifen with a broad smile. "That's settled. We'll do it once your arm has healed."

○

For seven weeks Baram swept the temple, replaced burnt-out candles, picked up things people dropped and generally made himself useful. He could use his left arm again, although it was weak and sometimes clumsy. He felt accepted and fairly contented. He missed his aunt but the only other regret he had was not seeing what had been Caseir's final appearance in the arena.

He waited in the antechamber for the noon chime. If it went well, this would be the last time he passed through the Boy's Gate. He was nervous. Raifen had assured him that he had enough of a beard for the sacrifice, but it would be so embarrassing to leave the sanctuary unshaven. He tried to keep his hand away from his face, but, when he wasn't paying attention to what he was doing, he found himself stroking his chin. He didn't think he had much to offer, just a few soft hairs. *Blessèd Raifen should know if it's enough*, he told himself. *Tugging at it won't do any good at this stage. What will I do when I'm a man, grow a beard or shave?* He imagined having enough of a beard to plait, dye or let grow long in honour of Huler. *Don't be silly. I'm never going to have that sort of beard. I'll stay clean shaven, or maybe grow a moustache.*

The sound of the gong made him jump. It was time. He stepped through the Boy's Gate into the magnificence of the sanctuary. Four columns of porphyry with lavish gold ornamentation supported a dome painted to look like the sun in glory burning its way through clouds. Directly under the dome was the altar, a massive slab of white marble carved with swords pointing north, south, east and west. A priest in red and gold vestments stood at the tip of each of the swords.

Baram went to his knees in front of the altar and waited.

Speaking in perfect unison the four priests asked, "Are you

ready to surrender the days of your childhood and assume the duties and responsibilities of a man?"

"I am."

"What do you offer to the god in token of this?"

"I dedicate my beard to the god. I will enter manhood with my face naked to his sight."

"Stand and turn."

In an alcove between the Boy's Gate and the Men's Gate Raifen stood beside a blackwood table with a razor shaped like a miniature sword in his hand. The table held a gold basin of water and a lamp burning with a clear blue flame.

At the table Raifen quickly and carefully shaved Baram until only a small patch just below his lower lip remained uncut. He dried the blade, passed it to Baram and stepped back.

Baram closed his eyes for a moment and made sure his hand was steady. Then he finished shaving with a single stroke and held the blade, with the last of his beard, in the flame. "Lord Huler, I beg you to receive this offering."

The hairs burned with a puff of acrid smoke. The flame went out. Then it flared up again brighter than it had been. Raifen clenched his fist over his heart, dropped to his knees and signalled Baram to do likewise.

"Your offering is accepted," said the four priests in chorus. "You are among the blessed. Great Huler has chosen you." Then they started singing verses in praise of Huler, Lord of the Sky and Illuminator of the World.

"Come," said Raifen and led Baram from the sanctuary through the Men's Gate and to a small chapel tucked into the extreme eastern end of the temple with a window that would catch the rising sun. He knelt in front of the statue of Huler depicting him as a smiling young man with his arms outstretched in welcome. With a gesture he indicated that Baram should kneel beside him.

"The relighting of the flame happens less than once in a hundred times," said Raifen. "It is an indication that Huler has chosen you to receive one of his gifts."

"Me?" gasped Baram, his hand going to his mouth.

"Yes, you. I know it's a surprise. I remember what it was like when it happened to me. I was as startled as you are. I don't yet know which of the gifts you have been given. We will find out tomorrow. For now, you must sleep here, in front of the Supplicant's altar."

"I won't be able to sleep."

"You will," said Raifen with a smile. "Huler will make sure of that."

Blessed by Huler. Imagine that, thought Baram as he waited to be snatched into sleep by Huler's hand. *What gift will it be? Something I can use against my uncle, I hope.*

◯

Raifen woke Baram the next morning and the first thing he said was, "What did you dream?"

Baram blinked sleep from his eyes and said, "I was walking through a crowd and everybody ignored me. It was as if they didn't know I was there."

"In that case I think I know what your gift is."

"Really? What is it?"

Raifen smiled, then took a quick pace towards Baram and shouted, "Hide!"

Baram jumped. For a moment everything blurred, as if he was looking through a layer of muslin. His vision returned to normal and he stood there blinking in surprise.

"I thought so," said Raifen. "You vanished for an instant. You're a Stealther. I'm sorry I startled you but it was the easiest way to make sure."

"A Stealther. Me?"

"Yes. It may be the rarest of Huler's gifts but it doesn't really surprise me that you have been given it."

"Why?"

"The temple records tell us that there are normally three Stealthers in Carrhen. Never more and rarely fewer. News reached us ten days ago from Getruva that one of them had died. We have been waiting for his successor to appear."

"Why me?"

"I cannot presume to answer that question. Huler chooses who he wills for all his gifts. However, you have something in common with all the Stealthers in the records. You came to the temple angry, having suffered an injustice which cannot be punished by the law. Tell me, what do you know about Stealthers?"

"They can't be seen or heard if they don't want to be…" Baram's voice trailed off.

"Go on."

"They're thieves and assassins."

"That *is* a common misconception. Yes, there have been instances where a Stealther has acted on his own account but mostly they act as the hand of the god."

Baram said nothing, gaping at the idea.

"You know of Huler's aspect as the Just Avenger," said Raifen.

"Of course."

"Then you know that people who have suffered injustice and are unable to gain redress through the law can appeal to the temple. What you won't know is what happens then. When it seems appropriate those appeals are passed on to one of the Stealthers. He can investigate the complaint and act as he sees fit, imposing any penalty up to and including execution of the oppressor."

"Execution!"

"You felt like killing your uncle, didn't you?"

"Yes, but…"

"That will be your first task, answering your own appeal against injustice. But you need to familiarise yourself with your gift before you do. About sixty years ago a Stealther wrote a book about it. You can read that – you can read can't you?"

"Yes. My aunt insisted I went to school for a few years and I learned to read and figure, but I'm out of practice."

"It will come back to you quite quickly. The Stealther's book will tell you what you need to know. Obviously you know a Stealther can become invisible but the book gives more details. For example, it says animals may be able to detect him when he's invisible and he can be discovered by accident if people bump into him. Also, he cannot stay invisible when holding a naked blade. I don't know why that should be. It must be the will of Huler. One more thing – you'll need to acquire weapon skills. I'll arrange teaching for you."

SPONGER

Anarya walked into *The Hopeful Swain*, a decent tavern in the district called Greenbank near the river that eventually flowed into the Carrh between the Western and Eastern docks. It had a special place in her memories. It was one of the first places where she had announced her availability as a quaestor and that had led to her first contract. The man who offered it was a merchant who was sure that one of his employees wasn't putting all the money he took into the strongbox and was keeping some for himself. He wanted her to confirm this. It was fairly simple. All she had to do was find a Voyanter, borrow his skills, use them to watch the suspect and find out where he was hiding the stolen money. The contract had only paid two bits, but it had been a start to her career.

This time she made her usual announcement to the indifferent clientele. She said who she was and how to get in touch with her, then turned to leave.

"A quaestor. You? Don't make me laugh." The voice came from an older man sitting alone next to the fireplace. He was big and muscular and towered over her when he stood up to glare at her in a most unfriendly way.

"And what's wrong with that?" she asked.

"For one thing, you're too young. For another, you're new to Carregis. The way you speak says you're from somewhere out west. Rustem, Hemeark or another of those insignificant little towns out that way. You can't know your way around the city well enough to be a quaestor."

Anarya studied him before saying anything else. The Oversight showed her the pink aura of a powerful Seeker who would be able to find people at long range and probably even find things, which was substantially more difficult. *Can I learn anything from him? It's got to be worth a try.* "You've got a good ear," she said, "Hemeark it is. But what makes you think I'm new to Carregis?"

"Cos I ain't seen you here before an' I'm here 'most every

day. *I'm* the quaestor around here. You got no business coming into my place an' advertising yourself like that. An' another thing, you ain't a Seeker, so you can't be a member of the guild."

There's a quaestors guild? Nobody's ever mentioned that before. I need to find out more. She waved to the server, collected two mugs of beer and took them to the big man. She gave him one and he sat down again.

"My name's Anarya. What's yours?"

He half emptied the mug without taking it from his mouth then wiped the froth from his moustache. "Aye. I know your name. I'm not deaf an' you said it loud enough in that announcement you made. I'm Janersh, an', like I said, this is my patch."

"Tell me," she said, settling herself on a stool nearby. "How do you know I'm not a Seeker?"

"See what I mean. You're too ignorant to be let out on your own. If you was a Seeker you wouldn't have to ask. You'd know we can recognise each other. That's how I know you're not one. Don't know what you are, but I know what you're not, an' that's a quaestor."

"I've been here more than six months and I've never heard that there's a quaestors' guild or that you had to be a Seeker to be a quaestor," she said, "I've heard of one who's a Voyanter and met another who's a Feeler."

The man snorted. "Aye, they can call themselves quaestors but that doesn't make it true. They're not members of the Worthy Association of Quaestors, 'cos that's restricted to Seekers."

"Never mind him." The interruption came from a small, elderly, rather overweight woman at a nearby table who stood up and came to join them.

"Don't you go buttin' in, Lurascha. This here conversation's private."

"And I suppose you think I'm going to ignore it when you start a private conversation with a young girl."

"I'm just puttin' her straight," said Janersh. "Ain't nothin' else."

"It doesn't bother me," said Lurascha, with a smile as she reached up to pat his cheek. "I know you don't rove. But talk sense and don't mislead this poor girl." She turned to Anarya and said, "'bout the only thing he's got right is my name and he should know that. We've been married long enough. There is a Worthy Association of Quaestors and, like he says, it's restricted to Seekers, but it don't mean much."

"But…"

"You be quiet, Janersh. Or tell her the truth."

He scowled, but said nothing.

"It's like this," said Lurascha. "Sixteen years ago, or thereabouts, a group of the quaestors in Carregis got together and started talking about forming a guild. Funny mixed bunch they were too, mostly Seekers, but there were some Voyanters, a few Feelers, a couple of Scratchers and one or two others – even an Aeromancer, although I'm not sure how useful a skill that is for a quaestor. Anyway, the meeting was nothing but arguments."

"An' you did a lot of the arguing," said Janersh.

"I did at that," agreed Lurascha. "Because there was a lot of nonsense being talked. For one thing, there I was, making a reasonable living as a quaestor and they all knew it. But they were all insisting that to be one you had to have a talent, although I don't."

"I've never heard of a quaestor without some sort of talent," said Anarya. "It must be difficult."

"Not as bad as you might think, all it takes is a bit of sense and a willingness to poke your nose in where it might not be wanted. Yes, it might have been easier with one but it don't matter. I was a good quaestor, until I got too old and stiff. What's your talent?"

"Voyanter," said Anarya, telling the lie calmly. She was used to saying that and she had borrowed that skill from Yisyena that morning.

"That's a useful one," said Lurascha.

Anarya thought it was worth learning more about the Worthy Association of Quaestors. She moved Lurascha's chair to the table she was sharing with Janersh and bought more drinks. "Tell me more about the guild."

"The meeting went on for two days without getting anywhere," said Lurascha. "Then the Seekers decided they'd had enough. There were more of them than everybody else together, so they formed the Worthy Association of Quaestors and made sure they were in control by making it exclusive. And," she said, pointing at Janersh, "to make things worse, they elected this fool as the first Worthy Master."

"It worked, didn't it. Gave quaestors some status."

"I'll grant you it did some good, but it's useless now, ever since that idiot Pifurk took over as Master."

Janersh scowled and said nothing.

"He's broken the Association. Even you've got to admit it means nothing now," said Lurascha. "Go on, tell her how many of the quaestors working in the city right now are Seekers and members of the Association?"

There was no answer.

Lurascha looked towards Anarya and said, "I'll tell you if he won't. Of the twenty-odd quaestors I know about, only four are Seekers, and one of those hasn't joined the Association. There's no need for you to worry about it. It's nice to see a young woman working in a mostly male business. You just carry on, and may Quarenna smile on you. If you ever need help come and see me."

O

From *The Hopeful Swain* Anarya visited most of the other taverns in Greenbank. Several times she stopped for a chat with acquaintances, but never for long. As she got closer to the Dip, the poorest area of Carregis, she stopped meeting people she knew.

In one pokey little establishment on the corner of Kitrel's Alley and Nelsway she didn't bother advertising her services. Instead she sat in a corner with a mug of beer that was almost drinkable and listened, for about half a chime, using the Voyanter skills borrowed from Yisyena. *It's nice that she's so strong. It lets me use the talent for a lot longer than I've ever been able to before.*

Most of what she heard was of no interest. On previous visits she had heard thieves talking about where they had hidden or fenced their loot and she was hoping to hear that sort of thing again. Selling information to the Duke's men about such matters didn't pay much but it was a reliable source of income.

A tall, gangling youth wearing a red and blue stocking cap

walked in. He went to a table occupied by an older man who had an orange and black scarf draped over the back of his chair. "Neutral ground," he said.

The older man looked up. "This is, as you say, neutral ground."

"Need a meeting. At Bisson's Cross, tomorrow night, eighteenth chime. No more than three of you."

"If you also have no more than three there then a meeting can be held." The older man looked down at the table and the arrangement of vurlo tiles on it.

Anarya saw the youth scowl and clench his fists. Then he turned and left, slamming the door behind him. The older man looked up again with a pleased smile.

That youngster didn't like being dismissed like that. Interesting conversation. I wonder what it's all about. It might be worth finding out.

O

Anarya's route back from Greenbank took her past the Coptomeruk Arch and the shrine of Quarenna she used as a message drop.

The warden had a message for her. She tucked it into her pouch and went into the shrine, touching thumb to forehead as she went through the gate.

The murmur of prayers, the quiet crunch of gravel underfoot and the occasional stroke of a gong made the shrine a peaceful place. She took a deep breath; ginger and lavender were the dominant scents in the incense of the day. She breathed deeply, feeling calmer in the familiar surroundings. The questions Yisyena had raised about talents and the role of the gods had been bothering her all day, making her feel insecure, as if she was on a tightrope swaying in the breeze.

She walked around the octagonal garden at the centre of the shrine, thumbing her forehead as she passed the altars of the Child, the Wife and the Warrior Maid, and going to her knees before the altar of the Friend and Comforter. That was the aspect of Quarenna she felt most affection for. There she stabbed her thumb and let blood drip into the bowl at the foot of the statue. She knelt there for a while silently begging for help and guidance before moving on to the altar of the Helper. There she offered more blood, sat back on her heels, closed her eyes, bowed her head and waited.

"How may I help you today?"

The voice made her jump because it was one she knew well but hadn't expected to hear. Lifting her head she looked up into a wrinkled smiling face framed by the green and gold scarf of a priestess of Quarenna.

"Blessèd Tilua, what a wonderful surprise. I'm so pleased to see you. I thought you were still in Hemeark. When did you move to Carregis?"

"I came five months ago when I was invited to join the Inner Circle of the Daughters of Quarenna."

"That's wonderful. May I offer congratulations, or would that be presumptuous of me?"

"Thank you. The invitation was unexpected but very welcome."

"I'm delighted it's you offering help today. I need your wisdom and advice."

"As always, I will provide what I can, but, as always, there is a price."

"I offer the blood in my veins, the tears from my eyes and the sweat of my brow to Holy Quarenna."

"She will accept any offering made sincerely. What is your problem?"

"Can we talk in private?"

Tilua raised an eyebrow but said nothing as she led Anarya to her study. "Tell me," she said, when they were comfortably seated in the cosy little room, rich with the scent of jasmine and cedar wood and with glasses of redleaf tea on the table in front of them.

"I have met someone... She's... She's from Sitrelk... and her beliefs are strange... She told me..."

"That she doesn't know our gods."

"Yes. And that the gods have nothing to do with the gifts of magic. Blessèd one, I'm frightened. Is what she says blasphemy? If I listen to it will Holy Quarenna turn her face from me?"

"This Sitrelker is important to you?"

Anarya bowed her head and whispered, "I think she is becoming so."

"I thought as much. You wouldn't be concerned if she wasn't. You can relax. I don't think you have to worry about blasphemy. While it is undoubtedly true that the talents are the gifts of Quarenna and Huler, the gods have chosen to do things differently in Sitrelk from the way it is in Carrhen. There they are not so closely involved with the gifts of talent."

"Why?"

Tilua laughed. "You would have to ask Quarenna herself that question and you probably wouldn't understand the answer if she gave one. The gods do things in their own ways for their own reasons."

STEALTHER

It was almost six months before Baram persuaded his teacher that he had learned enough. The ex-soldier Raifen had recruited to teach Baram the basics of how to use a sword and a long knife was hard to please. He had insisted on him learning simple unarmed combat techniques as well as weapon skills. The exercise this involved had put some muscle on him, although he was still quite slender.

He had also practiced with his talent and was comfortable with it, although it still felt strange to be close enough to touch someone without them having any idea that he was there. Learning to breathe quietly, move silently and give no clues to his presence was as difficult as anything his tutor taught him about weapons.

On an early spring afternoon with the air full of birdsong, Baram stood in stealth by the gate to the farm in Nuruye where he expected to find his uncle. He had spent a day watching what went on. The way the farmer and his family worked happily together made him wish his own childhood had been different. He envied their closeness and wished he could be one of them. *But they're not really my relatives, are they? They might be as mean to me as uncle.*

Noon had come and gone while he waited for any evidence that his uncle was there. He watched while the farmer and his family milked the cows, fed the pigs and went through the routine tasks of running a farm. There was no sign of him. *Did I guess wrong about what he would do?*

The farmer's sons, both big burly men built to the same scale as his uncle, led a horse and cart from one of the barns. One of them climbed aboard, the other walked alongside as they started down the track leading to the gate where Baram was waiting.

He couldn't see what, if anything, was loaded on the cart, but he was close enough to overhear part of their conversation as they went past.

"… lazy, that's what he is. He should be doing this, not us.

It's not as if he doesn't know how to drive a cart."

"All he ever does is drink. Pa won't stand it for much longer…"

That sounds like a conversation they've had before, Baram thought. *It's got to be uncle they're talking about. He is here!*

He waited until he was sure he knew how many people there were at the farm. The next day, when the farmer, his two sons, one daughter and the three farmhands were out working in the fields and farmyard, he walked cautiously through the farmhouse. The farmer's wife and another daughter were still in the house – and so was his uncle.

A delicious smell wafted from the kitchen. He sniffed and a wave of sadness flooded over Baram. It smelled just like the rabbit pies his aunt used to make, rich with onions, garlic, celery and carrots. His aunt had been so good to him and had been snuffed out by her brute of a husband. It was time he paid for that.

He climbed the stairs slowly making sure there were no creaks to give him away. Three doors opened off the upper landing and a ladder led to a trapdoor in the ceiling. Where would his uncle be? *Probably in the attic.* Listening, he heard muffled snores coming from above and he clambered up until he could see into the room. *Yes!* His uncle was there, lying on a straw-filled pallet.

Baram looked down at his uncle. *Got you,* he thought, *but I'm not going to kill you in your sleep. You deserve to know you're dead and who killed you.* With some satisfaction he kicked his uncle's ribs.

The man woke with a grunt, sat up, groaned, looked around, reached for the flagon lying beside the pallet and tipped it over his mouth. Nothing came out. He dropped the flagon and slumped back.

Baram kicked his uncle again then drew the long knife he had strapped to his thigh.

His uncle sat up again, his eyes went wide and he whispered, "Baram?"

I've got to do it now. He'll fight me and he's stronger. He could grab the knife from me. "Yes, it's me," he said. "Do you know that's the first time you've ever called me by name? Usually it's been 'boy', or 'you'. But I wouldn't worry about it. That's the last time you'll call me anything."

He stepped forward, thrusting for the heart.

"Didn't mean to kill her," shouted uncle as he fell backwards away from the knife. Instead of it being a killing stroke the blade sank into his shoulder and he screamed.

Baram froze. The scream would attract the farmer's wife and she would see him. Practice had shown him that he couldn't become invisible again for about a tenth of a chime after holding a naked blade. *What do I do now?*

"You be quiet up there," a woman's voice called from below. "I've had enough of you lazing around, getting drunk and waking the world with your nightmares. If you don't make yourself useful soon I'll have Derein throw you out, brother or not."

"No, please," uncle whimpered. "Derein'll protect me. He looked after me when Pa beat me. He'll protect me, like he always has."

Baram looked at the snivelling figure on the pallet. He felt an unexpected surge of pity. Uncle had been beaten as a child too. Maybe that was the only way he knew how to behave. *I can't kill him now. Not now that I've seen the fear in his eyes and heard the regret in his voice. Huler forgive me, I can't do it.*

○

Baram looked around Raifen's office. It was a small room with three bare stone walls. A window high on one wall let Huler's light into the room. A tapestry depicting Huler as the Craftsman hung on the fourth wall behind Raifen's desk and there was a rush rug on the floor. Books and scrolls were piled up on a desk in such profusion as to completely obscure the desktop.

"I'm pleased to hear you can be merciful," said Raifen, handing him a glass of wine. "It's one of the things Huler demands of his Stealthers for they are required to be judges as well as executioners."

"But I can't be a judge. I'm too young."

"No, I don't think that's a problem, Baram. I believe you will find that you can judge fairly. Huler chose you and he doesn't make mistakes. He will stand by you and help you."

"I suppose so."

"Are you ready to start work?"

"Yes."

"A Whisperer has brought an appeal from someone in Verenthe. The message said a sailor was stabbed on the dockside there two days ago. His attackers were careless and they didn't make sure he was dead before leaving him. Before he died he accused his captain of taking refugees on board in Sitrelk then robbing them and throwing them overboard instead of delivering them to safety."

"That's despicable. But surely the whole crew must be involved."

"I would think so, but that is for you to decide and take whatever action you think appropriate. The ship, the *Lady Visole,* will probably dock tomorrow." Raifen raised his glass and said, "May Huler guide your hand."

O

The *Lady Visole* was a fat-bellied lumbering cog which arrived in Carregis a day later than anticipated. Baram watched as she tied up at a wharf about as far away from the dock gates and the bustle of the loading area as it was possible to get. He admitted to himself that he wasn't familiar with ships but he thought she was riding high in the water, as if she didn't have much cargo on board.

The shouted orders and the backchat between the dockers and the crew competed with the screams of the gulls for a while. Then they faded once she was securely moored and the gangway run out. The only sounds were the gulls, the slosh of waves against the ship's hull, and a faint background of noises from other ships moored further along the wharf, plus creaks from the mooring lines and fenders as *Lady Visole* moved with the waves.

The dockers wandered off, apparently in no hurry to start unloading or loading. The crew, in ones and twos, went below and came on deck again carrying bags and bundles. They gathered in a loose cluster near the top of the gangway and waited. Eventually the captain came out of his cabin and climbed the stairs to the stern deck. He leaned on the rail, looking down on the crew, and started talking.

Baram couldn't hear what he said but he couldn't see any

way to get closer. He was fairly sure that sailors would notice the movement he would cause by walking up the gangway. All he could do was watch until eleven men made their way ashore leaving the captain and one other man on board. He was close enough to hear the mutterings of the crew once they were clear of the ship.

"Huler's balls. Back on board by fourteenth chime tomorrow, he says, then sailin' on first tide the day after. Hardly more than one Huler-be-damned day in port. Not enough for a decent drunk."

"You've never been a *decent* drunk in your life, you fool."

That comment provoked some good-natured jeering and shoving.

"Gotta be here tomorrow so those thievin' dockies don't steal the cargo."

"They're welcome to it. There's nothing worth having."

A small wiry man wearing an old pea jacket said, "Ye'll all be here tomorrow or ye'll regret it when ye do stagger aboard. The cargo's what pays ye. Gotta keep an eye on it and them dockies. We unload tomorrow an' then load whatever it is the Cap'n's found for us. Understood?"

There were grunts and mutters of, "Yes, bosun."

"Cap'n wants to do another trip like the last. Easy way o' making money, an' he wants to make as much as he can afore word gets out the *Lady* ain't a safe berth for refugees."

"Huh, how's that goin' t' happen? All the witnesses are feeding the fishes."

"I don't like it. It's not right," said a tall, burly man. He had a full black beard with tokens showing some of the aspects of Huler braided into it.

The bosun stopped at the bottom of the gangway and caused an obstruction while he turned to glare at the last speaker. "Newbie, you ain't got no right t' complain, so keep yer hatch shut. I'm warnin' ye. Keep quiet 'bout this here voyage. There'll be a knife waiting for ye if ye squeal."

"That's tellin' him, bosun."

"Nah!" said one of the others, "he won't say nuthin'. He's took the money just like the rest of us."

"He could always give us his share if he's feeling guilty."

"Aye, I'll take some of it."

"You, an' the rest of us, I reckon."

"Never mind 'im. Who's for Jezic's, eh? Lift a few beers…"

"An' a few skirts!"

That produced a laugh and shouts of agreement. Most of the men moved off in a noisy, jostling group, leaving two behind. One was the big, heavily bearded man who had been described as a newbie, the other had a thinner beard but looked enough like him that Baram thought they must be related.

"You've got to be careful what you say, Rodi. Bosun'll gut you happily if he thinks you're not part of the crew in this."

"Wish I wasn't. Why did I let you persuade me to jump ship? Should have stayed with the *Flying Fish.*"

"Didn't know it was going to be like that, did I. Wouldn't have been aboard myself if I had. Never thought Cap'n Lisort was like that. He's not usually a chesa. Always has an eye for a profit he does, why else does he always take the cheapest mooring available. He generally makes good money on each voyage, and he pays the crew well. That's why I suggested you when he was looking for a good ship's carpenter. Thought I was doing you a favour getting you a decent berth, but I was wrong. What he did was…"

"Evil, that's what it was, Kanu, evil. I've decided. Curse the bosun and his threats, I'm not sailin' on that damned ship again and I'm going to give my share of the money to Huler and beg his forgiveness."

"Sounds like a good idea, cousin, I think I'll do the same. I don't want to sail again with that on my conscience." He signed himself with Huler's lightning bolt, forehead, left shoulder, right shoulder and navel.

Baram trailed Kanu and Rodi as they went to the nearest temple. They didn't go into the sanctuary but went to one of the side chapels, the one occupied by the Penitent's altar. There they prostrated themselves in front of the tapestry which showed some of the faces of Huler, the Judge, the Grieving Parent, the Avenger and the Pardoner prominent among them.

A priest walked into the chapel about a fifth later, settled himself in the only chair and asked, "Why do you seek forgiveness?"

Hesitantly at first, but with growing confidence, Rodi and

Kanu guided each other through the recitation of a plea in the proper form, "Great Huler, Lord of the Skies, Ruler of the Waves and the Winds and Illuminator of the World, to my shame I have taken money stained with the blood of innocents and I seek to ease my conscience."

Baram listened as careful questioning by the priest drew out the story of the voyage. *Lady Visole* had sailed to Umbrett, a small port in Sitrelk, with a cargo of wine, copper and sheepskins. The wine in particular had been well received and all the cargo had been sold easily. Then Captain Lisort had discovered a problem. Another ship had left Umbrett the previous day and taken almost all the available cargo for Carregis. All that was left was some fruit which was already very ripe. He wasn't happy with that; too much risk of it rotting during the voyage and becoming unsalable. Sailing virtually empty seemed the only option until the bosun had been approached by two men who wanted passage for themselves and their families.

"They were desperate to get out of Sitrelk," said Kanu. "Don't know why. None of them had much Katelish and I don't speak Sitru. There were eleven of them. The two men and their wives, three older women, who I think must have been their mothers or their wives' mothers, and four kids."

"The captain looked well pleased with himself when they agreed a price and we sailed that afternoon as soon as they were aboard," said Rodi. "There was no trouble for the first three days, then an ignorant, foul-mouthed scumbag of a deckhand tried to force himself on one of the younger women. He got a knife in his belly for his trouble. Don't think anybody thought the worse of her husband for that, 'cept that right bastard of a bosun. He was all for killing the Sitrelker there and then but the captain stopped him."

Rodi and Kanu said they were taking their turn on galley duty the next day when they heard screams and shouts from the deck. They didn't know what had happened until it was done. They had to piece together the story from what their shipmates said.

According to what they heard, a deckhand called Rokesh, who was one of the bosun's cronies, went poking through the refugees' belongings and found a hidden cache of money. He told the bosun, who told the captain. There was a confrontation because the agreed fare for the passage was two-thirds of all the refugees' possessions and the hidden money hadn't been included in the calculation.

Kanu had gone to see what all the noise was about. "Blessèd one, a deckhand told me the bosun put a knife into the back of one of the Sitrelkers when he was arguing with the captain. Then the crew went mad. He said it was like seeing sharks feeding. I think one of the older women might have still been alive when I got there, but somebody crushed her skull with a belaying pin before I could do anything. The deck was covered in blood, even the children were dead. Everyone seemed shocked by what had happened. Then, when the corpses were stripped, it turned out the older women had gold sewn into their petticoats. That evidence that the Sitrelkers had been lying about how much they had seemed to justify the massacre for a lot of the crew, including the captain."

"I'd like to think I would have helped the Sitrelkers," said Rodi, "but, once it was over, speaking out would only have got me killed too. I'm ashamed of it but I took a share of the money once Captain Lisort sold off the gold in Verenthe. One of the others wouldn't touch it and the bosun stabbed him and left him for dead on the dockside."

"I took the money as well," said Kanu, "but I can't keep it. I want to give it to Huler. I will do penance and ask him for mercy."

"Is that what you want too?" asked the priest, addressing Rodi.

"It is."

"Very well. Huler has blessed me with the ability to know the truth of what men tell me and I know that both of you are truly repentant. Huler will accept the blood money, which will be used for the benefit of orphans. As penance he asks for an equal sum to be provided for the same purpose sometime in the next five years. It does not have to be all at once. You must also sacrifice your beards to him."

Rodi ran his fingers through his full beard, frowned, then sighed, "If it must be, it must be."

The priest insisted that the cousins keep enough to live on and accepted the rest of the money. Once they had left he said, "Stealther. Please show yourself."

"How did you know I was here?" asked Baram as he visualised himself removing a cloak that covered him from head to toe and made himself visible.

"You may be invisible and inaudible but you still have feelings and I tasted your rage when they spoke of the death of children. Raifen has spread the word that Huler has appointed his new Stealther. I'm pleased to meet you. Since you're here I assume you already knew of this incident. May I ask what you will do about it?"

"I don't know yet. I think I need to hear more to sort out the truly guilty from those that were carried away by events and by their emotions. Perhaps others of the crew regret what happened but are afraid for their lives if they speak. May I ask your opinion?"

"It's not for me to say," said the priest. "Huler guides his Stealthers and will make your path clear."

Baram prostrated himself in front of the Penitent's altar and said, "Great Huler, I beg you, let my judgement be right. And, if I must kill, guide my hand so that I strike true."

O

From the temple Baram went to the alley behind the tavern known as Jezic's where he waited in the hope that he could identify some of the crew when they came out. He was sure he would recognise the bosun and one or two of the others, but was less confident about the rest.

He tried not to breathe too deeply. The sweet, cloying smell of ganj was prominent, as was the sour stink of vomit and, overlying everything, the stench of the privy.

Two men staggered out into the alley, supporting each other. He recognised one of them.

"You all right, Bimel?" that one asked. "Never known you be so quiet."

"I'm fine, Rokesh. Just need t' piss." He started fumbling at the laces of his breeches.

"Not here, y' stupid chesa. Wait till y're in the privy."

"Who're you calling a chesa, eh?" Bimel shrugged himself free of the other man and reached for his knife.

"Huler! You're bloody touchy tonight. Calm down," said Rokesh, grabbing at Bimel's knife hand. "What's got into ye.

Never known ye t' be a sad drunk before."

"Can still hear the screams. Keep seein' them kids. Just lyin' there bleedin' into the scuppers."

"Best place for them. Less damned Sitrelkers in the world. Did for two of them meself, an' one o' the old bitches."

Baram had heard enough. *This one is guilty, the other at least shows some remorse. I hope this is Huler's anger I feel and not just mine.* He moved closer and drew his long knife. Remembering what he had been told about mortal wounds, he stabbed Rokesh, the blade sliding up under his ribs to his heart. The feel of the blade passing through flesh and the flutter as it touched the beating heart made him shudder and, anxious to get it over with, he pushed harder.

Rokesh didn't scream. He fell, like a sack of turnips, produced a gurgling, incoherent sound, twitched and lay still.

Baram watched his first victim bleeding out in the mud and filth of the alley. He sheathed his knife and thought, *It's odd. I expected killing someone would be harder, more stressful, more... significant, but I don't feel anything except satisfaction that he's dead and a conviction that he deserved to die. Huler must be protecting my emotions just as the Stealther's book said he would.*

He saw Bimel gazing at him in horror and took a step towards him.

Bimel shuffled backwards, tripped over something and fell into the mud. He wet himself.

"Are your crewmates still in there?" asked Baram and received frantic nods in answer.

"Tell them more will die for their crime. Rokesh was only the first." He watched while Bimel clambered to his feet and, carefully avoiding getting too close to Baram, shuffled back into the tavern. *That will bring them out,* he thought, *but they're not going to rush out. By the time they respond I'll be able to be invisible again. But I'm not sure how to handle eight of them by myself.*

When the sailors came into the alley they did so in two groups, one from each end, with knives in hand. "Ain't nobody here," said one of them, just before he tripped over Baram's outstretched leg. The sailor stumbled into one of the other group and pulled him down as he tried to regain his balance. Two more, already more than half drunk and unsteady, fell too. There was a bellow of rage when a knife found flesh somewhere in the tangle of bodies.

Baram stood back and watched as seven of the eight sailors finished up in a confused, cursing, vicious tangle. One of them ended face down in the mud and didn't move as the brawl rolled over and away from him. Another was bleeding his life out into the mud, vainly trying to stop the spurts of blood from his groin.

It looks as if they're going to do the job for me.

The eighth man was the bosun, who had managed to stay on his feet. He backed away from the others, looking around warily. Baram carefully positioned himself so that he was behind the bosun. When he was within touching distance he reached out and tapped the bosun on the left shoulder. Then he stepped back and drew his blade again.

The bosun spun to his left, lashing out with his knife but Baram wasn't there and he connected with nothing. He howled as his momentum carried him on to Baram's blade. It ripped through his jacket into his belly and his twisting motion enlarged the wound.

Baram looked down at the squirming figure and said, "You're dead, but you still have some time. Use it to think about the women and children you killed. I hope Huler won't spare your torment." He turned and walked away from the carnage. *Only Captain Lisort to deal with now.*

◯

It was still dark, about two chimes before dawn, when Baram got back to the dock and *Lady Visole*. Remembering that one man had stayed on board with the captain and expecting him to be on watch, he was in stealth as he walked up the gangway. However, there wasn't a watchman at the top of the gangway, or in the bow, or on the raised deck at the stern. It wasn't until Baram heard soft snores coming from the space between the mast and the hatch cover that he found the man, fast asleep.

Is the door locked? He took a hold of the handle and turned it carefully. *No, it's not.* He eased the door open, ready to stop if it creaked, and stepped inside.

Lisort was lying in a tangle of sheets in a bunk that looked cramped for someone of his size.

Baram prodded him. He woke with a snort but had to fight himself free of the sheets to sit up. "Wha... Oh... just another bad dream."

"No it isn't," said Baram, drawing his knife. "A nightmare, perhaps, but this is no dream."

Lisort jerked backwards and banged his head against the cupboard over the bunk. "Who in Huler's hells are you and how did you get past the watch?"

"It wasn't too difficult. I'm afraid your watchman is sleeping, rather more soundly than you appear to be."

"Chesa! He'll pay for tha..." Lisort broke off, looked at the knife, swallowed and said, "What do you want?"

"I've heard about your last voyage and I want to know more about it."

"You've heard... How?"

"Does it matter? I know you accepted payment for the return trip and then killed your passengers and that you're planning another voyage to do the same again."

"That's a lie," said Lisort, sitting up straighter and cursing as he banged his head once more. "It wasn't supposed to be like that. I'm not doing it again. One trip like that is more than enough."

"Your bosun said that's what you were going to do."

"That whoreson! Only reason he's on board is his sister's married to some sort of distant relative of the Beghroth family. They own the ship. He thinks he's captain and it's only because he can't read or navigate that he's not. I'd leave him on the dock or toss him overboard if I thought I could get away with it. Him, Rokesh and a couple of others are who really run this ship. The massacre was their doing, not mine. All I do is organise cargoes and make sure the *Lady* gets where she's supposed to go."

"You won't be sorry to learn he's dead then."

"Sorry! Hardly. I'd dance on his grave... You mean it, don't you. He is dead."

"Him, and Rokesh, and at least two of the others. The rest were fighting among themselves when I last saw them. None of them will be fit to sail tomorrow, even if they're still alive."

"But where do I find a crew?"

"I don't think you need to worry about that. At the very least I think you'll lose your command when the owners find out what happened, and they will because I'll tell them. If you can't control your crew you're not fit to be captain."

Lisort sagged back into his bunk. "You can't blame me. It's all the bosun's fault. It's my livelihood you're talking about. You can't take it away just because some damned Sitrelkers got themselves killed. It's not..." He surged up from the bunk with a gutting knife in his hand, trying to stab Baram.

Without thinking about it, Baram reacted. His parry swept the knife aside and his thrust took Lisort in the neck.

I guess I have learned something about fighting after all, he thought as he watched Lisort choking on his own blood.

He looked around the cabin. *Where would he keep his share of the money? If I can find it I'll give it to the temple.* A short search was all it took to find the loose plank. The cache contained almost two hundred regals. *Surely that can't all be from the last voyage. He's been saving up for a long time to get that much.*

Baram stepped out of the cabin and headed towards the gangway. A belaying pin slammed into his left shoulder. He rolled across the deck cursing himself for complacency. He had forgotten about the watchman. In the darkness the sailor had the advantage because he knew the layout of the deck. Stealth wasn't an option; he had held a naked blade too recently.

Crouching quietly against the bulwarks, Baram waited for the sailor to reveal his whereabouts. Staying still was something he had practiced; movement might give him away even in stealth. He hoped the sailor wasn't as patient.

A vague shadow loomed above him. He jumped up, caught the sailor in a bear hug and rushed him across the deck. The edge of the hatch cover caught him by surprise and he stumbled. He did manage to land on top of his opponent.

There was a grunt as the sailor had the breath knocked out of him.

Baram got back to his feet, and fell again when the sailor swept his legs out from under him. He rolled and kicked out, catching the sailor in the stomach and sending him staggering backwards.

The man fell through the gap in the rail and rolled off the

gangplank. The splash was followed by a panicked shout, "I can't swim!"

Too bad, thought Baram as he made his way ashore and headed for the temple. *That was a lot harder than I would have liked for my first assignment. I hope the next one is easier.*

SPONGER

"I thought I'd go to Westford today. I haven't done any advertising there for a while," said Anarya over breakfast.

"Good. It is time I learned more of this city," replied Yisyena.

"I don't think it would be a good idea for you to come with me, not there."

"Why not?"

"It's not the best area. Not the worst either, but you'd be too conspicuous there and you might attract the wrong sort of attention."

"I can dress appropriately."

"That won't help. It's your hair that's the problem."

Yisyena ran her hand through her hair. "What is wrong with it? I have seen women wearing their hair shorter than mine."

"There's nothing *wrong* with it. I love your hair. It's not the length that's the problem but the colour. The pale hair against your dark skin is gorgeous, but it does stand out. I've noticed people looking at it."

"It never occurred to me. I am used to it. Everyone in my family has pale hair. What can we do? I can't keep my head covered all the time."

"No. That would be too conspicuous. We'll have to dye it. Let's go to the Spice Market. I'm sure we'll find something there."

O

Anarya took a deep breath, she enjoyed the heady aromatic scent of the Spice Market. It was covered so that rain wouldn't spoil the spices and the roof held in the smells. She sniffed, trying to identify as many as possible as they made their way through the narrow alleys between the stalls; peppercorns, stinkroot, mustard, cloves, galal, cinnamon and many more.

Henna was easy to find but Anarya didn't think the aggressive red would be any improvement over Yisyena's normal hair colour so they kept hunting among the stalls until they found indigo. "We'll be able to get a decent brown by mixing this with the henna."

They left the market by a different doorway. Yisyena stopped at the sound of the newsmonger's voice. It was just audible over the clamour of the stall holders calling their wares and drawing attention to how fresh their spices were.

"News from Voro. News from Hemeark. Ships expected and ships sailing. Only half a bit for the news. News from Carregis and Firten. All the news from everywhere. Only half a bit."

"*Wenshul-ti,*" said Yisyena. "What do you call them here? A literal translation would be 'one who speaks rumours' – a rumourman? I did not know you had such here."

"What? Oh, him. We call them newsmongers. They're quite common around the markets and squares. Haven't you noticed them before?"

"Are they reliable?"

"Reliable? Depends what you mean. They have their own guild and the guildmasters make sure all of them give the same information. Factual things, like when ships will sail, are accurate. And so is the news, most of the time. They don't actually deal in rumours, they use Whisperers to get information from everywhere faster than messengers could bring it."

A man walked up to the newsmonger, tossed him a coin and asked for the latest news from Firten.

"The Guild conclave took place yesterday. It confirmed Fauthein as the new Master," said the newsmonger. "Don't know what the vote was, just that Fauthein is in and Horolt out."

"Where is that place he asked about?" asked Yisyena.

"Firten. It's three, maybe four, days travel north-east. It's where the best wine in Carrhen comes from. The Guild he's talking about must be the Vintner's Association. Let's go home."

"No," said Yisyena. "I want to watch this newsmonger for a while."

"They get a bit upset if people hang around them without

paying, hoping to overhear when someone else does pay. He'll spot you easily because of your hair."

"We can move back a short distance. I can use my talent and still be able to hear him. However, I am more interested in watching the way he works than in hearing the news. Let us go to the other side of the street."

"Why are you interested in him?"

"I will tell you later."

The newsmonger kept calling out where he had news from. If interest seemed to die down he would throw in a free snippet of information such as 'Benaur wins in Hemeark again. Only a quarter-bit for more details.' or 'Junielle still claims innocence. Half a bit for her speech.' Sometimes these teasers would result in someone paying for more information; much of the time nobody seemed interested.

About a third of a chime later a boy ran up to the newsmonger and handed him a roll of parchment. "That's the latest news come from the guildhall," said Anarya. "It gets delivered once a chime to every newsmonger in the city."

The newsmonger read and reread the parchment, then stuffed it into the satchel on his back and started calling, "Massacre at the docks last night. Ship's crew killed. Half a bit for the details. All the latest news."

"I have seen enough," said Yisyena. "Let us go home."

"You go. See what you can do about your hair. I'll go to Westford."

O

Anarya got home after her trip to Westford to find Yisyena looking dubiously at a brownish concoction bubbling in a pot. "Is that the dye? How long has it been simmering?"

"About a half."

"In that case I think it's had enough. Let it cool and we'll try it out later."

"Very well," said Yisyena, taking the pot off the fire. "There is hot water if you wish to have a drink."

"Yes, please. I think we have some chamil left. I'd like that." She took a message from her pouch and dropped it on the table. "Here's a possible job for us."

Yisyena poured hot water into a mug, stirred in a spoonful

of dried leaves and flowers, handed it to Anarya and set about making redleaf tea for herself.

"Tell me, Anra. Who is Rhyanek?"

"Where did you get that name? I'm sure I never mentioned it."

"That message. It is addressed to Rhyanek the Quaestor. Who is he?"

"He's me. I mean, I'm him. I told you I sometimes disguise myself as a man. That's one of the names I use when I do."

"I thought as much. That is good. It means we have a name to use that is already established."

"Use? For what?"

"I have been thinking about attracting customers. The way you do it seems inefficient. Watching the newsmongers has given me an idea. I told you there are rumourmen in Sitrelk who have a similar function. If paid enough they will also mention the name of a business or of someone providing a specialist service."

"You think the newsmongers might do the same?"

"I do not know. However, it seems possible. They are unlikely to be averse to a new way of making money."

Anarya sat down on the bed. She chewed her lip for a moment. "You know, that might work. It's worth trying to persuade the masters of the guild that it's a good idea. Might take a bit of effort, they tend to be rather conservative. But what's that got to do with Rhyanek?"

"It's better to have a man in charge, isn't it? We can call the business Rhyanek and Partner."

"What? No!" Anarya jumped up, almost spilling her tea, "It's my business and I get the credit for it, not some man, even if he is me."

Yisyena frowned, "You must think about this carefully. A business run by a woman is never taken seriously."

"Are you crazy? At least half the businesses in Carrhen are run by women, maybe more."

Yisyena sat down on the chair looking startled and said, "Really? I had not realised that the women I see in shops are working for themselves and not for a man."

"Yes, really. Oh, I get it, Yisa. This is another Sitrelker twist on the way things are, isn't it."

"In Sitrelk women can't own businesses or property unless

their husbands, fathers and any other close male relatives are dead. Even then there's pressure on them to marry again because men think women can't be trusted to run things. Except for a household of course."

"What a stupid idea."

"Didn't your Sitrelker friends tell you this?"

"No, they lived just the way everybody else did. In fact, Lutusha, who lived in the next street, ran one of the best bakeries in Hemeark. Still does for all I know. And she did it without a husband. Without any men at all actually, her employees were all women.

"You mean getting the newsmongers to talk about Rhyanek and Partner wouldn't have any advantage over Anarya and Partner."

"No, certainly not."

"I did not intend to upset you," said Yisyena. "I should make sure I know what I am talking about before speaking."

"You know," Anarya said after taking a couple of sips of tea, "there might be an advantage, but not the one you're thinking of. Suppose we said Rhyanek and Partners, plural. If we let people think there are several people involved then when I use different talents people will assume they were used by different people. I already use several different names depending on the talent I need to use. That'll make it easier to conceal that I'm a Sponger."

"You are not angry?"

Anarya hugged her. "I was, but now that I think about it, I believe you've had a good idea, even if it's for the wrong reasons. Let's go talk to the masters of the Honourable Guild of Independent Newsmongers tomorrow, once we've got your hair dyed."

"Should we not look at the message?"

"You're right, we should." She stretched across the table, picked up the message and examined the seal. "It's a bad impression, I can't recognise it. I wonder who it's from. I've only ever taken two contracts using the name Rhyanek." She broke the seal and fragments of wax fell on the table. "Oh, Holy Quarenna is smiling on us – that last contract, the one I had just finished when we met, didn't only pay well, it's brought another job offer. He was so pleased with the outcome that he's recommended me to one of his friends.

Just listen to this, 'To Rhyanek the Quaestor, I ask you to investigate the pilferage from my warehouses in the Western Docks as you did for Jemis Gotheer. I offer a fee of five dukals and will add a bonus of two if you succeed in identifying the thief or thieves within three days.' And it's signed Keiret Beghroth!"

"I have heard that name before. At the arena, I think."

"Do you remember seeing a green banner with a silver kraken?"

"There was one such just behind the beehive banner, was there not?"

"That's right. He sponsored the free-for-all race. The Beghroth family is one of the richest and most influential in Carregis. Being useful to them would be good for business."

"Then you must accept the contract. Start at the docks tomorrow and I will go to talk to the newsmongers."

"Will you be all right? You still don't know that much about Carregis."

"I am certain I can deal with them. After all, I have something they want, a way of making money."

"Right. Let's sort out your hair before I go out."

"Where are you going?"

"Oh, I never told you. I overheard a meeting being arranged in the Dip. It might come to nothing but I could learn something useful, you never know."

"Be careful, my love."

O

Anarya stood in a doorway at Bisson's Cross confident that, in dark clothes and with her ability to blend in to her surroundings in operation, she was effectively invisible. She wrinkled her nose at the sour, marshy smell of the Dip and the overlying stench of the rotten fruit and vegetables littering the ground. They had fallen from the carts that occupied this small square during the day, and were so bad that even the poorest inhabitants of the Dip hadn't bothered picking them up.

The moon was almost full and it was bright enough to let her see the three men approaching along Kitrel's Alley. They were all wearing something red and blue. One had a scarf in the gang colours, one a stocking cap and the biggest one wore a sad looking bunch of blue flowers pinned to a scrap of dirty cloth that had once been red.

They waited at the end of the Alley and didn't step into the square itself until another three men appeared from one of the intersecting streets. Then they slowly moved forwards, the man in the stocking cap looking around continually and muttering, 'All clear,' every few steps.

All six men stopped when the two groups were about two paces apart.

The newcomers' gang colours were orange and black, worn as ribbons pinned to their shoulders. One of them, who Anarya assumed was the leader, also wore a battered looking black hat with a badge, of two hands shaking, embroidered on it in orange. "What do the Angry Apes want from the Perfect Friends?" he asked.

"Nothin', 'ceptin' maybe your blood," growled the flower wearer.

"This is neutral ground, and you asked for the meeting."

"True enough," said the man wearing the red and blue scarf, "We got a truce?"

"A truce is agreed," said the spokesman for the Perfect Friends. "What is it you want?"

"Access to your streets."

"Why?"

"One of ours 'as betrayed us. He's gone legit, an' he's done good, but he's stopped paying his tithe an' we reckon he still owes. Hear tell he's living north of Ferras Street. That means we need to go through your territory to reprimand him."

"He's done well for himself if that's where he's ended up. What do you offer in return?"

"A third o' his tithe."

The spokesman snorted. "And if he doesn't pay we get a third of nothing, which is nothing. You'll have to do better than that."

"What would the Friends want then?"

"It's the *Perfect* Friends, apeface. Get it right. If you want access to our streets, give us access to yours. A secure corridor to the waterfront for one night."

"You're asking a lot."

"You asked first. How many would you need to deal with

your renegade properly?"

"Four would be enough."

The spokesman stepped back and muttered to his companions. They both nodded and then he said, "The Perfect Friends offer safe passage for four in return for access to the docks through the territory of the Angry Apes for four, to be granted within a week of the debt being incurred."

"Four is too many," said the scarf wearer. "You can't expect us to let you take whatever you want from dockside, it's our territory."

"And from here to Ferras Street is ours and you expect us to let four through, picking up anything they fancy. Won't happen."

"We'll let two through, and we'll accept an escort to Ferras Street so that you can make sure nothing is taken from your people."

"Make it three and you have a deal," said the spokesman for the Perfect Friends.

The scarf wearer nodded. "Agreed. We want to go three days from now. Gotta warn you, any attack on the men making the trip'll cause a feud."

"Naturally. And the same understanding will be in effect if there is any interference with the repayment of the debt. Three days it is."

The two groups separated, walking backwards until they were well clear of each other before turning and disappearing along their respective streets.

Anarya waited, thinking, *I'm sure there are other gang members waiting out of sight in case of trouble. I'll stay here a quarter chime or so and give them a chance to move away.*

O

"There wasn't a lot to it," Anarya told Yisyena, snuggling up against her in bed, "just two of the gangs in the Dip making arrangements to let each other through their territories."

Yisyena sat up. "Gangs? If they are anything like the *houln*, the street gangs of Jotuk, they are dangerous. I do not like the idea of you exposing yourself to such peril, my love."

"All I know about Jotuk is it's supposed to be the biggest city in the world."

"There are some parts of Jotuk where it is unsafe to walk alone. The *houln* and the gutter dwellers will rob and kill anyone who goes there without an armed escort."

"No," said Anarya, "It's not like that in the Dip."

"Tell me."

Anarya sighed and pushed herself upright. "It's late and I've got to be at the docks early tomorrow to make a start on the Beghroth contract, can't it wait?"

"I think it important that I know these things."

"I suppose so, but do you have to learn them tonight?"

"I wish to become an asset to your business. The quicker I learn the better."

"Oh, all right. But it'll have to be quick."

Yisyena wrapped her arms around Anarya. "So, tell me."

"There are three gangs in the Dip, the Angry Apes, the Perfect Friends and the Silver Wolves. They effectively rule it. The ordinary people there have to pay them for protection if they want to live in safety. A gang member can get away with almost anything if his victim hasn't paid, but payment does actually buy protection and the gangs are ruthless if one of their members steps out of line. They are very territorial and occasionally there are fights and one or two streets move from the control of one gang to another."

"Do the Duke's men not maintain control in the Dip?"

"No. They don't even go there except in strength."

"What did you find out tonight?"

Anarya briefly described the scene at Bisson's Cross.

"I do not understand the significance of the agreement you witnessed."

"The Angry Apes aren't the biggest of the gangs but their territory runs right up to the eastern arm of the docks. I don't know why the Perfect Friends want access to the dockside but I'm sure it's not for sightseeing. I can tell the Duke's men roughly when to expect them and they'll give a reward for that sort of information. It would be more if I knew exactly when they'd be going but I might get a bit or two out of it and you know the saying, 'enough bits'll make a dukal'."

"I do not know that saying," said Yisyena, with a slight frown.

"Oh, I suppose not."

"If the Duke's men intercept the Perfect Friends on the

dockside will they think they have been betrayed by the Angry Apes and start a feud?"

"Hadn't thought of that. It's possible. We should keep clear of the Dip until this is all over."

"What of the man the Apes want to punish?" asked Yisyena. "Should he be warned?"

"I'm sorry for him, but there's nothing I can do. I don't know who he is or where he lives. 'North of Ferras Street' isn't very useful as an address. Now can we go to sleep, please."

FEELER

I know these docks rather better now, thought Anarya when she arrived to start working on her contract with the Beghroth company. She went to warehouse seven in the Western Docks and asked for Threnisa, the supervisor. She was shown into the office where a skinny, almost emaciated, woman was sitting at a desk poring over a ship's manifest.

"Master Beghroth has hired Rhyanek the quaestor and his partners to identify your pilferer," she said. "I'm one of the partnership. My name's Gitra and I'm a Feeler."

"What! Get out of my head, creep."

Oh, no. Not one of those, please. A lot of people had a dislike of Feelers. They thought their ability to know someone's emotions was an invasion of privacy. Such people were always difficult, and sometimes impossible, to work with. It was an attitude Anarya couldn't understand. Feelers, on the whole, didn't go around sensing emotions at random, that would be overwhelming. Knowing what some emotions felt like, she thought it would be intolerable not to be able to escape from them.

"I'm not using my talent at present," she told Threnisa.

"How do I know that? You could be poking around in my mind without me knowing."

"I swear by Holy Quarenna that I am not."

Threnisa sniffed.

"All I want to do is accompany someone on a tour of the warehouse," said Anarya. "The idea is to frighten your thief. I'll spot anybody who's particularly worried by the inspection and tomorrow a Voyanter colleague of mine will watch the suspects and see what they get up to."

"I don't need you to tell me who to suspect," said Threnisa. "What if I tell you I already know who the thief is?"

"Then there's not much point in my being here, is there? I'll leave." Anarya shrugged and turned to go, with a sinking sensation in her stomach. *What a waste of time.*

"Wait," said Threnisa. "I do know who it is, but there's got to be more than one of them. Since the boss has hired you, you had better have a look and see if you can find out who else is involved. I'll take you round the warehouses myself. Just keep out of my head while you're snooping about."

"Why do you think there's more than one thief?"

"Believe it or not, we've had some big items, like a Getruvan rug, go missing. Things that would take at least two people to handle."

They had looked into every corner of the warehouse where most of the pilfering had happened. By the time they were done Anarya had been using the Feeler's talent for more than a chime and a half. She had to stop before running into trouble with talent exhaustion. She had to let it fade. For the last quarter chime she couldn't be a Feeler. It didn't worry her, she had identified two men and a woman who were very worried by the detailed inspection. The feeling of fear when she looked into one of the side rooms was intense. It was enough to make her hands shake and she felt sick.

Back in Threnisa's office she asked about that room.

"It's not used much, just occasionally for particularly bulky and valuable things. The last shipment in there was a crate of fine ceramics from Umbrett, and that was about four weeks ago. Why?"

"Because looking into it provoked a lot of worry. I noticed too, that the lock looks rusty but the key turned easily and the door didn't squeak."

"You're right!" said Threnisa. "Why didn't I see that? They could be using it as a place to hide stolen items. But there's one problem – I've got the only key."

"I don't think it's the only one anymore. But don't worry about it. I know you're not involved, you were much too calm when we were in there."

"You've been snooping!"

"Sorry," said Anarya. "I had to be sure. I'll go now. You can expect a Voyanter to turn up tomorrow to watch the suspects."

"Get out! Go on, get out and never come back. I never want to see you again."

O

Anarya very carefully didn't smile when she introduced

herself to Threnisa the next day as a Voyanter and had to suffer a tirade against 'that nasty, sneaky Feeler'.

"I suppose you know her," said Threnisa.

"We often work together," replied Anarya.

"I never really liked the look of her from the start. I hope we can get on together. You look much nicer than her." Threnisa ranted on for about a tenth.

Anarya had come across this before. She had found it difficult at first to believe that all she needed to do to be accepted as someone else was to wear other clothes, style her hair in an alternative way and demonstrate a different ability. People were so used to the talented having only one skill that they never suspected her of being the same person. The real danger lay in demonstrating multiple talents one after another while being obviously the same person.

She spent two days sitting in a lean-to at the back of the warehouse where she could use her borrowed Voyanter skill to watch the activity inside. Nothing happened.

Then, on the third day shortly before she would be forced to give up watching by running out of talent, she saw two of the suspects carry a bolt of fine worsted cloth into the warehouse. The third one reached into a pocket in her apron and produced a key. It opened the side room door. They carried the cloth into the room and left it there.

At last! She slipped out of her hiding place, ran round to the front of the warehouse and started to close the main door.

The thieves must have heard her. They burst through the door before she had it shut and scattered. Anarya followed the woman, hoping to catch her with the key. The woman knew her way around the docks at least as well as Anarya did and could run faster.

When they burst into the loading area Anarya knew the woman was going to get away. *How can I stop her? Is there anything I can use?*

The Oversight showed her a Scratcher. He wasn't very strong, but she absorbed his talent. She Scratched a glyph in the air and it fell apart. Cursing, she tried again. This time it held together and she released it. The glyph soared through the air and wrapped itself around the woman's ankles. She fell, heavily, and Anarya caught up with her before she could rise again.

The commotion attracted attention. Two burly men grabbed Anarya and she had to do some fast talking to explain why she had been chasing the woman. They were escorted back to the Berghoth warehouse where Threnisa confirmed what Anarya said.

"I was lucky she tripped," said Anarya. "Not sure I would have caught her otherwise."

"Didn't trip," the woman said. "I'd have got away if she hadn't used magic on me."

"Don't be silly," said Anarya. "Yes, I've got magic, but I'm a Voyanter. I couldn't trip you." She saw Threnisa studying her and said "She's got a key to the side room in the pocket of her apron. I saw her put it there."

Threnisa found the key and confirmed it was a copy of the one she had. "That's good work, Voyanter. I'll tell the boss you didn't just find out who the thieves were but that you went and caught one of them yourself."

Quarenna be praised, she's not suspicious. I've got to be more careful. I almost gave myself away.

"I've been careless," said Anarya over breakfast the day after the satisfactory outcome to the Beghroth contract. "I haven't been doing enough practice with the talents I don't use often. I almost let one of the culprits get away because I couldn't cast a hobbling spell fast enough."

"I should have realised you would need to practice. It took me a long time to fully understand my own talent after my Awakening. You must need to do the same for every ability."

"It's more than just needing to practice. I'm still learning the skills. I have to find out how to use them by watching other people. After all, I can't very well ask people for training in case they compare notes and discover I have multiple talents," said Anarya.

"I had not thought of that," said Yisena. "My talent was not a secret."

"Who taught you?"

Yisyena sniffled a bit, blotted tears from her eyes, and said, "My mother."

"Yisa, I'm sorry. I didn't mean to upset you."

"Do not worry, my love. I know I said that I had left my previous life behind me, and I have. Unfortunately, it has not left me and, sometimes, a memory sneaks up on me."

Anarya wrapped her arms around Yisyena and held her until she recovered her equilibrium. *She cries so easily*, she thought. *It must be a cultural thing because she's quite tough really.*

"Thank you, Anra, you are such a comfort to me." Yisyena kissed Anarya and wriggled out of her arms. "I do not understand how you can learn just by watching," she said.

"It depends on the talent. For example, I could see the magic the Pyromancers at the arena were using to control their display. I saw how they made fire cold by watching them. I need to keep practicing that."

"Is that what you are going to do?

"No, not this time. There's other things I need to practice

too. I'm going to be a Scratcher for a while."

"A Scratcher? Ah, yes. The translation of the Sitru name would be 'one who draws in the air'. Do you know where to find one?"

"I spent some time after I came to Carregis looking around and discovering where to find people with strong talents. That means I can observe experts using their abilities and try to work out how they get the results they do. It also means I always know where to find the skill I want to borrow. There's a hospice run by a group called the Little Sisters. They're not priestesses but they are dedicated to Holy Quarenna in her aspect of the Friend and Comforter. One of them is a really strong Scratcher. I'll go and see if I can learn something new from her as well as borrow the skill to practice with."

"While you are doing that I will go to the Newsmongers' Guild and get any messages they have for us."

"Good idea."

"I hope someone is offering a contract which needs my skills," said Yisyena. "I should like to be more active as a quaestor."

O

The bright yellow aura of a Scratcher was obvious as soon as Anarya walked into the hospice. The owner of the aura was a slightly stooped middle-aged woman who smiled when Anarya volunteered her services for a couple of chimes. "I remember seeing you here before. That's good. It helps when someone knows what to do. And it's good of you to come again, so few do. Please follow me."

When Anarya absorbed the Scratcher's skill she had the usual momentary feeling of being in two bodies at once. The warmth, humility and benevolence that she felt from the Scratcher in that moment almost overwhelmed her. She blinked away tears.

Much of what they did while caring for the sick was simple repetitive work and didn't require any magical intervention. However, there were times when the Scratcher drew glyphs in mid-air. Anarya paid particular attention to them.

The glyphs were visible in the Oversight as structures of

fine yellow threads which lingered in the air until the Scratcher made a gesture of completion. Then they drifted towards the person or thing they were aimed at and sank into them. Some of the effects were trivial, like the bedclothes tidying themselves without disturbing the patient. Different glyphs moved patients' limbs gently into more comfortable positions or helped them sit up.

Anrhya watched the woman and increased her knowledge of the, sometimes subtle, effects that variations in the glyphs produced.

While she tried to comfort a woman who was in pain and very restless she watched the Scratcher create a complex glyph. It was in two parts. In the centre there was a spiky structure which made Anarya feel uncomfortable just looking at it. She realised that this represented the patient's pain. Around it the Scratcher built a smooth octagonal box of gentle curves with no sharp corners. It was a cage for the pain. When the glyph was released the patient sighed, relaxed and rested more comfortably.

I've never seen anything like that before. I wonder if I can duplicate it. What would it do to someone who isn't in pain?

"Thank you for your assistance and may Holy Quarenna bless you," said the Scratcher when Anarya said it was time for her to go. Anarya was embarrassed by the thanks because she had come with an ulterior motive and not simply as a volunteer. She quietly dropped a small handful of bits into the collection pot at the door on her way out.

She still held the Scratcher's skills and wanted to practice with them. Instead of going home, she went to a secluded spot on the edge of the small stream that flowed through Greenbank and into the Carrh at the Western Docks. Rats were abundant there and she could use them as targets for her spells, some of which, she was sure, would only work on living creatures.

When she Scratched a glyph into the air she frowned. She was trying to copy one from memory and was dissatisfied. It wasn't as clear as it should be. However, she carried on and made the gesture of completion. The first attempt caused a rat to jump sideways, not what she expected. Other efforts made a rat spin in place or lurch about in an uncoordinated manner. Gradually she improved and, after about a chime, felt able to control a rat's movements with some precision.

Twigs and stones were easier to control and she was able to make them move in the way she wanted quite quickly. *Still enough left,* she thought. *I wonder what the two components of the pain relief glyph will do independently of each other.*

First she crafted the smooth octagon and aimed it at another rat, which promptly stopped moving and apparently fell asleep. *Hmm, that could be useful. I must watch it to see how long the effect lasts.*

Then she started on the spiky core which she was sure represented pain. It was more difficult to get the shape right and she made several false starts before she completed the first of the six spikes to her satisfaction. She added a second spike and stopped. Her skin was prickling all over. *What's going on? It's not talent exhaustion, I've still got enough.* With a third spike the prickling changed to a generalised ache and with a fourth the intensity increased to the point where it was actually painful.

The shape's wrong. The pain's reflecting back at me. What do I do now? Her heart rate increased. She started to sweat and twitch restlessly, trying in vain to find a comfortable position. *Should I carry on, or release the glyph now, or try to erase it?* Breathing hard she decided to continue and Scratched a fifth spike. The pain level shot up. Her breath caught in her throat, burning, as she tried to scream. She fell to her knees. *I can't complete it. I've got to stop before it's any worse.*

The pain made her lose concentration. She couldn't remember how to erase a partly drawn glyph. In desperation she released it although she wasn't sure what effect casting an incomplete spell would have.

The pain glyph soared through the air and enveloped a rat. It squealed and dropped dead.

The pain vanished immediately and she almost fainted with relief. *That could be a weapon,* she thought as her heart rate slowed and she regained her composure, *but I'd hate to have to use it the way it is now. I need a lot more practice to avoid being affected by it, but not now. That was too much.*

O

Anarya got home to find Yisyena busily chopping something. She walked up behind her, wrapped her arms around her and kissed her on the back of the neck.

"Be careful, my love," said Yisyena, putting the knife down, "I do not wish to cut you by accident." She returned the kiss. Then she sniffed and frowned. "You have been sweating. Why? What have you been doing?"

"Oh, I didn't realise it was that bad. I'll wash. What are you making?"

"Do not try to change the subject. That makes me think you believe I will be upset if you tell me what you have been doing."

Anarya sighed. "Perhaps you will. Is there hot water? I'll tell you once I've washed."

While Anarya washed she saw Yisyena pick up the knife again and attack the leeks, potatoes and carrots rather more vigorously than necessary.

"Now tell me," demanded Yisyena as soon as Anarya had finished and towelled her hair dry.

"I spent a bit over three chimes as a Scratcher," said Anarya, and carried on to describe what had happened and the pain she had felt. "I'll have to do it again and again, tweaking the shape of the glyph until I get it right and it doesn't affect me any more than it did the Scratcher I copied it from."

"You must take care, my love. You could have done yourself an injury."

"Don't I know it. I panicked at the end and threw the spell away even although it was incomplete and I know that can be dangerous. I once overheard two Scratchers talking about it. One of them had been temporarily blinded by what he described as 'flashback' from a spell that should have let him see in the dark. He said he was lucky it wasn't permanent."

"Have you tried that one?"

"No. I haven't seen it in use so I haven't had the chance to learn it."

"Good. It sounds too risky. I would prefer you not to take unnecessary chances. Please, do not practice that pain spell again, you might make it worse for yourself rather than better."

Anarya shuddered at the idea.

"There must be a better way to learn a Scratcher's spells than watching and copying," said Yisyena.

"There is. I was following a Scratcher one day and he looked at a book of glyphs. I managed to memorise a couple of them before he closed the book. The one he was studying was a privacy spell and the other was a way to mend broken ceramics. I've never found an occasion to use either of them."

"That sounds useful," said Yisyena. "Where can you get such a book?"

"I've no idea. I'd really like to have a book like that, or a Chemer's recipe book, if there is such a thing. At least I learned something today. I don't always find something new when I'm watching someone.

"Anyway, enough about me. What have you been doing today?"

Yisyena smiled. "I have been earning money. Only four and a quarter bits, but they are my first contribution to the partnership."

"That's wonderful, Yisa. What did you do?"

"The newsmongers had two requests I thought I could deal with. Both of them involved finding lost property. One of them was from a middle-class merchant who had lost an earring at her place of business. I found it easily enough. It had fallen through a crack in the floorboards and I was able to tell her where it was although I couldn't reach it. She was going to find a Lifter to get it out."

"I wonder if she has. I could borrow a Lifter's talent and get it for her."

Yisyena's face fell. "I did not think of that. I have not yet got used to the idea that you can have many skills."

"Don't worry about it, Yisa. What was the other one?"

"That was more difficult. A scribe had lost an important document. He had searched his office several times without finding it. He thought his partner must have taken it but wanted to be sure before accusing him. There were about a dozen knee high stacks of parchment in the room and he was most insistent that I did not disturb them. He said he knew where everything was."

"I wouldn't have any idea how to deal with that. What did you do?"

"I looked between the documents and read them. It is a very strange and distorted view and it gave me a headache. However, it is possible. Fortunately it was in the first stack I looked at. He is at a loss to explain how it got there."

"That's amazing. I couldn't do that, and I used to think I was a pretty good Voyanter."

"He was so pleased it has been found that he added another bit to the fee."

"That's good work, Yisa. I'm so happy for you. I know you were feeling left out."

"There is something else interesting. I heard a newsmonger talking about a gang attack near Ferras Street. Might it be related to the gang meeting you overheard?"

"It might well be. The timing is right. What else did he say?"

"The man who was attacked is called Veluth, and somebody was killed. Who is Veluth? His name seemed to interest a lot of people."

"He's a singer. He created a sensation about a year and a half ago when he first appeared in public. I heard him sing once. Wonderful baritone voice, makes you feel all quivery inside when he sings a love ballad, although he isn't much to look at. I think there was something about him – what was the phrase – Oh, yes, 'transcending the limitations of his humble upbringing'. I suppose that could include growing up in the Dip and being a member of the Angry Apes."

"The newsmonger said 'One dead'. I assume he would have been more specific if the dead man was Veluth. Do you think he could have killed one of his attackers?"

"I doubt it," said Anarya. "They wouldn't have left him alive if he had. It was probably someone who was unlucky enough to be nearby and got caught up in the fight."

FIGHTER

Caseir climbed out of bed rubbing the sleep from his eyes. Someone was hammering at the bedroom door.

"What's the matter?" asked Siklisha. "Who is it?"

He opened the door and Veluth, dirty, bruised and dishevelled, practically fell through it into his arms.

"She's dead, Caseir, she's dead. They killed her."

Caseir supported Veluth as he staggered. He guided him to the end of the bed where he collapsed, sobbing.

"Caerina?" asked Siklisha. "Is it Caerina?"

There was no answer. Veluth simply lay there moaning.

Siklisha got up, wrapped a sheet around herself and left the room. She came back moments later with a glass of avit which she thrust into Veluth's hands.

"Drink that."

He sat up, with help from Caseir, took a mouthful of the strong spirit and spluttered.

"Drink it. Then tell us what's happened."

Caseir felt as if he was detached from what was going on. His sister was dead. He had trouble grasping the idea. The words just didn't seem to make sense. He heard Veluth's voice a long way away then, gradually what he was saying penetrated and he started listening.

"We were coming back from the concert. It was late by the time we got away. We'd just turned out of Ferras Street and there they were."

"Who?"

"The Angry Apes."

"What were they doing there? That's well outside their territory," said Siklisha.

"They were waiting for me."

"Why?"

"I used to be one of them. That's where I grew up, in the Dip."

"I know that," replied Siklisha, "but you're not in the Dip anymore."

"Doesn't make any difference to them. They say I owe them."

"And they killed Caerina," said Caseir, feeling numb and wanting to be sure of what he was hearing. "Didn't they?"

"Yes. They snatched my pouch," Veluth managed to speak between sobs. "It only had about a dukal in it and that wasn't enough for them. Then they started beating me. Caerina screamed. I think she was trying to attract attention from the main street but they turned on her. Don't think they meant to kill her but she couldn't see the knife one of them was holding and she walked right into it.

"She just fell. Didn't say anything, just gave a quiet grunt. Then she fell and lay there. There was nothing I could do. And it's my fault."

"Nonsense," said Siklisha, "How can it be your fault?"

"I was one of them. They wouldn't have come for me otherwise."

"It wasn't your doing," said Caseir, feeling the cold numbness being replaced with red hot fury. "Who were they?"

"Angry Apes. I told you."

"I mean their names. Do you know them?"

"Yes. At least I know two of them. Mitrith was the leader. He was a master in the Angry Apes when I was a novice and Daconis was second rank. Don't know the third one."

"Which of them held the knife?"

"Daconis."

"What are you going to do?" asked Siklisha.

"Isn't it obvious? They're dead men even if they don't know it yet. I just need to find them."

"You can't do that, Caseir," said Veluth. "Mitrith is one of the men Duke Wurauf trusts to keep the Angry Apes under control. There are two or three more and I'm sure there are some in the other gangs too. Wurauf will protect him."

"Not from me he won't. My reputation will get me an audience with Wurauf. I'll persuade him to give me Mitrith."

"I hope you're right," said Veluth.

O

The splendour of the Duke's mansion made little impression

on Caseir. He had been there before. His status and fame had brought him several invitations, but this time he was indifferent to the statues, tapestries and furnishings which had previously attracted his attention. He simply waited, gazing into the distance but not seeing anything, barely aware of time passing.

"Ah, Caseir. So good to see you again."

He turned away from the window with its view over the ornamental lake and nodded his head to acknowledge the greeting from the man who had just entered the room. Jynder was a good head and a half taller than him, but so thin that he was only about half Caseir's weight. They were more or less the same age and had known each other for years. He was not one of Caseir's favourite people

"What are you doing here?" asked Caseir.

"I've been working with the Duke for almost two years now," said Jynder. "Didn't you know? I'm one of his advisers."

"I hope you give him better advice than you gave me."

"Oh, Caseir. You don't still hold that against me, do you?"

"You once gave me the Name of a daimon you thought would be too powerful for me to handle. I'm supposed to have forgotten that, am I? It's the sort of thing that tends to stick in your mind."

"It was nothing personal," said Jynder, with an ingratiating smile. "You know what Daimoners are like. We do tend to be rather jealous of each other and the strength of the daimons we can control."

"Speak for yourself. I've met others and they don't all have that attitude."

"But the ones who don't are usually weaker, aren't they. They can't afford to antagonise each other in case of reprisals. Those of us who can handle nine syllables haven't anything to fear from any daimon."

Caseir snorted and started to turn away from Jynder.

"Since you've brought up the subject, I must admit I've wanted to ask you how you ever managed to survive when the strongest daimon you had handled previously only had a six syllable Name."

Caseir turned back and said, "It wasn't all that difficult. I was just too stubborn for it."

"I suppose I should have guessed. That was always one of your strong points. Anyway, enough of catching up on old times. What's so urgent that you have to see the Duke immediately?"

"I'll tell him that."

"Now, Caseir, he's not very well and I can't let just anybody see him without knowing how important it is."

"'Just anybody'?" said Caseir. "I didn't realise I fitted that description."

"You know what I mean."

"I'll stay here until I can see him. I can wait as long as necessary. You know how stubborn I can be."

"Oh, very well. Follow me."

Jynder led Caseir through the mansion to the Duke's private study. He hadn't been in that room before and it surprised him. It was difficult to see the quality of the furnishings for the clutter. There were stacks of books and scrolls everywhere, on shelves, on tables, on chairs, even on the floor. Some of the piles were dusty and, from the smell, some were damp and mildewed. The only clear space in the room was in front of a bay window where an armchair was occupied by a thickset man dressed in black and red. His skin looked pale and unhealthy, there was a blue tinge to his lips and his breathing was laboured.

"Caseir. What do you want?" he gasped, pausing for breath after every few words.

"I want to know where to find a henchman of yours called Mitrith."

Wurauf picked up a pomander from a small table, held it to his nose and sniffed. He seemed to breathe a little more easily and gasped out, "Why?"

"Because he led the gang that killed my sister and I'm going to kill him." Caseir explained what had happened.

"Mitrith's a fool, but he's a useful one. I can understand why you want him but you can't have him," wheezed Wurauf. "Sorry about your sister but I'm afraid her death was just unfortunate collateral damage."

"What!"

"You heard the Duke," said Jynder. "I always liked Caerina and I'm sorry to hear she's dead, but a revenge killing isn't an acceptable option."

Caseir was stunned. For a moment he stood glaring at Wurauf, then he felt the rage building in him again and snarled, "From all you said when we met before I thought I could count on you for support. That's why I came to you. I thought it would be the easiest way to find him but if you won't help I'll find him anyway." He turned and stomped out of the study.

"Wait, Caseir, wait." Jynder caught up with him and tugged his sleeve. "Don't do anything foolish."

Caseir jerked his arm free of Jynder's grasp. "I know what can happen to people who cross Wurauf. I remember last year he had somebody flayed and hung from the Coptomeruk Arch for the ravens to feed on. But I don't care. Caerina's dead and those responsible are going to pay. Don't try to stop me."

O

"I need to find another way of getting to Caerina's killers. It was no use going to Wurauf, the chesa won't help," Caseir told Veluth. "He said Mitrith is 'too useful' to him."

"What are you going to do?"

"That's where you come in."

"Me? I want to kill them myself, but you know I'm no fighter," said Veluth. "That's why I never got higher than fourth rank in the Angry Apes."

"You can tell me where to look for them. I need to know everything about the gang's hideouts and safe houses."

"But I can't. I only know a few places, the ones that everybody used. The higher ranks had their own and kept them secret from the likes of me."

"There must have been rumours about them. You've got to have heard something."

Veluth frowned and said, "I did once hear about a carpenter's shop at the Nelsway end of Lussin Street that somebody said was a front for a high rank meeting place. But I don't know if it was true and it might have changed. It was almost four years ago that I got out of the Dip."

"It's a start. I'll go there and see what I can find."

"Can I come too?"

"I don't think so. You might be recognised."

"You're just as recognisable as me, probably even more so."

"But they won't expect to see Caseir the Unconquered wandering around the Dip, and they don't know about my connection to you and Caerina."

O

It looked like an ordinary carpenter's shop with stacks of timber leaning against the walls and the smell of sawdust and glue in the air. The only thing out of the ordinary was the number of people who came and went from the upper floor. Caseir saw seven in less than half a chime. He decided that one of the men in the shop, who spent all his time polishing the same, already shining, cabinet, must be a lookout. His eyes followed everyone who passed by and kept coming back to Caseir who was pretending to examine the goods on a leather worker's stall on the other side of the street.

Sooner or later he's going to get suspicious of me and send someone to investigate.

Veluth had told him that anybody he saw wearing red and blue was likely to be a gang member, few of the ordinary population of the Dip would wear that combination. Falsely claiming membership of the Angry Apes was discouraged rather severely. He was wearing black; a leather jerkin, corduroy trousers and sturdy boots. Nothing that could be misinterpreted as gang colours.

Two big men wearing the red and blue turned into Lussin Street from Nelsway at the same time that Caseir saw two more making their way along from the other end. Caseir got the impression that people were sensitive to their presence because he noticed several starting to walk away from the area. They didn't run but they did move fairly quickly. He guessed that they didn't want to attract attention from the Angry Apes by appearing to be running away.

"Well, are you going to buy something or not? You've had long enough to make up your mind," said the stall holder.

Caseir looked at the way the stall holder's eyes were flicking from side to side as he watched the gang approaching. Clearly he didn't want any part of what looked like potential trouble. He saw no reason to get the man involved in whatever was about to happen so he muttered, "Naw, nuthin' there I want," and started off along the street.

He was soon boxed in by the four gang members and one of them said, "Come with us."

Caseir thought the man was surprised when he didn't argue. He followed them into a building at the end of an alley next to the carpenter's workshop. It was scruffy on the outside with chunks of plaster missing from the walls exposing the wood beneath. The inside was different. It was clean and fairly well furnished, not luxurious but certainly better than he expected. Two of the men ushered him into a room, the others stayed outside.

There was an older man sitting in a deep armchair waiting for him. Steam and the spicy, resinous smell of mulled wine rose from the mug he was holding.

The man took a sip from the mug, put it down on the floor beside his chair and brought his fingertips together touching his lips. "You don't belong here. Why are you hanging about?"

"I'm looking for somebody" said Caseir. "Trouble is I don't know him. Was hoping one of you could help me."

"And why would you think we could do that?"

"I was told he was a member of the Angry Apes. That's what you are, aren't you. I recognise the colours."

"Who is it you want?"

"His name's Daconis."

Caseir caught the quick glance towards one of the men who had escorted him.

"And why do you want him?"

That's a bit of luck, thought Caseir, *I didn't expect to find him so easily.* He looked around assessing the situation. The one he thought was Daconis had a long knife in a leather sheath strapped to his thigh. The sheath was worn and cracked but the grip of the knife was in good condition and he had to assume the man knew how to use it.

The other one had no obvious weapon. He was big, but Caseir thought it was fat rather than muscle. The old man was at a disadvantage, he wouldn't be able to get out of the chair quickly. However, Caseir wasn't going to assume he was harmless. *There's at least two more of them in the building. Don't know if there's any more than that.*

He walked over to the man with the long knife and said, "Are you Daconis?"

"And what if I am?"

"Then I've got something for you," said Caseir. He half turned away, then slammed an elbow into the man's stomach and the heel of his hand into the side of his head. By the time the man hit the floor Caseir had possession of the long knife.

The spokesman made an incoherent noise. The big man was slow to react but, when he did, he took a couple of steps towards Caseir with his arms outstretched and ready to grapple.

"Keep still," said Caseir. "This doesn't concern you. It's just him I want."

"He's one of us, so it is our business," said the old man, rising from the chair. "You've put yourself in a lot of trouble. You can't take on all of us."

"Are you going to bet your life on that? You've probably heard of me. My name's Caseir."

The big man stopped moving and stared. "Huler's balls! I think it is him, Jussan." He let his arms drop and shook his head. "Sorry, Daconis, I ain't going against Caseir for you or anybody."

"Coward," snarled Jussan. His hand moved quickly and a triangular throwing knife embedded itself in Caseir's left shoulder. "Go get the others. Together we can take him."

Caseir kicked Daconis to make sure he stayed down, then ran across the room, knocked the old man off his feet and landed on top of him. A loud snap was followed by an agonised shout from Jussan as his arm broke under him. Another throwing knife clattered to the floor.

Caseir jumped back to his feet. He pulled the blade from his shoulder and turned towards the big man, who had backed into a corner. *Lucky nobody has heard the noise and come to investigate.*

"I won't do nothing," said the big man. "Honest. I'll just stand here. Please don't kill me."

"Did you go with this piece of scum to attack Veluth four days ago?"

"Me? No, no, wasn't me. That was Mitrith and Folvenu."

"In that case you can live," said Caseir. He turned toward Daconis who was trying to rise and dragged him to his feet.

"The three of them killed my sister in that attack and they're the ones who are dead."

He slashed the long knife across Daconis's abdomen and watched with satisfaction as his guts spilled on to the floor.

Leaving Daconis screaming Caseir opened the door and walked away. He expected somebody to investigate the screams. Two did. *I don't need to kill them*, Caseir thought, *they weren't involved.*

They got in each other's way and he had no trouble dealing with them, leaving them unconscious on the floor.

○

"You've got to be more careful," said Siklisha. "I thought I was done with patching you up."

"I'll try," said Caseir, rotating his shoulder and feeling the slight tension from the wound Siklisha had just closed. "I'm going to have to take some risks to get the others. I've got to get them. After that I don't care what happens."

"Well I care."

"I know you do," he said, putting his arms around her. "But you didn't argue about me hunting them down and you must have realised there was some risk."

"You'd probably have left me if I had tried. Not that I would. Carregis will be a better place without them."

He hugged her tighter. "I'm glad you didn't force me to make that choice. Let's go and see if Veluth can help with the next stage of the hunt."

"Folvenu? No, I don't know anybody by that name," said Veluth, "but there was a third ranker called Folkenu. I wonder if they might be related."

"It's worth a try," said Caseir. "Any idea where to look for him?"

"Not really. At one time Folkenu worked the pits, collecting the money the owners pay to the Angry Apes, but that's something that most third rankers do from time to time. I don't suppose he's still doing it."

"It's not much to go on, but I'll see if I can find somebody wearing red and blue around Stinky's tomorrow night and persuade him to help."

"There won't be just one of them, will there?" said

Siklisha. "Won't they have an escort for the money carrier?"

"They will," said Veluth. "There was usually six of them when I was doing it. There might be more if there's been any trouble with the Friends or the Wolves."

"Please be careful, Caseir," pleaded Siklisha.

O

Watching from the shadows Caseir had no trouble identifying the courier and his escort as they left Stinky's. One man had a canvas bag hung around his neck and walked between two men with drawn swords behind a third carrying a torch. The swordsmen also had crossbows slung across their backs.

Everything Caseir was wearing was black with nothing pale or shiny to pick up what little light there was. Even his sword and dagger were smeared with oil and soot to prevent reflections.

He followed them cautiously. *I don't want to have to fight any of them. I want information, not bodies.* There were others about, roaming around the route back to the Dip. Occasionally one of them would join the courier for a muttered conversation and then drop back into the gloom again, away from the torches outside the few late-opening shops and taverns.

Caseir was hiding in an alleyway waiting for the main group to get out of sight before moving to a new vantage point when one of the wandering escorts left the courier and headed straight towards his hiding place. *Coincidence? Or does he suspect something. He can't possibly see me. Must be going through this alley to wherever he's supposed to be next. Unless he's using magic. Can't be. He wouldn't come by himself if he knows I'm here.*

He moved back, away from the approaching man, as quietly as he could. There was a click as he kicked something he hadn't seen in the darkness. The sound wasn't loud but the gang member heard it and stopped. He whistled a repeated three note trill and waited. A whistled response was quickly followed by two more men appearing out of the shadows. They held a quiet conference, then two of them entered the alley while one held back.

Suspicious lot, aren't they. I can take the two of them but the third will raise the alarm and only Huler knows how many more will come to join in. Still, there's nothing else for it.

Caseir waited until he heard one of the men come close enough to his hiding place. He stepped forward and wrapped an arm around his neck to try to keep him quiet. He succeeded in preventing his victim saying anything but the man thrashed around and he was sure the scuffle had made enough noise to alert the others.

Caseir bounced the man's head off the wall, felt him sag and let him fall. He charged out of hiding into the other man and slammed him against the opposite wall. Running footsteps announced the approach of the third man and there was shouting in the distance suggesting that several more were on their way.

They'll know their way around better than I do. I'd better get out of here.

Caseir went deeper into the alleyway hoping it wasn't a dead end. He hurried as fast as he could while trying to keep quiet. Garbage underfoot made him slow for fear of falling. He turned a corner. The next street had torches burning outside a couple of taverns and small groups standing drinking in the street. He mingled with them.

When three men ran out of the alley, they stopped and looked around. Caseir felt confident that none of the gang had seem him well enough to identify him among the drinkers. *That's right, go away,* he thought when one of the gang members shrugged and said something to the others. He was relieved when they gave up the chase and went back into the alley.

O

"That didn't work," said Caseir. "Any other ideas?"

The scent of lilies filled the conservatory where Caseir, Siklisha and Veluth were sitting after breakfast the day after Caseir's trip to the pits.

Veluth shook his head. "No. I can't think of any way to find them, particularly since you told them who you are and why you're after them. They'll go into hiding."

"They can't hide forever."

"They don't have to," said Siklisha. "They could have you killed."

"She's right," said Veluth. "With one of the first rank at risk the Angry Apes might well pay for your death."

"I'll be careful."

"How does being careful stop a Lifter dropping a heavy weight on your head, a Pyromancer setting you on fire or an Aeromancer taking the breath from your lungs?" asked Siklisha. "You've got to get them quickly before they can organise something like that. There are just so many ways a magic user can kill. They could even get a Daimoner to send one of his creatures against you."

"At least that wouldn't work," said Caseir. "But you've given me an idea. I could use a daimon to find out where they're hiding. I won't use it to kill, just to find them. I'll do the killing myself."

Siklisha jumped to her feet. "What do you mean 'use a daimon'? You'd have to be a Daimoner to do that."

"I am," said Caseir.

"But… but…"

"I'd rather rely on my own abilities so I rarely use the skill, but I can handle the strongest daimons."

"But I loved you."

The despairing wail from Siklisha made Caseir look up at her and ask, "What's wrong?"

"You are."

Caseir stood and took a step towards her. She backed away, turned and ran from the conservatory leaving Caseir gazing after her in bewilderment.

"What did I say? She ran away from me! What have I done? Veluth, would you go and talk to her. Find out why she's upset."

Veluth followed Siklisha. Caseir forced himself to wait.

About a third later Veluth returned. "Get over there and sit down," he said, pointing to the far corner of the room. "Don't ask. Just do it." Then, when Caseir had seated himself, he turned to the door and beckoned. Siklisha took a few steps through the door and stopped as far away from Caseir as possible.

"What's wrong?" asked Caseir.

Siklisha's face was pale and she grimaced as if facing

something frightening.

"You never told me you're a Daimoner."

"Like I said, I almost never use the talent. Don't suppose I've invoked a daimon more than five or six times in the last ten years. I'd rather do things for myself."

"You deceived me. Why didn't you tell me?"

"The subject never came up. Why does it matter?"

Siklisha almost spat the words, "Gantur's Wells."

Veluth looked blank. "What does that mean?"

"Ask him," said Siklisha, pointing at Caseir.

"You're from there?" said Caseir, his face falling.

Siklisha nodded.

Caseir sank into a chair, head in his hands. "I had nothing to do with what happened."

"What do you mean? What happened?" asked Veluth.

"Gantur's Wells was a small village about three or four chimes ride from Firten," said Caseir. "Every Daimoner hears about it as a cautionary tale. Somebody lost control of a daimon, it destroyed the village, and everybody there died."

"All except me and Febrala," said Siklisha. "We had gone to Firten to buy cloth for Febrala's wedding dress. We got home to find it wasn't there anymore. Our families were dead. There was blood everywhere. I found my mother's body myself, ripped open like a side of beef. Never did find the rest of my family. Are you surprised I hate Daimoners? Are you?"

Caseir shook his head.

"I'm the only survivor now. Febrala was my cousin and my best friend. She couldn't stand it. She went mad. A year later killed herself. It wasn't you that did it. I know that. It doesn't make any difference. I hate Daimoners. All of them."

"Siklisha... "

"Don't talk to me. I'm leaving. And I'm never coming back." She stepped back, turned and ran from the room.

"Huler help me! What am I supposed to do? I can't help being what I am." Caseir looked up at Veluth. "I've lost her, haven't I?"

"I think so."

"Will you keep an eye on her for me? I need to know she's all right. Maybe you can persuade her I'm not a bad person just because I'm a Daimoner."

"I'll do what I can."

"And if I get myself killed make sure she gets everything of mine."

○

{Will be revenged. Make suffer forever. Will succeed. Somehow. Somewhen.} said the daimon Caseir had summoned, but he was in no mood to listen when it started threatening him.

"Be quiet," Caseir told the daimon. "You know you can't intimidate me so don't bother trying, just do what I ask."

{What want?}

"Find me the two men involved in my sister's death. Their names are Mitrith and Folvenu. They might be together and there might be other men guarding them. I need to know where they are. Don't kill them. Don't do anything to them. Just tell me where to find them and how I can get to them safely."

{After?}

Caseir shrugged. "After doesn't matter as long as I can get to them. Go!"

The presence vanished. Caseir shivered. Talking to a daimon always made him feel soiled and grimy. That was one reason why he rarely used them. The other reason was that he believed in himself and preferred to rely on his own abilities whenever possible. He was aware of the illogic since he was relying on himself when making a daimon do what he wanted, but he ignored it.

More than a day passed with nothing from the daimon and he was beginning to wonder if his instructions had been clear enough. He was restless and couldn't settle to doing anything. He tried to visualise a carving to commemorate Caerina and even went as far as setting up a piece of ash ready to carve. However, as soon as he picked up a chisel his inspiration waned and he put it down again with the wood untouched. He started pacing from one side of the room to the other, trying to stay patient.

○

{Found}

"At last. What took you so long?"

{*Not together until now.*}

"Where are they?"

{*Come. Take you.*}

"What do you mean?"

{*Go through door. Step here, step there. They there.*}

Caseir was startled at the idea of the daimon taking him on a shortcut through the Darkworld to his target, but he quickly scooped up his sword and made sure his knives were in their sheaths. "I'm ready. Which door?"

{*Any. All same.*}

"Are there guards?"

{*Said safe going, so safe going. After different.*}

I guess that means the daimon will take me there but not bring me back and I'll have to deal with guards after I'm finished with Caerina's killers. So be it. I don't really care what happens as long as I can kill them.

He opened the nearest door and stepped through. As soon as his foot crossed the threshold there was a brief sensation of movement, a blur of darkness and light, and he was standing somewhere else with a door banging shut behind him.

"What was that?" asked a voice from the next room.

"Look, youngster, I'm getting fed up with you jumping at every odd noise. We're safe here. Just relax."

"Sorry master Mitrith. It's just – well, he's Caseir."

"I know what you mean. But he'll be dead before too long. It's a shame, but it's necessary. He shouldn't get involved in our affairs."

Caseir looked around. He was in a small room with bunk beds along one wall. There were a couple of wooden chairs, which looked rather uncomfortable, and a hanging space for clothes, which was empty. A small window looked out on woodland. *Must be a servant's room. Where am I? Doesn't matter. They're here.* That was all he needed to know.

The door opened outwards and he burst through it, sword in hand, to find himself in a spacious room with a stone fireplace in the middle of the opposite wall. Large overstuffed chairs stood on either side of the fireplace and both were occupied. A young man, probably about eighteen, turned pale, jumped up and shouted, "Caseir."

The other man lifted a crossbow from the floor beside his chair and stood up more slowly. He aimed the crossbow at Caseir. "I don't know how you managed to get here but it doesn't matter. It's the last thing you'll do unless we can make a deal. We didn't mean to kill your sister and we're willing to pay a blood price if you give up this vendetta." He glanced towards the other man and added, "Folvenu, call in the guards."

"Yes, master Mitrith."

Caseir ignored the threat of the crossbow, took three quick steps across the room and knocked Folvenu to the floor with one punch. "You can't buy your way out of this," he said. "Nothing you could offer is worth as much as Caerina." He took one step towards Mitrith, then another. *He's only got one bolt. Unless he's a very good shot he's going to let me get closer to present him with a better target. I wonder how close can I get before he shoots? It depends on his nerve.* Another step closer.

Mitrith licked his lips. His hands shook a bit.

Ah. He's nervous.

Caseir took one more step, then a quick half step to the right before throwing himself to the left. He heard the deep twang of the crossbow and the thud of the bolt embedding itself in something. *Missed.*

He bounced to his feet and rushed Mitrith, leaving his sword lying on the floor. He heard a grunt of expelled breath as he put his shoulder into Mitrith's midriff, knocked him down and landed on top of him.

Caseir drew a knife. He put the point of it under Mitrith's chin and said, "Go tell my sister you're sorry." He thrust the knife up until it jammed against the base of Mitrith's skull. He twitched, his eyes went blank and Caseir rolled off the body.

"He's here! Caseir's here!"

Caseir looked around to find that Folvenu had picked himself up and was standing in an open door shouting for help. He grabbed his sword. Folvenu squealed when he saw him coming and dashed through the door. Caseir took a knife from his boot. It caught Folvenu in the small of his back. He fell screaming. A slash from Caseir's sword silenced him.

Caseir relaxed with a sigh. Caerina was avenged. His task

was over. He had a moment's satisfaction, then another six men came running into the next room. They spread out and stopped in an arc confronting Caseir. Two of them were armed with crossbows. *More of them. Huler's beard! Am I going to have to kill all the Angry Apes?*

One of the crossbowmen pointed to Mitrith's body. "Is master Mitrith dead?" he asked.

"Yes," replied Caseir, "do you want to join him?"

"Do you really think you can take all of us?"

"Are you going to bet your life I can't?"

The spokesman paused, glanced right and left at his men then lowered his crossbow and said, "There's no point in protecting someone who's dead."

"Sensible man. I'm going to walk out of here and you're not going to stop me. In fact you and the other man with a crossbow will come with me. Just in case you get any funny ideas, you understand."

Caseir saw the spokesman look around for support from the others and knew he had intimidated him. *I'm going to get away with this.* He walked forward, the arc of men opening up to let him through. The door opened into a small wood. When they reached the edge of the wood he recognised where he was. Caseir said, "That's far enough. Unspan your bows, put them down and go back. Don't follow me."

I'm going to have to do something about Wurauf, he thought. *Giving Caerina's killers shelter on his estate is too much.*

WHISPERER

Anarya didn't really like the dish Yisyena made for their evening meal. It was basically a bacon and vegetable soup but the Sitrelker flavourings Yisyena used weren't to Anarya's taste. The combination of fiery hot chillies and aniseed didn't work as far as she was concerned. However, she concealed her dislike because she didn't want to upset her.

Afterwards she said, "I'm going to be a Whisperer for a while. I'll go and borrow the talent and come straight back."

"Good," said Yisyena. "I will watch you. I am not aware of any risks associated with being a Whisperer, but I would prefer to be beside you to make sure you do not overexert yourself."

Anarya went to the nearest tavern. As usual there was a Whisperer there and she extended her aura to touch his. She was ready for the sensation of incurable nosiness she always found whenever she borrowed a Whisperer's gift.

When she went home she sat on the bed, tucking herself into the corner for support, closed her eyes and invoked the Whisperer's talent. The Oversight showed her a network of shimmering grey strands. She reached out mentally to touch one of the nodes where seven or eight strands came together.

There was a presence there and a wordless feeling of welcome.

<Hello, I'm Kirsa,> she muttered, remembering to use the name she was known by as a Whisperer and not her real name. The thread stretching from her to the node rippled as the message sped along it.

<Welcome, Kirsa. You're new.>

<Not totally new. I have been here before but I don't have much experience.>

<I can believe that. Your touch is rather clumsy. You need to be gentler or you'll end up garbling the messages you handle. Come and join me and I'll try to help you.>

<How do I do that?>

<Easy. Just imagine yourself sliding along the strand towards me.>

The sensation of rapid movement along the strand made Anarya feel dizzy, then she found herself in close contact with a benign, calm presence.

<My name's Onri. What do you want to know about being a Whisperer?>

<Everything?>

<That's asking a lot. You can't learn it all in one go. Let's see what you know already. How do you send a message?>

<That's easy. You just touch the strand and speak.>

<And how do you know where to send it?> asked Onri.

<All the nodes have names and you say which one it's for...>

<Which is fine if you know there's somebody waiting for it.>

<... Then it's just like an ordinary conversation.>

<Yes. Here's one like that I've just been given,> said Onri and muttered, <To Hepru at The Fat Donkey. Daneah will meet you at the Arch at the eighth chime tomorrow. Don't be late.>

<Where's The Fat Donkey?> Anarya asked.

<Nowhere really. The nodes aren't actually places. There's fifty or sixty of them and you can join any of them from anywhere, if you're strong enough. The geometry of the Whispermesh doesn't match geography at all. This node is called The Moon Maiden.>

<I don't understand how you can send a message to somebody who isn't expecting it.>

<Actually, there are two ways. The first is to give 'Full mesh' as the address. The message then bounces around from node to node until someone recognises the name of the person it's addressed to.>

<Then they get a local messenger to deliver it.>

<That's right.>

<What happens if nobody recognises the name?> asked Anarya.

<It bounces around the Whispermesh for about a day then fades out and never gets delivered.>

<But somebody's paid for the message.>

Anarya could feel the shrug as Onri said, <So it's cost them

a quarter-bit. Serves them right for wasting everybody's time.>

<You said there's another way.>

<There is. If you want to know about it we'll need to disconnect from the node and keep a private connection.>

Anarya agreed. She sent a message saying <Kirsa is out,> and watched Onri pinch out her own connection to the node.

<That's good,> said Onri. <You remembered to let everyone know you were leaving. But there's no need to shout. Just stroke the strands gently, don't twang them.>

<Sorry.>

<Don't worry about it. You'll get better with practice.>

<I hope so.>

<There's only us now. I'll teach you how to send a message to anyone, Whisperer or not. But first I want to have a private chat.>

<What about?>

<About you,> said Onri. <I didn't know there was a Sponger around.>

Anarya felt her heart speed up. She wriggled mentally but couldn't break the contact with Onri. *I'm trapped. How does she know what I am. How can I get away from her?*

<Don't panic, Kirsa. I don't know your real name or anything about you, and I don't want to. I'm a friend. At least I want to be one.>

Onri's mental presence was calm and Anarya took some comfort from that although she was worried that, somehow or other, she had given herself away. <Why should I trust you?>

<Because I once had a niece who was a Sponger. She was only nineteen when she died in a riot. That was about thirty-five years ago.>

<Geala? You're Geala's aunt?>

<You've heard of her. Yes. I loved that girl, she was so good and so caring. I wouldn't want the same thing to happen to anyone else so I promised myself that I would do whatever I could to help if I ever met another Sponger.>

<But how did you know what I am?>

<Because your touch in the Whispermesh feels just like Geala's. It's just different enough to be recognisable.>

<That means everybody that's connected knows what I

am!> The idea had Anarya panicking again. *I need to get out and never come back.*

<No, it doesn't. I know what a Sponger feels like from working with Geala, but she wasn't very strong as a Whisperer and rarely joined the Whispermesh. Anyway, it was a long time ago, the difference is slight and nobody else will have the experience to know what the difference means. I'll keep your secret.>

<Why can't I disconnect?>

<Because a one-to-one can only be broken by both people acting simultaneously.>

<I want out.>

<I really do want to help you. Please trust me.>

<Why should I? You didn't tell me you could stop me leaving.>

<I want you to think about it. I can teach you. You can speak to me anytime you join the Whispermesh. All you need to do is call my name.>

Can I trust her? I would like to learn more.

<I – I might do that,> said Anarya, <But what if you're not connected?>

<Look at this.>

Anarya saw Onri tie a knot in the strand linking them.

<If a message with my name as the destination hits that I'll be aware of it. It will pull me into the Whispermesh, even if I'm asleep. You can use it any time. It'll always be there.>

< You gave me quite a scare. I'm not sure right now. I might come back to talk to you, Onri. Will you let me leave now?>

<Next time I'll tell you how to send a message to a non-Whisperer if you have something belonging to them to work with.>

<That sounds like a useful trick. I'll think about it.>

<Quarenna's blessing on you, Kirsa. Look after yourself.>

The last strand vanished. Anarya opened her eyes to find Yisyena standing by the side of the bed looking worried.

"You have been muttering and making odd noises. Are you unwell?"

"No, Yisa. I'm fine. It's just that I've had a fright. Give me something to drink and I'll tell you about it."

SPONGER

As usual when Anarya got out of bed she knelt in front of the statuette, thumbed her forehead and asked for Holy Quarenna's blessing on the day to come.

With her morning devotions completed she turned round in time to see Yisyena wipe tears from her eyes.

"What's the matter, Yisa?"

"Nothing, there is nothing."

"Don't lie to me. You cry more easily than I do but you don't cry over nothing. There's got to be a reason. What is it?"

Yisyena waved a hand towards the statuette. "You are so fortunate to have a god to look to."

"But you have too. You've mentioned The God several times when you've talked about Sitrelk."

Yisyena shook her head and sniffed. "I did revere The God but now I do not. That is why I ran away. I cannot trust in him anymore."

"I don't understand," said Anarya. "You were a Godspeaker. You've been in the presence of The God many times. I envy you. It must be wonderful to meet your god face to face. How can you not believe in him?"

"I do, and I do not." Tears started running down Yisyena's cheeks again. "I mean he is actually there in the temple in Jotuk. I have stood at the foot of his throne many times and heard him speak. But he…" Her voice faded and she started sobbing.

Anarya wrapped her arms around Yisyena and made comforting noises until she stopped crying.

"I feel lost without someone to trust, someone to believe in and worship. Particularly today because it is Revelation Day. The God first appeared in Jotuk four hundred and sixty-three years ago today. It is a day of celebration. I feel I should be rejoicing and giving thanks for his guidance, but I cannot. I wish I could."

"Oh, Yisa. I don't know what to say. What happened to

make you lose faith?"

They clung together, Anarya desperately trying to comfort Yisyena, and Yisyena trying to regain her composure.

Between sniffles Yisyena said, "What happened is something I would rather not talk about. I do not even want to think about it. I am surprised by how vulnerable I feel. I did not think being without a god would make me feel so, so – empty. You are such a comfort to me but even you cannot fill that gap in my soul."

"*Galgalis*, remember. Perhaps this is why we are supposed to be together, to let you work through this crisis."

"Do you really think so? I wonder if your god would accept my devotion?"

"I'm certain she would. We can go to the shrine after breakfast. You can speak to Tilua. I'm sure she'll help."

O

"Tell me what to do, my love," said Yisyena as they walked into the shrine. "I do not wish to give offence."

"Just follow my lead." Anarya led Yisyena to the altar of the Helper and knelt in front of the statue. She pricked her thumb, let blood fall into the offering bowl at the feet of the statue, reached up to touch its outstretched hand and sat with her head bowed.

Yisyena copied her.

"How may I help you, daughter?" The enquiry came from a very junior priestess who appeared before they had been waiting long.

"Is it possible to speak to blessèd Tilua?" asked Anarya. "I mean no disrespect to you, but she already knows something of what we wish to talk about."

"It should be possible. I saw her in her study only a tenth ago. I will take you to her."

Anarya saw Yisyena take a deep breath when they went into Tilua's study and saw her relax a little as she inhaled the scent of jasmine and cedar wood rising from the incense burner.

"I presume this is the Sitrelker you told me about, Anarya," said Tilua, waving them to seats.

"It is. This is Yisyena."

"You didn't tell me she was a Voyanter."

"Didn't I?"

Tilua turned to Yisyena and said, "You are welcome, *hi-cranil*. What can I do for you?"

"I no longer have any right to that title," said Yisyena. "I gave it up when I left Jotuk and came to Carregis."

"I did wonder," said Tilua. "It's many years since a Godspeaker came here with the approval of The God. In fact I think it has only ever happened twice."

"I do not have his permission. I ran from him."

"I thought that might be the case when I realised you were *cranil*. Would you tell me why you ran and why you are here today?"

Anarya saw Yisyena take a deep breath before saying, "Do you know that Godspeaker is a bad translation of *cranil?*"

"Yes, I do," said Tilua. "I believe a better translation would be 'God-in-waiting'".

Anarya gasped. Then she said, "Don't mind me," when heads turned towards her.

"You are correct," said Yisyena.

"And why did you relinquish that status? asked Tilua.

Yisyena started to say something and stopped with a choked sob. "Forgive me," she said. "It is difficult, and painful, for me to think about it."

"I do need to know," said Tilua.

Anarya sat down beside Yisyena and wrapped an arm around her. "Be brave," she said. "I'm here."

Yisyena reached out to touch Anarya's cheek and gave a weak smile. "Ever since The God came to Jotuk," she said, "he has accepted the talents of the *cranil* as death gifts. He said that those who gave him their talents and their lives became part of him." She stopped.

"Please go on," said Tilua.

"I no longer believe that and that is why I am looking for a new god. Would Quarenna accept me?"

"Holy Quarenna looks after all women and will welcome you with open arms," said Tilua, smiling at Yisyena. "Will you tell me what happened to destroy your faith in The God?"

Yisyena hesitated, started to speak, stopped and then, in a rush, said, "He took my sister into himself a little more than a year ago. I watched carefully for months, but there was never any turn of phrase or mannerism to reveal her presence in The God. Nor was there any sign of any of the others who he took after her…"

"And?"

"And I stopped believing that he preserved the souls of those he took. I ran because I realised I did not wish to become part of The God."

"I understand," said Tilua. She turned to Anarya. "You are about to hear something known to the Inner Circle. It is not a secret, nevertheless it is something we do not normally talk about. You may stay because of your connection to Yisyena. If you do stay I must ask you to promise not to speak of it."

Anarya took her knife, stabbed her thumb and let a drop of blood fall into the flame of the incense burner. "I swear to Holy Quarenna that I will not repeat anything of this to anyone outside this room."

Tilua nodded. She said, "The Inner Circle of the Daughters of Quarenna knows what The God in Sitrelk truly is. He is a Thiever, a man who has a talent similar to that of a Sponger. It is probably the rarest of all talents"

"But he has been among us for more than four hundred years. No one lives that long," said Yisyena.

"The important difference is that when he takes someone's ability he is not duplicating it but stealing it from the original owner, who loses it. The God can keep the talent for a short time then the original owner has it again."

"But…"

"Let me finish. We don't know when it happened or how, but at some stage the person he stole from died before the talent reverted. He discovered that the talent was his to keep, presumably because it couldn't return to a dead man. So far his behaviour is understandable. However, he wasn't satisfied with one talent so he killed the next person he took from and again found he could keep the talent."

"That's why he has the *cranil* killed when they are invited to become part of him!"

"Exactly."

"We are told it is because a *cranil* cannot live without his or her talent and having them killed is an act of mercy."

"There's more," said Tilua. "He can hold several talents at

once. However, each stolen talent fades over time. We don't know how long they last but he has to keep stealing to maintain his powers. The reason he's lived so long is that having someone killed after absorbing their talent means he also absorbs part of their life force. He is younger now than he was when he became The God."

Yisyena's head drooped and tears fell with her making no attempt to stem them as she listened to what Tilua had to say about The God. "Oh, Gilearh," she whispered. "You do not live on in him. I feared as much."

"That's awful, Yisa!" Anarya's involuntary outburst brought her to her feet. She muttered, "Sorry," subsided into her chair again and tried to comfort Yisyena.

"The Inner Circle will be interested in hearing about your time at the court of The God. I hope you will be willing to talk to us and give us more details. Whatever you decide, I am confident Holy Quarenna will smile on you and I will undertake your education in her rites myself."

"How can I thank you enough," said Yisyena. "I will be her faithful servant."

○

Anarya looked up when Yisyena returned from the Newsmonger's guildhall. The worried look on her face made her turn away from the oven and ask, "What's wrong, Yisa?"

"Anra my love, what is an assured contract?"

Anarya had a sinking feeling in her stomach. "You didn't take one, did you?"

Yisyena slumped on to the new chair they had bought so that both of them had somewhere to sit at the table. Her head dropped and she said, "Yes, I did. What does it mean?"

"An assured contract guarantees completion with an amount equal to the contract fee as a penalty for failure. It's not something that's usually associated with a quaestor's contract but there's no reason it can't be."

"I feared it was something like that. I should have realised the offer was out of proportion to the task. It seemed too good to refuse."

"Holy Quarenna help us! Why didn't you ask me what it meant before accepting it? What have you committed us to?"

"I thought it would be a simple matter. A woman called Kairi Hemlos…"

"Hemlos! She's the trickiest lawyer in Carregis, maybe even in the whole of Carrhen. What did she want?"

"Some of her jewellery was stolen and she offered a contract for its recovery. She knew who stole it. It was a personal servant, called Mirsu, who she had dismissed for incompetence. She described the woman and even included information about where she lived in the contract offer. I thought it would be easy so I accepted the contract and went to the house where I used my talent to search it without entering."

"Let me guess. You didn't find it, or her."

"I did not. I asked neighbours and they said she had left to visit her sister in Voro."

"Tell me the worst. What was the value of the contract?"

"Twenty-five dukals."

"Oh, Yisa," Anarya sank on to the bed. "We can't afford that kind of money. I don't think we've got much more than six, if that. You know how slow business has been for the last few weeks." She took a deep breath.

"We could sell my earrings," said Yisyena.

"They'd be worth four, maybe five, dukals. Nothing like enough."

"What happens if we are unable to pay?"

"We'd probably end up in court. The best we could hope for is having to give Hemlos half our income until the debt is paid off."

"That does not sound too bad."

"No," said Anarya. "It would be difficult, but we could manage. The problem is Kairi Hemlos is notorious for always wanting the maximum penalty and she might well argue that we should be enthralled as slaves for a couple of years."

"What does that mean?"

"The court would get a Scratcher to put us under a spell of total and unthinking obedience to whoever would buy us as servants."

Yisyena's hand went to her mouth. She gasped and said, "Would we stay together?"

"Probably not, unless the same person bought both of us. And there's another thing. Enthrallment would mean we would have to answer truthfully any questions our owner asked."

"We would not be able to keep it a secret that you are a Sponger," said Yisyena, "or that I am a runaway *cranil*. It would be a disaster. What can we do?"

"I wish I was a strong enough Seeker to find this servant. I'm not, but I know someone who might be. I just hope he'll agree to help. We've never been on the best of terms."

O

On their way to Greenbank Anarya told Yisyena about her first encounter with Janersh and told her to stay in the background and let her do the talking, at least at first.

The Hopeful Swain was quiet in mid-afternoon but, as Anarya had hoped, Janersh was ensconced in his chair by the fireplace holding forth to anyone who would listen to his reminiscences. He looked up and saw her.

"Huh, it's the little girl who thinks she's a quaestor. I thought I told you this is my patch. What are you doing here?"

"I need your help."

Janersh's eyebrows shot up. "Well now, fancy that. She's got a job she can't handle, has she?"

"You're right," admitted Anarya. "I need somebody found and you know I can't do it myself. I'll pay you well if you're a good enough Seeker to do it for me."

"Don't need to prove myself so you needn't try to tempt and flatter me."

"Five dukals?"

Janersh pulled himself into a more upright position in his chair. "Five dukals ain't near enough. An' you needn't start haggling. I ain't going to help you."

"Yes you are," said Lurascha, from her seat nearby. "You've never been offered five dukals for a job in your life. Can't you see the poor girl's in trouble. Why else would she offer that much?" She turned to Anarya and said, "I told you to come to me if you ever needed help. Why didn't you?"

"Because I need a Seeker and I know you're not one."

"No, but I'm married to one and he *is* going to help you, whatever he says. He might as well get used to the idea."

Janersh said, "I sometimes think the only reason you married me was to have someone to nag."

"Why else?" said Lurascha, getting up and walking across to kiss her husband.

Janersh drained the mug he was holding and stood up. "Tell me what you know about this person you need found an' I'll see what I can do."

"See, I told you he would," said Lurascha.

Anarya beckoned Yisyena forward and had her tell what she knew about Mirsu, the missing servant.

"Oh dear," said Lurascha. "I heard about that offer. I thought you'd have enough sense to steer clear of it."

Janersh got a faraway look in his eyes as he cast his gift out into the city. Anarya copied his talent and tried to stay with him but to no avail. She was left far behind.

"Can't help you," said Janersh after a while, shaking his head. "Got her trail but she rode out of the city on the Voro road a good five chimes ago. She's way out of range now. Sorry."

Anarya sighed and reached for her pouch.

"Now you leave that alone," said Lurascha. "I'll not be letting him take five dukals from you when he didn't help. If you want to give him something make it a mug of ale."

Janersh snorted and said, "Like she says, I won't charge you nothing for getting nothing."

Anarya went off to get the ale while Janersh reseated himself. She saw Lurascha pull Yisyena off to one side and say something to her but couldn't hear what it was.

O

"Someone is looking for me," Yisyena told Anarya when they got back to their lodgings. "That nice Lurascha woman warned me that people are looking for a young woman with white hair. She said I should dye my hair again because the roots are showing. I think it is likely to be an agent of The God who is looking for me. I told you he does not permit *cranil* to leave Sitrelk. I am frightened. Should we be enthralled and I am revealed as *cranil* then I will be taken back to Jotuk and The God will have me killed."

"No," said Anarya, "I won't have that. We've got to find a

way of getting twenty-five dukals.”

"Or a way of completing the contract."

“Don’t see how we…” Anarya stopped and tipped her head to one side.

“What is it?”

“Just an idea. I think a daimon would be able to steal the jewels back from the thief and I know where to find a Daimoner. I’ll offer him all the contract fee if that’s what it takes. I’m not having you taken from me.”

“Where is this Daimoner?”

“I’ve seen him several times in a tavern near the fish dock.”

“Then we should go and find him.”

“I think you’d better stay here. If Lurascha spotted your hair then there’s a chance someone else will too. You’ve still got some of the dye mixture so you deal with that while I go to find the Daimoner.”

STEALTHER

Baram reached across the cluttered desk in Raifen's study, accepted a glass of wine and sat back. He was getting used to these discussions with Raifen. He seemed to have taken on the role of intermediary between Baram and the people appealing to the temple for help.

"That last one was difficult," he said, after tasting the wine. "I sympathised with the woman who lost her home but there was nothing I could do. I overheard a conversation which made it obvious that she and her new husband were trying to cause trouble for her previous partner."

He looked across the desk and caught Raifen's eye. "From what they said it was clear her complaint about her share of their common property being stolen just didn't hold up. She claimed her previous partner had destroyed the relevant documents but it was obvious that she knew, and didn't like, the details of the property settlement. I've no proof, but I think she was the one who destroyed the evidence, probably at the instigation of her new husband. He seems to be the dominant one of the pair."

"Have you taken any action against him?" asked Raifen.

"No, not yet. I might keep an eye on them because I suspect he's an opportunist who thought she had property and money. I think he's going to leave her now that he knows she doesn't. If he does then he might give me cause for action. The problem is, I think execution would be an excessive response and I can't steal from someone who has nothing."

"It seems to me that you've done all you can. Sometimes the appeals to Huler aren't valid."

Baram sighed and his head dropped. "I suppose so. But it's the first time it's happened to me and I keep thinking about it. Sometimes I think the woman is at fault and should be punished. Then I think it's one or other of the two men involved who is in the wrong. Do I need to do anything? I don't know." He looked at Raifen. "I need help to make that sort of decision. I don't have the experience to do it myself."

"Don't worry, Baram. Let that one go. You will get the experience you lack. And you can always come and ask me for advice. Trust Huler."

Baram nodded, made the sign of the lightning bolt and said, "Do you have anything else for me?"

"Yes," said Raifen. He rummaged among the pile of documents on his desk until he found the one he wanted. "There's this. It came in yesterday. It says the Gotheer and Erlosh brokerage company employed a man called Innotul. They discovered that he's been stealing from them for a couple of years. He's been moving money from account to account with inadequate documentation so that it wasn't clear how much was moving in which direction. He was quite clever about it because most of the transactions were honest, but sometimes a fraction of the money being transferred ended up in his hands."

"That doesn't sound like a job for me. From what you say there doesn't seem to be any doubt about his guilt. Anyway, although I can do some figuring I'd never be able to make sense of the sort of thing you're talking about."

"You're right, there is enough evidence against him. Unfortunately, it's useless. The Count's court were investigating and he was going to be arrested two days ago. Somebody put morttodt into his evening meal first. He's dead. Your job is to find out who killed him and take appropriate action."

"Was he killed to keep him quiet?"

"It seems likely," said Raifen. "He must have had at least one accomplice to get away with it for so long."

"And that accomplice must have some connection with the Count's court to know that he was about to be arrested. I think that's where I have to start. Can you get me the names of the court officials involved in the investigation."

"I'm far ahead of you," said Raifen, with a grin. "There are only three of them." He passed a piece of parchment to Baram saying, "Here are their names."

"What about his colleagues at the brokerage?"

"They were all investigated when Innotul's embezzlement became apparent. None of them were involved."

"I'd still like a list of them."

"I'll get it."

Baram finished his wine, said goodbye to Raifen and went into the temple. He knelt at the Supplicant's altar, as he had before each of his cases. There, he begged Huler for his blessing. "Great Lord, let me think clearly that I may punish the guilty."

O

There was a constant stream of people going into and out of the Count's court and Baram didn't see how he was going to get in without bumping into someone. Then he laughed at himself. He had become too used to thinking about moving while stealthed that he forgot that he could simply walk into the building with everyone else. In fact he had the perfect excuse. The court had ruled that his uncle's business was now his, but he had put off registering the change of ownership. It was something he would have to do at some stage if he wanted to sell, which he did. *I might as well do it now and have a good reason for wandering around the court if anyone questions me.*

After a trip back to the room he occupied at the temple to collect the relevant documents he returned to the Count's court. He walked through the archway into a crowded space and looked around. He had no idea where to go.

Several harassed looking men in black and gold livery were trying to answer questions shouted at them by the people packed into the quadrangle. Baram could see no option but to join the throng and add his voice to the hubbub.

"Business registry? That's second door on the left through there," said one of the liveried men when Baram got close enough to make himself heard. The man pointed towards another archway on the other side of the quadrangle. Then, as Baram started moving in that direction, he added, "No, you've got to go around. Keep off the grass. Only the Count and the judges are allowed there. Stay on the gravel."

It was with a sigh of relief that Baram turned into the relative quiet under the other archway. The second door on the left opened on to a staircase and the room at the top of the stairs held six people bent over ledgers. When one of them eventually deigned to acknowledge Baram's presence he dealt with transferring ownership quickly and efficiently. He was about to return to his desk when Baram asked, "Do you know Peragh?" naming the most senior of the people involved in the investigation of Innotul's embezzlement.

The sound of pens scratching paper and pages being turned stopped and the other people in the room turned their heads to look at him.

"Peragh? Why do you want to see him?"

"I've been told he might be able to help me with another problem I have."

"Huh! Must be nice to get recommendations. You'll find him in Business Liaison. Go back to the main entrance. Take the stairs on the right. That's where you'll find him, and his cronies."

Interesting, Baram thought, *sounds as if Peragh isn't too popular with his colleagues. I wonder if that's an indication of his character.*

Baram found a corner where he could go into stealth without being seen to disappear. He waited patiently until someone opened the door and he could slip into the room where Peragh worked. Then he settled down to listen. A man, presumably Peragh, and a short dumpy woman were there working at two of the three desks, but they weren't talking much, just getting on with whatever they were doing. They were interrupted a few times by people coming into the room with questions. Baram kept hoping that someone would say something about Innotul but nobody did. A couple of chimes later he was still waiting. He had learned patience working for his uncle and had discovered how useful it was in his new role. Things he wanted to see or hear rarely presented themselves in a nice, tidy, orderly manner. Waiting was something he found himself doing a lot.

When a tall, good-looking woman walked into the room and flung herself into the chair at the empty desk the others looked up.

"What did they want, Devhana?" the man asked.

"Are they suspicious?" said the dumpy woman.

"Of course they're suspicious," the newly arrived woman said. "They questioned me for ages and I expect they'll be after you or Peragh next. It was all about the money Innotul was skimming, how we found out about it and what can have happened to it."

"You didn't tell them anything."

"Of course not, idiot. Do you think I want to end up an enthralled slave? If they catch us out that's what will happen to us. Cholev Erlosh has enough influence to make sure of that. Remember, our story is that we only discovered what Innotul was doing three days ago. That's what I told them. Tell them the same. Stick to that and we'll be fine."

"Wish we'd never got involved," said the man.

"Too late for that. Just don't touch any of the money, not for a year at least. Spending more than you earn is sure to make them suspicious."

"Quarenna's tits!" said the dumpy woman. "This is your fault. If you hadn't been sleeping with Innotul you wouldn't have tried to protect him when we discovered his rotten little scheme and dragged us into it too."

"I didn't notice you complaining about getting an extra dukal or two every month," snapped Devhana.

"Shush!" said Peragh, "keep your voices down. Anybody might overhear you shouting like that."

That comment made Baram smile. They would be even more worried if they knew somebody was overhearing them from inside the room.

"What if they use a truth potion or get a Feeler to question us?"

"Then we're done for," said Devhana. "But they won't do that unless you give them a hint of a reason. They'd have to justify it to the Count, and Graumedel's been getting enough money from Innotul that he won't allow it to come out."

"I knew Graumedel was getting a cut but I wouldn't have thought a few dukals a month would mean much to him," said Peragh.

"Gotheer and Erlosh wasn't the only business Innotul was skimming from. It's just the one that caught him out. He was passing a lot more on to Graumedel from other sources."

"You never told us that," complained the dumpy woman.

"Why should I?"

"We should have got a share in that too."

"Do you think it was Graumedel that had Innotul poisoned?" said Peragh.

"Could be, I suppose," replied Devhana with a shrug.

"Huler preserve us. We might be next."

"Not unless you put the rest of us at risk by being stupid. That's what happened to Innotul."

"How do you know?" asked Peragh. Then he looked at Devhana in horror. "You killed him, didn't you?"

Devhana laughed. "Took you long enough to work that out. Yes, it was me. He was getting greedy."

"But he was your lover. How could you just kill him?"

"Because I'm more important to me than he was. Doesn't matter that he was the best lay I've ever had; he was putting me at risk. I couldn't allow that."

That's the question of who killed Innotul answered, thought Baram. *Now what? It's difficult to believe that Count Graumedel was involved. Think I'd better get advice from Raifen.* He listened to them arguing and worrying for a bit longer then took the chance to leave when someone else came into the room.

O

"This is exactly the sort of situation that needs a Stealther," said Raifen. "The Count is effectively immune from prosecution but he is culpable. I assume you are convinced of his guilt."

"I don't think there's any doubt. There's no reason the three of them in Business Liaison would dissemble. After all they didn't know I was there," replied Baram. "What I can't understand is why he would get involved in a petty crime like this. The money involved is nothing compared to what he has. Just the income from his holdings every day must be more than he's made from this embezzlement."

"Unfortunately, some people in positions of power forget that other people are real. And some can't resist the opportunity to see what they can get away with. I don't know which describes Count Graumedel. Is he involved in other schemes like this or is this the only one? What I do know is that something needs to be done about it. What will you do?"

"That's what I wanted to ask you. I need your advice."

"It's a difficult problem," said Raifen. "I don't suppose you remember what happened when Graumedel's father was killed. We had months of unrest and violence. The same could happen again if you killed Graumedel. Maybe even worse because he doesn't have an obvious heir."

"I've never thought about it," said Baram. "All I know is that he's not married and hasn't any children. Who's likely to succeed him?"

"I'm not sure. There are at least five nieces and nephews who might have a claim. Some of them are very young and probably out of the running. I'd have to say that the likeliest outcome would be for Duke Wurauf to take over Carregis and add it to the holdings of the Duchy of Carrh."

"That wouldn't be popular."

"I don't think popularity has ever been one of Duke Wurauf's ambitions."

"What do I do?" asked Baram. "From what you've said, I'm not sure that killing Count Graumedel is either appropriate or desirable."

"I guess you could steal enough from him to make up the amount Innotul embezzled. That's something on the order of six hundred dukals from the Gotheer and Erlosh company alone. But, from what this Devhana woman said, other companies have been robbed too and we've no idea who or how much is involved."

"He's very rich. Would he even notice if I stole from him?"

"More importantly, what would the result be if it became known he was a receiver of stolen property. It would be disruptive and the effects might be as bad as killing him. We'll need to do some serious thinking about this. I'll talk to some of the Brotherhood. Come back and see me in a few days."

Baram sighed, said farewell to Raifen and went into the Sanctuary where he prostrated himself in front of the altar and prayed for inspiration.

○

"It's been decided," said Raifen a few days later. "I put the question to the seniors and their recommendation is that you steal something small and valuable. Something he'd miss. His seal would be ideal. Then it can be returned anonymously with a warning."

"I'll do what I can," said Baram. *I know where Graumedel's mansion is but little else about it. How do I find out more? Does the city archive have any plans of the building?* He left the temple to take a look at the mansion.

On his return he asked the archivists for help. They denied having the plans and made it obvious that even if they had they wouldn't let just anybody examine them.

Well, that didn't work. I wonder if Raifen can find me someone who worked in the mansion and could describe the layout.

Raifen could, and Baram was present in stealth while he interviewed three men and two women who had been servants of Count Graumedel, or his father, and had worked in the mansion.

They talked about the history of the building. It was a big, square, two-storey, battlemented slab of a building with turrets at each corner and halfway along each side. It perched solidly on top the of the Rock on its eastern side, surrounded by parkland and next to Duke Wurauf's estate.

Typical of the houses built by the nobility almost a hundred years ago it was obviously meant for defence. That wasn't too surprising given the unrest during the time when king Duvereant II was still a child. The many disagreements between the members of the Regency Council had a tendency to flare into violence. The building had no doors at ground level. A wide staircase led to the main door which was on the upper floor in the middle of the western side. Originally the staircase had been made of wood so that it could be burnt if necessary to deny access to enemies but Graumedel's father had had it rebuilt in stone. Now it had wide treads and an ornamented balustrade in which bees and beehives figured prominently.

He heard that the Count's suite, comprising his study, library, bedroom and dining room, was on the east side of the upper floor and overlooked the garden which occupied the courtyard in the centre. Other rooms on the upper floor were occupied by the seneschal, the commander of the Count's Guard and an assortment of various court officials. Stairs in each of the turrets connected the upper and lower floors. The kitchens and other service areas were downstairs. There were dungeons, cut into the rock under the north-western corner. These were unused, said the ex-servants.

○

Quite a challenge, thought Baram, studying the movement of people up and down the staircase. *How do I get in without being obvious?*

The door at the top of the stairs stood open and people leaving did so without hindrance. However, there were two guardsmen in black and gold livery standing at the foot of the stairs and two more at the top. Everyone going in was questioned and quite a few were searched.

Baram watched for a while then decided he had had enough for the day. He had been invisible for almost seven chimes and was beginning to feel overstretched. The book he had read about his talent had warned against spending too much time in stealth. It said everyone had to find their own limits and experimentation had shown him that about eight chimes was the longest he could tolerate. *Stupid,* he told himself, *if I keep going for much longer I'll be useless tomorrow. I'd better get something to eat.*

Going down the zigzagging road on the eastern side of The Rock he passed a tavern called *The Halfway Point*. It had a reputation as one of the best, and most expensive, in Carregis. He had never eaten there. *It might be nice to treat myself. I've got enough in my pouch even after paying the land registry fee. I can't stand the idea of cooking for myself tonight. If I want to eat out it'll be half a chime before I get to any of the places I usually go and I'm hungry now.*

The tavern had a good view downstream to the Ferrahn Islands and beyond them to the estuary. As it was a pleasant evening he decided to eat outdoors and settled himself at a table from which he could watch the ships coming and going. He wondered if the *Lady Visole* was one of them.

He was taken aback by the list of dishes the server rattled off. *I don't even know what some of these things are. I didn't expect such a long list. The places I usually eat at have only one or two choices, often just one.*

"Sorry," he said to the server, "I was distracted. Could you repeat that?"

He broke into the recitation when something he recognised was mentioned. "Grilled flatfish sounds good. I'll have that."

"Certainly, Sir," muttered the server. "A good choice, if I

may say so. The cook advises a young light wine with it. Last year's Firten Bortu, perhaps, or Nessa Surric."

"The Surric, I think," said Baram, hoping that it wasn't obvious he was guessing.

The fish, when it came, was a surprise to him. It was bigger than he anticipated and had been stuffed with shrimps and mushrooms in a cheese sauce before being grilled. He took a rather tentative mouthful, then ate with enthusiasm. *I could get used to food like this. No offence, auntie, but this is a different class of cooking.*

O

He went back to Graumedel's mansion the next morning and waited for an opportunity to get past the guards. That came when a group of men and women arrived and demanded to see the Count. They were told he wasn't available but wouldn't accept that and tried to push their way past the guards at the bottom of the stairs. This drew the attention of the two at the top who came down to assist their colleagues.

A pushing, noisy, argumentative group formed and gradually drifted away from the bottom of the stairs. Baram took advantage of the gap between them and the balustrade to slip past before anyone drew a weapon or more guards were attracted by the noise. He hurried up the stairs and through the door.

The opulence that greeted him made him stop and stare. The walls, where they weren't covered in tapestries, were panelled in dark oak with goldenwood inserts. The floor was marble and plinths every few paces held statues or vases. There were doors on both sides of the corridor he stood in and he could see the staircases at each end that led down to the lower level. *I know the layout, but how am I going to find my way to something worth stealing? I'll just have to explore and hope.*

He shrugged. One way was as good as another when he didn't know where he was going so he went in the direction he was facing. He couldn't risk opening doors so he had to be content with looking into those rooms where the door was already open. Those on the inner side had windows looking into the courtyard and the well-tended garden there, full of trees and flowering shrubs. There was even a lily pond. He overheard servants talking as they worked and, when he got round to the east side, what he overheard helped him to identify which of the rooms was the Count's study. Unfortunately, and unsurprisingly, the door was closed.

He waited nearby, certain that Graumedel would put in an appearance sooner or later and only wandering off to take a look into other rooms when someone left a door open. He was awed by the quality and tastefulness of the furnishings. Eventually he heard noises and a small procession came round the corner. It consisted of a squad of six guards surrounding Graumedel. There was also a thin, lugubrious-looking man who Baram didn't know, and two women in the black and gold livery who were listening to whatever the Count was saying. They nodded, bowed and went back the way they came dodging around another man in livery who was holding the leashes of two big brindled hounds.

Oh, Oh. I could be in trouble here if those animals can sense Stealthers. Baram started to move away but he was too slow.

The hounds lifted their heads. They lunged forward and jerked their leashes from the handler's grip. Growling furiously, they rushed past the Count and stopped with Baram bracketed between them. They didn't attack him but prowled restlessly back and forth with their attention fixed approximately on his position

Huler protect me. They're not sure exactly where I am but they know I'm here. What do I do now?

"Kelam, Megra, come here," shouted the Count. "What are you doing? Come here!"

The hounds ignored the commands. The handler stammered out an apology for allowing them to escape his control and tried in vain to grab the leashes.

"What are they doing?" said the Count.

"You've seen them behave like this before, my lord," said the thin man. "That's what they do when they have something cornered."

"But there's nothing there."

"Nothing we can see, but they can hear or scent something. Wait a moment."

The thin man hurried along the corridor, entered a room

three doors away, then returned almost immediately carrying a small vial. He broke the seal, removed the stopple and splashed the contents towards the space the hounds were menacing. The liquid from the vial turned into a cloud of thin blue mist. One of the hounds was just on the edge of the cloud. It sneezed, started to back away then staggered and collapsed.

"I thought as much," said the thin man. "Look, my lord. Look where the mist isn't. There's a man in there. He's got to be a Stealther."

Baram tried to hold his breath but he felt himself slipping into darkness. He slumped to the floor and heard no more.

DAIMONER

Anarya didn't know the name of the tavern by the fish dock. It didn't have a sign and she would never have known it was there if she hadn't been passing it one day when two men staggered out of it, drunk enough to need each other's support as they stumbled down the street.

It was just as she remembered. The straw on the floor was broken, crushed and dirty, looking as if it hadn't been changed for weeks. The windows were grimy and little light managed to get in to relieve the gloom. Sour beer and stale sweat were the dominant smells, with an undertone of ganj.

She had never bothered advertising there. It felt like a sad place with a depressing atmosphere. The dozen or so customers sat apart from each other, there was no conversation and most of them didn't even look up when she walked in.

The only reason she bothered about the place was the old man sitting at a table in a corner with his hands wrapped around a mug, eyes shut and head drooping. His clothes were shabby and threadbare in places, his thinning hair hung in greasy strands and his skin had an unhealthy grey tinge. She wouldn't normally want to have anything to do with him, but in the Oversight he was surrounded by the dark blue aura of a Daimoner. He had been there the first time she visited and every time since. He was on her list of available talents along with a Scratcher, several Whisperers, a couple of Lifters and a Feeler, people she could count on to be in a specific place when she wanted to borrow a particular skill.

"Go 'way," he muttered when Anarya sat down beside him.

"Want to talk to you," she said.

"Go 'way. Don't want to talk to nobody."

She could see his mug was empty and said, "Not even if I buy you a drink?"

The old man lifted his head a little, peered at her and said, "Avit."

The barman grumbled when asked for the strong spirit and

insisted on Anarya proving she could afford it before rummaging under the bar for a stoneware bottle.

She took two mugs back to the table and gave one of them to the Daimoner.

He took a gulp, sighed and said, "Ganj."

I hope this is worth it, thought Anarya, paying the barman for the narcotic and wrinkling her nose at the thick, sweet smell.

The old man sucked hard on the pipe. The smoke set him coughing. He took another drag when he recovered but it was more restrained. He held the smoke for a moment, then exhaled with a satisfied sound. His head came up and he looked straight at her for the first time. "Whaddya want?"

"Hear tell you're a Daimoner."

"So?"

"Need a Daimoner to do some work for me."

"You've come to the wrong place then. I ain't never calling a daimon again."

"I'll pay you well."

"You can't pay me enough. I'm done with those... those things. They've got it in for me. Controlled them for years and years but can't hold them the way I used to. They'll do all sorts of things to me if they get me into the Darkworld and I'm not giving them the chance."

"But…"

The old man's voice grew shrill enough to attract the attention of some of the other customers. "But nothing, d'ye hear! I'm scared of them now. Didn't used to be, but I almost lost it the last time I called one an' there's no way I'm risking it any more." He sucked hard on the ganj pipe and set himself coughing again.

Now what do I do? Anarya asked herself. *I've got to have his help.*

"Can you introduce me to another Daimoner?" she asked.

"Could. But I'm not gonna. Ain't putting nobody at risk. Couldn't live with myself if they got took into the Darkworld 'cos of something I did. Worst thing that can happen to a Daimoner."

"Never understood about daimons and the Darkworld. I'm interested in learning more. Will you tell me about them."

He sucked on the pipe again and, after a short silence, said,

"Suppose it can't hurt since you're not a Daimoner, but it'll cost you. How 'bout ten bits?"

Anarya was about to agree when he said, "All right then, five bits – and a meal."

She realised he must have assumed she'd haggle. Putting a ten-bit coin on the table, she said, "There, that'll buy you dinner too. Now tell me about daimons."

The Daimoner shuddered. "They live in the Darkworld. Never been there and don't want to, but some people have, don't know how, and managed to survive. They say the Darkworld is everywhere. Distance means nothing to daimons."

"You mean they can be anywhere?" Anarya looked around. "They could be here?"

The old man nodded. "Yeah, they could be. Course, there's no reason they should be. Don't bother looking for them, you can't see them. There's none here. I'd know if there was one around."

"How?"

"Everything feels wrong and they talk at you all the time. They make all sorts of threats 'cos they hate being controlled."

Anarya felt cold trickling down her spine at the fear in the Daimoner's voice. She picked up the glass of avit and was about to take a mouthful. Then the strong smell of aniseed from the spirit struck her and she put it down again untouched.

"Course they wouldn't bother you 'cos you're not a Daimoner. They don't trouble ordinary people less'n they're told to. They got their own business to attend to, whatever that is."

"How does a Daimoner control them?"

"A Daimoner's talent gives him authority over them but they fight back, try to intimidate you. You gotta be strong, gotta command them. Never show weakness. They gotta obey if you're firm enough." He stopped and took a gulp of avit. "That's how I almost lost it. I got a really strong one and only just managed to dismiss it before it overwhelmed me."

"Didn't know daimons came in different strengths," said Anarya. *He wants to show off a bit, I just need to keep him talking.*

"Sure they do. Sometimes you have to invoke a strong one. All depends on what you want it to do. A powerful one will do more and do it faster. You have to be a lot more careful about the strong ones. They're more likely to get the revenge they all want."

"Revenge?"

"Like I said, they hate being controlled. Just about every year you hear of somebody being turned inside out by a daimon. Or going mad, or blind or something." He picked up his mug and drained it in a single gulp.

"So if they're that set on vengeance what's to stop one of them coming after you when you're finished with it?"

"Gotta dismiss it by Name, same as calling it. You've got to put a command into the dishmish… dismissal t' make sure it'll only come when called."

"You've got to call them by name? How do you learn that?"

"You could summon one without knowing a Name but that'd be taking a chance. You might get lucky and get a little one. They're kinda stupid and you can maybe fool it into telling you its Name. Huler help you if you get one of the big ones, 'cos nobody else will."

"Is that what you did?"

"Huler's beard, no. Do I look that crazy? Nah, I learned the way most do. Bought the Name of a minor daimon from somebody else."

"Can't you call one and command it to tell you what its Name is?"

He shook his head. "That's the one thing you can't force it to do. But it will tell you the Name of another, stronger, daimon in the hope that you'll go too far and won't be able to handle it."

I don't see any option. I'm going to have to borrow his talent and be a Daimoner for a while. But the longer she listened the more scared she became. *Quarenna give me courage.*

Anarya took a deep breath and said, "Tell me a Name, a minor one."

The old man peered at her, blinked a few times and said, "What do you want to know for? Won't do you no good. You gotta be a Daimoner or it won't pay no 'tention to you."

"I'm curious. I never thought about them having names. I suppose they're not like human names."

"That'sh right. The shtronger… stronger ones have longer Names. They're difficult to say and you gotta get them 'xactly right or daimon won't reshpond." He reached for his mug, found it empty and fell silent.

"If you teach me a Name you can have this," said Anarya, offering him the avit she hadn't drunk. "Where's the harm in telling me. You said I can't use it. What would happen if I said it?"

"Nuthin'. Need to be a Daimoner to make a way for a daimon to come from the Darkworld."

"Tell me. I'm curious to know what a daimon's Name sounds like, and what you've got to do to reach one."

He grumbled but eventually agreed. Between mouthfuls of avit he told her that just saying the Name wasn't enough. Nothing would happen even for a Daimoner if he hadn't opened the way to the Darkworld first. That meant visualising the threshold of the Darkworld. It appeared as a circle of complete darkness in which the daimon would be confined when summoned. Then he coached her through the, almost impossible, pronunciation of a three syllable Name. Finally she persuaded him to tell her the words of a safe dismissal. He gradually became less coherent as the effects of the avit and ganj combined. His head dropped, he fell asleep and started snoring quietly.

Anarya stood up and walked to the door. *I hope he wasn't too drunk to teach me properly.* She looked back at him. *I wonder what being a Daimoner will be like. Only one way to find out.* She visualised a thread extending from her own aura to his and duplicated his talent in herself. The two-body feeling that accompanied every borrowing was always strange but it was even odder when the other body was half asleep and drunk. She staggered, as if it was her that had drunk the avit and smoked the ganj. Staying awake for the few moments it took for the Daimoner's talent to establish itself in her mind was almost too much for her. It was only when she pulled the thread back to herself that she felt sober again. She shook her head. *That was weird.*

Concentrating on the feel of her new ability she was disappointed to realise it wasn't a good skill for her. The old man's ability was quite strong, which was good, but it chafed like a badly fitting pair of boots. She estimated she could probably hold it unused for one to one and a half chimes before she lost it. How long she could actually use it for was more difficult to assess but she guessed no more than half a chime. *Doesn't give me much time. I hope it'll be enough. It has to be.*

O

Anarya hurried back home, ran up the stairs and into the room to find it empty. *Where is she?* She was glad Yisyena wasn't home in case something went wrong; at the same time wished Yisa had left a note to say where she was going. *It's good I won't have to argue about doing this, it would waste time. But I wish I knew where she was.*

She went to her knees before the statuette, thumbed her forehead and said "Holy Quarenna aid me. This is something I don't want to do, but I must. I beg you, Holy One, lend me the strength of the Warrior Maid, the determination of the Guardian and the support of the Friend and Comforter. My blood and tears are poor payment for your grace but I offer them, such as they are."

The image of a circle of darkness came easily when she concentrated on the Daimoner's skill. Slowly and carefully she said the Name the old man had taught her. There was a feeling of resistance from beyond the circle, then, quite suddenly, it was occupied. She couldn't see anything, but there was a presence and something she could only describe as a wrongness. A rather nauseating taste, like pickled cherries gone bad, filled her mouth. She didn't vomit but it was a close thing.

{Not slave. Release, must release. Will punish. Be revenged.} The hollow, sighing voice of the daimon echoed round the inside of her skull and she had the impression that the circle bulged towards her for a moment before settling back to its original position.

{Will take bones from arms and legs. One at a time, one each day until none left.}

The old man had told her about the terrible threats daimons made and said strength was needed to resist them, but she hadn't realised how hard it would be.

{Change taste so no flavour good except excrement.}

The voice was the worst. The hissing, sinister sound seemed to slide straight into her head from all angles and its echo lingered long after it stopped speaking. She shivered, feeling cold with fear.

{Will turn head around so must walk backwards.}

"You will do as I command," she told the daimon and described the missing jewels and the woman who stole them. "Bring the jewels here to me and I will release you."

{Will make partner forget you.}

Anarya felt a lump form in her throat, but moments later she realised the daimon had made a mistake. There was nothing more likely to strengthen her resolve than a threat to Yisyena.

She summoned all the strength and willpower she could and said, "Be silent. You *will* do as I command. Go. Now!"

The daimon wailed, but it obeyed. The sensations accompanying its presence vanished. Anarya almost collapsed with the release of tension.

She realised it had taken about a quarter chime to force the daimon to obey her. *How long will it take it to do the job? What happens if it takes so long that the borrowed talent runs out before it comes back? I don't want to know.* "Holy Quarenna, I wish it would hurry up."

She waited. A quarter chime later she really began to worry. A headache started, like an ice-cold needle being driven between her eyes. Then shimmering coloured lights appeared in her peripheral vision and her skin started itching. She knew she was getting close to her limit and would suffer for it, assuming she survived the daimon's return. The borrowed ability was running out like sand in a timer. Her heartbeat sounded thunderous in her ears and she began to gasp for breath.

Suddenly the taste filled her mouth again and she gagged. The presence was back in the circle and there was a small brocade covered box there too. Being very careful with pronunciation she spoke the daimon's Name and said, "Be gone, be gone, and come not again unless I summon you. Trouble me not. Be gone."

{Will punish you. Will not forget. Will taste revenge.} Its

final threat lingered in the air as it vanished moments before Anarya lost control of the circle.

Anarya slumped to the floor. *That was close. Far too close for comfort. I was almost done there. Now I know why the old man is so frightened.*

She crawled across the room, opened the store cupboard and grabbed the first thing that came to hand. It was an orange. She bit through the skin, the bitterness giving her something to concentrate on. She squeezed and swallowed, squeezed and swallowed. The juice made her hands and face sticky but she didn't care. She managed to stand long enough to get some bread, cheese and watered wine from the cupboard before collapsing again. Still sitting on the floor and careless of how much she spilled or how many crumbs she dropped she ate and drank. Getting food into her stomach was urgent, she knew the signs of talent exhaustion and was well aware that she had pushed herself to the extreme edge.

The door opened and Yisyena walked in. She paused on the threshold as she saw Anarya on the floor, then ran across the room to kneel beside her. "What is wrong?" she asked, then answered herself without waiting for Anarya's response. "You have been overusing your talent, have you not? Why? You know it is dangerous. You must not stretch yourself so far."

"But I did it," said Anarya. "We're safe. Look." She pointed at the brocade box sitting in the middle of the floor.

Yisyena opened the box and looked into it. She turned to Anarya and said, "You did this! How?"

"The Daimoner wouldn't do it so I had to borrow his skills and make a daimon bring the jewels to me."

Yisyena's eyes went wide. She hugged Anarya and said, "You should not have taken such a risk, my love. Not without me beside you."

"I couldn't wait for you to come home. I've discovered I can't be a Daimoner for long, I had to do it quickly." She described the events of the day and finished by saying. "There will be times when being able to control a daimon could be useful to us but it's not going to happen. I'm never going to invoke one again. The old man is so frightened. He's stopped using his talent and I can understand why. I'd rather lose a contract than do that again."

"Was it that bad?"

"You have no idea."

"I agree I do not. However, Daimoners manage to work with daimons all the time."

"But I'm not a Daimoner, not really. What happens if someone nearby invokes that daimon and I'm not holding the right skills. Will that dismissal hold or will it be free to attack me?"

Yisyena looked thoughtful. "I confess I had not considered that possibility. It does provide a different view of the elephant."

"What? Oh, I get it. That's a nice phrase. I haven't heard it before. It's much more prosaic in Katelish. We'd say 'that's the other side of the bit'."

"How boring."

Anarya managed a laugh. "Let's take a look at the jewels."

"Later, my love. First you must eat more and rest."

O

Anarya discovered that Yisyena's instruction to eat and rest wasn't a suggestion but an order. Almost before she could do anything for herself Yisyena had her tucked up in bed with a handmeal of cheese and peppers wrapped in toasted bread. Eating it while trying to avoid dropping crumbs occupied her attention for a quarter.

Eventually Yisyena relented and allowed her to open the jewel box. It held a heavy silver collar encrusted with emeralds and a pair of matching earrings gleaming against the black velvet lining.

Yisyena held the collar against Anarya's throat and said, "These are very fine. They would look well on you."

Anarya snorted. "With my colouring? Don't be silly. They would look much better on you."

"These must be worth more than twenty-five dukals."

"More like a hundred and twenty-five, I'd think."

"It is a shame we have to return them to their owner."

"At least the contract is fulfilled and you know never to touch an assured contract again."

"That is true. While we are talking of contracts, the reason I was out when you returned is that I went to the newsmongers. I thought we had to take as many contracts as possible to at least try to pay off Hemlos. Just in case the Daimoner failed you understand. I never expected *you* to be the Daimoner."

"Did you find something?"

"Yes. There was one possibility. The housekeeper from one of those mansions on the south side of the Rock wants to have a member of the staff followed. She offers one dukal."

"One dukal for a simple surveillance? She must be worried about something. Who does she want followed? Her husband?"

"The man is a recent addition to the household, his name is Nasuren. He goes out late at night every Dinsday and does not return until early morning. She is concerned that he may not be trustworthy and wishes to know where he goes on these weekly excursions."

"Dinsday evenings, eh. I'd wager that means he's going to the pits. It should be easy enough to find out. The pits can be rather rowdy so I think this might be a job for Rhyanek. In the meantime, why don't you get in bed too and hug me. I need some comforting after that experience with the daimon."

O

Anarya woke in darkness and shuddered. She could feel Yisa cuddling her. What had wakened her? There was something wrong.

She screamed.

Yisyena was out of bed in a flash, grabbing her cane from the table. "What is it, my love?"

"I can't see!"

"It is the middle of the night and dark."

"No, you don't understand. I can't *see*. The Oversight's gone. I can't see your aura. There's nothing. I can't borrow if I can't see." Her voice changed to a wail. "I'm burnt out!"

"It cannot be so," said Yisyena. "Such a great risk for me took you. Suffer for me not must you."

Shaking with fear and moaning incoherently, Anarya spent the rest of the night in Yisyena's arms. She fell asleep occasionally, from sheer exhaustion. Then she would waken to find that she still couldn't use the Oversight and that started her crying again.

Anarya felt her world was falling apart. She had to be bullied into eating and she answered Yisyena's questions in monosyllables.

It was early evening when she caught a brief flash of orange from the corner of her eye. She turned to look at Yisyena. Her aura was there, not as bright or as clear as usual, but it was there.

She grabbed Yisyena, swept her off her feet and swung her round, shouting, "I can see! I can see again!"

"You must take great care never to stretch your talent so far again."

O

Anarya delivered the jewel box to Kairi Hemlos and enjoyed the look of surprise on her face when she accepted it. On her way back to her room she paused as she went through the market. The newsmonger's voice was clearly audible over the hubbub. "News from the arena you can rely on, brought to you by Rhyanek and Partners, the quaestors you can rely on."

Long after Yisyena had persuaded the newsmongers to advertise their business she still got a thrill from hearing their announcements. The city-wide advertising had generated quite a few contracts for them and was easily worth the one dukal a month she paid the guildmasters.

The newsmonger carried on. "The great Jurnean has agreed to appear at the next Arenafest. He's won seventeen times in the last three years, all to first blood. This will be his first death bout. His opponent is not yet known. Rhyanek and Partners give you this news free of charge. You can leave any messages for them with me."

She frowned slightly, *Jurnean, great? I don't think so. He's quite good, but Caseir's the only one who deserves to be called great. I wish he was still fighting.*

Hearing the newsmonger reminded her that she had to call in at the guildhouse and collect any messages. It wasn't far away, so she tucked the ham she had just bought under her arm and headed in that direction. She had just turned on to

Coverry Street, where the guildhouse was, when the Oversight showed her the aura of a powerful Chemer. Who was he? She didn't recognise him. If she could find out more about him and where he lived or worked then she'd be able to find a Chemer's talent whenever she wanted it.

She had borrowed a Chemer's skills before, but she hadn't had much success in brewing potions. This was, she knew, partly because she couldn't hold the ability quite long enough. This man had the brightest golden aura she had seen and she wondered if his strength would make a difference.

Abandoning her intention to go to the newsmonger's guildhouse, she settled down to follow the Chemer. It wasn't difficult. He walked briskly through the streets heading east and, to her surprise, climbed the steeper of the two roads leading up on to The Rock.

The ugly building perched on the eastern extremity of The Rock belonged to Count Graumedel and was obviously the Chemer's destination.

He walked up to the guards standing at the bottom of the stairs. Using Yisyena's Voyanter skill, Anarya could hear them greet him as 'Master Corvek' from two hundred paces away.

Corvek! Well, that's a surprise. I've heard of him as the count's seneschal but I never knew he was gifted. Oh well, he's not likely to be much use to me. Too bad.

STEALTHER

When Baram returned to consciousness he was lying curled up on his left side and had a thundering headache. He tried to sit up but he couldn't move. His eyes were open and felt gritty. Bare stone walls meeting at a corner, the edge of the straw pallet he was lying on and the hinges of a massive door met his gaze. That was all he could see. His eyes couldn't move any more than the rest of him.

Why am I still alive? When he'd breathed that mist and felt himself fall he'd thought that was it and he would never wake up again. *They must want to question me.*

He didn't know how long he had been unconscious but he lay there for more than half a chime before there was a jangle and clatter of keys and the door swung open. Another mist, this time pale yellow, enveloped him. Soon afterwards he found he could move but he ached all over, his joints had stiffened and his movements were slow and creaky. When he blinked it felt as if he had sand under his eyelids.

He managed to sit up and saw the thin man who had trapped him standing in the doorway, flanked by two guards with drawn swords. There were more guards, he wasn't sure how many, in the passageway outside.

The man offered him a carafe. "It's water. You'll need it."

Baram splashed some of the water into his eyes to get relief from the scratching sensation then realised he was very thirsty and gulped the rest.

"Don't try to disappear again. You won't get past the guards and I can immobilise you again if I have to. And you really wouldn't like what that would do to you. Stand up and follow me."

A nod was all Baram could manage. Despite the water his throat was too dry to produce any more than a croaking sound. He pushed himself to his feet, using the movements to check on his weapons. It wasn't a surprise to find that he been completely disarmed. Even the stiletto in his left boot was gone. He shuffled out of the cell. Four guardsmen led the way, then the thin man, who Baram had decided must be a Chemer. Baram followed him and another four guardsmen brought up the rear.

The procession passed another five doors, probably more cells, before the corridor ended at the bottom of a staircase. They climbed three levels. By the time they reached the top Baram was on his hands and knees crawling up the steps, his muscles quivering from fatigue. The thin man let him rest for a short time, then led him along a corridor he recognised and stopped at the door of Count Graumedel's study.

"In," said the Chemer, when there was a muffled response to his knock on the door.

Baram pushed the door open, stepped into the room and stopped. A magnificent goldenwood and ebony desk occupied one corner of the room. The Count was sitting in the throne-like chair behind the desk where he would have a good view of the courtyard and garden through the window in the opposite wall. A very fine black and gold rug with Graumedel's beehive emblem lay in front of the desk. The other furnishings were high quality and elegant. The only incongruous thing in the room was a heavy wooden chair standing on the rug.

"Sit," said the thin man.

With no alternative offering itself, Baram sat down. One of the guardsmen fastened strong leather straps around his wrists and ankles, binding him to the arms and legs of the chair.

The Count flicked his hand in a gesture of dismissal and the guardsmen left. There was silence for a while as Graumedel studied Baram. He turned towards the Chemer and said, "So, Corvek, this is a Stealther. He doesn't look like much, does he?"

"No, my lord, but he did manage to gain entry to the mansion and we'd never have known he was here if the hounds hadn't reacted the way they did."

"True," said Graumedel, then he turned his attention to Baram and said, "Who is paying you to assassinate me?"

Baram started to speak but couldn't. Anxious to answer, he worked his jaw to produce saliva and lubricate his throat. He managed to croak, "No one." *What am I doing? I meant to keep quiet but I didn't even consider not answering. I just spoke without thinking.*

The Count turned to Corvek and said, "You did give him the truth potion, didn't you."

"Yes, my lord. It was in the water he drank after I released him from the binding."

"Interesting," said Graumedel, then turned his attention back to Baram. "You, whatever your name is, why do you want to kill me if nobody is paying you?"

"My name is Baram. I don't want to kill you." The words left Baram's mouth without his consent. It was an eerie sensation, as if he was imprisoned in his own head as an observer while someone else spoke for him. He had no choice except to answer any question, or implied question, put to him.

"Then why are you here?"

"Because you trapped me."

"My lord," said Corvek, "allow me to remind you of the effects of the truth potion. He will answer any question truthfully, but he will interpret it literally. He takes 'here' to mean this room rather than the mansion. You must be careful what you ask."

"Hmm. Why did you come to this building in stealth?"

"To gain entry."

"I see what you mean, Corvek. Let's try this." He looked at Baram. "What did you come to do?"

"To rob you."

Graumedel sat up straighter. "Did you succeed?"

"No."

"What were you hoping to steal?"

"Money, jewellery, whatever I could carry easily."

"Did you have an accomplice?"

"No."

"Then how did you get in?"

Baram described the scene at the stairs.

Graumedel nodded. "Can you think of anything else to ask him, Corvek?"

"No, my lord. Nothing comes to mind."

"In that case call the guards in and put him back in his cell — No, that would take too long, I might want to talk to him again before the potion wears off. Put him somewhere nearby, restrained and under guard. I want to think about this."

Baram was taken to a small, windowless room with plain, basic furniture. He decided it must be a servant's bedroom. There he was strapped to the bed and two of the guardsmen stayed in the room with him.

I wonder how long the effect of that potion lasts and what he wants to think about. He's not going to let me go. Why didn't he just kill me? A fine Stealther I've turned out to be. I hope Huler will forgive me.

These and similar thoughts chased themselves around his head for a while until he realised that he wasn't as frightened as he should be about the prospect of dying. *Huler must be protecting my emotions again. Does that mean there is something he wants me to do? Will I get the chance to do whatever it is?*

He was still wondering why the Count was keeping him alive when the door opened. Two more guards entered and the straps were unfastened. He was allowed to stand and stretch before being escorted back to Graumedel's study.

"I could have you killed, you know," said Graumedel once Baram was safely restrained again.

"I know."

"However, I could find a use for a Stealther. Would you be willing to work for me?"

"No."

Graumedel turned to Corvek. "That confirms the potion is still working. I wouldn't have believed any other answer."

"It should last for at least another half, my lord. Plenty of time for what you want."

The Count looked at Baram again. "How long can you conceal yourself?"

"Seven or eight chimes if it's continuous. Longer if I have a chance to recover between episodes. After that it becomes more difficult, I get weaker and it can take me up to a day to recover from the nausea and dizziness."

"Long enough," said Graumedel, looking at Corvek.

"Yes, my lord. That would be very useful."

"Tell me, Baram, do you know how I came to be Count of Carregis?"

"You succeeded your father when he died eleven years ago."

"Almost correct. But my father didn't just die. Do you

know what happened to him?"

"He was stabbed…"

"Yes!" Graumedel jumped to his feet. "He was killed at a banquet – by men he called friends. But they conspired against him and murdered him. That's why I have no friends. I don't trust anybody. I need a bodyguard to keep me safe from assassins. A Stealther would be ideal. Nobody would know he was there."

Baram hadn't been asked a question so he said nothing.

Graumedel subsided into his chair again. He too said nothing but he was breathing hard and his face was flushed. Gradually he recovered his composure and spoke in a more normal voice. "That's what I'm offering you, a chance to live. There are two choices in front of you. Either you agree to work for me or you die."

Baram sat silently wondering if the offer was genuine. It made sense but there was no guarantee of survival. All it would take was for Graumedel to become suspicious of him and he was dead. He wouldn't be able to continue as Huler's agent, but he wouldn't be able to do that dead either. *Lord Huler, give me guidance, please.*

"My lord, you have to ask him a question to get a response," said Corvek.

"Well, Baram, it's time to choose. What will it be?"

"I will serve you," said Baram, realising as he did so that he hadn't made a conscious decision. *Huler must be guiding me.*

"Can I trust you?" asked Graumedel.

"No."

"Still telling the truth – good. That's what I expected to hear. So we will take precautions. Corvek has another potion for you to drink."

Corvek released Baram's left hand from the strap and handed him a glass containing a small quantity of a greenish liquid. "This is an unusual potion, very rare because it's difficult to make. It is a poison, but it is harmless unless you break the promise you speak while drinking it. If you do break it you will die instantly. Do you understand?"

"Yes."

"In that case, take one mouthful, say 'I take oath on my life that I will serve His Excellency, Count Graumedel of

Carregis, obeying all his commands and that I will not use my Stealther skills or any weapon against him', then drink the rest."

Baram did as instructed. The potion was surprisingly palatable, reminding him of celery and honey. He didn't feel any different after drinking it.

"I expect to be addressed with respect at all times," said the Count. "Henceforth you will call me 'my lord'. Also, I do not want you to speak to me unless I ask for your opinion or you see a threat and need to bring it to my attention. Do you understand?"

"Yes, my lord."

"Good. That's settled. You can release him now, Corvek. Find him suitable livery and a room that's not too far away."

O

Baram was given a small windowless room on the lower floor of the mansion. The only illumination came from a lamp burning sweet oil and he was warned to light it only when needed. He would be given a supply of oil every two weeks. If he used it all up before the next issue he would have to do without.

One of the doors next to his room concealed a private staircase which opened in a cupboard on the upper level directly opposite Graumedel's study. Baram was surprised; none of the people who described the layout of the mansion had mentioned it. He wondered if there were more hidden stairs he didn't know about.

The room had been occupied by a guardsman sergeant who, when Baram was given the room, was forced to move into one of the barracks rooms. That wasn't popular with either the sergeant or his men. As a result his relationship with the guardsmen got off to a poor start.

The first few days were confusing. He didn't know where to go or what to do and the guardsmen weren't inclined to help him. Corvek was his main source of information and he developed the habit of visiting his office every morning to find out what the Count's plans for the day were.

When Graumedel did leave the mansion he was always accompanied by a squad of at least six guardsmen, usually more. Baram went with him on those excursions. It was awkward at first. He had to stay close to the Count without getting in the way of the guardsmen. They knew he was there somewhere but they couldn't see him and he had to do the avoiding.

When the Count didn't need him as an escort Baram was free to do whatever he wanted. He was forbidden to leave the parkland around the mansion but he spent time exploring it and the house.

Raifen will start wondering where I am if he doesn't hear from me. I wish I could find a way of getting a message to him.

One of the guardsmen seemed a little less unfriendly than the others so Baram approached him and asked, "I need to practice my weapon skills. Will you be my sparring partner?"

The man grinned. "You sure you want to do that? I won't go easy on you."

"I'm sure. I expect I can learn something from you."

Another of the guardsmen overheard this and laughed. "You'll learn all right. Didn't you know Fedic is the best swordsman in the guard."

"No, I didn't know that, but who better to learn from than the best?"

"Ninth chime tomorrow then," said Fedic. "Don't worry too much. I won't kill you, the Count wouldn't like it."

They used blunt practice swords but even those hurt and Baram ended up bruised and aching after the first couple of sessions. The guardsmen realised he was serious about wanting to improve and their attitude towards him changed. He was soon accepted by them and his ability to be invisible wasn't the barrier it had been.

He noticed, after a couple of weeks, that Corvek's demeanour changed from day to day. Mostly he was calm and efficient but he started every fourth day in a cheerful, excited mood. On those days he left the mansion in mid-morning and returned in late afternoon sullen and morose with a foul temper.

Baram found himself speculating about where Corvek went on these trips and what he did. *I wonder if he might take a message to Raifen for me. I'll have to be careful about approaching him.*

He positioned himself to meet Corvek near the top of the stairs one day when he expected him to be going out on one of his mysterious trips.

"You look cheerful. Where are you going?"

"To see Beashli," said Corvek, with a smile. Then his expression changed to a scowl before he added, "not that it's any of your business," and stalked off.

Beashli? Who's that? And why wasn't he willing to say more?

He was waiting in stealth for Corvek when he returned that afternoon, followed him into his office and stood quietly in a corner. Corvek slumped into a chair looking miserable. He stayed there, with his head in his hands, doing nothing until the Count entered the room, then he stood up.

"Are you satisfied?" asked Graumedel.

"Yes, my lord. Beashli is thriving."

"And she will stay that way as long as you continue to serve me well."

"But she's unhappy, my lord. She wants to see me more often than once a week."

"You can see her more often if you want…"

"Yes, please, my lord."

"… but you won't see your wife if you do. It's either your daughter or your wife every fourth day, no more. Do you want to change the arrangements or keep seeing them alternately?"

"No, don't change it, my lord," said Corvek with a sigh. "At least this way I get to see both of them sometimes."

"I've been summoned to a meeting with Duke Wurauf tomorrow afternoon. You will come with me."

"Yes, my lord."

"Arrange for my carriage to be ready at the noon chime. I'll want a full escort, and tell Baram I want him there as well."

Graumedel left. Corvek slumped back into his chair and hammered his fist on to the desk. "I hate him."

"Then why don't you use one of your potions on him?" asked Baram, allowing himself to become visible.

Corvek jumped to his feet. "Baram! Why are you spying on me? How long have you been listening?"

"Long enough to get some idea of what's going on. He's forcing you to work for him, isn't he?"

Corvek sagged back into his chair and said, "Yes. He kidnapped my wife and daughter about a year and a half ago. I don't know where he's got them. It's not at the house in Greenbank where I get to see them, I know that much. He promised they won't be harmed if I work as his seneschal and put my skills as a Chemer at his disposal."

"He hasn't made you drink that potion you gave me?"

"No. He's smart enough to know that it wouldn't work on me, I'd find a way to nullify it. I'm not boasting when I say there's probably only one Chemer in Carregis stronger than me."

"Why don't you give him some sort of potion? – No. Forget I said that. It's a stupid question. You've too much at stake to take the risk."

"Before you ask, I'm not going to give you the antidote to the obedience potion. That would be too risky."

"I understand, Corvek, and I wouldn't expect you to under the circumstances. There's one thing puzzling me. How is it that I can despise Graumedel and even imagine myself killing him when I'm forced to obey him."

"That's easy. I phrased the oath you took carefully. You can't use your Stealther skills to harm him but it doesn't prevent you plotting against him. Who knows, you might think of something we could do."

"Perhaps there is something. You go by yourself to meet your family, don't you. Would you take a message for me next time you go out?"

"I…"

"I promise I won't take risks with the lives of your family."

"In that case, yes, I will. If it will help."

"Honestly, I don't know if it will, but it's worth a try.

The next time Corvek visited his family he carried with him a message addressed to Raifen explaining what had happened, and asking him to try to find Corvek's family.

○

Baram kept one hand on the sergeant's belt to let him know he was there. It wasn't ideal, but it was the only way he had found to accompany Graumedel's escort without the risk of them falling over him and revealing his presence.

It wasn't a long journey to Duke Wurauf's mansion. His estate was next to Graumedel's and only a narrow belt of trees separated the two. The Duke's residence was a much older and more attractive building than Graumedel's grim-looking fortress. It sat on the edge of an artificial lake, with a carefully maintained lawn and formal gardens on the side away from the water, and spoke eloquently of the power and prestige of the Dukes of Carrh.

Baram followed the Count as he was escorted through the corridors of the mansion to Duke Wurauf's study. He just managed to slip into the room before the door was firmly closed leaving Corvek, the sergeant and the rest of the escort outside.

"Your Grace," said Graumedel, bowing to the Duke.

Wurauf was slumped in his chair gasping for breath. He waved at the other man in the room and wheezed, "Jynder will…"

"Unfortunately," said Jynder, stepping forward from his position behind the Duke's chair, "his Grace is having a bad day. He has asked me to speak on his behalf."

"I understand."

"It is well known that His Grace is a member, indeed the leading member, of the Three."

Graumedel nodded in agreement.

"Do you know who the other members of the Three are?" asked Jynder.

Graumedel shook his head. "I have heard speculation that Duke Kuranesh of Voro or Latisec of Alrem may be among them, but I find it difficult to see either of them as serious possibilities."

There was a strange sound from Wurauf and it took Baram a while to realise that he was laughing between wheezes.

"You are quite right in dismissing them from consideration. They may well be competent enough in their duchies, although that is debateable in the case of Kuranesh. Neither of them have the stature, the influence required to rule the country." said Jynder. "Everyone knows that the king is a figurehead and that the Three are the real rulers of Carrhen. However, few know the identity of any but the spokesman for the Three."

"I am aware of this," said Graumedel.

"Of course you are," said Jynder with a knowing smile. "I assume you would be interested in knowing who the others are."

Graumedel nodded.

"In that case I'll tell you that two of the Three, and possibly a third, are present in this room."

"But there are only three people here."

"That's right," said Jynder. "We are inviting you to join us."

"Us?" said Graumedel. "You mean you're…"

"One of the Three? Yes."

"I trust Jynder," wheezed Wurauf. He started coughing and waved at Jynder to carry on.

"I have been working with His Grace for about two years. He invited me to join the Three seven months ago. You may not know that the Three have in fact numbered anywhere from two to six over the years since the three members of the original Council of Regents for His Majesty Duvereant II were appointed."

Baram listened to the conversation, fascinated by the insight he was getting into the politics of the kingdom.

"At the time His Grace invited me to join them the Three had actually been only two for several years. Now that Hirgessa has died and brought us back down to two we would like you to take her place."

"Hirgessa? The lawyer?"

"Yes, she was one of us."

"I'd never have guessed."

"I'm not well," said Wurauf. "Haven't been for years. I'll be lucky to last much more than another year or two."

"We have discussed this at length," said Jynder. "I'm a commoner. I can't become the voice of the Three. Nobody would believe it. You, on the other hand, are a noble. Nobody would be surprised if you were suddenly revealed as one of us."

"I'm flattered and honoured that you've chosen me," said Graumedel.

Wurauf snorted, and said between gasps, "Don't try to fool me. All you're thinking about is what you can get out of it. You're just as greedy for power as we are."

"You see, my dear Count, we are realists," said Jynder.

"Power is all that matters, even if it has to be exercised in secret. You are going to join us, aren't you?"

Graumedel nodded. "Yes, of course I will."

"Thought so," said Wurauf, before another coughing fit shook him.

"I have a suggestion, your Grace. One of my party, a valuable member of my staff, is a Chemer. He may be able to brew a potion to help your breathing."

"Tried Chemers before. No good," wheezed Wurauf.

"He is very powerful, your Grace. It would be worth trying him."

"Bring him in."

Jynder bent over Wurauf while Graumedel opened the door and called Corvek into the room.

Baram had to move to avoid him and stumbled over a pile of scrolls. He saw Jynder's head jerk up to look around at the sound. *Hope he's not suspicious.*

The sound was repeated as Corvek kicked some scrolls and staggered.

Did he do that deliberately? Quick thinking if he did.

"I understand you are a Chemer," said Jynder to Corvek."How strong are you?

"Probably the second strongest in Carregis. Praukel is the only one I know who is stronger."

"Are you a friend of Praukel?" asked Wurauf.

"No."

"Good. I hate him and he hates me. Wouldn't trust a friend of his." After this speech Wurauf sagged back in his chair gasping for breath.

"Can you do anything for Duke Wurauf?" asked Graumedel.

"I can try. But I must examine his chest. Please leave."

Baram slipped out of the door behind Graumedel before Jynder had a chance to close it. He went to his usual position behind the sergeant and took hold of his belt. The man twitched then nodded. Baram hoped that meant the sergeant was aware of his presence.

"Come again next week," said Jynder as Graumedel settled himself in his carriage. "We have much to talk about."

O

"Your Chemer's potion has worked wonders," said Wurauf. "It has a foul taste that I must endure three times a day but I can now breathe more easily. I still get breathless at times but it's nothing like it was before. What's more, I can enjoy a good wine without fear of choking."

"I am pleased to hear it, your Grace."

"Help me up, Jynder. We must go. His Majesty is expecting us."

Baram trailed behind as they walked through the magnificence of Wurauf's mansion, his eyes flicking from a piece of statuary, to an array of antique daggers and swords, to a portrait, to a display cabinet containing three delicate pieces of enamelled porcelain, to a tapestry. He was overwhelmed by the artistry on display.

"Look," said Wurauf, stopping in front of a display of armour. "That gorget is my latest acquisition. I now have every piece of armour made for Fereathlin IV which is known to survive."

"It is in amazingly good condition," said Graumedel, "considering it must be a hundred and fifty years old."

"A hundred and sixty-one," said Wurauf. "It's listed in the records of the royal armoury as being made by an apprentice called Huratiel."

"I've heard of him," said Graumedel.

"I'm sure you have," said Wurauf. "He's probably the most famous weaponsmith in history. I have three other pieces by him. Now that my collection of Fereathlin's armour is complete I'm going to start collecting Huratiel's work."

"Your Grace," said Graumedel, "I am fortunate enough to have a hand-and-a-half sword made by Huratiel. May I gift it to you as a step towards repaying the honour you have given me?"

Wurauf smiled. "I was hoping you would. I knew you had it of course, just as I know the whereabouts of many of his other pieces."

Jynder coughed, attracting Wurauf's attention, and said, "Your Grace, we should proceed."

"True. Mustn't keep royalty waiting. It looks disrespectful."

Jynder made a noise which sounded derisive. He led them along another corridor to a gilded door where two guardsmen in the Duke's black and red were standing. He walked up to them and said, "Announce us."

The taller of the guardsmen opened the door, stepped through it and said, "Your Majesty, Wurauf, Duke of Carrh, Count Graumedel of Carregis and Master Jynder of the Duke's household seek admission to your presence."

"Bid them enter."

Baram followed them into the room. The king, Sulereath III, was sitting in a chair which, although lavishly decorated with the pelican emblem of the House of Ereath, wasn't quite a throne. For one thing it wasn't raised above the other chairs in the room, and they were all similarly embellished.

They bowed to the king. Baram did likewise although he remained in stealth and the king wouldn't have noticed if he hadn't. It just felt right. Despite knowing how powerless the king was he still felt that he should show him some respect. He had seen Sulereath at a distance in various parades and was curious to see him at close range. His aunt had always made his birthday a special day because it was the same day as the king's.

Apart from having the bright red hair and blue eyes of the House of Ereath, the king looked a lot like Baram. Same size and build, slightly longer nose and slightly bigger ears. His lips were pressed together and he looked sullen.

"I suppose this is about my marriage again."

"Yes, Your Majesty. It is important that you marry and ensure the succession. We would like to be able to announce your betrothal at your next birthday celebration."

"That is not the way I would choose to celebrate."

"We are truly sorry you feel that way," said Jynder. "We propose giving you a choice of consorts."

"A choice?" said the king, raising one eyebrow.

"There will be a banquet at Count Graumedel's residence next week."

Baram saw Graumedel twitch and look towards Jynder. Obviously this banquet was news to him.

"Several suitable young women from Carregis and the surrounding countryside will be invited," continued Jynder.

"You get to pick the one you want," said Wurauf.

"And if none of them please me?"

"Then more banquets will be arranged and eligible young

women from Voro or Getruva or somewhere will be invited until you find one you do like."

"Or," said Wurauf, "if you don't choose one before your birthday we'll pick one for you. After all you don't have to like her, all you have to do is bed her and ensure that the House of Ereath continues."

"So that you can have another puppet to play with," said Sulereath.

"Don't feel bitter, Your Majesty," said Jynder. "Look at it this way, the most beautiful women in the kingdom will spread their legs for you for the opportunity to call themselves queen. You can have as many of them as you want and marry the first one to get pregnant."

"I could curse my ancestors back to my great-grandfather for being weak enough to sign away the crown's authority. I will *not* choose a consort. I would rather let my House die out than submit any child of mine to the sort of domination I have experienced. As my namesake Sulereath I said when he set out to unite the five duchies, 'A struggle against odds is the way a man proves himself'. My struggle is taking the kingdom back from the Three, or dying in the attempt."

"Then we will put someone in your bed who you cannot resist," said Jynder. "Do we have your permission to leave your presence?"

"As if you need my permission. Go!"

Baram's head was spinning as he followed the others from the room. He had known that the Three ruled, but he thought it was with the agreement of the king. This display of power shocked him.

Back in his study Wurauf lowered himself carefully into the chair and said, "Why has he suddenly become intransigent?"

"He's not normally like that?" asked Graumedel.

"No," said Jynder. "He usually accepts whatever we suggest, although he has always been resistant to any suggestion that he should marry. We don't know why. He has lived a very isolated life and hasn't had an opportunity to get to know women. He may be frightened of the unfamiliar, or he may prefer men. As far as we know he's a virgin."

"Where did he get that quotation from Sulereath I?" said Graumedel. "The only place I've come across it is in *The*

History of the Unification by – by – oh, what's his name?"

"Dezzian."

"That's him."

"Right," said Wurauf. "Find out who gave him that to read and let him feed the ravens. It's given him ideas."

"Let's carry on with the banquets. You never know, he might fall madly in love."

"Thanks for telling me about the banquet next week," said Graumedel. "It's really going to take some organising. Fortunately, Corvek is good at his job."

"He's also a good Chemer," said Wurauf. "I'm sure he could brew a potion that would make sure Sulereath falls in love with whoever we choose."

"I once asked him why love potions aren't commoner," said Graumedel. "He told me there's no such thing. He said that what are usually called 'love' potions would be better described as 'lust' potions and their effects are transient."

"That wouldn't matter," said Jynder. "As long as the effect lasts long enough for him to get an heir on somebody. Still, let's hold back on the potion until we see what happens at the banquets."

"We will meet again next week, Graumedel."

"Yes, your Grace. I shall look forward to it."

O

Back at his own residence Graumedel asked Baram, "Were you at the audience with the king?"

"Yes, my lord."

"You will not speak of it to any living person except me. Do you understand?"

"Yes, my lord."

"I think you need not come with me when I visit the Duke. I am sure we will discuss other things that you do not need to know.

"As you wish, my lord."

VOYANTER

"I would like to come with you," said Yisyena.

"I'm not sure that would be a good idea," said Anarya, "Not many women go to the pits. That's why I'm going as Rhyanek."

"I should go too. If I am going to be an asset to our partnership I need to do more and learn my way around. Also, I have an idea which I think will be useful and this would provide an opportunity to try it out."

Anarya stopped rummaging through the wardrobe. "An idea? I hope it's as good as the one about the newsmongers. Tell me."

"If you borrow my talent we should be able to hear each other talking even if we are separated and without speaking above a whisper. That would give us the opportunity to coordinate our activities and, if necessary, change our plans without having to meet."

"You know, that might work," said Anarya after a moment's thought. "It would certainly be useful. Let's give it a try. You'll need to dress for the pits. What have we got that'll fit you?"

A shabby knitted shawl over a rather tight blouse and waistcoat, a slightly crumpled ankle length brown skirt and scuffed leather boots produced an appearance that Anarya felt would let Yisyena blend in at the pits. Her own outfit was a plain linen shirt and needlecord trousers topped off with a sleeveless jerkin. The embroidery on the facings of the jerkin was worn and had loose ends showing in some places. She was confident they could pass as a couple from the edge of the Dip.

The last thing she did before they left was absorb Yisyena's skill. It was something she relished doing because it let her experience Yisyena's love for her during the moment she felt she was in two bodies. She hugged Yisyena and said, "I love you too."

O

"Anra my love, can you hear me?"

"Yes, as clearly as if I was standing next to you."

"Good. I was speaking so quietly that you would not have heard me if you had been next to me. Did you speak aloud?"

"I did, but I'm not now. This is barely a whisper," said Anarya.

"It seems my idea works."

"It does. I must admit I was sceptical, but you were right. Where are you?"

"In the street opposite the side gate. I am far enough back that the guard will not be able to see me."

"I can see the main gate from where I am. Now we stay here until Nasuren appears. The waiting is the unexciting part of a surveillance job."

"The contract offerer said he goes out at about the seventeenth chime so we should not have long to wait."

Yisa was right. Talking like this is great. It lets us cover both gates and we can stay in touch.

The main gate opened at the expected time. A man stepped out into the street and nodded to the guards before setting off westwards. He fitted the description of Nasuren – about forty, short, clean-shaven with thinning hair worn in a short pigtail and limping slightly because his left knee was stiff.

Anarya examined Nasuren with her Oversight. No aura. *Good,* she thought, *no magic to confuse me. This'll be easy.*

Their quarry headed towards the Dip. They could follow him easily and at a safe distance thanks to their Voyanter skills.

"I thought as much," said Anarya when he turned into Osterc Lane. "Three of the pits are along here, including Stinky's. That's the most prestigious of them and I expect that's where he's going. It's not the biggest one but it attracts the owners of the most ferocious animals. Winning there can make a beast very valuable."

Anarya sighed when Nasuren's destination was confirmed. She didn't care to see animals starved and goaded into fighting each other. Her preference was for the arena, although even that had palled a bit since Caseir had retired. At least professional arena fighters had chosen to be there and take the risks involved.

○

The way the doorman at Stinky's treated Nasuren suggested he was a regular customer. He was allowed through the narrow door without delay. Anarya and Yisyena were stopped. "Ain't seen you here before," the doorman said.

"Been here before but not for a while," said Anarya.

"Two bits, each, or three if you want a seat," said the doorman, "and y' gotta show y' got enough to cover at least one house bet, that's two bits minimum."

"Since when?" said Anarya. "Not showing what I've got." She reached into her pouch, identified coins by touch, put five bits into the doorman's hand saying, "We'll take one seat." She concentrated on her ability to blend into her surroundings.

It must have worked. The doorman rubbed his chin, producing a rasping sound from the stubble. He studied her for a moment then handed her a wooden token. "For y'r seat. In y' go."

They started up the creaky stairs towards the sound of the crowd. Anarya handed Yisyena the token and muttered, confident that she would hear her, "He might have a seat, so you take that. Go left at the top. I'll go the other way in case he likes standing."

It was crowded at the top of the stairs. Anarya pushed her way through the throng and looked around. The pit itself was at ground level with the spectator's gallery looking down into it. The seats were at the far end of the oval. She saw Yisyena making her way towards the seats but couldn't spot Nasuren.

"Have you got him?" she asked.

"Yes. He is going to the seats."

"I'll go around the other side and get as close as I can."

The crowd was starting to get raucous, stamping their feet and shouting for action. She looked down into the pit where three men were raking the sawdust flat. There was no sign of the animals or their handlers yet.

Some of the spectators were already half drunk. There was a faint aroma of ganj in the air. It combined with the smells of sweat, sour beer and animal dung to make Stinky's live up to its name.

Anarya saw Nasuren. He claimed a seat in the second row and started a conversation with the man in the next seat. She carried on making her way around the gallery trying to get as close as she could to the seats. A man wearing the brown sash of a house approved bet-taker stopped her.

"Bet on the first fight?" he said.

There was a surge of noise from the crowd as the doors at pit level opened. He repeated his question.

"No," said Anarya. "Don't know these beasts. Not betting on this one."

"Take a look at them. Give you three to one on the green."

She looked into the pit. Two men were straining to hold back big lizards who were tasting the air with their forked tongues and hissing at each other. One of them was all green. It was a little smaller than its opponent, which was muddy brown with a yellowish stripe along its back.

"Like I said, don't know these beasts. No bet."

"Green lost first fight then won four in a row, last two were kills. Stripy's won all eight fights, with three kills. Three to one on green for a win, five to one for a kill. Stripy's at evens, win or kill."

Anarya looked across the gallery to where Nasuren was deep in conversation with a well-dressed man who looked familiar. The bet-taker was stopping her hearing what was being said

"I'll take green for a bit," she said, anxious to get rid of the man.

"House bet. Got to be at least two bits."

"Two then."

"Good man." The bet-taker handed her a token marked with her bet then walked off to accost someone else.

Anarya carried on round the gallery, pushing her way between the people in the standing area. It was a little less crowded towards the seating section and she found a relatively quiet spot near the back where the borrowed Voyanter skill let her hear what Nasuren was saying.

"… not good enough. You can do better than that. I expect to learn more about what Graumedel's planning next week, or he'll be hearing about…"

The crowd roared. The lizards had been released. They lunged at each other. The bigger animal tried to get a grip on the green's throat but both were wearing spiked collars to prevent such an easy kill. It bellowed in pain then tried to heave itself on top of the smaller animal. The green twisted around and raked a hind leg across its opponent's belly. Stripy bellowed again. The sound encouraged the crowd and the noise level soared.

Anarya ignored the events in the pit. She watched Nasuren and the familiar looking man he was talking to. *I know why I recognise him.* The Oversight showed her a shimmering gold aura. *That's Corvek, Count Graumedel's seneschal. Why is Nasuren interested in him?* She could barely hear over the din. *Hope Yisa can hear him better than I can.*

She turned back to the pit when there was a loud groan mixed with cheers and applause from the spectators. Stripy was bleeding from several gashes in its sides and belly. However, it had gutted its opponent. The green's tail was still twitching but the fight was over, another kill for Stripy. Two bits lost.

The spectators got noisier and more drunk with every fight. The place got hotter. Anarya was sweating, contributing to the stink. More people pushed their way in, jostling her and making it even more difficult to hear anything. Nasuren talked to a succession of different people. She did manage to hear a few scraps of each conversation, but that was all.

Between fights the bet-taker shoved his way round the gallery to corner Anarya and get her to place another bet. He took other bets on the way but she thought he had picked her out as an easy target. He talked and talked at her giving her little choice but to bet if she wanted to have any chance of overhearing Nasuren. She picked the wrong animal every time. *This isn't going well,* she thought. *If I keep losing I'll have spent all the contract fee by morning, and I haven't even got it yet.*

It wasn't until the fifth fight that Nasuren showed any interest in the action. He called a bet-taker over. Money changed hands but Anarya couldn't tell which animal he was betting on. This fight was different. It was a mêlée. Four lizards of a different breed were released into the pit at the same time. Smaller and faster than the others had been, they prowled around the pit hissing furiously. Unlike the bigger animals in the earlier fights they didn't get involved in a brawling mass. Instead one of them would suddenly dash at one of the others, take a quick bite, then disengage.

Soon one of the lizards was bleeding from a mangled hind

leg and limping badly. Its handler got a loop of rope around its neck and pulled it from the fight. Two of the others ganged up on the third and it too was removed by its handler.

The fight distracted Anarya. Her lizard was still in the fight. She had picked one flecked with light grey splotches on black because it was the most attractive. It looked in better condition than its remaining opponent. She forgot about Nasuren, who she couldn't really overhear anyway, and watched the action in the pit, getting more and more excited.

She realised the atmosphere of the pit was getting to her. It was something she had never been aware of until Yisyena noticed it. The 'blending in' worked both ways and she could be affected by her surroundings. A noisy tavern where many of the customers were drunk could make her feel drunk too, even if she hadn't had much to drink herself.

The enthusiasm of the spectators enveloped her and she started cheering for the smaller of the two lizards. If it won she would recoup most of her losses. *Come on, little fella. Get him! Yes! Well done.* A shout of triumph erupted from her as the bigger animal turned and ran.

"Got lucky, didn't you," said the bet-taker when he gave Anarya her winnings. "What about the next fight? Which do you fancy?"

Just then Anarya saw Nasuren stand up and leave. "No more tonight. I'm off," she said, yawning.

"Up to you. There's four more fights. If you change your mind I'll give you good odds."

"No, I've had enough for one night. I'm off."

She escaped from the bet-taker and wasn't far behind Nasuren when he walked out into the night.

O

"Can you hear me, Yisa?"

"Yes, my love."

"He's leaving."

"I know. I heard him say goodbye to his companions, anticipated him leaving and I am on the stairs a little ahead of him."

"Good. I'll meet you outside. Did you manage to overhear him?"

"Oh yes, quite easily. Did you not?"

"Hardly anything. It was too noisy for me during the fights and between them I kept getting pestered to place bets."

"Did you win?"

"No, curse it. Overall I lost seven and a half bits."

"I did better," said Yisyena. "I won all but one of my wagers and made thirty-three bits."

"Oh! Well done."

Anarya caught up with Yisyena two streets away from Stinky's and wrapped her arms around her. "I'm glad we're together again. We'd be losing touch soon. I can't be a Voyanter for much longer, it's starting to fade."

"Release it. I do not want you to make yourself ill again. I can follow him, he is only one street ahead of us."

"What did you hear?" asked Anarya.

"He seemed to be gathering information about various people and appeared to be blackmailing his informants."

"Yes, I heard him talk to Count Graumedel's seneschal about him."

"He also questioned someone about that shipping company, Beghroth, and several other names I do not know."

Anarya identified the other names she gave as being a judge, two other wealthy merchants and a woman who owned a bank. "I wonder why is he interested in all these people?"

"He has turned uphill," said Yisyena. "That is not the way to his employer"s house."

They followed him to a gate in the fence surrounding Duke Wurauf"s estate. The guard waved him through without hesitation.

"I don't understand," said Anarya.

"I believe he must be a spy for the Duke," said Yisyena. "He has gone straight to the mansion and he was admitted as if he was expected."

"We can't tell our client that. She'd tell her employer and he's bound to dismiss him. The Duke won't be happy if his spy is exposed and he might find out that we're responsible. The last thing we want to do is get embroiled in the affairs of the Three."

"I think, my love, that we do not tell her he is a spy, just that he went to Stinky's. It is the truth, although not all of it."

STEALTHER

"Stay near me once the guests start arriving," said Count Graumedel to Baram before the banquet. "Huler knows I don't trust any of them."

"My lord, I need more information about what to expect. I have never experienced a formal banquet."

"Huh," grunted the Count. "You'd better talk to Corvek. He'll tell you all about it."

"Yes, my lord."

Baram set off to find Corvek. The mansion was bustling with activity; he had never seen it so busy. He eventually found Corvek in the pantry, giving instructions to some of the servants. The seneschal was already dressed for the occasion in a short, sleeveless, rust-coloured velvet gown over a green doublet. He looked harassed.

"Well, what is it?" asked Corvek when he had dismissed the servants.

"His Excellency wants you to tell me what will happen at the banquet so that I can be in the right places at the right times."

Corvek clucked his tongue and sighed. "As if I didn't have enough to worry about already. I've got things to do and check on. You'd better come with me. We can talk as we go."

"How many are expected?" asked Baram.

"Ninety-four."

Baram winced. "I can't stay close to him with that many milling around, they'll find me by bumping into me."

"It won't be that bad. His Excellency will greet the guests at the top of the stairs then they'll be escorted to the Hall of Portraits where they'll be supplied with wine." Corvek scowled. "The greedy amongst them will demand Miros and start on the road to a drunken stupor."

"So far it doesn't sound as if the Count is at risk."

"No, you fools. Not there! Those go in the west anteroom." Corvek berated a couple of servants struggling along the corridor with great bundles of flowers. "Sorry, Baram, sometimes it seems as if nobody can do anything right without my supervision. What were we saying?

"About the risk to His Excellency."

"Oh, yes! You'll need to watch him during the greetings. The last time anyone was murdered at a banquet it happened when she was greeting her guests. The weapon was a poisoned needle concealed in the killer's glove. One stab, when they touched hands, was sufficient."

"I couldn't stop that sort of thing," said Baram.

"No, but it's not likely to happen now anyway. It was eighteen or nineteen years ago and that incident resulted in a change of practice. The greetings no longer involve contact of any sort, but you should be there anyway."

They looked into the entrance hall at the top of the stairs. Two full squads of guardsmen, resplendent in their black uniforms with gold trim and the golden embroidery of their beehive badges were waiting there. Corvek nodded to the sergeant in charge who came over to confirm that they were ready for the guests.

"Have you got a chair ready?" Corvek asked the sergeant. "Musart Erlosh is coming and he'll need to be carried up."

"Ready and waiting at the bottom of the stairs," said the sergeant, "with four of my strongest available to carry it."

"Good," said Corvek and led Baram back into the corridor.

"The guests will stay in the Hall of Portraits until His Excellency has escorted the king to the dining room. Once they are seated at the great table the rest of the guests will be admitted and the meal will be served. There will be fourteen courses."

"Fourteen! How can anybody eat that much?"

"They're all quite small."

"I should hope so."

"You need to be near the Count during the meal. The greatest risk to him is probably from the transients."

Baram was shocked. As Graumedel's father had been killed at a banquet, he hadn't expected the Count to observe the tradition of the transient guest. The seventh place at the great table would be occupied by a different person for each course. Supposedly the idea was to allow people to say they had shared a meal with whoever the banquet was intended to honour. The transients could be chosen by lot or at the whim of the principal guest. Knowing why the banquet was being held, Baram suspected the transients at this meal would all be eligible young women being paraded in front of the king.

"His Excellency hates the custom," said Corvek. "Unfortunately, it can't be avoided and he will be in a foul mood until it's all over."

"And after the meal?" asked Baram.

"They'll go back to the Hall of Portraits, which should have been cleared during the meal. There will only be two chairs left, for the king and the Count. The guests will mingle and some of them will try to have words with the Count. There is a tradition that any interview with the host or principal guest will last no longer than a twelfth. It's the ones that want to go on longer that are the ones you need to watch – Oh! Those idiots." Corvek dashed into the kitchens leaving Baram standing.

What's upset him? I didn't see anything wrong.

O

The guests started arriving, the lower ranking first. Jynder was among them, one of the early arrivals. *Of course,* thought Baram, *he's just a well-off commoner as far as anyone knows.* About halfway through the arrivals two priests of Huler appeared. Raifen was one of them, to Baram's surprise. He was wearing a red robe stiff with gold thread embroidery. Around his neck was a collar of golden links from which an enamelled sun dangled, and he had dyed his beard red. *I must find a way to talk to him.*

There were no other surprises during the greetings, nor during the meal. Soup was followed by shellfish, then a cheese tart, a sour salad with chilli dressing, slivers of crisp bacon with quail eggs, and so on, and on. Baram lost track of the dishes, many of which he would have liked to try.

He was right about the transient guests. All, except one, were young women. The exception being Veluth who joined the great table for the sixth course. He was questioned by the king and Graumedel on the state of his health, congratulated on his recovery from the beating and commiserated with for his wife's death.

The women were all attractive. Many of them were dressed to the extreme edge of fashion, a couple of them almost scandalously so. The king was polite to them all but showed no real interest.

Jynder was at a distant table and Baram couldn't see him well enough to gauge his reaction.

After the meal Baram took his place between and slightly behind the chairs occupied by Graumedel and the king. He was close enough to hear all the conversations although they were conducted in quiet voices. While his main attention was on those who approached the Count, he also listened with interest to the king's conversations.

One of those was with Raifen and another priest, a vigorous-looking man in late middle age wearing a heavy gold pectoral ornament in the shape of a sun disc.

"Your Majesty, it is a rare privilege to be able to speak to you," said the other priest. "I am Rupesc. I have the honour to be the head of the Brotherhood."

Baram blinked in surprise. This was the highest ranking priest in the temple.

"It is a pleasure to meet you, Rupesc," said the king. "I hope you may be able to answer a question for me."

"I will, if I can."

"Last week I was reading about my ancestor Linereath II. A loose piece of paper was wrapped up in the scroll. It must have been there since the scroll was last read, or possibly since it was written. It said that the temple uses Stealthers to avenge injustices. Is this true?"

"If the law cannot act then the temple may, your Majesty," said Rupesc after a thoughtful pause.

"In that case, your Eminence, may I appeal against the injustice practised by the Three. They have usurped control of Carrhen from my family."

"As I understand it, your Majesty, the Three were originally the regents for your great-grandfather Duvereath II. When he was old enough he effectively abdicated, signing a document which kept them in power. There is no injustice there."

"There is! It was not his choice. He was forced to sign that document, and my grandfather and father were forced to cede even more power until I cannot even sneeze without permission."

"What would you have the temple do?" asked Rupesc.

"Kill the Three and let the House of Ereath rule again."

Rupesc looked around. "We cannot speak any longer, your Majesty, others are waiting. I can promise you that the Brotherhood will consider the matter." He bowed and turned away.

Interesting, thought Baram. Then his attention was caught by two men starting an argument on the other side of the room. It quickly degenerated from name-calling to pushing and wrestling. He stepped in front of Graumedel in time to intercept a man pulling a stiletto from a pocket in his cape. *That fracas was a diversion. Thought it might be.* The knife wielder tripped over Baram's leg, falling forward and embedding the knife in the polished floorboards. The guardsman on the other side of the Count's chair gasped. He jumped on the fallen assailant, calling for help.

Baram was sure the guardsman and his colleagues had the would-be assassin under control. He stayed in stealth in case any others who hadn't revealed themselves were involved.

Graumedel and the king were hustled away from the Hall of Portraits by guardsmen.

Corvek appeared at the door and said, "Honoured guests. Count Graumedel, regrets this disturbance and asks that you leave as quickly as possible."

The guests sorted themselves out and prepared to leave, discussing the events with a mixture of excitement, horror and disbelief. Their departures were less organised than their arrivals had been and they went in whatever order their coaches and sedans appeared.

Baram took the opportunity to get next to Raifen and mutter, "I'm here."

Raifen didn't jump or act surprised. He pulled a small scroll from his waistband and held it in a position where Baram could take it without anyone noticing. Then he and Rupesc started walking down the stairs.

In the aftermath he found, as he had hoped, that the scroll was an answer to his message. It told him where Corvek's family were being held.

CHEMER

"To Rhyanek the Quaestor, Greetings.

I have a task which requires skill and discretion. You have been recommended to me by someone whose opinion I respect and I would be pleased to discuss my requirements with you. Should you wish to know more you may visit me at any time in the next three days," said Anarya, reading the latest message aloud.

"And it's signed, Praukel!

"It was his housekeeper who set us to follow Nasuren," said Yisyena.

"It was. I wonder what he wants."

"There is but one way to find out."

"Yes," said Anarya, with a smile, reaching out to touch Yisyena's cheek. "Rhyanek had better go and see him."

O

"You're younger than I expected," said Praukel.

"I'm sorry to disappoint you," said Anarya, more calmly than she felt. Before coming to the meeting she had absorbed a Feeler's skills. They told her that Praukel was experiencing a mixture of antagonism and resentment directed at her. *Why? We've never had any dealings with him before.*

She was also surprised to see the bright golden aura of an exceptionally strong Chemer around him, even brighter than Corvek's. She had heard of him as one of the richest men in Carregis but had never heard that he was a magic user of any sort.

"I'm not disappointed," he said, "it's just a little unexpected. My housekeeper tells me you did a good job for her. Please sit."

Anarya settled into a comfortable leather upholstered chair and accepted a glass of wine from the servant who had ushered her into Praukel's study. She raised her glass towards Praukel in thanks, took a sip and smiled. It wasn't the best wine, she hadn't expected it to be, however it was perfectly acceptable.

Praukel waited until the servant left the room before saying, "I understand you are the source of the information that set my housekeeper so strongly against my secretary that she asked for his dismissal."

Anarya said nothing. *He's really angry, but if it's me he's angry with why would he give me wine?*

"When you told her that Nasuren's weekly excursions took him to the pits she assumed he was gambling. She insisted, quite correctly, that I could not trust a gambler as my personal secretary. However, you know what he was really doing, don't you?"

"Yes, he was gathering information from various people." She was shocked by what she was saying but couldn't stop. "I think he's a spy for Duke Wurauf."

"Not just a spy but his spymaster," said Praukel. "Oh, by the way, don't be surprised. You have no choice but to answer my questions. There was a drop of my favourite truth potion in your glass. I trust it did not spoil the wine."

"No, it didn't," said Anarya, helplessly answering the implied question.

"Good. It's a pity my housekeeper grew suspicious. I knew Nasuren was a spy. He told me so himself after drinking that same potion and then promptly forgot he had done so, as you will forget this conversation. It's very convenient for me to get the same information Wurauf does and to feed him disinformation through Nasuren."

"Why?" asked Anarya.

"Because Wurauf and I hate each other. We have for years. Your meddling, although it wasn't intentional, has inconvenienced me. It forced me to use potions to change my housekeeper's mind about Nasuren. I said you would forget this conversation. By the time the truth potion wears off you will also forget all about Nasuren. You may leave now."

Anarya had held a Chemer's skills before without being able to do much with them. *Will his strength make a difference?* She reached out to absorb his talent before leaving the room. The characteristic sensation of a Chemer's mind, very precise and tidy, filled her while she shared bodies.

She looked at the wine glass. In the residue there was a faint golden glimmer. She studied it. *It's just very, very pure water with the Chemer's magic added. No fancy ingredients at all. No wonder it didn't have a taste. Can I do anything about it?*

She used the Oversight to look at herself. It was something she rarely did because it was disorientating and made her feel dizzy. The rainbow aura was stained with gold in her stomach and round her head.

She was puzzled. *Why am I looking at myself?*, she wondered. *What's that glow? Don't think that should be there. Whatever it is, I don't want it. How can I get rid of it?*

She imagined pulling mental fingers through the glimmer, trying to scrape it together into one place. As she teased it out of her head into her stomach she started remembering again. Indignation made her feel sick. *That's it*, she thought and forced herself to vomit. *People will think I'm drunk. Doesn't matter. That got rid of it. He's not going to force me to forget.*

FEELER

Anarya was scowling when she got home. She dumped her pack on the table with unnecessary force. It tipped over. Two oranges, a cabbage and five eggs spilled out. One of the eggs rolled off the table and smashed. She grabbed at the others and managed to prevent any more breakages.

"What is wrong, my love?" asked Yisyena.

"This," said Anarya, waving a folded sheet of buff parchment. "I picked it up at the newsmonger's. It was the only message for us."

"What is wrong with it?"

"It's sealed with Count Graumedel's beehive. Why should he be writing to us?"

"I wonder what have we done to attract his attention? Open it."

Anarya sat down beside Yisyena and hugged her. She broke the yellow wax of the seal, unfolded the parchment and read it aloud. "His Excellency, Count Graumedel, invites Rhyanek the quaestor to meet him at his residence at the eleventh chime on the third day of Jekleb to discuss a business opportunity."

"I really don't like this," said Anarya, passing the parchment to Yisyena. "What does he mean by a business opportunity?"

"I can only imagine he means to offer us a contract."

"I suppose so. But I wouldn't have thought we were prominent enough for him to notice us."

Yisyena reread the message and said, "This is phrased as an invitation but it is not. It is a summons."

"You're right," said Anarya, with a sigh. "I'd rather he'd never heard of us. He could make life very difficult. We really don't want to get involved with him but we can't afford to antagonise him by not going to the meeting."

"It might be profitable if we get a contract from him."

"Yes, but you've heard the gossip. You know how little people trust him. It could cost us in the long term if it gets about that we're working for him."

"Nevertheless Rhyanek must go to the meeting tomorrow."

"Yes, he must," said Anarya. Her stomach was churning at the prospect. "I think I'll borrow a Feeler's talent before I go. It might give me an insight into what he wants from Rhyanek. That's another thing that's bothering me. Don't you think it odd that the message was addressed to him? The Count's spies are supposed to be good but they can't be that good if they haven't worked out that Rhyanek is really me dressed as a man."

O

The guardsman at the foot of the stairs examined the invitation and made her wait until a tall man came to the top and beckoned her up. She recognised Corvek and thought. *He's a Chemer, isn't he. I'd better be careful about what I drink in case he tries dosing me with a potion of some sort like Praukel did. I think I might risk borrowing his talent even if it means losing the Feeler in the process.*

Anarya had taken care to dress well, with a dark green velveteen waistcoat over a spotless white linen shirt with a touch of lace at the cuffs and collar and black needlecord breeches tucked into half boots. Despite this the supercilious look Corvek gave her made her feel shabby.

He sniffed, and said, "I will take you to the Count. Be respectful, call him 'my lord', answer his questions and keep your opinions to yourself." He stalked off, obviously expecting her to follow.

One of the guardsmen fell in behind her and the small procession walked through the corridors to the Count's study. She caught glimpses into some of the rooms as they went and was awed by the sumptuous and tasteful quality of the furnishings.

Corvek tapped on a door, opened it a little without waiting for a response and said, "Rhyanek the quaestor, my lord."

The Count's profile, with its prominent hooked nose, shoulder length hair and neat pointed beard was familiar to her. It was portrayed on every half-bit coin. She was fairly sure she would have heard if he was a magic user of any kind but she used the Oversight to check for an aura anyway.

There was none.

He dismissed Corvek and the escort with a nod and studied her in silence for a few moments. Eventually he said, "I understand you are a Voyanter, Rhyanek."

Anarya said nothing. It suited her to have her talent misidentified. She certainly didn't want him to know what she really was.

"I have a task for a quaestor, particularly a Voyanter," he said, "and I hear from Keiret Beghroth that you and your partners are competent."

Ah, that's how he's heard of us. I just hope the job is as easy as the one we did for Beghroth. She inclined her head slightly and said, "We endeavour to give satisfaction, my lord."

"I want you to follow someone. Can you do that?"

"Yes, my lord."

"I want to know who he meets, what they talk about and everything he does for the next three months. Are you good enough for that?"

With the two of us sharing the job it should be possible, but I'd better play it safe, just in case. "My lord, I have to warn you that even the best Voyanter has limitations. For example, a privacy spell can make it impossible to overhear a conversation."

"I am well aware that there are limits to any magic user's talent. I employ several but at present I do not have a Voyanter on my staff. Prove to me you are good at what you do and I will have more tasks for you."

Turning down an offer of employment from the Count might not be good for our health. We can't risk doing a poor job, but I'm not too keen on the idea of this one leading to others and us ending up on his permanent staff. I suppose I could try to make us too expensive to use often. "For our exclusive services for three months we would ask for thirty dukals." *I hope he doesn't know that's more than double what we'd usually make.*

She was surprised when he didn't haggle.

"Who do you want us to follow, my lord?"

"Do you know Caseir?"

"The Unconquered? Yes, of course. I mean I've never met him but I was there for all of his last few fights."

"Then you will recognise him."

"Yes, my lord."

"Good. My information is that he is meeting someone at the House of Silken Delights in Hemeark at sunset five days from now. That would be a good place to start following him."

Anarya relaxed slightly, they were going to get out of working for Graumedel. "I am sorry, my lord but we can't do that. We don't work outside Carregis."

"You will this time, or you won't work inside Carregis again. Your arrangement with the newsmonger's guild is clever but it will not hold if I instruct the guildmasters to stop mentioning Rhyanek and Partners and to refuse to accept messages for you."

He can't do that! Anarya invoked the Feeler's talent. It let her experience the Count's emotions second-hand. A sensation of suppressed rage and gritted teeth was enough to let her realise the Count was angry at being refused. He meant what he said. *Yes, he can do it!* Her heart started hammering and there was a lump in her throat as she said, "You leave me no option, my lord. We will take your contract."

He grunted and smiled. The self-satisfied sensation she got from him made her squirm. *I don't like him and I don't trust him.*

"Your pardon, my lord, but if we are to be away from Carregis for long periods we must make arrangements for reporting to you. I will need a token. Something of yours that a Whisperer can use to contact you, but preferably nothing easily identifiable as yours."

"One of your partners is a Whisperer? I was not aware of that."

Anarya said nothing, hoping he would take that for agreement.

He rummaged in his desk and produced a small ebony rectangle. It looked like a vurlo tile, with a bird on one side and an animal on the other. The animal, as always, was a lion but Anarya didn't recognise the stylised bird with its long plumage, it wasn't the usual owl.

"Will that do?"

"Yes, my lord." She paused briefly. "There is one more

thing, my lord," said Anarya, swallowing hard. *I hope I can pull this off, otherwise this contract is going to break us.* "We will need travelling expenses on top of our fee."

The look he gave her, and the surge of annoyance she experienced through the Feeler's talent, made her quake. She almost retracted the request but she knew they couldn't rely on credit when travelling. *Holy Quarenna, aid me.* "We will be travelling for an unknown length of time, my lord. We will need money for lodgings, and we may have to hire horses."

He grunted. "I suppose so, but don't get greedy. Half the fee now, half at the end of the contract and, let's say ten dukals in advance for expenses." He scrawled something on a piece of parchment, rang a bell and gave the note to the guardsman who answered. "Give this to Corvek."

Anarya bowed and followed the guardsman to another room where Corvek was working at a desk.

Corvek looked up, took the parchment, clucked his tongue and told her to wait. The guardsman stayed with her while Corvek went into the next room. When he returned he handed her a purse which jingled nicely and said, "Here you are, my good man. Remember your duty to His Excellency," before dismissing her.

O

"At least he has been generous with payment," said Yisyena, when Anarya told her what had happened. "And the coins are a good mixture. Gold may be nice but smaller denominations are more useful for everyday use."

"I don't like being bullied," said Anarya.

"Nor do I. However, it is the nature of power that the powerful can do as they wish."

"I guess you would know about that."

"I do. *Cranil* can do almost anything they want. Learning to live at a lower rank has been about the hardest thing for me to do. I do not think I would have managed without you, my love."

Anarya reached out to lay her hand against Yisyena's cheek before rummaging in her pouch for the vurlo tile. "He gave me this too."

"Where did he get that?"

"He didn't say. Why?"

"That bird. It is called a tree-dancer. It is the emblem of the Neyen family."

"I've never heard of them."

"They are one of the great families of Sitrelk. He must have a very good relationship with them to be given that. I am very surprised to see it."

"I think we'll take the coach to Hemeark tomorrow. Hiring horses would be faster but we've got enough time and the coach is cheaper."

"It is fortunate that we do not have any outstanding contracts."

"Yes," agreed Anarya. "The Count would probably have insisted we cancelled any we had and that wouldn't have done our reputation any good."

TERROMANCER

"This must be halfway," said Anarya as the coach clattered across a bridge and pulled in to the inn on the outskirts of Harrsev.

"Is that all?" said Yisyena. "It feels as if we have been travelling forever. This coach is not very comfortable."

"That's an understatement. It doesn't seem to have any springs at all."

The door opened and the coachman looked in. "We'll be here for about a chime while we change horses. Plenty time for you to eat if you want to. Food's good and so is the ale. Tell the server you're on the Hemeark coach, give him my name, it's Dersic, and he'll ring a bell to warn you when we're ready to go again."

Anarya and Yisyena climbed down, stretched and looked around. The two-storey, timber built inn stood in the shade of a clump of trees. Looking back across the bridge they could see the monotonous farmland they had been travelling through for most of the day. Fields of grain with only slight variations in colour stretched as far as they could see. Ahead was a small town where two roads met and beyond it a suggestion of purple on the western horizon hinted at the hills to come.

On earlier stages of the trip the various coachmen had always described the food, drink or beds at their stopping places as good, with varying degrees of accuracy. They were pleasantly surprised to find that this one was telling the truth, the food was very good. After eating they went outside again hoping to stretch their legs before being cooped up again for another two or three chimes.

It wasn't long before the server rang a bell and called, "Coach for Hemeark! The Hemeark coach is ready to leave."

Anarya and Yisyena had got used to being the only passengers, they had had the coach to themselves until then so they were slightly surprised when someone else climbed aboard. He was a middle-aged man conservatively dressed in dark grey worsted with black frogging. There was little ornamentation on his clothes; only a touch of silver embroidery at his collar.

He bowed, but the effect was spoiled by him staggering as the coach lurched into motion. "Ladies, as we are to be travelling companions permit me to introduce myself. My name is Sontau, I am a stonemason."

"He's more than that," said Anarya under her breath, knowing that Yisyena would hear her. They were well practiced at using Yisyena's Voyanter skills to communicate quietly. "He's a Terromancer."

"What a useful skill for a stonemason. Sontau? Where have I heard that name before?"

"I've heard it too. Isn't that new statue of the king they put up outside the temple in the Great Square by Sontau."

When questioned, Sontau admitted to being the sculptor and they spent part of the journey chatting about statuary, and art in general.

At the next staging point another passenger joined the coach but otherwise the journey was unremarkable and every bit as uncomfortable as previously until mid-afternoon. Then they came to a stone bridge which carried the road over a wide river which was running very full. The road was blocked and half a dozen men were working at the base of one of the piers.

The coachman went to investigate then opened the door and told the passengers, "There was a big storm upriver yesterday. A large tree has been swept down and it's damaged some of the stonework of the bridge. It might be dangerous to take the coach across and we may have to go back to the last inn until repairs are finished."

"How long will that take?" asked the new passenger.

"The workmen don't know. They're not sure how much damage has been done."

"I'm in a hurry. Got important business in Rustem that can't wait."

"Sorry," said the coachman. "Nothing I can do about it."

"Perhaps I can," said Sontau as he climbed down from the coach. "I am a Terromancer, I will take a look and see if I can do anything.

Anarya murmured to Yisyena, "I'm going to borrow his

ability and watch him. I might learn something."

The violet aura of the Terromancer brought with it a feeling of strength, security and implacability. Anarya watched as Sontau crouched by the bridge and laid a hand on one of the stones. She followed his examination of the stonework as closely as she could. One of the facing stones was slightly out of alignment and he nudged it back into position. Then a crack in a keystone attracted his attention and she saw a shimmer of violet as he fused it back together again.

A quarter later Sontau straightened up with a grunt, massaged his back and said, "The bridge is secure. There was little damage and I have repaired what there was. If you will pardon me, I must rest now." He clambered back into the coach, wedged himself into a corner and promptly fell asleep.

Anarya renewed the Voyanter skills she had lost when she absorbed the Terromancer's. She muttered to Yisyena, "That was amazing. His touch was so delicate, almost as if he was persuading the stone to do what he wanted it to rather than forcing it. Terromancy is by far the best of the elemental skills for me. I can break stone down, even influence metal to some extent but I couldn't do anything like that."

"I remember you being a Terromancer once before, when you recovered that key someone dropped into a crack in the street. That was quite delicate."

"Not really. All I did was destroy a bit more of the cobbles to make the crack wider. Destruction is easy."

"I do not think I have ever seen you use the other elemental skills."

"Yes, you have. Sometimes I've borrowed Pyromancy from the blacksmith in the next street on my way home and used it to light the stove. It's easier than using flint and steel. I haven't used the other elemental skills for a long time. I remember telling you I'm a very poor Aquamancer and an even worse Aeromancer. It's pointless me even trying to use them."

O

On the last stage of the journey they had the coach to themselves again. The scent of apple blossom filled the air as the coach passed through the orchards surrounding Hemeark.

"This is pleasant," said Yisyena. "Despite being coerced into this journey I find I am enjoying seeing more of Carrhen. You were born here, were you not? Why did you leave?"

"Yes, I was. It's nice enough, but it's a boring little town with not much to recommend it. Everyone is obsessed with fruit growing. That's part of the reason I left."

"What is the other?"

"My mother kept trying to marry me off and I wasn't interested in any of the boys she pushed in my direction. They were all too – too earnest and unexciting. They would talk for hours on the harvest prospects, or the latest varieties of plums. Or the weather, always the damned weather, particularly at this time of year, forever terrified that a late frost would catch the blossom. The arena was much more exciting. I loved it and went to every event. I even saw Caseir fight there once, before he became famous. But the boys my mother wanted me to meet weren't interested in it. I eventually left when I was twenty-one. The place was so tedious I just couldn't stand it anymore."

"What did your parents think about you leaving?"

"My mother didn't like it. We fought a lot before I eventually left. She had this idea that I should be like all the other girls. She expected me to get married, have children and settle into family life with my own circle of friends who were just like each other. And that's not me."

"What about your father?"

"He died when I was three. I don't really remember him. I know my mother missed him terribly. That's why I stayed around for as long as I did, because I owed her something for bringing me up by herself."

"You have not visited her since you left?"

"No. And I'm not going to either. She'd be wanting me to come back to Hemeark and I don't want to get all tangled up with her emotional blackmail."

"Oh, Anra, my love. My mother was my friend and I am so sad to hear that the same was not true for you."

"Don't worry about it," said Anarya. "I couldn't have stayed anyway. I had this idea of becoming a quaestor and using my talent instead of concealing it. I couldn't have done that in Hemeark. There was only one quaestor there when I was growing up and he didn't have much to do. I had to go to the big city to find my dream."

"How could you afford to move to Carregis and start your own business?"

"I saved up. Most of the money came from my virginity sale."

"I do not understand."

"I sold my virginity at the House of Silken Delights shortly after my fifteenth name day. Did well out of it too."

"You were a whore?"

"Certainly not. That was the only time I have been paid for sex. It's like that for almost all the girls around here. It's a tradition. Yes, there are a few who carry on going to the House but for most of us it's just a step towards becoming an adult."

"Do the men not expect virginity when they are betrothed?"

Anarya looked round at Yisyena. "Why should they do that? It's none of their business what a woman does before she marries."

"Oh!"

"Now you're going to tell me it's different in Sitrelk."

"Yes, my love, it is. At least it is among the *cranil*. And since the middle ranks of society tend to copy the doings of the Twenty-three Families they place great store on celibacy for both sexes. I do not know much about the doings of the lowest classes."

"But you're not a virgin, Yisa."

"I was betrothed and it is considered acceptable, perhaps even mandatory, for a betrothed *cranil* couple to experiment before they are married. The God wishes to be sure that any marriage is fertile."

"Oh, Yisa. That's awful. He wants more lives to play with."

"I fear so."

They carried on in silence for a while. Then Yisyena said, "Tell me more about Hemeark. Who controls the town?"

"There is a Baron of Hemeark, but he's a nonentity. The real power is a woman called Melauthua. She owns about half the town including a lot of the orchards and the House of Silken Delights."

"Do you think Caseir will stay there?"

"At the House? No, it's not that sort of place. It may be principally a whorehouse but it's also a high-class dining establishment and a place people go to for private discussions with privacy guaranteed by magic. Unless he's got a friend to stay with he'll probably go to *The Golden Apple*. It's the best inn in town, not that there's much competition. With all his winnings Caseir must have got used to living well."

SPONGER

Anarya was relieved when Caseir walked into the common room of *The Golden Apple* shortly after noon the next day. *Glad I got that right, although we know where he's going and we could have picked him up later. Still, it's nice to be right.*

"Do we dress well, my love?"

"Yes," said Anarya, "I think we do. We will get better service if we look prosperous and you're going to stand out anyway so we might as well take advantage of it."

It was Rhyanek who escorted Yisyena to the House of Silken Delights that evening, both dressed in the best they had available in their packs. They arrived in time to see Caseir being ushered towards one of the more expensive private rooms.

Anarya used the Oversight and spotted the yellow aura of a Scratcher surrounding a rotund, middle-aged man sitting in a corner of the entrance hall. *I'll borrow his talent and see how he constructs a privacy spell.*

She was fascinated to see the way he built a barrier around the room Caseir was in. It wasn't static, it kept changing and shifting. The result was that it didn't stop sounds but fragmented them and rearranged them into a nonsense order. Without being able to watch him and know exactly what he had done she wouldn't have had a chance of negating the barrier. As it was Anarya waited until she and Yisyena were settled in an adjacent room before gently easing aside some of the yellow strands that formed the barrier and making a hole to listen through.

Once she was satisfied with her spell she looked around. The room was very different from the one she had been in on her previous visit to the House. Then it had been a room barely big enough for the well-padded bed which was its reason for existing. This one had a black marble floor with a sunken pool filled with rose scented water, thick soft towels, cream and scarlet draperies stiff with embroidery and soft cushions everywhere. There was incense, a selection of very good wines and a bed big enough for – well she wasn't sure how many.

"What a room," she said.

"Adequate," said Yisyena with a sniff after glancing around. She poured wine for both of them.

"I've solved the privacy spell," said Anarya. "Can you hear anything from the next room?"

"Yes, I can hear movement. Are you still holding whatever skill it took? You must not do too much."

"I'm fine. It was a Scratcher's spell and I can hold it for ages. But I won't borrow your talent until you tell me there's something worth listening to."

They snuggled up together on the bed while waiting for whoever Caseir was meeting to arrive. "Although I enjoy being close to you," said Yisyena, "it is pleasant to have a little more room in bed."

Anarya smiled and kissed her. "Let's get really close."

"Later," said Yisyena. "Somebody just opened the door in the next room."

Anarya invoked the borrowed Voyanter skill and they settled down to listen.

"It's good to see you looking so well, Melauthua," said Caseir. "It's been a long time."

"Too long," said a light soprano voice. "I see you've acquired a few new scars since I saw you last."

"They happen," said Caseir.

"And I hear you've acquired a wife too."

"I did, but she's left me."

"She has! Why would she do a foolish thing like that?"

"Doesn't matter why. You don't need to know."

"Hmm. I don't think you've come to renew our acquaintance just because you've been abandoned. It's four years since your last visit and you could have come anytime if you'd wanted to. I'm sure you haven't come to show me your latest scars, although I would like to see all of them, not just these two on your forehead."

"I know you like scars, Melauthua, but business first."

"Oh, very well," she said. "So what brings you to Hemeark?"

"I'm doing some information gathering for the busy man. He has a project in mind and wants to know how you and some others would react to it. Specifically, he wants to know what you think of people like Fauthein and Kuranesh."

"Probably much the same as he does. There must be more to this than you're asking." She paused briefly, then, when there was no response, said, "Duke Kuranesh of Voro is a self-important nobody. He's very fond of his own voice but he says nothing of substance. He doesn't seem to be able to hold an opinion against any sort of resistance. I wouldn't want to be associated with any project he's involved in."

"And Fauthein?"

"Now he's a different breed of cat. He's pulled himself to the top of the Vintner's Association in Firten. Doing that has given him a taste for politics. I suspect he'd like to branch out and take control of the town, not just the Association. He'll probably do that without too much trouble. After that, who knows?"

"What about Wurauf?"

"What about him?"

"Do you think he's vulnerable?"

Anarya almost choked on a mouthful of wine when she heard Caseir ask that question.

There was a sharp intake of breath from the next room, then a pause before Melauthua said, "So that's what this is about. That is a very dangerous question."

"You've taken risks before," said Caseir.

"There are risks, and risks. Wurauf is…" Melauthua's voice trailed off as if she couldn't find suitable words.

"Arrogant, domineering, self-centred," suggested Caseir.

"Yes, all of those. Also intolerant, unforgiving and, above all, powerful."

"He won't last forever. He has no obvious successor and the busy man is interested in replacing him."

"No obvious successor that we know about," said Melauthua. "I wouldn't put it past him to have some sort of arrangement in mind."

"True. But I need to know if you'd be interested in making different arrangements."

"I might. I'd want to know more about the busy man's plans before committing myself."

"That's enough for now. He'll be in touch later. All I'm doing is testing the waters. I'm going to see Fauthein next.

I'm sure I don't need to tell you not to say anything about this to anyone."

"I'm not stupid. The busy man and I may not be the best of friends but you can tell him I don't dislike him enough, or like Wurauf enough, to talk about this."

"Good."

"Business over?" asked Melauthua.

"Business over," agreed Caseir.

"Now let's have a look at those scars."

The rustle of clothing replaced the voices from the next room. That was followed by rhythmical gasps, grunts, groans and moans. Anarya and Yisyena didn't need the additional stimulus, but they took advantage of it anyway.

Afterwards, their conversation turned towards what they had overheard.

"I can't believe someone is plotting against Wurauf," said Anarya.

"It is bound to happen," said Yisyena, "he is not popular and, sooner or later someone will throw him over."

"You mean overthrow him."

"Overthrow him. Yes, thank you for correcting me, my love."

"You don't often need correction now. Your Katelish is getting better all the time."

"I am pleased you think so. I wonder who Caseir can be working for. Who is the 'busy man'? And why is Count Graumedel interested?"

"I don't know. We'll need to find a Whisperer and report this to the Count. Then we'll have to follow Caseir to Firten. I think we'll hire horses tomorrow. It will give us more flexibility."

O

"He's not in a hurry, is he?" said Anarya.

They had been following Caseir for two days, staying about half a chime behind him. That was well within Yisyena's range and all she needed to do was check which way he had gone whenever they came to a fork in the road.

"I wish he would hurry up," said Yisyena. "I do not like sleeping rough."

"It was only one night."

"One is too many."

"But we couldn't risk staying at the same inn as Caseir. We don't want him to start noticing us."

"I accept that. Nevertheless, I do not wish to do the same again."

"We're surrounded by vineyards. That must mean we're close to Firten. It's big enough that it's got to have several inns."

"What do you know about Firten?"

"Not a lot," said Anarya. "I've never been there. All I really know is that the region has a reputation for excellent wine."

It was mid-afternoon when Yisyena announced she could see buildings ahead. They urged their horses to a canter and shortened the distance between themselves and Caseir. As a result they were not far behind him when he rode into the market square.

People crowded around the thirty or so stalls set up in the square which was dominated on one side by a temple of Huler and on the other by a building with a frontage elaborately carved with vines. A mixture of shops and workshops occupied the other two sides.

Caseir dismounted in front of the Guildhall, handed his horse's reins to one of the men waiting at the door, and went inside.

"He asked for the Master," said Yisyena as they tied up their horses. "An underling is taking him upstairs. It is getting more difficult for me to follow him – now I have lost him. There are too many walls between us, I can no longer hear him."

Now what do we do? Anarya asked herself. *It won't look good if our second report to the Count says we've lost our target.*

She scanned the square. *There must be some magic users among all these people. Is there anything useful?*

Five auras showed themselves to the Oversight. There was the usual assortment of the commoner skills. A green aura marked a Feeler, two red ones showed her Lifters and there was the silvery-grey glow of a Whisperer. Of the rarer ones she could only see a Pyromancer working at a forge. None of them useful.

Then she saw a sixth aura. A very faint pink haze surrounded a young woman walking towards one of the side streets. She was only just close enough for Anarya to see the aura. The woman was rather weak, but she was a Seeker.

A moment later Anarya had the woman's skill. She turned towards the Guildhall, concentrating on Seeking Caseir.

Nothing.

Anarya knew she wouldn't have long as a Seeker, particularly when using such a weak gift. Probably only a dozen or so breaths. *Got to find him.* She ran for the street on the left side of the Guildhall.

Still nothing.

She ran down the street, her head pounding and her eyesight fading. Round the corner to the back of the building.

There it was. A pink halo showing her the position of the object of her search.

She stumbled and fell. Her tongue felt thick and she managed to gasp out to Yisyena, "Up there – top floor – second window – from left."

Then darkness closed in.

O

Anarya opened her eyes and promptly closed them again. It was too bright for comfort. She felt weak and shivery and had a terrible taste in her mouth. The only pleasant sensation was the faint smell of lily-of-the-valley coming from the bedclothes. She grunted and rolled over.

"Are you awake?"

Reluctantly she opened her eyes again. It wasn't quite as dazzling because Yisyena was bending over her and shielding her from the direct sunlight.

"Yisa?"

"Yes, my love. I am here."

"Where's here and how did I get to it?"

"You managed to walk here with me supporting you. Fortunately you could assist yourself, I could never have carried you. It was as if you were sleepwalking," said Yisyena. "We are in a room in an inn near the market square. I had to pay extra to persuade them to let us stay. They thought you were drunk."

"I don't remember any of that."

"What do you remember?"

Anarya winced as she tried to sit up.

Yisyena pushed her firmly back down. "You must eat something before you think about rising. You have overextended yourself."

"But we needed to overhear Caseir. We couldn't tell Graumedel that we'd failed."

Yisyena sniffed. "Your health is more important. I will be seriously displeased if you continue putting yourself at risk."

"I'll be more careful in future."

"Until the next time you feel you must stretch yourself to the limit."

"My head feels like a grape in a wine press. What happened after I told you where Caseir was? I did tell you, didn't I?"

"You did, and I overheard most of his meeting with Fauthein. I will tell you more after you have eaten."

Cheese and ham pancakes, buttered fresh bread with winterberry preserves and several mugs of honey and ginger tea made Anarya feel much better.

"Now tell me," she said.

"The meeting proceeded much like the one with Melauthua. Caseir asked Fauthein for his opinion of her and of Kuranesh and Praukel."

"Praukel? The same Praukel that employed Nasuren?"

"I think so," said Yisyena.

"Interesting. What did Fauthein say?"

"He dismissed Kuranesh in much the same terms as Melauthua did but he approved of the others. Then Caseir raised the question of supplanting Wurauf and Fauthein was enthused by the idea. It seems that, apart from anything else, Wurauf owns two of the best vineyards nearby and is one of Fauthein's main rivals. He'd like to see that change."

"Did Caseir identify who he's working for?"

"No. He referred to whoever it is as 'the busy man' or 'my sponsor'. It is most unfortunate because I am sure Count Graumedel would like to know who it is."

"Where is Caseir?"

"He is staying here too. I heard him say he was staying until tomorrow."

"No suggestion of where he's going next, I suppose."

"None."

"Well, we did all right here."

"Not so," said Yisyena. "We learned very little. Not enough to make up for the risk you took."

Anarya wrapped her arms around Yisyena, stroked her hair and kissed her neck. *I've got to be more careful. I shouldn't upset Yisa.*

Yisyena sniffled. A few tears dropped on to her breasts. Anarya licked them off.

"I feel better now," said Anarya, as one intimate contact led to another.

O

"Why is he going east again?" asked Anarya. "He's wandering all over the map as if he doesn't know where he's going."

"Where are we?" asked Yisyena.

"At a guess I'd say we're now in the duchy of Alrem, maybe somewhere near a little town called Nuruye, but I'm not really sure."

"Is there anyone or anything of interest there?"

"Not that I can think of."

"Perhaps he is lost."

"I hope not. I'm starting to get saddle sore. I don't fancy chasing him all over the countryside while he finds himself."

They rode on, glumly following Caseir. It started to rain, a fine drizzle that had them soaked within a quarter. They were on a little used road and the surface quickly turned to mud.

"He's got to stop somewhere soon," said Anarya. "He can't be enjoying this weather any more than we are."

The road led through a succession of villages, each of about a dozen buildings. The sun had almost set when they reached a village with an inn. They brightened up at the prospect of shelter, but Caseir rode on without stopping.

"Where *is* he going?"

The rain stopped, but it was too late, they were already wet and miserable. It was getting dark when Yisyena said, "There's a crossroads ahead. He has stopped and dismounted. There is another man waiting there."

"We'd better stop and listen without getting any closer in case they hear us."

Anarya borrowed Yisyena's Voyanter skills and was just in time to hear an unfamiliar voice say, "*Te-verun-li.*"

She had just translated that as 'We are well met' when Yisyena gasped.

Anarya turned to her. "What?"

"Ssh!"

Anarya made a mental note to ask Yisyena what had surprised her. Then she concentrated on overhearing what Caseir and the other man were saying. Surprisingly the conversation was conducted entirely in Sitru with the other doing most of the talking. He gave Caseir his opinions of various people, including Graumedel and Wurauf, in a didactic tone.

The discussion didn't last long. At the end of it the stranger mounted his horse. He looked down at Caseir and gave him instructions before riding off.

Caseir watched him go, then remounted his own horse and set off back towards the village they had passed through.

"I think he's going to the inn," said Anarya. It's not very big and I don't think we'll be able to get a room there too. Means another night camping rough. Quarenna curse it."

"We do not have an alternative," said Yisyena. "We have already stayed at the same inn as him twice and he would become suspicious if he sees us again, particularly in an out-of-the-way place like this."

"I know, but I don't have to like it."

They pitched camp just inside the wood on the edge of the village, ate a cold meal and snuggled up together for warmth.

"Something upset you, Yisa. What was it?"

"I was not upset, merely surprised at hearing a familiar accent in an unexpected place."

I think there was more to it but I'm not going to pressure her. "What did we learn?" asked Anarya.

"Did you follow the conversation well enough?"

"Yes, I think so. The man told Caseir 'Be at the drinking place called *The Seventh Step* in Verenthe at noon five days from now. Someone who may be of great value to this enterprise may meet you there. You should speak to him.'

"Then Caseir asked who he was supposed to meet and was

told, 'I may not tell you his name without his permission. Nor can I promise he will be there in five days, it may take him longer to reach that place. If he has not arrived by sunset then do the same each day for a week. Should it be that he has not appeared by then assume that he does not wish to become involved and go about your business.'"

"That is correct," said Yisyena. "Then Caseir said he could not wait more than three days because he had other people to meet."

"He kept his hood up and I never got a good look at him. Did you?"

"No, I did not."

"I wonder who he was. There's one thing, Yisa. Caseir used a word I didn't recognise when talking about his patron. What does *Gelefth* mean?"

"It means beekeeper," said Yisyena. "I think Caseir used it instead of 'busy man' because that would not convey the same meaning in Sitru. 'Busy as a bee' is not a Sitru saying."

"Why would he call his patron a beekeep… Holy Quarenna and her angels! The beehive badge. It's Graumedel. It's got to be. He's even called him 'my sponsor' a couple of times and the Count did sponsor his last few appearances in the arena. Why would Graumedel need to know what Caseir is doing if he's working for him?"

Yisyena said, "It may be that he has set us to follow him to make sure he is doing whatever he is supposed to be doing."

"Perhaps to ensure that he knows what happens in case Caseir meets someone who would side with Wurauf."

"This is dangerous, my love. I do not think we tell the Count what we have deduced. We simply report what we have seen and heard. In this case we say we could not identify who Caseir met."

"At least we know where he's going next and when he's supposed to be there," said Anarya. "We can get ahead of him again. That'll be better than traipsing after him."

"Do you know anything of Verenthe?"

"Not much. I've never been there. I believe it's built on a marshy island connected to the mainland by a causeway. The only reason it exists is because it's a good place for ships heading up or down the Carrh to pick up and drop pilots."

O

They reached Verenthe with a day to spare before Caseir's appointment. It wasn't as dull a town as Anarya thought. The island was marshy but there was a rocky core to it. Most of the buildings were on the solid ground but there were also many buildings built on piles driven into the mud. Towards the dockside the piled buildings were a bit shabby and a few of them were sagging. However, on the whole, the town looked prosperous.

"That inn looks promising," said Yisyena as they reached the island end of the causeway and a small market square.

"I don't think we should go there," said Anarya. "It's the first decent looking place you see when you arrive and it's likely to attract Caseir's attention. I think we should find somewhere else nearby."

They settled on a smaller inn a couple of streets away. It had a bath house and they spent a blissful half chime soaking in hot water, relaxing and easing the aches and pains of days in the saddle. That was followed by a hot meal they didn't have to cook for themselves, then they settled into chairs in the common room with glasses of decent wine.

Anarya asked the server who brought their wine for directions to *The Seventh Step.*

He scowled and walked away without answering.

"Never mind him," said a man sitting nearby. "He's a Gwyrrist."

Anarya looked blankly at him.

"Never heard of Gwyrrim?" he asked.

"No, never."

The man emptied his mug and said, "They brew some pretty good ale here. Fill that up again and I'll educate you."

Anarya studied him. No aura of any description. He looked like a moderately prosperous shopkeeper. *Might just be a way of getting a free drink but it can't hurt to find out more about this place Caseir is supposed to go to.*

The shopkeeper, if that's what he was, took a sizeable draught from the new mugful and belched. "About eighty years ago there was a magic user here called Gwyrrim. The stories about him disagree on his talent. Some say he was a Chemer, some a Scratcher, but whatever he was he was really powerful. One day another magic user turned up and challenged Gwyrrim for control of Verenthe. They fought over by the docks and Gwyrrim lost. The story is he staggered off down the street, collapsed, transformed himself into a sea-eagle and flew away. A bunch of gullible fools saw this and decided he must have been a god in disguise. That's how the Gwyrrist religion was born. It's not caught on anywhere else and it's not too popular even here." He took another mouthful of ale.

Anarya touched her thumb to her forehead, muttered a brief prayer to Quarenna and said to the man, "You're not a believer."

The man almost choked on his ale. He laughed and said, "Certainly not. I think Gwyrrim was a Sponger. You know what they're like, they can do any sort of magic. I think he used a Stealther's skill when he was beaten, went invisible and just crawled away."

"What about the sea-eagle?"

"Coincidence. It happened to be there and when Gwyrrim vanished everyone saw it fly off and jumped to the conclusion it was him."

"This is all very interesting," said Yisyena. "However, it does not explain why that Gwyrrist did not answer our question."

"That's easy. If you turn right out of this inn and take the third street on the left you'll come to the small square where the fight took place. One of the streets leading from the square is called the Street of the Six Holy Steps, because that's how many steps Gwyrrim was supposed to have taken before his transformation. That's where you'll find the tavern you were asking about. The Gwyrrists think its name is blasphemous and refuse to talk about it.

"What happened to the winner of the fight?"

"Oh, he decided Verenthe was too small for him and moved on after about a year. Don't know where he went."

O

They found *The Seventh Step* without difficulty by following the shopkeeper's instructions. The square he described was on the edge of the high ground and the Street of the Six Holy

Steps sloped sharply downwards towards the docks. They recognised the inn by the outline of seven footprints scratched into its green-painted, weather-beaten plank door.

It was bigger than they expected. Benches lined the walls under the balcony that ran around three sides from stairs in the back left corner. One server manoeuvred her way among the two dozen battered and scarred tables with ease, dispensing drinks and food which she brought from a door in the other back corner. Tallow candles on the tables and in sconces on the balcony provided reasonable light. The tables had two, three or four chairs around them, mostly unoccupied as the tavern was quiet in mid-afternoon.

Anarya looked around using the Oversight. She saw the silvery-grey aura of a Whisperer around a woman sitting under the stairs. She was the only magic user present.

Three of the fifteen or so other customers were sitting with their heads close together talking quietly. They were well dressed in a variety of styles but each of them was wearing a soft, floppy velvet beret pulled down over the left eye where it was pinned with a silver badge featuring a pair of scales. *They're probably merchants,* Anarya thought, *and the ones in those knitted sweaters are sailors. The rest could be anything.*

Anarya noticed several heads turn towards them when they walked in but everybody looked away again quite quickly. *Good. Looks like this is the sort of place where people mind their own business.* She wrinkled her nose. *Smells a bit of overheated cooking oil but I've been in worse. At least it's clean.*

They sat and ordered wine. Yisyena took a sip and made a face. "That is barely drinkable. It is thin and halfway to being vinegar."

"It's not that bad," said Anarya, "but I suppose you're used to better." She called the server over and asked if they had any better wine.

"It'll cost you."

"I will pay extra to have something drinkable," said Yisyena.

The server shrugged and went off to get the wine. While she was gone another man entered, sat down at a table and stuck his knife into the tabletop. When the server returned

Anarya asked about this behaviour.

"Means he don't want to be disturbed and don't want company."

"I've never come across that before."

"Local custom," said the server before moving away again.

○

The next day they made sure they arrived at *The Seventh Step* well before noon in case Caseir arrived early. They found a vacant table in the front left corner and Anarya stuck a knife into the table top. Anarya was inconspicuous in a well-worn blue cotton shirt, canvas jacket and breeches. Yisyena, as always, attracted more attention despite dressing as unobtrusively as possible in a faded tan-coloured blouse and black skirt.

Their timing was good. About a quarter later Caseir walked in, took a seat on one of the benches with his back to the wall, got a mug of ale and settled down to wait. The tavern gradually filled up to the extent that two more servers were needed to cope with the demand for food and drink for the next chime until the midday rush was over.

In the afternoon the tavern was occupied only by Caseir, the Whisperer at her seat under the stairs, Anarya, Yisyena and a variable number of others. Sometimes there were as many as twelve, often as few as four. It stayed like that for most of the day and started getting busy again towards evening. Caseir managed to make three mugs of ale last until sunset, then he left. Whoever he was waiting for hadn't arrived.

Anarya and Yisyena left soon afterwards and went back to their inn.

"I'm glad you insisted on better wine. I couldn't have drunk the other stuff for long, certainly not for as long as we did," said Anarya. "That was boring."

"You should remember your own advice, my love. You did warn me that waiting was the tedious part of surveillance."

Anarya laughed and started to say something at the same moment as Yisyena. After apologising and deferring to each other, she eventually said, "I'm worried. At times the tavern was almost empty. If that's the normal pattern then there's a chance that Caseir will start wondering about the same people being there each day.”

“You mean he may become suspicious of me. He is not going to notice you when you blend in.”

“Yes. Someone as beautiful as you stands out in a place like that.”

“Do not try to flatter me.”

“I wasn’t. It’s true. You are beautiful.”

“*Olyunces-va!*”

“Yisa!”

Yisyena clapped her hand over her mouth and dropped her gaze. “I am sorry, my love. I should not use such language.”

“I didn’t think a *cranil* would know words like that.”

“They are known. As children we would use them deliberately to shock each other. Of course our parents did not approve and would punish us. However, that did not stop us. We only stopped using them when we were old enough to understand exactly what they mean.”

Anarya laughed. “The Sitrelker children I grew up with used them regularly. I learned the words but not the meanings.”

“And I am certainly not going to teach you!”

They fell, giggling, into each other’s arms.

“I am sorry, my love. You are quite right about my visibility. I objected because I want to contribute to our partnership and not be left out. However, I feel that in this case I can contribute most by not being seen.”

O

Rhyanek went alone to *The Seventh Step* the next day and it was almost a repeat of the first day. The only difference made Anarya shiver. She was using the Oversight to look at some new arrivals when she saw Caseir’s aura flicker and become a circular opening into nothingness. *He’s called a daimon. Why? He can’t know I’m here, can he?*

She watched warily in case the daimon made any move towards her, not that she had any idea what she could do about it if it did. Without knowing the daimon’s Name she had no chance of controlling it.

The longer the daimon stayed the twitchier she got. When

it vanished about a third later she almost collapsed with relief. *Quarenna's grace. It had nothing to do with me after all.*

Back at the inn Anarya didn't tell Yisyena about the daimon.

O

The third day at *The Seventh Step* was busier. When Anarya arrived all the tables and benches were occupied. She had to be satisfied with leaning against the wall close to the door. Listening to the conversations around her she discovered that the tavern was benefitting from the arrival of a new cook. Apparently this woman had a good reputation. She moved from tavern to tavern a couple of times a year and always attracted customers to wherever she went. Certainly the food smelled more appetising than it had previously.

Caseir arrived, looked around and grunted. He got a mug of ale from a server and stood beside one of the pillars supporting the balcony. About half a chime later an elderly man levered himself out of his chair at the corner table next to where Caseir was standing. He reacted quickly and his dagger was embedded in the tabletop before the old man had moved far.

Anarya was too far away from Caseir. Without using Yisyena's Voyanter skills she wouldn't be able to overhear if whoever was supposed to meet him actually arrived. She looked around the tavern with the Oversight. As well as Caseir's Daimoner aura she saw the Whisperer in the corner as usual, muttering quietly to herself. *She must use this as her place of business.* Then there was a priest of Huler, who was a moderately strong Scratcher, and a young man who was a rather weak Lifter, so weak that he likely needed physical contact with whatever he was Lifting and was probably thought of as just a strong man.

Anarya pushed herself upright. *Hope the crowd thins a bit soon. I'm getting stiff leaning all the time.* She looked across at Caseir's profile. *Bet he's glad he's got a seat.*

She was looking at him when the Oversight showed a dull brown aura appear behind him. A man materialised and metal flashed as a blade slashed across Caseir's throat. He lurched to his feet, hands going to the gash in his neck. It looked as if he tried to say something but he was choking in his own blood. He crashed to the floor in an untidy heap, twitched a few times then was still.

A man overturned an adjacent table as he jumped to his feet, spilling drinks and a couple of platefuls of sausage and pickled cabbage. People cursed, a few screamed. Those closest backed away from the spreading pool of blood. Several drew weapons. The priest of Huler crossed the room to kneel beside the body but shook his head almost immediately. There was nothing he, or anyone else, could do.

Amid the shock and turmoil, the killer ran for the door. Anarya followed him, just managing to get out ahead of the jostling, pushing crowd as many of the customers hurried to get away from the scene.

She saw the killer turn into the alley on the downhill side of the tavern and followed him. She forced herself to go slow, concentrating on blending in, trying to convince herself she wasn't noteworthy and thereby convince everyone else too.

The killer slowed from a run to a brisk walk and carried on down the hill towards the docks.

Why am I following him? she wondered, *It could be dangerous.* Then she answered herself, *Because Graumedel will want to know what happened and there's a possibility I'll find out who paid for the killing.*

At the bottom of the alley the killer turned left and went to a jetty where small boats were tied up. He called to a boatman, tossed him a coin and clambered into the boat. The boatman rowed away from the jetty as soon as the killer was seated.

Now what? I could hire another boat and follow him but that would make me too conspicuous. She looked out at the broad sweep of the Carrh estuary. As usual there were several ships in sight going both up and down river. The boat looked as if it was heading towards one of them, a brigantine heading upriver. *That settles it. If he's getting on a ship I'm not getting on it too.*

She used Yisyena's skills to read the ship's name and listen as the killer negotiated with the captain for passage to Carregis. He was a young man, probably in his early twenties with a thin face, pale blue eyes, a faint wisp of moustache and long brown hair worn in a loose braid. He called himself Baram, although Anarya thought that probably wasn't his real name.

She watched *Fortunate Lady of Nerysaun* continue on her way upstream for as long as she could to make sure he stayed on board. Then she went back to the inn to tell Yisyena what had happened.

O

"A Stealther!" said Yisyena.

"What else could he be? I don't understand why I didn't pick up his aura before he struck."

"Have you ever met one before?"

"No. It's a very rare skill."

"Do you think it possible that his aura is invisible when he is?"

"Oh. That would make sense, I suppose. I wonder why he became visible at all."

Yisyena hesitated, then said, "Stealthers are also very rare in Jotuk, but I knew one. He told me he could not remain invisible when holding a naked blade. I do not know if this is always the case but it could explain why this Baram revealed himself."

Anarya stared at Yisyena. She so rarely said anything about her past. "I'd think he'd want to keep that quiet. Why did he tell you?"

"He was the one to whom I was betrothed."

"Oh."

"I wonder," said Yisyena, "why he cut Caseir's throat rather than stabbing him. Was it to prevent him calling a daimon?"

"That's a good question. And I've got another. Did that man send Caseir to *The Seventh Step* so that the Stealther knew where to find him?"

Yisyena looked thoughtful. "Yes, my love. I think that very possible."

"In that case, he wasn't a good choice for Graumedel's plot, was he?"

"No, but in the opposite seat…"

"On the other hand."

Yisyena glared at Anarya and said, "Wait until I have finished speaking before correcting me. Do not interrupt."

I've upset her again. Sometimes she can be so touchy. "Sorry, Yisa."

"I do wish to learn to speak better Katelish, I truly do," said Yisyena, hugging Anarya. "I was about to say that it may have been one of the others Caseir spoke to who is responsible. One of them may have wished to ingratiate himself with Wurauf."

Anarya returned the hug. "If we can work out that Graumedel was behind Caseir then others can too. The Stealther took ship to Carregis. Perhaps the Count is next on his list, we must warn him."

"Why?" said Yisyena, frowning. "He must know that what he is doing is dangerous. We do not need to be involved or the danger may embrace us also. We would not want that."

"No, but he needs to be alive to pay us."

"That is true. Find a Whisperer and send him a message."

"Easy. There's been one at *The Seventh Step* each time I've been there."

SURVIVOR

Anarya changed clothes and went back to *The Seventh Step* wearing a buff linen jacket over a faded dark brown blouse and skirt. Not shabby enough to look poor but not well enough dressed to look out of place.

The tavern was quite busy. Everything seemed normal except that nobody was sitting at, or even standing close to, the table where Caseir had been killed. There were blood stains on the table top and on the floor under it. *Surely that's not enough to put people off sitting there when there aren't any other tables vacant.*

Anarya shrugged. Whatever others thought of the idea of sitting at that table it didn't bother her. She weaved her way through the crowd overhearing snippets of conversation. The murder was the main topic. Two out of every three people seemed to be discussing it.

She called to a server for wine and sat down. From the way people were behaving it wasn't likely anyone would want to share the table but she pushed the candle to one side and stuck her dagger into the tabletop anyway.

When the server brought the wine she thumped the mug down so hard a little slopped out. Then she moved away as fast as she could. Anarya opened her mind to the Oversight and saw the silvery-grey aura of the Whisperer where she expected it to be. She saw a Feeler's green aura around a dumpy merchant three tables away. There was also a pimply-faced youth who was a rather weak Scratcher, but she wasn't interested in either of them.

She absorbed the Whisperer's talent. With it came a feeling of aching bones and joints; the Whisperer was older than she realised. The mesh of connections to other Whisperers around the country came into view. She saw the Whisperer initiate several messages about the murder and send them rippling on their way.

Anarya didn't announce her presence in the Whispermesh but carefully detached herself from the network of threads, knowing that doing so wouldn't attract attention, people joined and left all the time. She held Graumedel's token in her hand and concentrated on it. Very quickly it felt as if she was standing beside him. She spoke into his ear, telling him of Caseir's murder and the name of the Stealther. Not being a Whisperer himself he couldn't acknowledge the contact. In fact he probably wasn't aware of the communication and wouldn't be until his mind was quiet enough, probably on the edge of sleep. Then he would hear her message. *Hope it keeps him awake all night worrying.*

Satisfied that she had done all she could, she broke the connection and put the token back in her pouch. She was drinking the rest of her wine when a quiet voice said "You're a Sponger."

O

She looked over her shoulder. There was nobody there. Her heart thumped. After seeing, or failing to see, the Stealther she didn't like the idea that someone she couldn't see was talking to her.

The voice said, "You were Whispering to Count Graumedel. I heard you."

She recognised the voice.

It was impossible.

Cold crawled up her spine. She didn't know what good it would do but she grabbed her dagger from the table top.

"I'm sure you think I'm dead," said Caseir's voice. "Well, you're almost right."

The tightness in her throat made her voice almost inaudible when she said, "I don't understand. I saw what happened. How can you not be dead? I mean dead is dead, isn't it?"

"It really is me. I'm here. Not exactly dead but not exactly alive either," said the voice, which she couldn't believe was Caseir's.

She frantically surveyed the available magic. *Can I use the Scratcher's skill in this situation? Holy Quarenna help me. What is this situation anyway?*

"Don't worry. I can't do anything to you."

That didn't reassure her at all. She had no idea what might or might not be possible for the disembodied voice of a dead man.

"I'm a Daimoner," said Caseir. "I tried to call a daimon when my throat was cut. I couldn't say the Name, but it came anyway. Years ago I made it promise to preserve my life when I called and was in danger. Since I couldn't summon it properly it didn't have to obey me. It decided to come because it saw its chance to get its revenge on me for compelling it for years. It preserved my life by binding it to the bloodstain. I'm part of the tavern now. I will be until the bloodstain wears away and the daimon said it's made sure that it can't be just scrubbed away. It wants me to suffer."

"Oh!" said Anarya, thinking, *That's why the bloodstain hasn't been cleaned up. I did wonder. After all it can't be the first blood to be spilled in here over the years and there's no sign of other stains.*

"You're the first person who hasn't run away when I started talking to them," said Caseir. "Now they all think this table is cursed."

Anarya looked around. Several people were watching her. Most of them turned away rather than make eye contact. She scowled and most of those still watching dropped their eyes. A few thumbed their foreheads, briefly linked their little fingers or made some other warding gesture.

She reached out to the Feeler she had noticed earlier and absorbed his ability to sense emotions. Some of the people watching her were fearful, some curious and some suspicious. There were two who seemed sympathetic and ready to come to her aid when she swooned or screamed. As if any woman on her own in a place like *The Seventh Step* would be the swooning type. *That's quite sweet of them,* she thought, then she realised they were hoping their help might lead to a closer acquaintance in one of the upstairs rooms.

"Talk to me," said Caseir. "Please stay and talk to me. You don't have to speak loudly, muttering like that Whisperer is good enough. Talk to me and I could help you. It's bad enough knowing I'm dead. I don't need to make it worse by frightening everybody I try to talk to."

The initial shock of talking to a dead man was wearing off and her heart rate was returning to normal. "What do you mean, help me?"

"I can only talk to people at this table, where the bloodstain is, but I can hear everything that goes on in the room. Since

I've been stuck here I've heard talk of expected cargoes, about quarrels in the Guilds, robberies being planned, and so on. I can listen to every message that Whisperer passes. You want to know which daughter of a noble house is upstairs with her low-born lover right now? I can tell you. A lot of that information could be quite profitable."

He's right. Information like that could be very valuable to the right people. But why would he share it with me? What's the catch?

To give herself time to think she asked, "Why did you call me a Sponger? Does being half dead make you believe in wild tales for children?"

"Two reasons. Firstly, you've got too many skills. You were Whispering to Graumedel just now. I heard you tell him the Stealther's name and what ship he's on. A Whisperer couldn't find that out. And, from what you said, you've been following me and a Whisperer couldn't do that either. Spongers may be commoner in children's stories than in real life but there's got to be some basis for the tales. The other reason is even more convincing. I spoke to my daimon yesterday about something else. It said you were watching me and that you're a Sponger. I believe it."

Anarya didn't want to admit to being a Sponger, even if Caseir was convinced of it, so she avoided talking about it and asked, "Why should you help me? What's in it for you?"

"Revenge. I can't get it myself so I'll need help."

"How? I don't know anything about the Stealther except a name, and that's probably not his real one."

"It would be nice to get him too, but who I really want is whoever paid him."

Anarya nodded. "I guess I can understand that, but I know even less about whoever that was."

"There aren't too many possibilities. It's got to be somebody I spoke to for Graumedel. You've been following me. You know who they are."

All except the cloaked man who spoke Sitru, thought Anarya, but she didn't say anything about that. She wanted more information about Caseir's motives so she asked, "Are you angry about me following you?"

"I would have been if I had known about it. Wouldn't do me any good now, would it? I can't do anything to you."

"Except give me bad information," said Anarya. "You could get me killed quite easily by doing that."

"Why would I? I don't want to lose the only person willing to talk to me."

Anarya still held the Feeler's skills, including the ability to know if someone was lying. Would it work on Caseir? She had no idea but it was worth a try. "Why should I trust you?"

"I don't know why you should," he said. "All I can say is I won't betray you. It's not in my interest, but I don't know how to convince you of that."

The Feeler's talent didn't work on a dead man. There was neither the hum of truth nor the rasp of falsehood. *Too bad. Now I've got to decide if I trust him or not.*

"It must be nice to be able to use any sort of magic," said Caseir.

She said nothing. Oddly enough that comment made her feel more relaxed. It was such a common response to any discussion of Spongers that its familiarity was soothing.

"There's something else I want," said Caseir.

Anarya was immediately suspicious again. "What?"

"Company. You're the only person who's spoken to me. I can see myself getting very lonely. Come here often and talk to me."

Anarya though he sounded sad. She quite liked the idea of being able to talk to one of her heroes but it wasn't practicable. So she said, "I can't. Now this job is over I'll be going back to Carregis and staying there."

"You don't have to. You're a quaestor, aren't you. There's something else I can tell you, something that'll be very useful to you. Something my daimon did."

"It's not taking an interest in me, is it?" asked Anarya, feeling sick and weak at the idea.

"No."

"Holy Quarenna be thanked," she said, touching thumb to forehead.

"You don't have to worry about daimons. They hate Daimoners but are completely indifferent to other people."

"So what is it you think will be so useful?"

"How do I know you won't listen to me, then walk away and never talk to me again. Promise me you'll come back often and I'll tell you."

"No promises. You'll just have to trust me," said Anarya, shaking her head vigorously.

"I haven't trusted anyone since my mother died."

"Not even Graumedel?"

"Trust Graumedel! You've got to be joking."

"You've been working for him."

"Working for him, yes. Trusting him, no, definitely not. He sent me to canvas opinions then sent you to follow me. That shows you how much trust there was."

I've got to talk this over with Yisa before settling anything. Anarya drank the last mouthful of wine and wished she hadn't. The dregs were bitter.

"I have a partner," she said. "I'll bring her here tomorrow and we can talk then."

O

The Seventh Step was fairly quiet when Anarya and Yisyena arrived, well ahead of the mid-day rush. The Whisperer was there as usual but there were no other magic users present.

A group of merchants huddled around a table in one corner were arguing in hushed tones. Their bodyguards sat at the next table, nursing mugs of ale and glancing suspiciously at each other. The rattle of dice came from another table where half a dozen men were laughing and swearing over their mixed fortunes. A balding man in a long broadcloth jacket stained with gravy and vomit was sprawled along one of the benches, snoring loudly.

The server remembered Yisyena from their previous visit and produced mugs of better quality wine without being asked. That earned her a half-bit but she still looked oddly at them. Anarya thought it was because they chose to sit at the bloodstained table when there were others available.

"I realised I didn't give you my name yesterday. I am called Anarya and my partner is Yisyena."

"And I am Caseir. I'm very pleased to meet you, Yisyena. I wasn't sure Anarya would come again."

Anarya was impressed with how calmly Yisyena accepted a greeting from a disembodied voice. *Anybody would think it's something she does every day.*

"Let us begin our business. I understand that you have

information for sale."

"I do," said Caseir. "Come and talk to me often and the things I hear will make you rich. Just as an example, I overheard a discussion between two fences last night and I can tell you where to find the diamonds stolen two nights ago from Jeinas Gulest. Her husband has offered a substantial reward for their return."

"That would be useful to know. But yesterday you said you had more than that sort of information to offer. Something more useful, you said."

"I did and I do. I know something which, if it works out, will be very valuable to people in your business."

"If it works out," repeated Yisyena. "You would have us buy an unhatched egg not knowing what laid it." She turned to Anarya and said, "I am aware that I have translated a Sitru expression word for word. I do not know the Katelish equivalent, please tell me later what it is. For the moment I think the meaning is clear enough."

"We've talked about your offer," said Anarya. "We are prepared to take a chance. I will take an oath to Holy Quarenna that I will come to visit you three more times this year. Then we will judge how useful your information has been and decide what happens after that."

"Make it six times a year for the next five years," said Caseir.

"Too much. I've a business to run in Carregis. Three times a year for five years."

"Four times a year."

"Very well, but for three years, not five," said Anarya. "But only if the information is good."

"Both of you come. Not just you, Anarya."

"We will come three times more this year whatever the value of the information."

"Agreed. As long as each visit is at least two days long."

"Done," said Anarya. "I will make a promise to Quarenna if you will make one to Huler."

"Promising what?"

"That the information and advice you give us will always be as good as you can make it."

"I'll do that," said Caseir, "but I don't know if Huler will accept a promise from a dead man."

Anarya pulled her dagger from the table top, nicked her thumb, let a drop of blood fall into the candle flame and spoke her promise to Holy Quarenna. Then she scraped at the bloodstain with the dagger and dropped the shaving into the flame while Caseir made his promise.

"It is done," said Yisyena. "Tell us."

"The daimon wanted to torment me more than simply trapping me in the bloodstain. It wanted to remind me constantly that I am imprisoned here. It has done something to the door so that doesn't just open on the Street of the Six Holy Steps. It also opens in Carregis, Getruva, Hemeark and lots of other places. Every time the door opens I get a glimpse of somewhere else. I don't recognise all of them so it's not just places I've been.

"Think about it. If you can find a way to make it work for you, you can go anywhere in the country, maybe anywhere in the world, just by walking through the door. No need to spend three days on a ship or seven on a horse to get from here to Carregis. You could make this your base, as it is for that Whisperer, but be anywhere else you wanted to be in no time at all."

"The door cannot work that way all the time," said Yisyena. "There are constantly people passing through it. What do we need to do to use it in the way you suggest?"

"I don't know," said Caseir, "but I think whatever it's done to the door is permanent. It must have better things to do than wait by a door I'm never going to be able to use just to torment me with a different view every time it opens. You can be a Daimoner, Anarya. Why don't you take my talent and see what that shows you."

"I can't," said Anarya. "There's not a trace of that particular ability in this room."

"Are you sure?"

"Quite sure."

"Oh," said Caseir. "I haven't tried summoning the daimon since I was killed. I don't even know if it would respond and I've been afraid of making things worse. That ability has been part of me for so long – even although I rarely used it I'm going to miss it."

O

Anarya tried to imagine what it would be like to lose her magic. She had come close when she had exhausted her talent on a couple of occasions. To some extent she did it every time a borrowed ability faded and became unusable. There was always a feeling of loss, but at least she knew she could borrow again. She sympathised as Caseir came to terms with his loss. To give him time to grieve she turned in her chair and looked at the door. There was nothing remarkable about it. "I'm going to take a closer look," she said.

When she got back to the table Yisyena said, "What is the matter? You look pale."

Anarya picked up her mug and took a big mouthful. "It's true about the door. There is something strange about it. It looks – blurred. As if there are many doors occupying the same space. One of them looks a bit – a bit – more real than the others, if that makes any sort of sense, but there must be hundreds of them, all in the same place. I was afraid to touch any of them."

"But you've been through it several times since I was killed," said Caseir, "and you didn't notice anything peculiar those times."

"That's true but I wasn't looking for magic before."

"I don't understand."

"You always knew another Daimoner when you met one, didn't you. And you could tell roughly how strong they were."

"Yes."

"Well, I can do the same for any magical ability if I look in a certain way. I looked at the door that way, and that's when it looked blurred"

They sat in silence for a while, then Anarya said, "I've got to try it. I don't see any alternative."

"Be careful, my love."

Anarya walked to the door, pushed it open and stepped through into the Street of the Six Holy Steps. It was just as she had last seen it, a short cobbled street sloping down to the docks and lined with coppersmiths' workshops from which the sounds of hammers echoed. As usual there were some Gwyrrists meditating on the footprints carved into the cobbles.

From the outside the door looked perfectly normal, even in the Oversight. She went back in. When she looked from the inside she could see many overlapping doors. She chose one of them and concentrated on it. It started to look more solid. She reached out to touch it, pushed it open and stepped forward.

One step was all it took. The door knob vanished from her hand. She felt she was falling forwards. There was a flash of multi-coloured light. She didn't have time to scream before her foot landed on a level surface and she was standing somewhere else, the door thudding closed behind her.

"Holy Quarenna," she muttered, thumbing her forehead. She knew where she was, and it wasn't Verenthe or anywhere near it. She had never been there before. However, she had heard the double peak of the gently smoking mountain that dominated the scenery described. It was unmistakeable. She shook her head in disbelief. She was in Voro, so far to the west that the sun was noticeably in a different place in the sky than it was in Verenthe.

How do I get back? It'll take weeks if I have to go overland. Yisa will worry. I might have to find a Whisperer to let her know I'm all right.

Then she saw the door. It looked out of place on the end of a one-storey building which was nothing like *The Seventh Step*. It was the same battered plank door outlined by a faint shimmer. She pushed at it and had a moment's panic when it wouldn't open. Then she tried pulling and stepped through into the familiar warm atmosphere of the tavern.

She sat down, grabbed her mug and took a deep draught. She inhaled a little of the wine and that set her off on a coughing fit. "Voro," she gasped when she could talk again. "I've just been to Voro and back. The door works."

"Are you sure?"

"What did you see that makes you think it was Voro," asked Caseir.

"The smoking mountain."

"That certainly sounds like Voro."

"Have you ever been there?" asked Yisyena.

"I haven't," said Anarya at the same moment as Caseir said, "Once, years ago. I fought there once when I was just getting started. All I saw of the town was the arena and the fighters' barracks but you can see the mountain from everywhere. Interesting that the door took you somewhere I knew and not somewhere you do."

"Anra, my love, do you feel like trying again?"

"I think so."

"This time try thinking of somewhere first before opening the door."

Feeling more confident, Anarya watched one of the doors solidify in front of her and then stepped through. It took her to a street in Hemeark, a street she knew well. She had been born there. She knew every door in it, and none of them were green with scratched footprints. She turned around. There it was, where it had no business being, between Lutusha's bakery and Diraut's workshop. It was impossible. In that position the door would open into Lutusha's oven, but it didn't and a moment later she was back in *The Seventh Step.*

Anarya barely made it back to the table before waves of heat and cold washed over her and she started shivering. She collapsed into her chair gasping for breath and with every muscle twitching. She fumbled for the mug and gulped down the wine, spilling as much as she swallowed, desperate for the liquid and not caring what it tasted like.

Yisyena swept her arms around Anarya and held her, muttering gentle, soothing, wordless sounds until the shivers eased.

Eventually Anarya stopped gasping and her heart rate slowed to something approaching normality. She tried to sit up straighter. "I'm fine now. I think we have discovered that the door works but it has limitations. Use it too often too quickly and it's like talent exhaustion."

"In that case you need to eat," said Yisyena. She looked around to see the server and several of the customers watching them. "Bring hot food," she told the server, "and send to the nearest vintner for some really good wine."

A plateful of eels in mustard sauce arrived quickly, followed shortly by a bottle of six year old Mephala Grise, which Anarya, and even Yisyena, found acceptable.

Anarya looked around when she had finished eating. The other customers had stopped watching them, at least overtly. "Are we a topic of conversation?" she asked Caseir.

"You were," he said. "Your reaction was quite dramatic but

interest seems to have died down now. Tell me, do we have an agreement?"

"We'll need to experiment and find out how frequently we can use the door without side effects, but I think it will prove useful."

"It might even make sense to make this our base as you suggested," said Yisyena. "You knew it would so why did you haggle over the number of visits we would make?"

"Would you have believed me if I hadn't? Anyway I wasn't sure you would be able to find a way to make it work and I had to get whatever agreement I could."

Anarya laughed. That sounded more like the confident man he had been before he was killed.

"Anra, my love, I think we have a new partner. *Gu-merin-li tisseta.*"

When they had finished toasting the new partnership Caseir said, "I have something else for you. You've heard of Miros, I suppose."

"Of course," said Anarya.

"Ever tasted it?"

"Are you mocking me? Two regals for a thimbleful! That's way out of my price range."

"Well those merchants in the corner have got hold of an eighteen year old cask and are shipping it upriver. They've been arguing about the best way to market it."

"That is a nice problem for them," said Yisyena, "but I do not see how it affects us. We could not possibly afford to buy into whatever scheme they come up with."

"They've decided to wait until the ship reaches Carregis before making an announcement," said Caseir. "You could use the door to get there before the ship does. Tell the connoisseurs of Carregis that a cask of eighteen year old Miros is on the way and you could have them bidding for the name of the ship so they can get to it first."

Anarya and Yisyena looked at each other and nodded. They could see the possibilities.

"We can go tomorrow," said Anarya," and collect the rest of our money from Count Graumedel at the same time."

"No, my love. We should wait at least another day. It would cause suspicion should the Count realise tomorrow that we have arrived faster than any ship could carry us."

"He'll find some way of forcing you to work for him if you give him any hint of what the door can do," said Caseir.

"He already has," said Anarya, and explained how they came to be following Caseir. "Is that why you were working for him, because he had some sort of hold on you?"

"No, that's not it. I suppose I'd better tell you if we are going to be partners. I told you I wanted revenge on whoever paid to have me killed. That's true, but it's not everything. I was feeling out possible conspirators for Graumedel because he promised it would help me get the vengeance I really want."

"I don't understand. What vengeance?"

Caseir sighed and told them about Caerina's death and Wurauf's refusal to help him track down her killers.

Anarya shook her head vigorously. "I understand why you were recruiting for Graumedel and why you want to do something against Wurauf. But I'm not going against him. No way."

"I also sympathise," said Yisyena, "but I must agree with Anra. It is too dangerous."

"What about your daimon," said Anarya. "You could have sent it to deal with Wurauf."

"No, I couldn't. One of his minions is a Daimoner at least as strong as me – I mean as strong as I used to be. I've tried to find a way to reach Wurauf but now he's warned against me and I can't get to him. I need your help."

"Sorry, the answer is still no."

"But we are partners. *Gu-merin-li tisseta*, remember."

"I do not think attacking Wurauf is covered by our agreement," said Yisyena.

"Not specifically," said Caseir, "but think about this. It might be Wurauf who paid the Stealther because I was becoming a nuisance."

"Holy Quarenna aid us," said Anarya. "That's a frightening thought."

O

That night Anarya and Yisyena spent chimes discussing Caseir's desire for vengeance, what to do about the Miros, and the door, and what their future relationship with Count

Graumedel should be. They talked, and talked, and kept repeating the same ideas over and over before they went to bed.

When they did Anarya couldn't stop thinking and couldn't sleep. Her restlessness disturbed Yisyena.

"Anra, my love, calm down. We cannot do anything until tomorrow."

"But the possibilities…"

"Will still be there tomorrow."

"You're so practical," said Anarya, and kissed her partner. Yisa returned the kiss, hands slid between thighs and it was some time before they finally slept.

SPONGER

They went back to *The Seventh* Step again the next day. Their plans included letting Yisyena have the experience of travelling through the door and finding out more about how often it could be used without provoking a reaction.

After greeting Caseir, who had a few snippets of gossip for them, they went to study the door.

"I see nothing unusual," said Yisyena. "It looks like a perfectly ordinary door."

"Take my hand," said Anarya. "Does that make a difference?"

"No. It remains unchanged."

"I thought touching me might let you see it as I do but I guess it was too much to hope for. Do you suppose that means it's not going to work for you?"

"We must try," said Yisyena. "There are but three possibilities. It may be that both of us travel to whatever destination you select, or neither of us do, or you go and I do not. We must know."

"Let's try Hemeark." Swallowing nervously, Anarya concentrated on her intended destination, reached for the door handle, pushed and stepped forward. Just then she realised there was another possibility, they might both travel but to different places. How would they find each other again if that happened? She started to pull back. Too late. The sensation of rapid movement caught her and she lost her grip on Yisyena's hand.

She screamed. She wasn't in Hemeark. She wasn't anywhere. Blackness surrounded her. Blackness so absolute that her eye movements produced little flashes of colour. She couldn't feel anything underfoot, couldn't feel her heartbeat, couldn't hear anything, not even her own scream.

What's happened to Yisyena? How do I get out of this?

Then she became aware of a presence nearby and a hollow, sighing voice said, {*Who uses this portal?*}

She screamed again. It was the voice of a daimon. *I'm in the Darkworld!*

{How is it you can use this portal? What is your relationship to the confined one?}

Anarya tried to speak. She guessed 'the confined one' meant Caseir so she tried to explain to the daimon how she came to use the door. She couldn't hear her own words but the daimon seemed able to hear them.

{Promises of blood and fire link you to the confined one – it is well – he will suffer more in consequence of being bound while you are free. You may continue to use the portal for yourself.}

Relief swept over Anarya and she started to relax. Too soon.

A second presence appeared and another voice said *{Mine – Revenge.}*

{Hold. Meaning?}

{This creature compelled.}

{Impossible,} said the first voice, *{It has no ability. Are mistaken.}*

{Taste known – This creature – Revenge – Mine}

Anarya was beyond frightened by this time and well into terrified. Her throat constricted until she could hardly breathe and she felt cold sweat trickling down her back. She recognised the second voice. It was the daimon she had used to recover the stolen jewels.

She heard the two daimons arguing but didn't understand some of the concepts involved. All she could do was remember the threats the daimon had made, even as it obeyed her. She still had occasional nightmares about them. She felt sick at the idea of being at its mercy and started shivering uncontrollably.

{Explain,} said the first daimon, *{You are not one with ability to compel but small one certain you did. How possible?}*

She tried to explain about being a Sponger and borrowing skills. The daimon seemed to understand.

{Comprehension – Wait.}

The instruction to wait almost made her giggle because she couldn't do anything else, she was helpless. With an effort she managed to prevent it because she was afraid that if she started she might never stop.

Eventually the daimon spoke again, *{You have compelled obedience.}*

She admitted it.

{You will never do so again.}

That sounded so much like a threat that Anarya almost resigned herself to being trapped like Caseir, becoming a plaything for a daimon, or some other fate she couldn't begin to imagine.

{Small one wants you but has submitted to me. Will take no action against you but vengeance will follow if you compel again. Go.}

With that, Anarya found herself completing her step through the door and into the familiar street in Hemeark. She was shaking. Tears filled her eyes. She tasted bile and came close to vomiting. The quiet bustle of the street was reassuring. *Safe! I'm safe!*

Only the need to know what had happened to Yisyena allowed her to even think of going through the door again. Before she did, she went to the local shrine and offered blood and tears to Holy Quarenna in thanks for her survival.

Yisyena was sitting at the table when Anarya stepped through the door into the tavern. She jumped up and ran to meet Anarya halfway across the room. They wrapped their arms around each other, sobbing with relief.

"You have been gone for chimes," said Yisyena. "What happened?"

"Where did you go," asked Anarya at almost the same moment.

"Nowhere," said Yisyena, "except into the Street of the Six Holy Steps. I've been so worried about you."

They sat down and Anarya described her experiences.

"I can't believe it," said Caseir. "You survived meeting Amgw…"

"Don't say it. Don't say that Name. Just in case you attract its attention. I never want to meet it again."

"I don't blame you," said Caseir. "Sorry, I wasn't thinking. I was just so surprised that you met it and survived unscathed."

"Not unscathed. I'm going to have nightmares about it for a long, long time."

"The daimon did say you could use the door," said Caseir.

"Yes, it did. What it said was 'for yourself'. I think that means I can't take anybody with me."

"That is unfortunate," said Yisyena. "It means you will have to do all the travelling, my love."

O

Anarya dressed as Rhyanek again for her trip to Carregis. She had a lump in her throat at the idea of using the door to get there. Even the prospect of collecting the rest of their fee from Count Graumedel and of making money by selling news of the cask of Miros wasn't enough to let her look forward to opening the door again. *The daimon did say I could use it for myself. Holy Quarenna aid me. I hope it meant what it said.*

She took a deep breath. Her hand shook as she reached for the door handle. She pushed the door open and stepped through it. Then she let the breath go with a gasp of relief and a mutter of thanks to Holy Quarenna. She was somewhere real, not lost in that desolate empty blackness.

It took her about a tenth to realise where she was. The door had opened into an alley not far from the Sailmaker's Guildhouse on the edge of the Western Docks, inconveniently far from the Rock and Graumedel's mansion. It took her a bit more than a chime to get there.

The guardsmen summoned Corvek who took her to a room and said, "Wait here my good man. His Excellency will join you shortly."

She took one step into the room and stopped in surprise. There was already one person there, one she hadn't expected to see. Baram's ship must have been faster than anticipated.

Her only weapon was her belt knife. Baram was wearing a shortsword and she could see at least two knives in his boot tops. *Why is he still visible if he's come to kill Graumedel?* She did the only thing she could think of, reached out to his dull brown aura and absorbed his skills. It was a new, and shocking, sensation for her. The feeling that came with the talent was ruthlessness with a touch of do-unto-others-before-they-do-it-to-you. She was expecting it to be as difficult to hold as Seeking or Aeromancy instead it was as comfortable to hold as Yisyena's Voyanter skills.

What must a fight between two Stealthers be like? He's more familiar with his talent so he's got the advantage. On the other hand he doesn't know I've got the same skills as him. Should I attack first?

Before she could make up her mind the door opened and Graumedel walked in. "Ah, Baram and Rhyanek. How fortunate that you are here at the same time. You must get to know each other. I can see you working together sometimes."

Anarya blinked. *Baram is his real name? No, perhaps not. Not any more than Rhyanek is mine.* It was the discovery that he worked for Graumedel that really shocked her. Why would Graumedel have wanted Caseir killed? It didn't make sense.

"Baram," said the Count, "Rhyanek is a Voyanter. His reports were what got you into place to eliminate Caseir. He saw you kill him so he knows what you are. It was well done by both of you. Getting him out of the way is a good result. His vendetta against Duke Wurauf was becoming a nuisance." He handed jingling purses to both Anarya and Baram and they bowed themselves out of his presence.

Anarya was really confused. Graumedel wasn't plotting against Wurauf after all, he was supporting him. She wanted to discuss this with Yisyena and Caseir.

"Rhyanek."

"Oh, yes. Sorry, Baram. My mind was all up and down the river."

"I was just wondering if you have time to join me for a meal. There's a really good place on the road down to the bottom of the Rock. It's called *The Halfway Point.* Do you know it?"

"No, I don't know it. I mean, I know where it is but I've never been there. I'm in no great hurry so, yes, I will join you."

On their way to the tavern Anarya kept her Oversight in action. She was hoping to find a Feeler to borrow from so that she could get a measure of Baram. She was beginning to despair of finding one until she saw a green aura surrounding a man leaving the tavern as they entered. Baram led the way to a small courtyard looking east towards the river, surrounded by lilac trees and the rich scent of their blossoms.

He ordered wine for both of them. "I hope you like this. It's one of my favourites, although I must admit to being a bit of a novice as far as quality wine is concerned."

"It's very good," she said, after a sip. *As if Firten Dramish would be anything else. Four-years old. Very drinkable.*

"I was really sorry I had to kill Caseir," said Baram, "but I didn't have a choice. He was one of my heroes and having his throat cut in a tavern seems an ignominious way for somebody as great as him to die."

"Why did you do it then?"

"Like I said, I didn't have a choice. I have to obey the Count's commands and if he says 'kill' then I kill."

"He's got some sort of hold on you."

"You could say that. It's the way he operates. Like the pressure he put on you to work for him."

"You know about that?"

"I was there when he gave you the contract. He's afraid of assassination and he often uses me as an invisible bodyguard."

The Feeler's talent let Anarya know that Baram was telling the truth. In general he came across as friendly and curious. It was more than a year since she had had a man in her bed and she might have been tempted if it wasn't for two things. She didn't know what Yisyena's reaction to sharing her bed would be and he was too closely associated with Graumedel for her liking.

They chatted through an excellent meal, reminiscing about Caseir's victories and speculating on who would succeed him as the next great fighter. Neither of them was particularly impressed by Jurnean, who seemed to be the current crowd favourite but neither of them had another name to offer.

"How strong are you?" asked Baram "If the Count wants us to work together we'll need some idea of each other's skills. What's your range?"

"It all depends on the surroundings," said Anarya. "In the open I can see and hear up to about a thousand paces. Reduce that by one or two hundred for every wall that's between me and what I want to pay attention to."

"Really? I've never met a Voyanter as strong as that before."

"Well, I've never met a Stealther before at all. What's it like being invisible?"

"I'm sort of used to it now but it was very strange at first. I don't really know how to describe it. In a way it's as if everyone else has agreed among themselves to ignore you. At times you can wonder if you're really there."

Anarya shivered. "That sounds really weird."

"Why do you think you're a Voyanter?"

Anarya looked across the table at him. "Are you one of those who thinks that childhood experiences influence the ability you've been gifted with?"

"Yes, I do. Don't you?"

Anarya said, "Yes, I think so. However, I'm more interested in why the gods chose to give some people talents and not others and less in why a particular ability is given."

"That's trying to get inside the mind of a god," said Baram. "I don't think it's possible. You haven't answered my question, why do you think you're a Voyanter?"

Anarya had heard this sort of speculation before. She was familiar with the idea of experiences influencing the nature of a talent and had an answer ready. She couldn't very well admit to her own childhood feelings of wanting to know and do everything. That didn't fit with the Voyanter she was supposed to be, so she said, "Curiosity. I always wanted to know what was round the next corner or over the next hill. I can't think of anything else it might be." That was more or less what Yisyena said. "There's nothing unusual about that. Most of the Voyanters I've met have said something similar. What about you? What do you think made you a Stealther?"

A slight crease appeared between Baram's eyebrows, not quite enough to be called a frown, but Anarya thought he didn't really want to talk about it. She didn't want to press him but the expression piqued her curiosity. It was him who had brought up the subject, so she simply waited until he said, "Hatred."

The reply made her blink. "You can't leave it there," she said. "Tell me more."

It took some persuasion but Baram eventually related his story. Anarya surprised herself by feeling sad for him and indignant at his treatment. She wanted to wrap her arms around the young Baram and comfort him.

Sunset colours were staining the river when they finished their meal. Anarya stretched and said, "Thank you. I really enjoyed that. Now I've got to go home. I have a busy day planned for tomorrow."

Anarya walked back to her room above the carpet shop. Unexpectedly she found herself liking Baram, but she didn't trust him. *Is he following me in stealth? How could I tell?*

She rose early the next morning, ate a quick breakfast and then, using her best calligraphy, wrote fifteen copies of a message informing the recipient of an auction for news of a shipment of Miros. '*The auction will be completed today and bids should be left with the Warden at the shrine of Quarenna by the Arch before the fourteenth chime.*'

With that done and the messages tucked into her pouch she climbed up the stairs and on to the roof. At one point the gap between buildings was narrow and she could jump it with ease.

The stairs on that building led to a different street with no direct connection to the street she lived on. She walked off along it, confident that she must have left Baram behind, even if he had been following her.

The announcements of the auction were addressed to rich patrons such as the Gotheer, Gilruan and Beghroth families, to well-known dining establishments like *The Halfway Point* and to individuals like Praukel, Wurauf and Graumedel.

When she opened the bids that evening she was astonished. She wasn't offering the Miros, just information about which ship was carrying it and when it was expected, but that was apparently worth eight and a half regals to the highest bidder.

The door took her back to Verenthe. Yisyena wasn't in the tavern so she left immediately and made her way to the inn they were living at. She shook her pouch as she went into their room, wrapped her arms around Yisyena and fell, laughing, on to the bed.

○

"We should go and tell Caseir how successful the auction was," muttered Yisyena into Anarya's ear.

"I'm too comfortable," said Anarya. Her head was pillowed on Yisyena's breasts with an arm wrapped around her neck and her legs tucked up behind Yisa's knees.

"I think you should get less comfortable quickly, Anra my love. We also have news to tell him about why he was killed."

Anarya sat up with a jerk. "Holy Quarenna forgive me. I had forgotten about that. You're right. Working out how we fulfil our obligations is going to take some delicate negotiations. That's quite spoiled the warm, cosy feeling."

O

They walked into *The Seventh Step* and came to an abrupt halt. The table was missing!

A brand new, unscarred table stood where their table had been and there was a cordoned-off area where the bloodstained floor had been sanded and re-varnished.

Anarya looked around the room. The old table was nowhere to be seen. "Caseir, are you still here?" She asked, under her breath.

There was no answer.

She moved closer to the varnished area and asked again.

This time she got a reply. "Yes, I'm still here," but Caseir's voice sounded weaker than usual.

"What's happened?"

"The landlord decided to use the old table for firewood since nobody else will sit there. It's out the back waiting to be broken up and burnt."

"Burnt! What will that do to you?"

"How should I know?"

Yisyena looked around and summoned the server. "I wish to speak to the landlord. Bring him here," she said, adding a peremptory "Now!" when the server looked as if she was going to object.

"I am Limabur," said the burly man who appeared in response to the server's call. "What do you want?"

Yisyena looked calmly up at him. Anarya was amused to see him wilt under her gaze and rephrase his question.

"What can I do for you, lady?"

"Restore the table that stood there to its place."

"But, lady, almost nobody sits there. It's bad for business."

"*I* am going to sit there. I associate it with good fortune in my business. Reserve it for me and my partner and I will pay you ten bits a month."

Limabur licked his lips. "Thirty-five bits a month and it's yours for as long as you want it, lady."

"Twenty, and you will also profit by supplying me with better quality wine than you usually keep."

Anarya was watching the reactions of the customers with the benefit of a Feeler's talent. Many of them were amused to see Limabur faced down by a woman less than half his size.

Limabur, shrugged and said, "Twenty it is, lady. Paid in advance, five bits a week." Then he turned to glare at the spectators and said, "Two of you lot go out back and bring that table in again."

"Cost you a mugful," said one of them.

Limabur scowled but agreed.

Caseir's voice returned to normal as soon as the table was restored to its usual place. "You were overgenerous," he said. "That Whisperer only pays ten a month for her place."

"We can afford it," said Yisyena. "Graumedel paid us the rest of our fee for the three months he hired us for and Anarya did a good job selling the information about the Miros."

"The bloodstain is still there under the varnish, isn't it?" asked Anarya.

"Yes."

"That means you were in two places at once when the table was out in the yard. What was that like?"

"Strange. I could concentrate on either the floor or the table and still be just aware of the other. I could hear what was being said in here and, when I paid attention to the table, I could hear people talking as they passed through the alley behind the tavern."

"Caseir, I've got more news," said Anarya. "You were right to tell me not to trust Graumedel. It was him who sent the Stealther after you."

"What!" Caseir's voice was so loud that Anarya thought it must be audible throughout the tavern but, when she looked round, nobody was paying particular attention to them.

She described the scene at Graumedel's mansion, her story punctuated by a stream of curses from Caseir. Then she sighed. "I know it means we will have to work against the Count to get you your revenge. I don't like it, but I made a promise to Holy Quarenna and I can't break that."

"I have been thinking," said Yisyena. "I wonder if it would be possible to create a genuine conspiracy among those to whom you spoke, Caseir. If Wurauf could be persuaded that Graumedel's conspiracy was real and not the ruse it turned out to be then he might take care of Graumedel for us."

"No, I don't think that would work," said Caseir. "You witnessed the meetings I had. They would be happy to see Wurauf fall but none of them are going to expose themselves in anything resembling a genuine conspiracy."

"What about the cloaked man who sent you here?" asked Anarya. "Who was he? We didn't hear anything to identify him. Can we use him in some way?"

"I don't know much about him. He was on the list of people to meet that Graumedel gave me. His name is Aynesh."

Yisyena started to say something and stopped.

"What is it Yisa?"

Yisyena shook her head. "I think I must tell you. His name is not Aynesh. It is Aethurt ve Neyen. He is one of the envoys of The God in Carregis."

"How do you know that?" asked Caseir.

"I recognised his voice."

"How do you know a *cranil* well enough to recognise his voice?"

"Oh, I am sorry, Caseir. I had forgotten that you do not know much about me. I was *cranil*. My true name is Yisul cra Neyen. Aethurt is my cousin."

Yisyena turned toward Anarya and said, "Please forgive me, my love, for not telling you at the time that I recognised him. Did it not seem strange to you that, with my talent, I could not see his face even if it was hooded?"

"I never thought about it. Why didn't you say something?"

"It did not seem particularly relevant. He belongs in my past, and I wish he had stayed there."

"It's nice to learn your real name but I think I'll continue as if I had never heard it and call you Yisa."

Yisyena hugged Anarya. "Thank you, my love. I think that would be preferable."

"Very touching," said Caseir. "Now stop being so sentimental and think. What has this Aethurt got to do with Graumedel?"

"When I last met him, which would be about four years ago, Aethurt told me he was being sent to Carregis to look after matters of trade between Sitrelk and Carrhen. The God keeps people in Carregis for that purpose."

"I didn't know the trade delegation were *cranil*," said Caseir.

"They are not. Occasionally people are born into the Twenty-three Families who never have an Awakening. The God uses them for various purposes, one of which is as envoys. He does not permit *cranil* to leave Sitrelk."

"But you're a Voyanter," said Caseir. "How did you get here, and why did you want to?"

"The how is simple. I stowed away on a fishing boat. It was easy. My skills let me sneak through the docks without being seen. When the boat was at sea I used my rank to intimidate the captain. He was not averse to docking in Carregis. Fish prices are higher here than in Jotuk and many Jotukil fishing boats make two catches in one voyage, selling the first in Carregis and the second on their return to Jotuk."

"And the why?"

"It is not of significance at present and I would rather not speak of it. Suffice it to say that I did not wish to become part of The God."

"Well, if you're sure it's not relevant," said Caseir. "Let's get back to Aethurt. I still don't understand how he fits in."

"He must have had business with the Count at some time. Aethurt is very…" She paused, turned to Anarya and said, "I do not know how to translate *diturshik*."

"Personable, or charming, something like that. I'm not sure."

"Thank you, my love. Aethurt is very personable and may have made friends with the Count."

"I don't believe Graumedel is capable of making friends."

Yisyena frowned slightly. "In that case Aethurt must expect some favour in return for acting as the Count's messenger."

"What would he want?"

"Almost certainly something, some accomplishment, that would let him return to Jotuk and the regard of The God. Being part of the trade delegation to Carregis is not considered an honour."

"What could Graumedel offer him?" asked Anarya.

"I do not know."

"That hasn't got us very far," said Caseir. "Anarya, are you going to meet Graumedel again?"

"He said he would be in touch when he needs my services," said Anarya.

"That means you're going to have to stay in Carregis where he can find you," said Caseir.

"I'll have to spend time there anyway. Graumedel isn't our only customer."

"You should not go to Carregis," said Yisyena.

"Why not? That's where our business is."

"We agreed that this would be our base."

"I've asked around. There are already three quaestors in Verenthe. There's not enough business for another one, the town is too small."

"I am not happy about you travelling back and forth."

"It's safe," said Anarya. "The daimon said I could use the door."

"I was not talking about using the door but about being excluded from our partnership. If I am stuck here I cannot contribute."

"Don't be silly."

"I am not accustomed to being called 'silly'," snapped Yisyena.

"Oh, we're getting all high and mighty, are we? I'm sorry, *hi-cranil*, I'm not prepared to abandon the business I put so much effort into establishing just because you don't like the way it's going to work from now on. I'm off to Carregis to wait for Graumedel to call me. See you in a day or two."

Anarya used the magic door to leave *The Seventh Step*, feeling sad. *That's our first real quarrel. But I can't give in to her. She wants to leave Sitrelk behind her; she'll have to accept that it means she doesn't get things all her own way.*

"Baram, I have another task for you."

"At your service, my lord."

"I have sent for Rhyanek and I want you present when she comes."

"She, my lord?"

Count Graumedel laughed. "Didn't you realise that Rhyanek is a woman? Her real name is Anarya but she finds it advantageous in her profession to pretend to be a man at times."

Baram was startled. He had liked Rhyanek and now was trying to picture him as a woman. They had had a pleasant meal together. He couldn't remember anything being said that would give her away. He broke off that line of thought because the Count had more to say.

"I have been asked by one of the members of the Sitrelker trade delegation to find a particular refugee. There are quite substantial trade benefits available if we find this woman. I am told Rhyanek has a partner with a Sitrelker accent. It might not be the woman they want but it's a possibility. I want you to follow Rhyanek when she leaves and see if she leads you to this Sitrelker."

"Yes, my lord."

"That's all for now. I will have you told when Rhyanek gets here so that you can be in position to overhear our conversation without her knowing you're there."

○

Even knowing that Rhyanek was a woman, Baram found it difficult to see her as one when she arrived. She didn't have noticeable breasts; of course the waistcoat she was wearing would act as a binder to some extent. Her voice was a pleasant baritone, not obviously forced into a lower register than normal, and she walked like a man.

"Good of you to come, Rhyanek," said the Count. "I need

you to find someone for me."

"That need not be difficult, my lord."

"It might be more difficult than you think. If you are successful I will pay you fifty dukals. Ah, I thought that would get your interest. There will be no payment during the search because the person you are looking for may not be in Carregis."

"Who is it you wish found, my lord?"

"The person you are looking for has disappeared from Sitrelk and she needs to be found. She is a criminal called Yisul cra Neyen."

Baram was watching Rhyanek closely and saw her response to the fee being offered. He was surprised himself; the trade advantage must really be significant. He carried on watching and saw a slight flinch as her target was identified. *She does know where to find her. It must be her partner. I'll have to trick her into admitting it. Perhaps if I pretend to want the reward money.*

Baram was close behind Rhyanek when she left the mansion. She seemed distracted as she took the road down from the top of the Rock, stopping every ten or twelve paces and looking round as if unsure of where she was. Past *The Halfway Point* she suddenly changed direction and went back up the hill to the tavern.

Baram waited about a quarter then allowed himself to become visible and made his way to where Rhyanek was sitting glumly under a lilac tree with an almost untouched mug of wine on the table in front of her.

"May I join you?" he asked and sat down assuming she would agree. "You look troubled, Anarya. Can I help?"

"No, I… What did you call me?"

"Anarya. That is your name, isn't it. Did you really think that the Count doesn't know who Rhyanek is? I've got to admit your disguise is very good. Even knowing you're a woman I have trouble seeing it."

The blank expression on her face amused him. "There's something about your latest commission that bothers you, isn't there?"

"I suppose you were there, watching when he spoke to me."

"The Count thought the woman he wants might be your partner, but she seems to have vanished. I'm looking for her too. Fifty dukals is a lot of money."

"Why does he want her?" she asked.

"I don't know. All I know is that she's wanted alive. He's been in discussions with the Sitrelker trade delegation and they want her for some reason. It makes sense if Yisul cra Neyen is an escaped criminal."

"She's not a criminal."

"So, you do know her. She *is* your partner."

Rhyanek flushed, clearly annoyed at being trapped into admitting she knew Yisul cra Neyen.

"I'm sure you know where to find her."

"Yes, I do, but why should I tell you?"

"I'll help you catch her and we can share the finder's fee."

"She trusts me. I don't need your help."

"The Count's had people searching Carregis for her without finding her so I think she's left the city for some reason. If you have to bring her back from wherever she is you're going to need another pair of hands."

"Well..."

"Since you know where to find her you get most of the money. How does thirty dukals sound?"

Baram looked steadily back into Anarya's eyes as she thought it through.

"Thirty-five," said Anarya, sounding reluctant. "And don't tell anybody else. We don't want to split the fee too many ways."

"Thirty-five it is," agreed Baram. *That was too easy,* he thought. *She's up to something.*

"Right," said Anarya. *I need to talk to Yisa and work out what to do. I'll put him off for a while.* "Meet me eight days from now, about the ninth chime, at the tavern where you killed Caseir and I'll take you to her."

"Eight days! That gives her a lot of time to move on."

"That's where and when she's expecting to see me. I can't go any earlier, I've got things to take care of here before I go to meet her."

"It's not as if there's a time limit on finding her," said Baram, "so I suppose eight days is fast enough. I'll see you in Verenthe."

He stood and walked away. As soon as he was out of sight he went into stealth and went back to where he could see her and follow her. Suddenly, for the first time, he could see Rhyanek as female. *She's quite attractive.*

SPONGER

Anarya hurried away wishing the door wasn't so far away from the Rock and berating herself all the time for being so careless. *What are we going to do? I've got to warn Yisa. We need to make some plans. At least we've got eight days to think of something. We're going to have to leave Carregis. It won't be safe here. Holy Quarenna aid me, what can we do?*

Part way to the door she realised she might be about to make another mistake. If Baram was following her he was going to realise there was something strange going on when she walked into the alley at the Sailmaker's Guildhouse and never came out. Instead of going straight there she went to her room and used the same strategy as before. Up on to the roof, across the gap and down into another street. Then she headed for the Western Docks as fast as she could.

She stepped into the familiar surroundings of *The Seventh Step* and stopped. The table was empty.

"Where's Yisa?" she asked as she sat down.

"Gone," growled Caseir.

"What do you mean gone? Where to?"

"Where you can't find her, traitor."

"What are you talking about?"

"I never thought you'd betray her."

"Hold on. Tell me what I'm supposed to have done. I haven't betrayed anybody. Certainly not Yisa. I'd never betray her. I love her."

"You've a funny way of showing it."

"Tell me! I don't know what you're talking about."

"Telling Graumedel where to find Yisyena when you know he wants to send her back to Sitrelk."

"But I didn't…"

"So how did he know she was here? I overheard the Whisperer pass a message to one of Graumedel's agents. It was from somebody called Baram – he's the one who killed me, isn't he? The message described her, said she was here or hereabouts and told the agent to catch her. Then he's supposed to put her on a ship for Jotuk."

"Baram. That sneaky whoreson. He must have told Graumedel." She grabbed her knife, stabbed her thumb and let blood drip into the candle flame. "Holy Quarenna be my witness. I wouldn't willingly do anything to harm Yisa. I swear it."

Caseir didn't respond immediately. Then he said, "I suppose I've got to accept that since you swore to Quarenna and it's well known she doesn't like oath-breakers. You'd better tell me what happened. Oh, by the way, you're still bleeding."

Anarya looked at her thumb in surprise, then squeezed it to stop the flow of blood. She described the interview with Graumedel and the encounter with Baram. "I thought Baram was only interested in the finder's fee and would keep the information to himself. I guess I was wrong."

"Maybe you didn't mean to, but you had that argument and you've given her away. Now she thinks you've betrayed her," said Caseir.

"Did she say where she was going?"

"No. When I told her about the Whisperer's message she burst into tears and rushed out of here as if Huler's hounds were at her heels. That would be a bit more than a chime ago."

"I've got to find her. She'll be killed if she's caught and taken back to Jotuk."

"So that's why she doesn't want to go back. Look, you can be a Seeker. Find her that way."

"I can't. There isn't a Seeker here I can borrow from and it's not something I can do very well in any case. It'll take me time to find one and by the time I do she'll be well out of my range, particularly if she's taken a horse."

"Then hire a Seeker instead of becoming one. I've heard of one called Kiplaun who works out of the dockmaster's office. He's supposed to be very strong."

"That's an idea. I'll go there," said Anarya and started to rise.

"Wait a minute. You remember when the table was moved and I seemed to be in two places at once."

"What's that got to do with finding Yisyena?"

"Just an idea I had. Try taking a piece of bloodstained

wood from the tabletop with you. If it works I should be able to hear what's going on around you and talk to you without anyone else knowing. It might not work but it's worth a try."

Anarya studied the tabletop. It was battered and scarred from having knives stuck in it. At one place overlapping cuts had almost isolated a piece about the size of her thumbnail. She carefully prised that piece out and tucked it in her pouch before leaving.

"Can you hear me?" she asked once she was in the Street of the Six Holy Steps.

There was no response.

Oh, well. It was a nice idea but it didn't work. Pity. It could have been useful. And it would have let Caseir partially out of the daimon's trap too.

O

The dockmaster's office was near the downstream end of the island, at the land end of one of the jetties where the pilot boats moored. Unfortunately Kiplaun wasn't there, but one of the dockmaster's assistants told her that he was working on the causeway. She had to make her way back along most of the length of the island, getting more and more frustrated by the time it was taking.

Kiplaun was an inconspicuous little man but the brightness of his aura said he was as strong a Seeker as Janersh. *Good. He's going to have to be strong to find Yisa after she's been gone for more than three chimes.*

He listened to one man, who gave him a ten-bit coin. Then Kiplaun nodded, pointed towards the landward end of the causeway and gestured as if giving directions. His customer walked off looking pleased. The next man in line didn't fare as well. He received a shake of the head from Kiplaun and left wearing a dissatisfied expression.

The Seeker then listened to a prosperous-looking merchant and nodded. He beckoned to a young man with a Lifter's aura. Together they walked thirty-odd paces along the causeway. Kiplaun pointed down into the water. The Lifter peered into the water and moved his hands as if feeling for something. Then he crouched and stood up with a grunt of effort. The water parted. A small brass-bound chest broke the surface and was deposited on the edge of the causeway.

The merchant exclaimed, "That's it, that's it!" He took a key from a chain around his neck and, apparently unmindful of the water and mud dripping off the chest, opened it and examined the contents. "It's all there, master Kiplaun. Thank you."

"Two dukals, as agreed, master merchant," said Kiplaun.

I suppose the fee depends on how difficult the search is. I'd better be ready to pay whatever he asks. Anarya put her hand into her pouch. She came in contact with the piece of wood and heard Caseir shouting repeatedly, "Don't talk to him." It was faint but perfectly clear.

"Calm down," she said. "I can hear you. Why shouldn't I talk to him?"

"Because he's already been asked about Yisyena. That was Graumedel's agent he sent off looking glum. Kiplaun doesn't know where she is but he's agreed to tell the agent if he hears anything about her, so don't give him anything to pass on."

"Now what do we do?"

"You're the quaestor. What would you do if you were looking for any other missing person?"

Anarya thought about it as she walked back across the causeway. "I know. We'll go to our inn, see if she's been there or taken anything that might give us a clue. You know, it's useful being able to talk to you like this."

"It's nice to know it works. You didn't seem to be able to hear me at first."

"I couldn't, not when the wood was in my pouch, you were too quiet. It was only when I was touching the wood that I could hear you. What was it like for you?"

"Odd, but not too bad. I could hear all the conversations within a few paces but I had to concentrate on one at a time and when I did I lost awareness of *The Seventh Step*."

"I think I'll bore a hole in the wood, thread it on something and wear it as a necklace."

"You could make one for Yisyena too. Then the two of you could talk through me however far apart you are."

"We need to find her first."

There was nothing to see at the inn and no sign that Yisyena had been there since they had left together that morning.

"The only thing I can think of," said Caseir, "is waiting until Baram gets here and squeeze information out of him."

"He might not even bother to come. He can use other Seekers to find her now that he knows roughly where to look."

"That Whisperer's message called her a criminal. All the stories that come out of Sitrelk say the Godspeakers make the rules and can do anything they want. What would make one of them a criminal?"

"She's not really a criminal. Not in our terms. All she did was break The God's rules about leaving Sitrelk and that's why they want her back."

O

Anarya spent the next few days restlessly wandering around Verenthe. She had no idea where to go to look for Yisyena. She knew she must have left the town or she would have been found but she was worried that someone had caught her. The idea that her carelessness might be responsible for Yisa's death was intolerable. *I wish we hadn't argued. That makes it worse.*

Caseir was getting fed up with her constant rehashing of events. At length he said, "Why don't you be a Whisperer for a while. You might hear something about her. Then you can use the door to get to wherever she is."

Anarya brightened slightly at the prospect. "That's not a bad idea. At least it's better than doing nothing." She touched the grey aura and slipped easily into the Whispermesh. The messages and gossip rippling along the strands normally fascinated her, but this time they couldn't hold her interest. She listened for anything that might relate to Yisyena, but there was nothing. Four chimes passed. She started feeling light-headed and forced herself to stop before she exhausted her talent. It would do Yisyena no good if she collapsed.

The next day she did the same.

And the next.

She had just stopped listening on the third day when Caseir said, "Did you get that?"

"What?"

"Baram's on his way. He's about halfway between

Carregis and here and he's coming to meet Graumedel's local agent. He wants backup here in *The Seventh Step* when he comes to meet you."

"That means they haven't found Yisa. Quarenna be praised."

"We've got three days to work out how we're going to deal with him. Any ideas?"

"I'll need to be a Feeler to know when he's lying about something," said Anarya. "What else will I need?"

"Something to nullify his agent," said Caseir, "and something to frighten Baram and keep him under control."

"Too many somethings. I can't hold more than two skills at once. How about if I'm a Scratcher? I can have one spell ready to put the agent to sleep and one to keep Baram still while we question him."

"I like it," said Caseir.

"I wish we were in Carregis," said Anarya. "I know exactly where to find a strong Scratcher there but I haven't been here long enough to be sure of finding the abilities I need when I need them."

AVENGER

Anarya was frowning as she walked into *The Seventh Step* and took her usual place at the table on the day they were expecting Baram to arrive. She slammed her knife into the tabletop with a bit of extra force and muttered, "It's all going wrong."

"What's the matter?" asked Caseir. "The bit of wood you're carrying only lets me hear what's happening around you. You've got to talk to me too."

"It's the Scratcher. She's gone. I told you a couple of days ago that I'd found a good strong one. She works for the Baron and he's gone and sent her off on an inspection somewhere. Quarenna knows where; I've never heard of it. Doesn't matter anyway. The important thing is she's not around and the only other Scratchers I've found are too weak to be useful."

"What about the Feeler?"

"I've got that," said Anarya, "but our plans depend on having a Scratcher's spells available. It would take me too long to go to Carregis to find a Scratcher there. A couple of chimes at least by the time I got from where the door opens to where I'd expect to find the Scratcher and back again. Baram should be here before that."

"What talents are available here?"

"Not much. There's the Whisperer, of course, then there's a middling-strong Lifter and a rather weak Chemer."

"Better think of something quick. That thin fellow with the red beard that's just come in is Graumedel's local agent. Is he a magic user?"

"No."

"Well that's something at least."

Anarya watched the man ease his way through the drinkers. She had an idea, reached out and absorbed the Lifter's skills. The agent's elbow jerked as he passed a man raising his mug to his mouth. His elbow bumped the other man's arm. The mug and the ale hit the drinker's face. A wordless bellow accompanied the spillage and the victim smashed his fist into the agent's jaw.

Limabur bustled his way towards the developing mêlée. "No brawling! You know the rules. If you want to fight, you do it outside. No, I don't care whose fault it was. You can settle that amongst yourselves, but you don't do it in here. Get out. Go on, get out."

The agent looked groggy as he was hustled out, followed by the man whose ale had been spilt. Several people went with them, apparently to enjoy the fight.

"That was a very convenient accident," said Caseir, "or wasn't it an accident?"

"It wasn't. I just saw the chance to get rid of him."

"Well done. Now we only have Baram to deal with. Can you keep on being a Lifter?"

"Yes, for another couple of chimes."

"Good. Use it to pin Baram to his chair. I'll talk to him, scare him, make him think it's me holding him down. Follow my lead."

Baram was late. He walked in about a tenth before the noon chime. He looked around with a slight frown, then walked across to join Anarya.

As soon as he was seated Caseir said, "So you're the one who killed me."

Baram jumped, or tried to. He couldn't move.

"Nothing to say? No excuses?"

Baram started sweating. "Who are you?"

"Caseir the Unconquered."

"But…"

"You see, even death can't defeat me."

"Caseir could squash you like a fly," said Anarya, "or he could let you live."

"Killing you would be satisfying," said Caseir, "but I'd rather get the man who sent you to kill me."

"That was Graumedel," said Baram. He looked at Anarya with fear in his eyes. "You know that."

"I do. And now, if you want to live, you're going to kill Graumedel."

Anarya Felt panic building in Baram's mind.

"But I can't," he said. "I would if I could, believe me. I hate him but I can't kill him."

"That's too bad," said Caseir. "Goodbye."

Anarya increased the pressure holding Baram into his chair and started squeezing his chest.

"No… No… Wait…"

"What for? If you won't kill Graumedel you're no use to us," said Caseir.

Anarya let the pressure relax a bit.

"It's not that I *won't* kill him. I would if I could, believe me, but I *can't*."

"He's got some sort of hold on you," said Anarya.

"Yes, I went to steal from him but I was overconfident and clumsy. Corvek, that Chemer who works for him, caught me with a spell and I had to swear an oath. After that it was work for the Count or die – I didn't have a choice really."

"That oath," said Caseir, "what did you swear?"

"To obey him and never to use my skills to harm him. It doesn't stop me plotting against him. I spend quite a lot of time imagining how I could get free of him."

"He said something about Wurauf's involvement with sending you to kill Caseir," said Anarya.

"Yes. I told you he often uses me as a bodyguard. Well, one day I was at a meeting he had with Wurauf and his seneschal when he was invited to join them as the third member of the Three."

"Jynder is one of the Three?" said Caseir, sounding astonished.

"Yes."

"Jynder! That's difficult to believe. He's a nasty, slimy character."

"Wurauf complained about what you did to his henchmen, Caseir. It was Graumedel who sent me to kill you, but it was Wurauf who wanted it done."

"Could you kill Wurauf?" asked Anarya.

"I think so," said Baram, after a thoughtful silence. "My oath wouldn't stop me, but I'd need some sort of distraction to get Jynder out of the way. He's a Daimoner and a daimon might be able to find me, even in stealth."

"Is that possible, Caseir?" asked Anarya.

"I don't know. I suppose it is. Daimons have all sorts of abilities."

"In that case," said Anarya, "take an oath not to hinder us

killing Graumedel and to help us kill Wurauf. Do that and I think we can let you live."

Baram's relief was obvious to the Feeler's talent that Anarya was holding and she could Feel his sincerity when he spoke an oath to Huler.

She relaxed her grip on him and watched him stretch.

"Is Wurauf behind the search for Yisul cra Neyen?" asked Anarya.

"Not as far as I know. Only Graumedel is involved. You said you were meeting her here. Where is she?"

"She's disappeared. Where have you looked for her?"

"Be easier to say where we haven't. She's vanished. There's no sign of her anywhere."

"We'll need to keep looking," said Anarya, "but you'd better realise that I'm not giving her to Graumedel."

"I think that's fairly obvious," said Baram, "and I don't blame you."

"How do we get to Wurauf?" asked Caseir. "He rarely leaves that estate of his. When he does it's with an escort."

"I've got an idea about that," said Anarya. "I think I need to visit your friend, Caseir. The one who saved your life."

"You're not serious," said Caseir.

"Yes. Scared, but serious. If I can get away with it, it will help us find Yisyena and get at Graumedel too."

"Don't tell me," said Baram. "Just in case the oath compels me to act."

Anarya walked to the door, licking her lips. Her heart was racing, her mouth dry and her palms sweating as she concentrated, opened one of the doors and stepped through into darkness.

Relief flooded through her. The first part of her plan had worked; the door *was* a way into the Darkworld. She was taking a terrible gamble but couldn't think of anything else to do.

She waited. After a while, she wasn't sure how long it was, there was a presence. The, by now familiar, sighing voice of a daimon said {*Why bring confined one here?*}

Panic. She had forgotten about the piece of wood around her neck with Caseir in it. The daimon didn't sound pleased. She tried to explain.

{*Ingenious – possibility not considered – permissible – why come here?*}

"I want to make a bargain."

{What bargain – you want what?}

"I would like to have more control of the door."

{Door? Mean you portal?}

"Yes, the portal. I would like to be able to choose where it takes me, to a particular place or person. And I would like to be able to take someone with me."

{What benefits me?}

"I seek revenge on one who has wronged me but the one I want is protected by one who compels obedience. I offer you revenge on that one."

{Who?}

Very faintly she heard Caseir's voice say "His name is Jynder."

{That one! – Strong – Revenge much wished – You offer this?}

"Yes."

{Acceptable – Bargain made – Portal takes you, others touching you, to place or person chosen by you – Warning, must fulfil bargain within two uses of portal or suffer revenge.}

Then she was back in the Street of the Six Holy Steps, relieved to hear the cacophony of the coppersmiths' hammers.

"Huler's beard! That was a gutsy thing to do," said Caseir. "I'm glad you didn't tell me exactly what you were planning. I've never heard of anybody bargaining with a daimon. I'd have tried to talk you out of it."

"How long have I been away, I wonder."

"Getting on for three chimes," said Caseir. "And it's weird. The me in the tavern and the me around your neck weren't in contact when you were away. I'm only just catching up with myself. Makes me feel dizzy."

Back in the tavern, Baram was sitting at the table with a mug of ale and the remains of a mutton pie in front of him. He looked up and smiled as Anarya sat down. "Caseir's been filling me in on what happened to him now that we're partners. He's hinted that there are even more surprises to come. He's got some news too, but he wouldn't tell me what it is until you got back."

"It's about Yisyena," said Caseir. "About a chime and a

half ago the Whisperer passed a message saying that a passenger disembarking from a ship at the next port downriver saw someone on board fitting her description."

"Quarenna be praised. We should have thought of a ship. She used one to escape from Jotuk and probably associates them with safety. I'll go to her now."

"What do you mean 'go to her'? She's days downriver," said Baram.

"You can't," said Caseir. "You've got to give Jynder to the daimon first."

Anarya groaned. "You're right, curse it. Still, if she's on a ship she's safe until it docks. Let's deal with Wurauf and Jynder first."

"How are we supposed to get to them?" asked Baram. "Wurauf's estate is well guarded."

"Explain about the door please, Caseir. I want to think," said Anarya.

Baram's jaw dropped when he heard about the door and the daimon.

"Right," said Anarya. "You've both been in Wurauf's study. I need a really good description of it so I can picture it and tell the door where I want it to open. I think this should work if you can describe it well enough. Then I'll open the door and hope it takes us there."

"And if it doesn't?" asked Caseir.

"Then we'll try again."

"Baram had better have a piece of the table top too, so that I can talk to him."

"Good idea," said Anarya, prising out another piece of wood. "Keep that somewhere touching your skin."

Baram nodded. "I'm sure Graumedel was wrong when he told me you're a Voyanter, Anarya. I think I can guess what you are."

He paused when Anarya glared at him. "Wurauf's study – Well, the most obvious things about it are the clutter and the smell. There are piles of scrolls and books everywhere. Nowhere for anybody except Wurauf to sit…"

"… and there's an ebony inkwell in the shape of a raven on the left hand end of his desk. That's it. I can't think of anything else to add," said Caseir about a third later. "Is that good enough?"

"I hope so," said Anarya. "There's only one way to find out."

Anarya led the way to the door. She carefully built the picture of where she wanted to go in her mind. One of the overlapping doors solidified in front of her. She was surprised to find that she could see her destination as a faint image overlain on the door. That was something new since she had bargained with the daimon. She was looking into the room she had imagined. There was nobody in it. She took Baram's hand, opened the door and stepped forward.

"Huler's mercy!" The exclamation burst from Baram. "That's…"

"Ssh."

"How do we get back?" asked Baram, keeping his voice low as he looked around.

"Back through the door."

"I can't see it."

"You're standing right in front of it."

"I am?"

"Turn around," said Anarya, "now a small step forward. Reach out. A bit more to the left. That's it, you're touching the door knob."

"No I'm not. I'm touching the wall."

"Interesting," said Caseir. "Makes sense, I suppose. If anybody could see it they might be able to use it."

"There's nowhere for you to hide," said Baram.

"Don't worry about me," said Anarya. "I've got another trick or two. You hide yourself."

Baram vanished.

Anarya waited until she heard the sound of someone turning a key in the lock then went into stealth too. The room became hazy. She could see Baram, standing in a corner. *But he's supposed to be invisible.* He looked as surprised to see her as she was to see him.

Two men entered.

She heard Caseir identify the tall, thin one as Jynder.

Wurauf shuffled across the room, almost bumping into Anarya. He settled into the chair by the window, wheezed a couple of times and said, "Have you managed to find out what hold Graumedel has on that Chemer of his?"

"No, not yet."

"I want him working for me. His potions have made a huge difference. Breathing is so much easier now. I'm not leaving him in Graumedel's control."

"What do you want to do about Graumedel anyway?"

"At the moment, nothing. He's useful, in a small way. As long as he carries on thinking he can become one of us we'll have him on a leash. It won't be too difficult to dispose of him when it becomes necessary."

There was a tap on the door. Jynder went to answer it and held a quiet conversation with someone in the corridor outside. He closed the door and turned back into the room. "Got him."

"Got who?"

"The man who gave the king that book about Sulereath I."

"Good," said Wurauf. "Who is he?"

"He's a priest of Huler."

"And how did he get his hooks into the king? You know what those priests are like, always preaching about personal responsibility. They're supposed to be kept well away from Sulereath. What have you done about him?"

"Nothing yet. First we need to find out how he got access to the king. We couldn't stop the priests talking to Sulereath at the banquet but they didn't have long enough with him to have a bad influence. Another contact should never have happened. I'll find out how, then we can deal with whoever else is involved."

Jynder bumped into a small table dislodging the pile of books on it. He grabbed at them and ended up stooped in an almost perfect position in front of the magic door. Anarya moved towards him, then her foot hit one of the scrolls lying on the floor. It rattled across the floor unrolling as it went.

She saw Jynder look around. His aura flared.

Anarya grabbed him before he had time to say a daimon's Name, wrenched the door open and pulled him through it into darkness.

{*Mine.*}

She heard Jynder scream, the only real sound she had heard in that place. She shuddered at the terror in his voice.

{*Bargain kept – Portal yours – Use well.*}

The awareness of the daimon vanished and she was left on her own in complete darkness. She concentrated on visualising Wurauf's study again and imagined herself taking a grip of the door knob and stepping forward. Her foot hit something solid. She stumbled, as if tripping up a step, and fell on to her knees in Wurauf's study. She lost control of stealth.

Wurauf was half out of his chair. "Who are you? How did you get here? What's happened to Jynder?"

Anarya didn't answer. She took the piece of wood from around her neck and tossed it to Wurauf, saying, "Here, catch."

He caught it without thinking. Colour drained from his face and he fell back into his chair gasping, "Caseir!"

His hand scrabbled across the desk towards a bell.

Baram appeared in front of Wurauf and knocked his hand aside. He said, "I'm sure Caseir has told you already, but I'll say it again. Giving shelter to his sister's murderers isn't acceptable behaviour. What's going to happen to you isn't 'unfortunate collateral damage'. It's intentional."

Baram's sword ripped into Wurauf's abdomen.

Wurauf shrieked. A nasty, gurgling noise that made Anarya shudder. She forced herself to watch as he vainly tried to stuff his intestines back inside.

"That's a very nasty, slow way to kill somebody," said Caseir. "I did it to the chesa who killed my sister but I prefer to kill more quickly. Finish him off, please."

Baram thrust his sword back into the wound and blood gushed when he opened a major artery.

When Wurauf stopped moving and the blood stopped flowing, Anarya made sure she recovered the piece of wood he had dropped.

"Are you still there, Caseir?"

"Where else would I be? Hadn't we better go before someone comes to investigate that noise he made?"

"Don't suppose it carried very far," said Baram. "There's one more thing I want to do. I'm going to leave a message on his body. Probably won't do any good but I've got to try."

"Why? What message?" asked Anarya.

"Can't tell you. My oath to Graumedel is involved. 'Don't tell a living person' he said."

"That description doesn't fit me," said Caseir.

Baram looked thoughtful, then said, "Maybe not. I'm not

sure though, and I don't think I'll risk it. You'll just have to carry on wondering about it."

Baram scrawled something on a scrap of parchment and placed it on Wurauf's chest.

It said, 'Your Majesty, it gives me great pleasure to offer the death of Duke Wurauf to you as a delayed birthday present. I can also confirm that another member of the Three, one Jynder, is dead too, although I cannot offer his body as proof. The last of the Three will be dead soon. You are free of their domination. Trust in Huler and rule wisely.'

Anarya opened the door back to *The Seventh Step*.

CHEMER

Anarya stood in front of the portal concentrating on Yisyena. A door started to solidify in front of her but it wouldn't open. *What's wrong? The daimon said I could control the door.*

She tried a different door and had no difficulty concentrating on the well-known street in Hemeark.

What about somewhere I've never opened a door to? The square in front of the Vintner's Guildhouse in Firten took shape in front of her.

I don't understand. Why won't it take me to Yisa?

She tried again. The image of the destination was blurred and moving constantly. The door still wouldn't open for her.

Suddenly she realised what the problem was. "Yisa's still on a ship," she said. "Ships pitch and roll all the time. That's why the door won't stabilise. The other end is moving too much."

"That makes sense," said Caseir and Baram nodded his agreement.

"At least you know where she is now," said Caseir. "She's safe on the ship until it docks again. We know somebody saw her on board when the ship left Ghusert yesterday. It won't get to Westruth until late tomorrow afternoon. There's plenty time to eat and deal with Graumedel before then."

"You're right," said Anarya. "Food and rest sounds good. It's such a relief knowing where Yisa is. I'll be ready to tackle His Not-so Excellency, Count Graumedel tomorrow."

"Remember, I can't help you against him," said Baram.

"I remember. It might be as well if you're not involved in the planning at all, just in case. Can you meet us here about the tenth chime – No, it's too busy here at noon, make it the eighth."

"Fine. I'll leave you and I'll see you back here tomorrow."

"Then Caseir and I can go to deal with Graumedel. Afterwards we can all go and find Yisa."

◯

Anarya slept poorly. Desperate to see Yisyena again, she couldn't rest. It was still dark, about the fourth chime, when she gave up the idea of sleeping and decided to make preparations for the day. *I wish I could get to Corvek or Praukel but I'll have to make do with a weaker Chemer.*

The strongest Chemer she had found in Verenthe worked in an apothecary's shop near the upstream end of the island. She went there and waited, with growing impatience, for him to rise and open the shop. *Thank Holy Quarenna he's an early riser,* she thought when she saw a candle being lit. She urged him silently, *Come to the window.* He did and stood there long enough for her to borrow his talent.

Back in her room at the inn she examined the ingredients she had available. *I can't make anything too elaborate,* she told herself, *I haven't got the time. I'll try several things that might be a distraction, and something to make sure I'm not disturbed.*

She worked as quickly as she could, making four potions and sealing them into vials. They went into her pouch and she went to *The Seventh Step* in time to meet Baram.

"You're going to borrow my talent again, aren't you?" said Baram.

"Yes."

"My oath to Graumedel says I can't use my skills against him. I hope that doesn't stop you using them."

"Shouldn't do," said Anarya after a moment's thought. "You're not in control if I take your talent, and you can't stop me doing it. In fact I've already done it."

"There's one more thing," said Baram. "If you get the chance, tell Corvek to look in the clothes shop in the street behind the lower Greenbank shrine."

"What does that mean?"

"He'll tell you, if it seems appropriate at the time," said Baram. "See you soon, I hope."

Anarya turned to the door. There was no difficulty about finding her destination, she had been in Graumedel's study before.

O

The elegance and sophistication of the room, made all the

more imposing by comparison with the clutter of Wurauf's, welcomed Anarya.

She stepped on to the beautiful rug with the beehive motif in front of the desk and came to an abrupt stop.

"What's wrong," asked Caseir. "You can't just stand there."

"I can't do anything else. There's an immobility spell on the rug."

"Can't you just undo it? You got up early and spent chimes making potions this morning. You said you wanted to be ready in case you got caught like Baram."

"That's the problem with being a Chemer. Potions are great, but you can't prepare them at a moment's notice. If you haven't got something ready for whatever it is you come up against then you can't counter it."

"You'd better do something about it."

"Just be quiet and let me think. I've stood here before when Graumedel gave me the contract to follow you. Nothing stopped me moving then. I think it must be something Graumedel can use to immobilise somebody threatening him. Something must have set it off, probably me standing on the rug without him being present."

"Then you had better go invisible. If it's a trap somebody will be along to find out what set it off."

Anarya slipped into stealth shortly before the door opened and two guardsmen with drawn swords looked into the room.

"Nobody here. Told you."

Corvek entered the room behind the guardsmen and looked around. Despite her predicament, Anarya was amused by the look of puzzlement on his face. "Something set the spell off. I felt it. I told you."

"The spell must have gone wrong."

"Don't be a fool. Spells like that don't 'go wrong'. Somebody set it off and managed to escape. I am going to my room and I will come back to reset the trap. Nobody gets in until I return. Understand?"

The guardsmen looked at each other, shrugged and followed him from the room.

"Good job they're not very observant, isn't it," said Caseir.

"What do you mean? They can't see me."

"No, but they might have noticed footprints on the rug

where your feet are flattening the pile."

"Holy Quarenna! I never thought of that."

"Can you move at all?" asked Caseir.

"No, I'm stuck, like a fly in amber."

"Do something."

"What? I came with a Scratcher's skills and some potions prepared, but I can't use any of them because I can't even twitch. Got to admit it's a bit scary being stuck like this. Don't worry, I've got a way out. I can always borrow Corvek's talent. That'll let me cancel the effects of any potion he uses. *I hope*.

The door opened and Corvek entered, alone. He was carrying a small vial of murky brown liquid.

If that's to renew the spell it'll activate again immediately and he'll know there is somebody here. She let the Scratcher's skills she was holding drain away, like water being poured from a jug. Then she pushed a thread from her aura out to touch Corvek's and watched as it turned golden.

The curious sensation of restrained excitement she felt while she was in both bodies puzzled her. Then she pulled the thread back and held Corvek's talent. As soon as she did she could see a web of shimmering golden strands wrapped closely round her. *They must outline me enough to let Corvek see where I am.*

"Who are you?" he asked.

She said nothing.

"Hmmm! Is my little trap too tight to let you talk. Here, I'll ease it a bit."

She saw one of the strands break. A section of the imprisoning web faded away and she had a little freedom of movement.

"Is that better?" asked Corvek. He removed the stopple from the vial and said, "Tell me who you are or I will add this potion to the one that's trapped you. Then, if you don't answer it will get tighter and tighter until you can't breathe. Eventually you won't be able to answer even if you wanted to."

"My name is Aethurt ve Neyen," said Anarya, mimicking Yisyena's accent.

"Impossible," said Corvek. "Aethurt isn't a Stealther. The Count would have told me."

"Would he? I do not think he tells you everything. In any

case he does not know what my talent is. I have never told him, nor have I used it in his presence."

Anarya could see the doubt on Corvek's face. She couldn't risk having him demand that she become visible so she said, "Bring the Count here. He will recognise my voice and vouch for me."

When he hesitated she added, "I am securely wrapped in your spell. What can I do but wait for you to release me. Bring Graumedel."

"I would like to know how you managed to get into the mansion and this room. Even with you being invisible someone should have noticed something."

Anarya said nothing.

"I have to assume you've come to kill the Count," said Corvek. "Why? What has he done to break your alliance?"

Having seen Corvek break one of the strands of the web, Anarya knew she could break the others with the skills she'd borrowed from him. She didn't want to do that because it would show him that she had more than one talent and reveal her secret. She had never killed to keep it but she had, long ago, decided she had to be ready to do so.

Corvek glanced at the door, licked his lips and said, "If you *are* here to kill him, I'll help."

"What!" Anarya was so surprised that the exclamation was involuntary.

"Don't trust him," said Caseir. "It's a ploy to make you confess, then he'll kill you with that other potion."

"I hate Graumedel. I only work for him because he's got my family. He only lets me see one of them at a time, days apart. He said they'll suffer if I don't do what he wants. I can't harm him, but you could kill him for me."

"No, don't believe him. It's a trick," said Caseir.

"Why didn't you make this offer to Baram when you caught him?" asked Anarya.

"You know Baram? Yes, stupid question, you've just told me you do. I didn't catch him alone, like you. The Count was there when Baram was trapped so I didn't have a choice. I left him as much freedom of action as I dared. He said he would try to find out where Graumedel has imprisoned my family and have them freed."

"I think he might have done so," said Anarya, still

mimicking a Sitrelker accent. "He did not tell me what it meant, but he said to tell you to 'look in the clothes shop in the street behind the lower Greenbank shrine'."

Corvek's normally lugubrious expression brightened. "Thank you, Aethurt. You give me hope."

"Then release me. Go find your family."

Corvek licked his lips. "Forgive me, but I am not quite stupid enough to stay in the same room as an unrestrained, invisible Stealther. I will break the bonds when I leave the room."

"That will be sufficient," said Anarya. "Fortune and the favour of The God go with you."

"I hope I'm doing the right thing," muttered Corvek, restoppering the vial and tucking it into his pouch. He glanced briefly into the room as he closed the door behind him.

"Ow," said Anarya as she stretched. "Being stuck like that hurt. I'm so stiff. What a useful potion. I must remember it."

"I suppose we have to trust him."

"I think so. He could have used that other potion and I'm not sure if I could have countered it in time."

"Now we wait for Graumedel."

"Yes. The plan hasn't changed. I can still be a Stealther for a while but there's no point in hiding when there's nobody around to hide from, so I'll stay visible until we hear Graumedel arrive."

Anarya sat down on a comfortable chair where the opening door would conceal her from anyone coming into the room and give her time to become invisible again. She waited, growing impatient with the delay. It gave her time to worry about Yisyena and she was caught up in that, and in anticipating their reunion, when the door finally opened.

As Graumedel entered he said, over his shoulder, "Send somebody after Corvek. I want to know why he's left the mansion so suddenly. He wasn't supposed to be going anywhere today. Get him back here as soon as you can."

Anarya waited until Graumedel closed the door, seated himself and bent over something on his desk. She took one of the potions she had prepared and poured it over the handle of the door. It solidified and jammed the mechanism. Nobody was getting through that door for the next four or five chimes.

She coughed, watching to see how Graumedel would react.

His head came up and he looked around the room with a puzzled expression. It made her laugh. He jumped up, grabbed the knife from his belt, banged a gong and retreated into a corner, putting a small table between himself and the source of the laughter.

She had planned on frightening him first, as a payback for frightening and using her. It looked as if she had succeeded.

Baram had said he was afraid of assassination and implied that he was a coward. However, his reaction suggested caution rather than cowardice. "Who's there?" he said. "Is that you, Baram?"

"No," said Anarya, once again mimicking Yisyena's accent, "It is not Baram."

"Aethurt? But…"

"You thought I was without talent. It suited me to let you think that."

"Why are you here?"

"Why do you think? Your usefulness is over. You are a loose end which I have come to tidy up."

"But why? I've done what you wanted. You've got her."

"What!" The exclamation burst from Anarya. She dropped the Stealther's concealment. "What do you mean Aethurt has her?"

Graumedel gaped as Anarya appeared in front of him. "But you're a Voyanter, not a Stealther."

"Neither, actually," she said. "Who does Aethurt have?"

"Yisul cra Neyen, of course."

"But she was on a ship."

"She was. One of my ships took her off that ship yesterday. They're taking her directly to Jotuk. She'll be there soon, by tomorrow afternoon at the latest. You're out of luck. No share of the finder's fee for you."

Anarya's vision closed in until she could see nothing but Graumedel's face. She stepped towards him but he retreated to the other side of the desk. She couldn't get close to him.

I can't get to him. She heard shouting from outside the door. *They can't get in but I've got to do something quickly.*

Working by feel she found the vial she wanted in her pouch. She threw its contents at Graumedel.

It was one of the potions she had prepared as a distraction. It didn't actually do any damage; what it did do was produce an uncontrollable, excruciating itch wherever it touched. Graumedel dropped his knife and started scratching.

Anarya stepped around the table and picked up the knife. "This is from my partner, and me, and Caseir," she growled. She drove the knife into Graumedel's chest with a mixture of satisfaction and relief. *He's not manipulating anybody else.* Graumedel grunted, fell forward on to his desk, driving the knife in deeper, then he slipped off and landed in a heap on the floor.

Anarya bent over him to check his pulse and breathing. *He's dead.* She turned and walked away from the body. It was the first time she had killed anyone, but she was too caught up in the need to get to Yisa that she didn't even think about it. "We're going to Jotuk," she told Caseir.

"Wait!" he said.

He was too late. Anarya had already opened the door.

"Wait," said Caseir again, as Anarya stumbled back through the door into the tavern. "You need to rest."

"No! I'm going to help Yisa."

"You've done a lot today. It'll catch up with you and you'll be in no fit state to help Yisyena."

"I'll be with her."

She turned just inside the door and started reaching for one that would take her to Yisyena.

The door wouldn't open for her. She slumped into her chair. "Yisa must still be on a ship."

"Thank Huler. You can't dash off like that. You've got to give yourself a chance to recover. Eat something before you try again."

"But Yisa's in danger. I've got to get to her."

Baram walked across the room to join them. "Is Graumedel dead?" he asked.

"Yes," said Caseir. "Anarya made sure of that, but now she won't listen to reason. She's got to eat something or she won't have any strength left to help Yisyena."

"Caseir's right," said Baram. "You must eat."

"I suppose so," said Anarya. "I can't do anything else."

"Good," said Baram. "I've got to thank you for freeing me from Graumedel. That means I can go back to my proper work for the temple. But I'll come with you to help when you do go to find Yisyena. It's the least I can do."

SPONGER

Anarya grew restless. She took a few mouthfuls of food without paying attention to it. At intervals she got up, walked across the room and checked the door again. It wouldn't stabilise. This went on for almost two chimes and she became more and more impatient. After one trip to the door she looked at her plate and blinked in surprise when she saw the skeleton of a fish that she didn't remember eating.

"At last," said Anarya when she checked the door again. It showed her an image of Yisyena surrounded by many other people. *Can't go there,* she thought. *I need a clear space near her.*

The image blurred and she was looking into a large room with a spot of bright light at one end. *That'll do.*

"Time to go," she said, opened the door and stepped through.

"Wait for me," called Baram as he grabbed for her hand. He touched her but didn't get a good grip and felt himself lose contact part way through the blur of motion.

O

Anarya looked around. She was standing in an archway near one end of a vast room. Rows of fluted pillars supported a barrel-vaulted roof smothered in gold ornamentation.

Where am I? This has got to be the temple of The God, she thought. *Stealth, quick!* Her view of the room became hazy. She had noticed this before and Baram had confirmed it was how he normally saw things when in stealth.

Baram! Where is he? What's happened to him?

Sunlight pouring in through high windows at one end illuminated a figure sitting on an ornate ebony and goldenwood throne, decorated with gold and rubies. It stood on a dais of five steps, each one a differently coloured marble.

"That's a bit ostentatious," said Caseir.

Anarya had to smother a laugh.

The God sat on his throne, apparently a young man with a pale complexion and long dark hair. He was wearing a simple white robe and was crowned with a circlet of gold.

In the Oversight, his aura was mostly a dull, matt black, which soaked up the light. There were a few spots of colour in it, gold, red, yellow and pale blue. Anarya had never seen anything like it and didn't know what it meant. The room blazed with the auras of the twenty-three richly dressed men and women standing in an arc around the base of the dais. *They must be cranil.*

Behind each of the twenty-three there was an attendant wearing a floor length black robe with the hood pulled up to cover his head. *Who are they?*

Yisyena stood directly in front of the throne, plainly clothed, and in chains.

I've got to let her know I'm here, but how? I'll bump into somebody if I try to get closer and she won't be listening for me.

Only the quiet rustle of clothes as the members of the Twenty-three Families shuffled and moved around broke the hush in the temple. The God leaned forward to study Yisyena who stood with her head bowed.

The silence was eventually filled by the voice of The God. A light tenor, it wasn't what Anarya expected to hear. She thought it should be deep, dark and sinister.

"Join me," he said, pointing to one of the *cranil* with the green aura of a Feeler.

"Gladly," shouted the man. He fell to his knees and started a prayer of thanks. His aura vanished. The God nodded. The black clad figure standing behind the Feeler flipped a garrotte around his neck and the prayer of thanks came to an abrupt end.

Anarya saw a green spot appear in The God's aura. *Those must be the talents he's stolen. He's a Scratcher, a Lifter, a Chemer, and an Aquamancer as well as a Feeler.*

The God watched the killer pull the body away. He turned to look at Yisyena.

She lifted her chin and stared back at him. Anarya wanted to cheer. Despite the discrepancy in their sizes and positions Yisyena managed to give the impression of looking down at The God.

"Not fear," said The God. "Resignation, and a sense of an aching loss. What could have caused that? Tell me Yisul cra Neyen, what have you lost that makes such a void in your life."

Yisyena said nothing.

"Neyen! Always the most stubborn and recalcitrant of the Families. If the line did not produce so many strong talents I would have ended it long ago. Did you know that?"

Yisyena shook her head fractionally, but it was enough.

The God saw it and said, "So you do respond. I was beginning to wonder. I want to know why you ran from me. Do you know how many times that has happened over the years?"

"No," said Yisyena, so quietly that Anarya could barely hear her.

"Eleven," said The God. "In the four hundred and sixty-three years since I became your God only eleven people, including you and five more of the Neyen Family, have not wanted to join me. None have ever run far enough to escape their destiny. A few, like you, have managed to stay hidden from me for a while, but all have become part of me in the end."

"Murderer," hissed Yisyena.

The God frowned. "Your emotions say you want revenge on me for someone's death. Whose?"

"My sister Gilearh."

The God looked uncertain.

"You don't even remember one who is supposed to be part of you," said Yisyena.

"That does not explain why you do not wish to join me. It will reunite you with your sister."

"I do not believe you. Until you took Gilearh, I stood here as I am now when it was my turn. I did so freely, hoping that the day would come when you would choose me and let me feel the glory of godhood. Then you took her and there was never anything to show that she was alive inside you. I kept watch and never saw any evidence that any of your victims survived. I stopped believing and did not wish to die for no reason."

"I understand. It is the same story again. It has always been a loss of faith that has caused someone to run. Look around you. Your family have heard what you said and they still believe. Why are you different?"

Yisyena shook her head.

The God turned to the man in green and scarlet robes at one end of the arc of the Families. "Muhan cra Neyen, do you have anything to say before I decide what to do with your daughter?"

Yisyena also looked in his direction and said, "Father, you heard what he said about our Family. Please do not give him any reason to act against it. Do not worry about me; I am resigned to my fate."

Muhan shook his head and said nothing.

"What about you, Hessilt cra Jerut? Do you have anything to say to your betrothed?"

"I repudiate her," said a muscular young man in black and silver from the middle of the Families. "Her behaviour puts her out of my regard."

"You see, Yisul cra Neyen, you are all alone." The God paused then said, "I will be merciful. I will allow you to become part of me in due course. You will stand before me every day until I choose to accept you. It *will* happen. It may be tomorrow or it may be months hence."

"Knowing all the time that I am to die uselessly," said Yisyena. "It would be kinder to kill me now."

"Why should I wish to be kind?"

Anarya heard The God condemn Yisyena and without thinking shouted "No!"

Everybody in the room looked around to see who had spoken. A Seeker was the fastest to react and shouted, "It must be a Stealther."

"Where is he?" called The God.

"I don't know, Holiness. I can't detect someone if I don't know who to look for. There's nobody there at all as far as I can tell," said the Seeker.

"Hessilt cra Jerut," said The God. "Join me."

Anarya remembered that Yisyena's betrothed had been a Stealther and saw him bow to The God then fall to his knees. A garrotte went round his throat.

A brown spot appeared in The God's aura.

Anarya wasn't surprised when The God became more visible, she remembered being able to see Baram when they were both in stealth. *He'll be able to see me now. What can I do?*

"There are two of them," said The God. "One over there, by the third column and the other by the fourth. Send them fire."

Anarya looked behind her and saw Baram on his knees ten paces behind her. She ran back to stand over him in time to see the one Pyromancer among the *cranil* send a wall of fire racing down the aisle towards her. The purple aura was within her reach. She managed to copy the Pyromancer's talent before the fire reached her and wove the purple threads into a braided tube around her and Baram. The fire swept past her, but it was cold. The practice she had put in after watching the display at the Arenafest had come in useful. *Lucky being a Stealther is so easy for me that I can hold another talent at the same time.*

"Are you all right, Baram?"

"Dizzy," he replied. "Can't stand."

Now what? How can I fight him? She dropped the Pyromancer's skill and took a Terromancer's instead. With it she attacked the dais on which the throne stood. It crumbled and the throne started to topple. The God lost control of the Stealther's talent.

Anarya moved down the aisle towards the throne staying well clear of the people trying to avoid the collapsing dais. She dropped the Terromancer's talent before exhausting it and threw a vial at The God. She didn't expect it to do more than inconvenience him but it might give her time to think. It was one of the potions she had prepared for use against Graumedel. The glass shattered when it hit the floor and billows of choking black smoke rose from it. The *cranil* scattered, trying to avoid the fumes.

An Aeromancer's aura vanished and a wind blew the smoke away. Then the Aeromancer's aura reappeared. *He really can't hold it for long if he doesn't have the donor killed.*

"You don't have to die," Anarya shouted into the babble of noise coming from the confused watchers. "He takes your talent but he has to have you killed to keep it. If he doesn't you get it back when he can't use it any more. You don't have to die. Resist him."

"The Stealther's right. My talent went and I didn't die and now I've got it back," said the Aeromancer.

The God gestured and the Aeromancer fell shrieking, his body jerking violently and his bones breaking audibly even over the cacophony in the temple.

He's a Scratcher. I can do that too.

She became a Scratcher and felt the Stealther's skill fade. With care she constructed four spikes of the pain glyph and tossed it at The God.

It didn't kill him, she hadn't had time to create enough spikes, but it made him fall to the floor in agony.

Without the Stealther's skill she couldn't see what had happened to Baram who was still in stealth. *Hope he doesn't do anything stupid.*

Anarya started to construct the smooth octagon, hoping it would send The God to sleep. She gave up the attempt when he struggled to his knees after weaving a protective shield for himself. It was something Anarya hadn't come across before, but she could see its structure clearly and duplicated it for herself.

"Stealther, Pyromancer, Terromancer, Chemer and now a Scratcher. You're just like me," said The God.

"I'm *nothing* like you," she snarled.

"Why are you doing this?" said The God. "Stop fighting me and we can work together, ruling side-by-side."

"Working with you doesn't tempt me at all. Even if it did, I wouldn't be able to trust you for a moment. I've come to rescue my partner. Killing you wasn't in the plan but I'm going to do it anyway."

"Anra! You came for me," shouted Yisyena.

"You just made a serious error telling me that. Your partner is dead." The God turned towards Yisyena and started gesturing.

"No!" screamed Anarya. She ran towards Yisyena. *She's too far away. The shield won't reach!*

The God staggered dand blood stained his robe. He lost control of the glyph he was constructing. A half-formed fireball bounced off the floor and rolled into the distance.

Baram appeared among the debris of the broken throne with a knife in his hand. He was shaking. "Sorry, Anarya. Missed him," he managed to splutter before collapsing in a twitching heap.

The God looked down at Baram. "How dare you! I'll deal with you later." He turned his attention to Anarya and started gesturing again.

She pushed people aside in her hurry to reach Yisa. Ignoring the headache that was building she took time for a quick kiss and extended her shield to shelter Yisyena. It also covered several other people who were close to her.

The God's thunderbolt slammed into the shield. The impact knocked Anarya, Yisyena and the others protected by the shield to the ground. The thunderbolt bounced off and went skittering away into the distance. In the process it burned two of the *cranil* and five of the black-clad attendants to ashes.

Holy Quarenna aid me! I can't take another like that. The shield's weakened by covering so many. What can I do? I'm getting close to my limit and he's got other lives to sustain him.

"Do something," said Caseir. "You're not dead so it's not over."

"Great advice, thanks. Any bright ideas?"

The God was getting back to his feet.

I wonder...

Anarya reached out to touch the black aura. For a few moments she shared the mind of The God. There was fear but the dominant feeling was a pure lust for power. It nauseated her. To her horror, it tempted her at the same time. Then she was back in her own body with The God's talent available to her.

She used it; to steal the ability from The God.

He screamed, then fell, whimpering.

Anarya picked herself up off the floor and started towards The God, trying desperately to hang on to his borrowed talent. She could feel it wasn't a good skill for her. Already tired from using so many talents so quickly, she could feel she didn't have long before she lost it.

She fell and vomited, shaking and shivering from talent exhaustion. Her vision closed in until she could see nothing but The God in a quivering heap ahead of her.

I'll crawl if I have to. It doesn't matter.

Yisyena's face filled her vision. "Hold on, my love. Stay with me, please."

"Kill him... quick. Can't hold on much longer."

O

Baram opened his eyes and blinked. He was still shaking and he had trouble making sense of what he saw. Anarya and Yisyena were lying in a heap. Yisyena was trying to take Anarya's belt knife but she couldn't reach it. Her chains restricted her too much and Anarya was lying on top of the knife.

Somebody he didn't recognise rolled Anarya over and took the knife.

"I will do it, Yisul," the man said.

Baram tried to rise, thinking that he had to protect Anarya. He was wrong. The man who took the knife walked over to The God, and cut his throat.

O

Anarya woke up in a soft bed. It was better than she expected. Wakening hadn't seemed likely at all. The scene in the temple replayed in her mind. She couldn't remember what had happened after taking The God's talent.

She tried to sit up.

Yisa kissed her and said, "Lie down. It's all over."

"It is? Tell me…"

Baram said, "Later. You need to rest."

"Tell me!"

"The God is dead," said Caseir. "Yisyena's father killed him. Later you've got to tell us what you did. For now you need to rest."

Anarya tried to sit up and was pushed firmly back down again.

"I will forgive you for exhausting your talent again, Anra my love, but this has to be the last time."

THE END

APPENDIX

The talents and their auras

Aeromancer	Affinity for air	White
Aquamancer	Affinity for water	Pale blue
Chemer	Makes magical potions	Gold
Daimoner	Summons and controls daimons	Dark blue
Feeler	Empathy	Green
Lifter	Telekinesis	Red
Pyromancer	Affinity for fire	Purple
Scratcher	Casts spells by gestures	Yellow
Seeker	Finds people and things	Pink
Sponger	Uses other people's talents	Rainbow
Stealther	Invisibility	Brown
Terromancer	Affinity for earth	Violet
Thiever	Steals other people's talents	Black
Voyanter	Clairvoyance	Orange
Whisperer	Telepathy	Grey

Sponger is an exclusively female skill, Stealther exclusively male.

Acknowledgements

With many thanks to everyone who helped me create the world.

David M Allan, July 2019

Elsewhen Press
delivering outstanding new talents in speculative fiction

Visit the Elsewhen Press website at elsewhen.press for the latest
information on all of our titles, authors and events; to read our blog; find
out where to buy our books and ebooks; or to place an order.

Sign up for the Elsewhen Press InFlight Newsletter at
elsewhen.press/newsletter

THE EMPTY THRONE
by DAVID M ALLAN

Three thrones, one of metal, one of wood and one of stone, stand in the Citadel. Between them shimmers a gateway to a new world, created four hundred years ago by the three magicians who made the thrones. When hostile incorporeal creatures came through the gateway, the magicians attempted to close it but failed. Since that time the creatures have tried to come through the gateway at irregular intervals, but the throne room is guarded by the Company of Tectors, established to defend against them. To try to stop the creatures, expeditions have been sent through the gateway, but none has ever returned.

On each throne appears an image of one of the Custoda, heroes who have led the expeditions through the gateway. While the Custoda occupy the thrones the gateway remains quiet and there are no incursions. Today, Dhanay, the newest knight admitted to the Company, is guarding the throne room. Like all the Tectors, Dhanay looks to the images of the Custoda for guidance.

But the Throne of Stone is empty. The latest incursion has started; a creature escaping into the world, a kulun capable of possessing and controlling humans.

The provincial rulers, the oldest and most powerful families, ignore the gateway and the Tectors, concentrating on playing politics and pursuing their own petty aims. Some even question the need for the Company, as incursions have been successfully contained within the Citadel for years. Family feuds, border disputes, deep-rooted rivalries and bigotry make for a potentially unstable world, and are a perfect environment for a kulun looking to create havoc…

ISBN: 9781911409359 (epub, kindle) / ISBN: 9781911409250 (304pp paperback)
Visit bit.ly/TheEmptyThrone

Thorns of a Black Rose

David Craig

**Revenge and responsibility,
confrontation and consequences.**

A hot desert land of diverse peoples dealing with demons, mages, natural disasters ... and the Black Rose assassins.

On a quest for vengeance, Shukara arrives in the city of Mask having already endured two years of hardship and loss. Her pouch is stolen by Tamira, a young street-smart thief, who throws away some of the rarer reagents that Shukara needs for her magick. Tracking down the thief, and being unfamiliar with Mask, Shukara shows mercy to Tamira in exchange for her help in replacing what has been lost. Together they brave the intrigues of Mask, and soon discover that they have a mutual enemy in the Black Rose, an almost legendary band of merciless assassins. But this is just the start of their journeys...

Although set in an imaginary land, the scenery and peoples of *Thorns of a Black Rose* were inspired by Egypt, Morocco and the Sahara. Mask is a living, breathing city, from the prosperous Merchant Quarter whose residents struggle for wealth and power, to the Poor Quarter whose residents struggle just to survive. It is a coming of age tale for the young thief, Tamira, as well as a tale of vengeance and discovery. There is also a moral ambiguity in the story, with both the protagonists and antagonists learning that whatever their intentions or justification, actions have consequences.

ISBN: 9781911409557 (epub, kindle) / 9781911409458 (256pp paperback)
Visit bit.ly/ThornsOfABlackRose

Bookworm series by Christopher Nuttall

Bookworm

Elaine, an inexperienced witch in Golden City, has her life turned upside down when she triggers a magical trap to end up with all the knowledge in the Great Library stuffed inside her head. Avoiding the Inquisition she tries to understand what has happened to her. But she is a pawn in the dark plans of one who wants the Grand Sorcerer's power.

Bookworm won the Gold Award in the Adult Fiction category of the 2013 Wishing Shelf Independent Book Awards.

ISBN: 9781908168320 (epub, kindle) / 9781908168221 (368pp, paperback)

Visit bit.ly/Bookworm-Nuttall

Bookworm II – The Very Ugly Duckling

Not every ugly duckling becomes a swan ...

In the wake of the disastrous attack on the Golden City, Lady Light Spinner has become Grand Sorceress and Elaine, the Bookworm, has been settling into her positions as Head Librarian and Privy Councillor.   But any hope of vanishing into her books is negated when a new magician of staggering power appears in the city, one whose abilities seem to defy the known laws of magic.

ISBN: 9781908168382 (epub, kindle) / 9781908168283 (432pp, paperback)

Visit bit.ly/Bookworm2-Nuttall

Bookworm III – The Best Laid Plans

Elaine and Johan prepare to leave Golden City, with Daria and Cass, to search for the Witch-King. But Elaine is arrested on the orders of a new Emperor, puppet of the Witch-King. She must escape and destroy him. Privy Councillors and Heads of the Great Houses have bowed to the Emperor. Only Elaine and her friends can prevent an all-out war.

ISBN: 9781908168764 (epub, kindle) / 9781908168665 (400pp, paperback)

Visit bit.ly/Bookworm3

Bookworm IV – Full Circle

Until now the Witch-King had remained hidden as a lich. But Elaine was intent on his destruction. Bonded to the unknowingly powerful Johan, she was the only other magician who understood the deeper layers of magic. As they slowly made their way towards the catacombs in Ida where his lich was hiding, he had to rely on the new Emperor to stop them.

ISBN: 9781908168948 (epub, kindle) / 9781908168849 (416pp, paperback)

Visit bit.ly/Bookworm4

Now available as audiobooks from Tantor

About David M Allan

David M Allan got hooked on reading at a young age by borrowing to the max – 3 books, twice a week – from the public library. He was caught up and transported to fabulous other worlds by the likes of Wells, Verne and Burroughs (and later by Asimov, Bradbury, Clarke, Heinlein, Le Guin, Wyndham…). Alas, the journeys were temporary and he had to return to Earth.

His love affair with science fiction and fantasy had him thinking vaguely about writing but he didn't follow through until after retirement and his relocation, with wife and cat, to a houseboat on the Thames. It was reading one book which he didn't think was very good that led him to say "I could do better than that" and then setting out to prove it. David has since had a number of short stories published in online magazines, and his debut novel *The Empty Throne* published by Elsewhen Press. *Quaestor* is his second novel.

www.ingramcontent.com/pod-product-compliance
Lightning Source LLC
Chambersburg PA
CBHW060756190726
48285CB00002B/452